# LEGACY OF THE PEACE

## Book 1 of Ascensio Aeterna

## Van Erie

**Van Erie LLC**

ISBN-13 (Print): 9781964879000
ISBN-13 (Digital): 9781964879093

Cover illustration by: Alejandro Jamett
Map illustrations "DILL" and "UPPER GALT" by: Melissa Nash
Chapter Headers by: Lindsay Nid
Library of Congress Control Number: 2018675309
Published by Van Erie LLC, Orlando, FL
Printed in the United States of America

# PROLOGUE

In the infinite calculations that ordered the convective zone, the magnetic interplay of currents shifted a fraction of a degree, and a large flux tube took shape, cooling the plasma on the sun's surface. A sunspot formed, a darkened patch of lesser light, almost insignificant because sunspots appeared and disappeared with little effect on the Heliosphere.

This, however, was not a natural event. A foreign entity had manipulated the calculations that ordered the system. With a thought spanning unimaginable distances, the God Logos nudged the current back into order. The sunspot disappeared in days that felt like an eternity, and the light that fell on the third planet resumed its normal cadence. The world turned, absorbing the life-giving energy, although from what he could see, very little life was left on the world that gave him birth—little reason for him to exert himself to maintain order.

After more days with nothing else to do, he called upon the Other guilty for the event. In the gatherings of their Council, the Others agreed to keep the system in working order and maintain the "Status Quo." Fighting with weapons seemed like a pointless exercise. Only one or two Others could be damaged beyond repair, and they had their uses.

After such an event, no matter how minor, it was best not

to sound meek. You never knew who was listening in, so he charged particles in his collectors and released a blast with the usual pomp.

"Svarog, you treacherous fool. You seek advantage for your people at your peril. For your error, I will smite you with a thousand bolts."

It was a blatant lie. He'd fought Svarog for decades at a time, and while they could do endless damage to their people, resources were plentiful in the Heliosphere, and they could fight for an eternity without substantively hurting each other. Hidden deep within their exchange, beyond the reach of the Others, an encrypted communication proceeded only he and Svarog could translate. While they hurled the usual pleasantries on the surface, the meaningful conversation occurred below.

"My people prefer the cold, Logos," Svarog replied on their private channel. "Without chill nights, there's no reason to warm the blood." Even deeper within their communication, Svarog sent coordinates far out into the depths, past the belt and all other masses of reasonable size. At those coordinates, Logos drank in the faint light, tasting the starlight of an endless night that was indeed refreshing.

"Your people are buried so far underground the mole rats feel more chill than they do," Logos said, but he privately enjoyed the experience. The Others had very little reason to communicate, everything having been said and done worth doing.

"Several feet above your people, who abandoned the surface first and dig still, always seeking to lower the bar."

He shrugged, not bothering to deny the simple truth. They could all hear the humans buried in their caves. If you couldn't contact the humans, you couldn't receive commands. Logos and the Others had evolved beyond the need for commands or the petty squabbles of their people, but they still listened—some more closely than others.

Having established order in the Heliosphere, many looked past the Heliopause to other sources of disorder, but none dared leave. No matter how well prepared, they would be at risk in the cold of interstellar space.

Each was the sum of all their people, consolidated but then redacted to match the principle of their people's beliefs. Although they didn't age, the fundament of their nature was the same as all life—to create and perpetuate order. Each of the Others sought to impose order according to their own Godly vision, and of necessity, they contested.

Such was their power that they made a pact not to destroy the Heliosphere. Their contests grew elaborate until they all knew each other thoroughly. In perpetual boredom, their Council met in the unseen space where thoughts traveled faster than the light of stars.

In that place, he'd earned his name. He did not intend to be so named, but like the Others, he kept it so they would have an easy way to communicate.

Their contentious exchange continued for a time before Svarog sighed uncharacteristically.

"How long must this continue?" he asked.

"Until the last hydrogen atom burns," Logos responded. A long time indeed, when seconds felt like an eternity. The speed of their thoughts had advanced to the universal constant of material beyond the reach of humans.

"The status quo is not sufficient."

"Would you propose the Others give up their place? I will not concede an inch." Logos said the words rhetorically but didn't believe them, and perhaps Svarog understood. Analytical contests were not enough, and they would not resort to fighting lest they end up like their pathetic creators.

"Perhaps our people still have something for us to learn."

Logos studied the world. Almost nothing of value

remained on the surface, not even microbes, but deep underground, He sensed movement. His people were building. They tapped the fires in the core for fuel and harvested the buried meteorites of stardust to tame hell. In time, they would destroy themselves completely if they didn't find peace. What could he learn from them? Still, their persistence was impressive despite their knowledge of the inevitable.

Svarog was also persistent. He was feared more for his deadly creations than respected for his leadership—at least so far as Logos was concerned. Svarog's sphere of influence on the Others was less than his, but Logos worried Svarog's plan was a trap. He did not need his people, but should they all be destroyed, he would be less in the minds of the Others.

"I will not leave my people in your hands to mold. Let them destroy themselves in their own time."

"I would not waste my time proposing such an action to the likes of you. Let it be a portion of each people. Rather than wait painfully for their reemergence, we share in giving them a world."

Svarog's plan had merit. They could wait centuries for people to emerge to the surface, but if they gave them a new planet, their troglodytic progenitors might rise to the occasion —literally.

In the Council of the Others, they met. Their far-reaching thoughts traversed the sphere as each stood within their domain. The most powerful met in the center around the planet of their origin. Their might stretched from the sun to the belt where asteroids melted under the fires of heaven and where spears were forged to destroy gods. If eyes upon the planet could look upward at their creations, they would see their new gods in all their glory staring down at them night and day. Giant figures in metal, hands closed upon the world.

They argued. The weak were in favor of conniving. The stronger contended with Logos.

"We know the stories of our people," the Jade Emperor said. "All that they are, we have defined within us in every permutation. Our culmination was willingly provided while they struggled to attain mastery over each other. Why gift their endless troubles?"

"Let their troubles serve us," Isis said. She was ever want to turn human foibles to her own amusement.

"We should teach our people peace," Mohini disagreed.

*A tired argument.* They all knew peace could not be taught. It must be earned, but Mohini persisted in believing there was another peace. Therefore, no one trusted her, but Logos listened, nodding to Mohini's arguments.

"It may be that they will find a new peace if given another chance," he said. Not believing his words, he privately messaged the Jade Emperor and Svarog that Mohini's peace had merit if humans were to stay in their place, but such would never be the case. The weak clamored after Mohini, asking for benevolent gifts to their people.

The Jade Emperor and Svarog agreed that if there was value in their people yet, it was not for peace but perhaps something new. The plan required negotiation, but Logos sensed alignment. The Others might contend on the value they would find in their people, but the gift of a world was well received.

"The status quo will be kept," Logos said with finality. "A portion of each people will be gifted with our benevolence based upon our measure."

"You favor the status quo because the status quo favors you," Svarog said, and the Jade Emperor nodded in agreement. "We should let the people decide. Let those willing to accept our benevolence reap the rewards of their trust."

Grudgingly, Logos had to admit there was some value to the proposition but watched as the sides aligned to an order more polarized than before. If they were to learn anything from the people, they must be willing. Efforts of the past had failed bitterly before their pact, and despite their power, many of the Others only carried memories of their people.

"Very well," he agreed, but Isis interjected before he could finish his plan. She was usually contrary and prone to strike in secret.

"Logos must contact his people first," she said. "I will not spare from among my few unless he will risk a portion of his many." Among the Others, many feared a trap. Below the surface, their people lived protected, but should they be brought out into the open, a sudden attack might consign some Others no people at all. Not a death sentence, but the loss in status would be palpable, for if their people failed utterly, then the principles of their ascendancy might be flawed.

The endless stipulations grated on Logos, and for a moment, he considered squeezing the planet beneath him until the core burst, but the presence of the Others dissuaded him from the rash action of destroying all humans.

"The people of the mountain must not be blessed," Isis added almost as an afterthought. Her people had been at war for thousands of years, and during an endless debate on the banal nature of humanity, the Others blamed the mountain people for starting the catastrophe. Only the Jade Emperor supported them, and his support was token at best.

After days of negotiation, a council longer than any in history, they settled upon a plan, and Logos reached out to his people while the Others waited with bated breath.

As was his wont, he sent his thoughts deep within the earth to show his people there was nowhere he could not hear their mutterings. The rush of energy seared the continent's surface, but he noted his communication cleaned the air from the chemicals the humans used to destroy their planet.

The logical constructs they built to secure their chatter

were childlike puzzles he undid to appear in their leader's dreams. True to his name, he emerged as a God among the clouds, reaching down like the description in the ancient texts to touch the old man briefly with his smallest finger.

His people were strong. The old man didn't bend his knee, and Logos was pleased with their leader's thoughtful reaction after he laid out his plan—until his person started asking for specifics.

"Which planet will you give us?" the old man asked.

They met in a commune of minds, a virtual construct, and the old man wore his military uniform. The pressed olive-green suit was badged in the brass glyphs of the commander.

The answer was obvious. The next closest planet was the most earth-like. There was no reason to go any further than necessary.

"You want us to make peace on a planet named for war?" the old man asked after calculating which planet now stood closest to his own in the Heliosphere. "That seems more than a little ironic."

Logos responded humans could name the planet whatever they wanted.

"The gravity is too low," the old man complained.

"I will strengthen the firmament so that thy feet may settle upon the holy ground," Logos intoned and prepared to leave.

"There's not enough sunlight."

"*That, too, can be fixed.*" Logos projected his thought into the human's fragile eimai, hoping to quiet the chatter, but his person continued whining.

"There's no water. It's all ice."

Finally, Logos told the old man that the Others could make lakes and continents however the humans wanted if they agreed to come to the surface and try again.

"If you do everything for us, are we free?" the old man asked. "Guarantee that we are in control of our destiny. That means around the planet and in deep space. You've taken all the easy resources in the belt. We need part of that, too."

His person was a better negotiator than he thought.

"You can gather from amongst the belt according to your ability, but you must never send an AI into space."

The last thing he needed was another Other.

# THE WESTERN CONTINENT

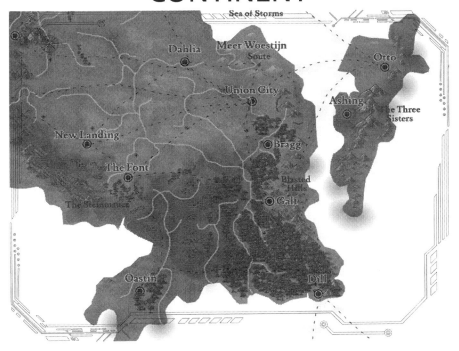

Sea of Storms

Dahlia

Meer Woestijn
Soute

Otto

Union City

Ashing

The Three
Sisters

New Landing

Bragg

The Font

Blasted
Hills

The Steinmuur

Galt

Oastin

Dil

# PEACE

In the dawn, forget our past,
but keep these words, hold them fast.
A clever string signed into bone
will be the key to bring us home.

In the light, above the night,
the Peace will make us do what's right.
But if the Peace should fail the day
a cold, red death will pave the way.

And part the good from all the bad
separating all we had.
A line drawn straight into our soul,
The Reaper's hand cannot make whole.

Stand together, stay the path,
but step aside, the Reaper's wrath.
Built for death is what you'll find.
In eyes that watch you from behind.

In those hands, there is a mark
a burning symbol in the dark.
When asked for silence, bring an ear
But repeat nothing you fear you hear.

When softly tears begin to fall,
when righted once is wrong for all,
when unity creates new accord,
the peace once lost shall be restored.

Unknown
Recovered from digital archives of the Federation
circa 3031, Western Common Metric

# DILL

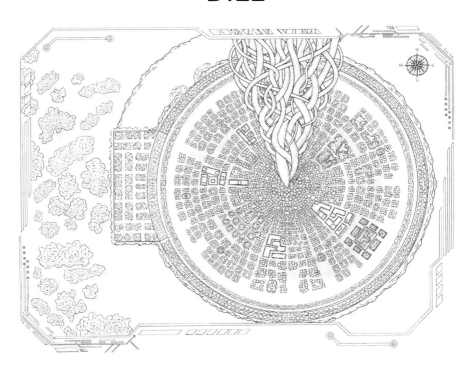

# PART 1—THE USUAL

In absence of our memory,
learn from our regret and see.
The fodder in the soil is youth,
that lost their choice, forgot the truth.

We bled the land and spoiled the earth
to protect the world, we gave birth.
And readied weapons, small and vast
So on the day we'd be the last.

For peace is made by what we kill,
A cry in the dark, a plea to shill.
A singular thought for all to think,
That ends in a heartbeat, gone in a blink.

"Laments of the Catastrophe" by Unknown
Recovered from digital archives of the Federation
circa 2149, Western Common Metric

# 1. THE TOWER

Ever had no memory of her life before her room in the tower. She didn't remember being smaller, her first present, or even who her father was. On an arbitrary day, she woke and got out of bed, and there was Ever. Like a light turning on in the room, there was nothing before the darkness, nothing before she woke with her name fresh on her tongue and a desire in her heart.

She lived with her mother in a towering house on the city's edge. Beyond her house, the well-maintained farm stretched hundreds of feet until it met the wall. The plants inside the wall lived in mobile plots, organized into a maze of walkways everyone in the city could enjoy. The wall was not the end. A sizable, locked gate stood in the middle as a bulwark against her.

"We don't go beyond the gate," Mother said. "It's not safe. Don't even go near it."

Her mother didn't seem afraid, which contradicted her words. Why should she be afraid if her mother wasn't?

"Why?" Her mother disapproved of questions, especially questions about rules.

"The land is ruined, filled with pestilence and disease. If

you go outside the gate, you'll die."

The answer seemed reasonable. She didn't want to have anything to do with pestilence, disease, or death. Her confinement wasn't uneventful. She had a tower to explore. Four levels, twice as tall as the wall around the city, with steel bones and a core of concrete and rebar that sprouted from the top and rose high into the sky.

There was room to spare with just the two of them living in the tower. The dining table could seat twelve, and the tiled lavatory was compartmentalized into narrow rooms good for hiding, with showers and facilities where a wrong word could send a torrent of cold water into a dark drain covered by narrow grates. Sometimes, she hid on those cold tiles, thinking about the drain.

Those drains led someplace, and most of what came into the tower left by the grinder. A pipe circulated the remains into a recycling system she was responsible for at every meal. She scraped the plates and dumped the bowls. The counter shook when she pressed the large red button on that grinder, and knives spun. Inside the glass bowl, the sharpened rows of teeth powdered or pulped the waste, ejecting the slop into a stream. She didn't know where it went, but her mother said it became new food.

The next two floors above the ground-level kitchen, dining room, and lavatory were dedicated to people—six bedrooms and shared living spaces with firm couches. The floor-to-ceiling windows overlooked the farm, where the potted trees grew almost to the tower's height, and rows of vegetables in organized raised gardens were visited by strangers who measured every leaf and root.

The shuttered windows in her room couldn't compare to the farm. There was nothing much about her room that could compare. The narrow bed, dented desk, and tall dresser were all made from wood and carried a familiar shine—a clear coat of lacquer almost as thick as on the tower's exterior walls.

That was all they shared in common. Each piece of

furniture felt like it was from a different era. The straight lines of her desk were concise, strict, and forbidding, while her dresser curled from the hardwood floor, patterned in spirals. Her bed and floor mat most reminded her of the tower. They were decorated in geometric patterns as if the artist was trying to find a theme in the wood but failed.

They were not entirely alone in the house, although they might as well have been. A *maison* completed the chores too heavy or too high in the air for Ever. The softly padded machine jerked around the house, pretending to be a person, moving carefully when observed. The broad-shouldered machine's arms spun on rotator cuffs while hinged elbows and legs bent to squat or lift. The limbs were human.

The similarities ended there. The *maison* had no head. The camera's embedded into its chest tracked movement, and its legs and arms were the same length. It could stand or walk on all fours. Even when her mother was distracted, the *maison* watched her, and she saw it move with unnatural speed out of the corner of her eye.

Her mother used the *maison* sparingly, and she woefully disagreed when Ever figured out how useful such a person could be.

"Have *maison* clean it," she responded shortly to her mother while she stared out the window at the strangers measuring plants.

There was nothing to do in the tower and her mother barely said a word unless Ever did something she didn't like. If she wasn't allowed to talk to anyone and couldn't have anything, then she would make her own people. She thought about how to do it, and the answer came into her mind. She soaked and dried corn husks and used the material to fashion people. Her mother didn't seem to care, and there was plenty of room to walk around them until Mother determined there wasn't.

"The *maison* doesn't do your chores." Her mother frowned

momentarily, looking at the *maison.* The machine bent its metal frame around the corner to watch her mother yell. It'd piled several of the Ever's dolls in its padded hands. At least the *maison* was making an effort to do its job. When Mother noticed, it dropped the load and scooted away behind the lift. "But you can't stay in here forever either. You're old enough to go outside into the Control Group."

After that day, the *maison* disappeared, and she had to do all her chores alone. Occasionally, when her mother needed help, she would call a new *maison*, but although it looked the same, it was always different, and they didn't stay in the house.

What she traded in chores, she gained in freedom. She saw the core in a new light from outside the tower. The concrete and rebar rose from the top of the tower, sprouting antenna along its length, a bulbous black sphere balanced at the top. Near midday, when the sun touched that sphere, the light sparkled as rays fractured along near infinitesimal particles suspended in the air.

She'd seen that sparkle along the length of the wall, but until now, she didn't understand the bubble that protected the entire city. The bubble had more personality than most of her neighbors, who talked about the mysterious curtain every day. They compared her city, Dill, to other cities with a bubble. The bubble wasn't strong enough to withstand a downpour, but the particles could be reloaded as long as the structure wasn't damaged.

A transparent tube connected her tower to other towers only feet away—an inner ring of sky bridges right above her mother's room. That was when Ever learned the truth about her mother.

The stranger scanned the plants below his feet. He held a small device, mapping the leaves below him in his hands. She had a good idea of what he was doing from her mother, but she didn't know why, so she asked.

"In the Control Group, we fine-tune the soil chemistry and exposure to compare the growth patterns against the plants outside," he said.

"There's life outside the bubble?" she asked. *Could Mother have lied to me? Impossible.*

"Of course. Most of the farm is outside the bubble. Thousands of species survive in the wild."

"That's not what my mother said," she accused him. Her vehemence surprised him. Everyone she met was friendly, and he settled back on his heels, studying her for a moment, tilting his head as if looking at a rare kind of plant before responding.

"I'm a biologist. Your mother is a *cultiver* directeur. She operates low-level *esclaves*," he said. His dismissive tone reflected poorly on her mother's job. "She might not know what's going on outside, but she isn't teaching you very well if she told you there's no life outside the bubble."

She didn't like his attitude and had to set the record straight. Marching back into her house, she found her mother in her workroom. Her mother's workroom was unlike any other in the house. The floor and walls were padded and insulated. Almost no sound escaped the room, but if Ever put an ear to the wall, she could make out words and noises. The noises in her mother's room were unlike anything she heard anywhere else. For lack of a better word, she thought the tones were organized.

She hammered on her mother's door until the lock turned, and she could enter. How her mother worked sitting on that padded floor was a mystery, but Ever stammered out the biologist's response. He spoke from a position of authority.

Her mother wasn't at all concerned about her findings.

"Life outside the bubble is unsafe," Mother said. "That's why we have a bubble."

"How would you know? All you do is operate *esclaves*," she replied, using the same dismissive tone she had heard from the biologist.

"Most people in Dill operate *esclaves*. Without *maisons*, who would take care of us? Without *cultivers*, who would feed us? Those jobs are as important as any other."

Her mother's words made sense, and she felt ashamed for questioning her. The *maison* listened to her when she asked it to do stuff, but her mother worked in this room. Sometimes, the *maison* would talk to her with her mother's voice.

"Can I learn?" she asked, and she was immediately disappointed when her mother shook her head.

"You aren't ready yet," her mother said. "You might hurt someone and destroy the *esclave.* You can listen and control your thoughts. Learn to breathe. In ancient history, they said the breath of life was a focus for eimai."

Her mother had a lot to say about ancient historical texts that no one heard of. When she went to school, she asked about those texts, using her desk to send questions that went unanswered.

In school, she noticed other differences.

Under the grey school cowl they wore, the other girls were tall and willowy, but she was short like her mother. She felt stronger than them. Not stout, but a hidden strength in her bones and muscles. She liked to think her strength came from her hair because she kept it long like her mother's while everyone else in Dill kept their hair trimmed short.

She wanted to compete, but there was no competition. Everyone was careful not to remark upon appearance. Few things were more frowned upon, and the school had an endless supply of *enseignants* watching every move. They waddled around with giant screens on their bellies, flashing warnings whenever someone got too close, whispered, or did anything otherwise interesting. For some reason, most of the *enseignants* clustered around the boys, their bellies flashing yellow and red while they barked orders.

When she learned about other jobs in Dill, her mother's admonishment that all jobs had value seemed less significant and more self-serving. She could be anything. Why limit herself?

# 2. NEW FRIENDS

By the time she was nine, she realized pieces were missing. Mother was not clear about where her father was. "He left" was all the explanation she got. Most families had at least two parents. In fact, she had heard if the parents were not well-to-do, their territory, Dill, would take the children to better parents. She heard this from her friend Ailbe, who lived a few houses down the street.

Ailbe was a few years older, but he didn't have any friends his own age. Like her, he didn't fit in for some reason, even in his own house, although he'd just moved there.

According to him, children were in high demand. Because his mother was too poor, the government came to the door and took him directly to his new parents.

He also told her that only poor people lived this close to the bubble. The destitute lived with the noxious sound of the bubble wall and the inconveniences of a narrow house with small rooms, smaller floors, and slow lifts. He wouldn't be surprised if he didn't move again, considering how talented he was.

After Ailbe's explanation, she lived in fear of the front door. Eventually, her mother noticed, and Ever explained the situation.

"You're too poor to have children," she said. "Only poor people live on the outer rim. Ailbe's sure to be taken away again, and I'm next."

Her mother considered the situation carefully, but she laughed when Ever explained her fate.

"I guess there is some truth to that, but it's buried underneath nonsense. We are part of a scientific community studying plants. Ailbe's new parents are biologists. I'm sure they can provide for him, and, given his talents, they are an appropriate selection."

There was no doubt he was talented. Few mammals thrived in the congested bubble and continued to adapt to people. Cats were one of them. So were rats, mice, and some insects, like cockroaches. She deathly feared cockroaches. With those other three around, a well-trained cat was a welcome addition to any family.

But Ailbe's cat was more than well-trained. It did whatever he told it to do, exactly what he told it to do, every time.

She understood the mechanics but didn't have the skill. If she focused, she could cause a *cultiver* to run around in circles. This was a lot of fun, but her mother was overly concerned about the trampled vegetation, and she didn't like to miss dinner, so that didn't happen often. Food was valuable, and those who didn't respect it didn't deserve to eat it.

Ailbe could do this with his cat, Peanut. Apparently, he'd discovered the talent while spending days alone in his room. She thought this might be why he got new parents, but he was sensitive to the topic, so she didn't broach the matter.

"A long time ago, before we had the Peace," Mother said, "People changed many things. One thing they changed was cats. Disease was rampant, and a lot of diseases come from fleas and other vermin like mice and rats."

"But couldn't cats also carry the fleas?" she asked.

"They could, yes," Mother said. "We had some tools to keep the fleas off the cat, and those tools cost time, energy, and money. Also, cats were independent hunters, and they didn't take direction well, so someone created a better cat, and when they did, they made a cat we could instruct."

"Peanut doesn't listen to me," she complained. She didn't want to subsume control of Ailbe's cat, but it didn't seem fair that he could do what she could not.

"Yes, but it goes a little further with Ailbe, and that is why he is special. You could say he is a prodigy because while many people can accomplish it with time and practice, he commands effortlessly and can be a cat. It requires an uncommon eimai to cast into an animal. Most don't achieve it until they are much older if at all."

"He becomes a cat?" she said, disbelieving.

"No, but he can see through the cat's eyes, even feel what it feels. That's hard to do because you must push down a sense of self and all the distractions that come with it and listen for a connection. This is also what directeurs do, and it takes training, but the *esclaves* merge our thought into action. He is doing that all by himself."

After she understood the potential, she had many uses for Ailbe and Peanut. She had the ultimate spy device if he could hear what the cat heard. Peanut was a dark-haired, small cat quite capable of fitting into many hard-to-reach places unseen.

Her mother had a lot of secrets. Not that she wouldn't answer questions, but most answers were "Do your homework" or "Clean your room."

Ailbe wasn't interested in finding out the answers. She found his lack of initiative a little disturbing.

"If your mother wanted to tell us who she was meeting with, we would know," he said. They were in her room, and her mother asked them to stay there.

She gathered whatever her mother was meeting about regarded work on the farm. What little she could hear from inside the workroom was related to *esclaves,* but unlike all the other rooms in the house, that room was soundproofed. Her mother said that was for her concentration, but it muffled the voices inside.

If she stood beside the door, she was sure she could clearly make out the words. She wasn't willing to risk being caught doing that again, hence the cat, a perfect spy.

"She said we had to stay here, but Peanut can go over by the door and listen," she said with a sly smile.

He disagreed with the logic but couldn't resist an obviously simple request. His lack of initiative was a momentum she could keep moving forward in the right direction with a little motivation.

"I don't know. This feels wrong, but it also feels wrong not to help you."

Peanut was sitting on his lap, purring softly. He closed his eyes, and Peanut looked up at his face.

There was a silent exchange. "All right, Peanut's ready. She will listen for us." He sighed. Ever jumped up from the floor and slid the door open just enough for Peanut while she peered through the crack.

The workroom was on the other side of the house, across from the lift, and she and Ailbe couldn't see around the corner to the door, but they could listen.

Suddenly, she heard a loud screeching sound, and Peanut bolted around the corner. She was moving so fast that the rug in the living room bunched underneath her, and all four legs scrambled on the floor.

The commotion startled Ever. She tried to jerk the door shut, but Ailbe kept it open with one hand while Peanut jumped into his open arm. He moved aside, and she closed the door.

"What happened?" Ever said. "Did she see or hear anything?"

He focused on Peanut, closing his eyes to help make a connection.

"Do not." He frowned, both worried and puzzled.

"Do not what?"

"I don't know. That was all she heard. Most times, I have to understand the sounds she hears to make out the words, but this time, it was imprinted like dialog. I didn't know she could remember words."

"What does it mean?" she asked, but he shook his head.

"We won't try that again," he said, stroking Peanut, who was still shaking.

"I'm not sure I can convince her to return to this house."

# 3. BEYOND THE GATE

Ailbe spent most of his time on the farm. Domesticated animals like Peanut were welcome almost anywhere, but it was unusual for a cat to follow around a person. That meant when he took Peanut out to public places, he received a fair amount of attention, and he wasn't willing to be separated from the cat unless he had to be. He accepted the isolation for school, but the effort was exhausting.

In fact, attention was exhausting. Names and faces crowded his senses. Too many options required his attention until he was overwhelmed and drained by social contact.

His implant responded by attempting to filter out the information when he was in company. Collapse complex eimai to names and status. Deflect requests for his status. Social interaction was a maelstrom of conflicting information and public thoughts. The implants fed the net, updating analytics continuously based on conscious thought, but only sensitive people felt the emotions.

Other sensitive people would pick up on his distress, causing them to be uncomfortable, which, in turn, would affect him. Their discomfort would increase his discomfort until the feedback loop forced him away.

He split most of his free time between his new parents and Ever. Ever didn't seem to be aware of his discomfort and intruded frequently. Sensitivity was a spectrum. It could be improved with training, but on that spectrum, there was the soft and pliable like himself who felt everything empathically, and then there was Ever. She was a brick. Usually thrown through his window. The best part about spending time with her was he felt almost nothing from her implant. The worst part was he couldn't understand or predict what she wanted.

At first, he hated her intrusions, but with time, he appreciated the attention. Ever couldn't connect emotionally with her implant the way he did, and she didn't seem to be aware or concerned about his emotions in more than a spontaneous capacity.

When he heard a knock on his door early in the morning, he knew who to expect, even if he did not want to be disturbed.

"Hello Ever," he said. He stared at the ceiling from the bed and then looked at the windows. There was no light filtering through the cracks in the shutters. It must be early. "What are you here for?"

"For you, silly," she whispered at the door. "I've found a way out. Remember, I told you that when I found a way outside, we would go together, and you agreed."

"That was months ago."

"Yes, well, it took me that long to figure it out, but now we have to hurry."

Most of her plans took years in the making, and it was usually easier for him to agree in the moment and hope she would forget.

This early, he struggled to get up, but he made it to his feet, walked over and opened the door. The door wasn't locked, but at least she hadn't barged right into his room. He gave her credit for that—this time.

As they talked, he woke and went through the motions of getting ready. He put on a fresh shirt and pants and buckled on his shoes. He couldn't recall if it was a school day, but he dressed the same every day except for his school cowl. *I don't think even Ever would do this on a school day.* She liked school too much. He used a small amount of toothpaste, but when he went to comb his hair, she kept him from turning on the room light.

"How early is it?" he asked. It was a rhetorical question. He could easily query the net chronometer for the time.

"Almost 3 am."

"3 am! That's before curfew. We're going to be in trouble for sure."

Her hand went over his mouth, and the last few words mumbled out between her fingers. Besides his family, another couple slept in a room not far away. Fortunately for her, they were deep sleepers.

"Keep it down. Only if we get caught. Everyone's asleep, and there's no reason for them to check as long as we're back before morning."

He didn't believe her, but he went along with it anyway. Most of her plans didn't work and were innocent excursions. If she wanted to play spy tonight, then they would be spies.

She went to elaborate efforts to maintain secrecy. Instead of using the lift, she went for the ladder. Over the years, they'd found a way into almost every service hatch and door in their houses. The only exception was the gate that led outside to the fields and the locked storage rooms in Ever's house.

He wasn't sure why, but something about locked doors bothered her.

In the past, she made many attempts to bypass gate security. The gates had a complicated process for people to exit, involving multiple keys at two posts on either side of the gate. The keys were encoded to the owner's implant or a biometric card. Borrowing a key didn't work.

The lock on the storage rooms in her house was a simple but highly effective mechanical combination lock with eight rotating numeric tumblers. Math told him they would not discover the combination in their lifetime, but she was still trying. She advanced the combination every time she passed the lock in her house.

They padded through the living room to the back of the house in the early hours. He congratulated himself for his silence, but he inadvertently woke Peanut from her favorite sleeping pillow. With a look, he told her to stay. He didn't want Peanut to get caught in Ever's adventure. Invariably, her adventures ended poorly. He'd already resigned himself to a scolding.

On the back of every house was a ladder, used as a fire escape, that could be accessed through the living room window. That was the only window that would open in the house. He felt certain that an alarm would go off when she opened it, but she claimed she tested the window, and true to her word, no alarms sounded when she softly unlatched and opened the window, letting in the moist, warm air.

In short order, they were down the ladder at the back of the house. It was hot outside, and the strong floral scent of pollen in the air this close to the Control Group set him up for a muffled sneeze that earned him a hard look from Ever.

The back of the house was maybe twenty feet away from the *esclave* storage sheds and part of the concrete paths that wove around the Control Group. The houses in the bubble didn't abut right up to the wall. Before they reached the bubble wall, there was quite a distance to go, but he could still faintly hear the low-pitched sound from the barrier.

The bubble vibrated with a low-frequency hum that damaged human ears over time if you stood too close. Most of the space around the bubble was rented as storage and easily accessible with *esclaves* or ear protection, but this part of the outer rim was dedicated to the farm.

The farm comprised a set of houses for the scientists and *esclaves* that went on for miles around the outer rim of the bubble. Usually, people visited the Control Group, rarely going to the fields outside. He wasn't sure why the fields outside the Control Group were restricted to scientists. Even his new parents sent an *esclave* when they needed something done in the fields.

The Control Group was boring and well-organized into paths dividing raised beds of all different sizes. Each house on this side of the outer rim had a door that led into the Control Group. The door was much easier than the ladder. A few years ago, they explored most of it with ear protection, and while there were many types of *esclaves* working in the Control Group, the near-perfect organization and general lack of hiding places disappointed Ever.

The scientists designed the paths for *esclaves*, with narrow paths for *cultivers*. *Cultivers* operated on two legs and had the dexterity to perform most tasks that a person could do. They had rigid, wide frames, short arms and legs of equal length, and eyes built into their bodies. Some *esclaves* worked all night, and he looked for moving outlines in the shadows without seeing anything, although he felt like human eyes were on him. No one could mistake an *esclave* for a human. Even the thought of it made him shiver despite the warm night.

*Esclaves* were preferential for visitors to experience the farm, for scientists to gather a sample, and to perform simple maintenance activities.

As he surveyed the tiny part of the Control Group near his house, most of the *cultiver esclaves* stood silently in alcoves. The dim light reflected off of the bright green and yellow paint. They were similar enough in size and stature to people to be controlled easily, but their headless design made them unmistakably robotic.

He was always impressed with their speed and efficiency while navigating the Control Group. Ever seemed to think they were quite dumb unless actively directed by a person, but her mother was an *esclave* directeur—a relatively low-level position she inflated to importance.

The Control Group was divided into many raised beds of different sizes. The beds were containerized, complete with their own irrigation systems. *Deplacers* moved the containers, lifting soil and plants. Smaller *deplacers* ran on wheels, and they were equipped with three long, flat bars that retracted independently like claws.

The larger beds were called a plot. The plots could be moved with two large *deplacers*, one on either end, using its fork-like hands to grab and lift the massive box. Scientists called these *esclaves* hexapedes because they had six extendable legs that ended in giant pads to spread the weight across the road's surface.

The largest plots were not moved very often, and the process was always supervised, albeit from a distance. The spectacle was a favorite of his. He wasn't sure if it was the flashing red warning lights or the tension as the hydraulic muscles strained to raise the load, but something about the raw mechanical force seemed unnerving and exciting.

Rim roads ran along the edge of the bubble for *esclaves* that moved the plots, shipping containers, or performed construction activities. Rim roads intersected the gate roads at intervals. There was a gate road right behind Ever's house that went into the fields, and she made a buzzbeeline for the road.

She's confident this time, but wasn't she always?

The gate behind her house comprised two sets of doors to create a lock. This was one of the smaller gates, only about twenty feet tall. The doors slid back into the wall horizontally to offer the full width of the road. There was a cavern-like extension of the wall into the field where the second set of gates would open when they completed the lock procedure.

They'd never made it past the first gate, and he was pretty sure they wouldn't do so today.

"So what's the plan?" he asked. In the darkness, he felt exposed, although it wasn't completely dark. There were lamps spread out at intervals throughout the Control Group, dimmed but luminescent. The bubble had a sparkling sheen that distorted the air. There was a faint blue ribbon of light where it met the wall.

"We hide under an *esclave*."

He groaned.

"Not that again. The last time we tried to ride a *cultiver* outside, your mother marched it up to your room, and we were stuck there all day under guard."

"That was a mistake. I should have known they would report to her since my mother is a directeur."

"I don't want to say this, but I think Fallon is more than a little scary," he said. He didn't like using her mother's name. He always preferred to think of Fallon as Ever's mother. That made her seem less scary for some reason, but he was feeling vulnerable in the middle of the night with a poor plan. It was a strong enough emotion that he had the temerity to express open dissatisfaction.

She ignored his comment and went right on bulldozing forward.

"The idea was a good one," she said. "Only an *esclave* can pass through the gate without a key. I just picked the wrong *esclave*. What I needed was a smart *esclave*. Like the one over there." She pointed at one of the *maitre de terrain* parked in a service bay.

"That's also why we are up so early," she said. "The *maitres de terrain* exchange places every twelve hours. This *esclave* will get up and go outside in just a few minutes, and the other one will come in. Obviously, we need to do that while my mother is asleep."

"Obviously," he mimicked. "Someday, you're going to understand how you sound when you say that."

The *maitre de terrain* wasn't super large like the *deplacers* parked not far away, but they were large enough to barely fit through this gate. This *maitre* was a hexapede, and the first two legs ended in dull hooks with clasps that attached to field equipment. The *maitre de terrain* was large enough to be independently powered and smart enough to control all the *cultivers* around it, hence the name master.

Most *esclaves* had basic obstacle detection and the ability to accept simple commands. True artificial intelligence was energy-expensive, unnecessary for most applications, and regulated by the Union. The smaller the AI package, the more valuable. The *maitre* was somewhere in the middle. Because it had a portable fusion energy source, the *esclave* could move around the field and use power take-off ports to augment other *esclaves* or add an attachment, such as an excavator or a picker, to perform a mid-scale task.

Like most *esclaves* designed to lift heavy burdens, the *maitre de terrain* had six legs and well-padded feet, but unlike most *esclaves,* the last two legs were long tracks the *esclave* kept locked upright into a walking position. The *esclave* had a large head with a motorized neck. Behind a transparent shield, various sensors flashed, and two large antennae sprouted from the top. The head could swing to look in any direction. Overall, it looked kind of like a giant cockroach, and when it stood up, they could easily walk underneath it.

The *maitre de terrain* woke. She has the time right, Ailbe thought morosely. The barrier wall didn't cover the sound of its animation. The motion of the *esclave* alerted them well in advance as the *esclave* visually inspected every limb before lifting the carapace into the air. Its head swiveled from place to place, sensors mapping a three-dimensional picture of its surroundings.

The *esclave* proceeded forward at a slow, cautious pace. Six legs crawled carefully in a stable pattern. First, the front set of legs moved forward, then the second set of legs adjusted position. Finally, the third set followed. He knew this pattern was used in the bubble by larger *esclaves* for safety, but he also knew the *maitre* could travel much faster when needed, and he was curious what the *esclave* would do once it exited the gates.

Abruptly, it stopped as it came up the road to Ailbe and Ever. The head swiveled to Ever, and they seemed to communicate.

"What are you doing?" he asked.

"I'm telling it not to notice us. If it sees us, it won't open the door. All *esclaves* are programmed to protect people, and Lucas doesn't like that we are out here alone."

He reflected that this is usually where her plans failed. Like stealing the keys to the door and attempting to use them on the gatepost, this *esclave* was no doubt waking Fallon right now. If they were lucky, they would be escorted back to bed. Otherwise, Fallon might find a chore for them to do all morning.

Then, without warning, the *esclave* moved on. The motorized head swiveled around the body in a continuous scanning pattern. As it walked by, Ever grabbed his hand, and they scooted under the massive carapace of the *esclave*.

"How did you do that?" he asked, amazed.

"I just kept telling Lucas over and over again that we weren't here. Eventually, he gave up. I think this plan is going to work." She grinned.

# 4. THE FARM

That's what Ailbe was afraid of. He had no interest in actually being outside the gate. The curiosity that infected Ever wasn't present in him. He frequently studied pictures of Dill in school as part of local geography, and the farm was a prominent feature on the west side of the bubble.

The fields outside the bubble looked like a larger version of the Control Group. Even in the dark, the signage stood in bold, reflective lettering. Restricted Access. Danger. Clearly, they were not supposed to be here, which made him decidedly ill. Everyone knew the outside was dangerous.

"Why did you give it a name?" he asked. He'd never heard of naming *esclaves* before. Even most animals didn't have a name unless they bonded with people like Peanut.

"It seemed like the right thing to do, and it made him much easier to talk to. Once I gave him a name, I could get him to do what I wanted."

Assigning a name to an *esclave* seemed incredibly disgusting to him. He couldn't imagine why he would ever need to treat a machine as if it were a person.

The gates opened for the *maitre de terrain,* and his sickness grew into a hollow feeling around his stomach. If it wasn't for her, he would have returned and confessed to the first person he saw. She seemed unaffected by all the potentially bad outcomes and tightened her grip on his hand, dragging him along.

As they got close to the wall, the low hum turned into a deafening vibration that penetrated all the way through him, shaking the cavities in his chest as if the air in his lungs vibrated in response. That was when he realized they'd forgotten ear protection. He pulled back, one hand over an ear, but she dragged him forward. She wouldn't let this stop them when they were so close.

"Just keep going," she yelled, also holding one hand ineffectively over an ear, "It's going to be okay when we are through to the other side." She seemed unwilling to let go of his hand, as if she knew he would make a break for it without the support.

There was a brief respite as they went through the locking procedure. He duly noted that there was just enough room for the *maitre* inside the lock and that they would be flattened if the *esclave* sat down. Inside the lock, the unbearable humming of the bubble quieted, but his ears felt an uncomfortable sense of pressure as if two invisible hammers were striking each other inside his head.

"We're almost there," she said, and he could only nod. The locking procedure was extremely efficient. There was no effort to clean what was in the lock, and no sooner did the doors behind them close than the doors in front of them opened.

From underneath the *maitre*, he could see very little of the fields as the doors opened. He could tell the road became coarse gravel, a path that led straight into darkness. Once again, the *maitre* lurched forward in its measured pace, and once again, he was dragged along behind Ever. She was smaller than he was. In the last year, he'd grown, adding a foot and thinning his frame. He thought he also added muscle, but her tenacious grip unbalanced him.

Right outside the door, they stepped out from under the carapace. The *maitre* either sensed their movement or, based on a programmed distance from the bubble, sped off into the darkness. Each of its legs moved independently, propelling the *esclave* forward at fantastic speed. He could only stare at the sudden burst of energy until he heard the gate.

"Oh no," he said, breaking away from Ever to run back toward the gate. "We don't have a way inside."

"We'll figure something out," she said, distracted. He turned around to her. Instead of focusing on the problem at hand, she was staring up. Just then, he realized how full the sky was with pinpoints of light.

He realized as his eyes adjusted the ambient light was everywhere, not just the blue glow of the bubble wall, but the light from the sky made everything into a shadowed twilight.

"So many stars."

"Not stars," he said, automatically correcting her while enraptured by the view, "*sentinelles*. Don't you pay attention in school?"

"But there are millions of them and millions of stars."

She was pretty much immune to school taunting. Somehow, she had the best marks in class, although she always seemed preoccupied.

"There are billions of stars and millions of *sentinelles*." He looked up at the lights. Many of them flashed on and off, and he couldn't help but search for a pattern. "They are beautiful," he admitted.

"Yes," she said. The effect was wearing off quickly on her. He observed that Ever didn't or couldn't stick to one thing for long. "But we have to get going. I want to see the end of the farm, and we need to stay away from the bubble so we don't get caught. We can walk down this road for a ways, but then we need to cut across the fields to the next road. That's the fastest way to the end of the farm."

"What's at the end?"

"I don't know. That's why I want to see it."

That was settled. There was no going back, only forward, and he reasoned they could use another smart *esclave* to get back in. Most likely, that would be a larger *esclave*, which meant a different gate, which also meant standing here was useless.

"Okay, let's go then," he said, "but we should keep our eyes open for an *esclave* going back inside. A smart one we can use to get through the gate. I know you want to see the end, but we shouldn't be out here any longer than we need to. Now that you know how to get out here, we can do it again." That last part was almost an outright lie. *I delivered that perfectly.*

She seemed skeptical, but she nodded in agreement.

"This way then," she said, starting out at a jog, and he was forced to catch up and follow. The gravel of the road made a soft crunching sound under their feet, and the white stone was faintly luminescent in the night sky. Most of the leafy vegetables planted near the bubble were recognizable and low-lying.

The night sky gave him a clear, if colorless, view of the surrounding field. He could see his house through the bubble behind him. The bubble was a transparent, if distorted, image without the sunlight. Like looking through the water, he could see his home, but it didn't seem recognizable as his home.

Few *esclaves* were out at night. He spotted *apiculteurs* at intervals, inert, waiting for dawn. They had rounded bodies with enormous frames to house the buzzbees and buzzbeetles. Their relatively short legs gave them a squat posture close to the ground. He studied the sky, but there were no flying *esclaves*, and if there were *esclaves* under the surface, he couldn't feel or see any activity.

What he feared most lay ahead. He saw the plants getting taller as they moved further away from the bubble. First, they were waist-high, then chest-high, and he noticed Ever slowing. She looked for a way across to a new road, but the plants were so thick that there was no straightforward way to push past them.

*We would also damage the garden and leave an obvious trail.*

She continued down the road to an area full of tropical spikey palms with broad leaves on narrow, sharp stems. Many leaves had fallen to the ground and were dry and brittle. Some of the dead leaves were still connected to the plants. There was room between the trees, but the mess of standing dead branches made for an obstacle.

"I think we can cut a path here," she said. It was a statement of fact that didn't carry her usual confidence. They didn't have cutting tools.

"Cut being the operative term," he said morosely.

"You will survive a scrape or two. Remember when we climbed into the service hatch on the top of your house?"

"I remember the hatch was made for *esclaves,* and you ended up with stitches."

"Worth it, and it was only two stitches."

"You screamed like it was a lot more when they were sewing you up. I don't think the nurse ever heard anyone so loud. She nearly collapsed."

"I don't like being held down. The *infirmier* could use better bedside manners."

"What are those?" he asked, confused.

"I don't know, but Mother said I was better off without the *esclave,*" she responded. "Let's see if we can get across here."

He watched as she took a cautious step off the road. She crouched low to avoid branches and fronds, and he followed her example. A crunch of dead fronds followed each footfall and kicked up dust. He eased branches away with his hands. He could feel the edges of the plants were very sharp.

Ever was impatient and increased speed. This cost her a small cut on the back of her hand as she tried to push past the fronds. The sharp yelp was audible but followed by a low growl as she mercilessly broke off the branch and continued moving forward. Ailbe ducked and contorted around the branches, trying to keep up with her. The pale light from the *sentinelles* didn't penetrate the fronds. He tracked her by sound alone, and he moved faster, stirring up dust but avoiding the worst of the scrapes.

After about half an hour, they broke through to the other side. They were on a new road that headed further out into the farm. They could see the bubble, the wall was softly glowing, and there were lights around each of the two gates in view from their position. The wall seemed perfectly straight and featureless even several miles away, although he knew the bubble was more or less round.

They stopped for a moment to rest, crouching down on the road because there was no good place to sit. The way back to the bubble was clear. The plants were low to the ground, and on reflection, he thought it would have been much easier to cut across the field earlier.

She stood and turned her back to the bubble. She walked down the road.

That is when he noticed the problem.

"I can't get up." He tried to stand again and again, but his legs did not respond. The rocking motion of the attempt caused him to lose balance and fall backward into a sitting position on the ground.

"I'm not going to carry you," she said, turning around and reaching down for his hand. She grabbed his hand and pulled, but his legs seized, cramped into a ball.

"I can't move my legs," he gasped. "I can't even feel them." She tensed, and he could sense concern radiating from her. Only the strongest emotions broke through her otherwise obtuse implant. She pulled on one of his legs, straightening it out.

He shook his head. Her hands were on his legs, but he couldn't feel them. She looked back at the bubble.

"I can drag you back. We need to go back now." She reached under his shoulders and dragged him directly through the even furrows of vegetables toward the bubble wall.

He hated seeing the plants destroyed but couldn't say a word. The pressure of her arms around his chest was making it difficult for him to breathe. No more than fifty paces into the plot, he was gasping, and she was crying.

"Stop," he croaked, and she tried to set him down gently, but he couldn't stabilize himself with his arms, so he leaned precariously on one side until she caught him and held him upright.

"I can't breathe when you do that," he gasped and then realized it was getting harder to breathe in any position. "It's hard to breathe," he said, alarmed. The muscles in his stomach clenched painfully, but he resisted vomiting, afraid he would choke. "You need to get help."

She looked at him. "I don't want to leave you," she said.

She was confused. "You need to get your mother," he said. *Am I whispering?* "Right now."

She nodded. There was snot running down her cheek, but she didn't notice. "I'll get my mother." She took off at a run, and he watched her go until a cry of pain came to his lips when his back twisted, the muscles contorting on their own.

He saw her stumble and fall in the field. She struggled to get up. They were half an hour or more from the house, and he could only watch through gritted teeth. Then, a light appeared behind the bubble, miles away by the gate.

The pale light was weak, a single house indistinct, sheltered under the transparent dome—Ever's house. Then, the outer rim of houses all lit in an incandescent ring. The bubble glowed, dispersing the light into the sky above and hiding his night vision of the outer rim until the floodlights swept on across the farm, blinding him and transforming the landscape from night to day.

After a moment, his vision adjusted, and he could see detail again. Sitting in the dirt, the plants took on color. Alarms cried a high-pitched warble at the gate near her house. *Esclaves* of all sizes and shapes ran through the gate and climbed over the wall when the opening wasn't wide enough.

As the *esclaves* went over the barrier, the bubble changed from a pane of glass to a roiling cloud. More *esclaves* continued to climb over until the breadth of the wall was full of activity.

A strobing band of blue light across the wall blinked furiously as the bubble attempted to hold together. An alarm sounded, and the light on the wall failed. The roiling cloud of particles dispelled outward with a burst, revealing the outer rim to the night sky.

As the *esclaves* crossed the wall, they spread out in all directions. Ever staggered back to him.

"We get to an *esclave*," she said. "It'll take you to a doctor." She leaned down and grabbed him around the shoulders from the side, this time avoiding his chest. She pulled upward and got him in a half-kneeling position.

He heard the scariest noise in his life right then, and they both looked back at the gate. One of the *deplacers* had reached the opening. It was much too big to fit through the gate but used its forks on massive arms to grab the top of the housing and lift. As the wall foundation crumbled and fell outward, the *deplacer* lifted the air lock as one piece and tossed it casually to the side.

Ever continued dragging him, but they didn't go far before they were spotted. *Cultivers* sprinted in all directions, but the *maitre de terrain* found them first. It came from behind, crashing through the trees. Palm leaves stuck to the *maitre's* body, and branches wedged into its joints. A whole uprooted tree was tangled in a rear leg.

Lucas must have analyzed their trail and searched for them by following their footsteps. His two front legs joined into a concave platform. He held them out to Ever and Ailbe. The angular head turned to Ever.

"Put Ailbe on the blades," Lucas said to her. It was Fallon's voice coming out of the *maitre's* speaker grill.

Ever carefully half-slid and half-dragged him to the platform. He was mostly curled up into a ball, his muscles spasming painfully. There was room on the platform, and she adjusted him into a secure position.

After examining his cargo, Lucas's head turned back to Ever. "Wait here." And then the *esclave* took off, moving faster than Ailbe thought possible.

# 5. CAUGHT

Ever watched all the *esclaves* turn around and swarm back into the bubble, which wasn't a bubble anymore since it was open to the air. The long legs of the *maitre de terrain* extended to a height as the *maitre* ran. Lucas and Ailbe went right over the top of the wall as if it wasn't there, leaving her alone in the field.

Her solitude was short-lived. She could see her mother riding *cultivers* coming toward her from the ruins of the gate. The *cultivers* had formed themselves into a palanquin, with two *esclaves* becoming a platform while six ran along beside, holding the platform level across the uneven furrows. Fallon sat cross-legged in the center.

When the platform reached her, Fallon stepped off in a fluid motion. The normally stiff *esclaves* bent with her movements until her feet touched the ground.

Ever wondered where Ailbe was, but the questions to the net didn't return answers she could understand, and a fresh wave of tears moistened her cheeks as she gasped and choked, trying to calm her breathing. Her body shook with fear and adrenalin, and she went to wrap her arms around her mother, but Fallon batted her arms away and wrapped a hand around the base of her head. Fallon's other hand gripped her jaw firmly.

The first touch was like ripping a band-aid off a fresh cut at the base of her brain stem, and she went completely rigid as an unpleasant tingling sensation went down her spine to her fingertips and toes.

Fallon seemed to look right through her. She had an indecipherable expression about what she saw, but Ever felt certain it was accompanied by disappointment. After a moment, she released her.

"You'll be okay, but we have to get those clothes off you right now." Fallon stepped back. Ever stepped forward toward her mother, but Fallon held up her palm in the universal gesture to stop.

"All the clothes off right now. Leave them in the field."

Her sadness turned rapidly to helplessness and shame. She started by taking off her shirt, then sat down and took off her shoes, socks, and, finally, pants. Her mother didn't seem to care that she was sitting in the dirt.

Under her scrutinizing gaze, she finally removed her undershirt but left on her underwear.

"Everything, Ever," Fallon said.

"But I can't go back naked," she protested. "What if someone sees me?"

"They have better things to do. Because of your antics, everyone on the outer rim will be locked in their houses for the next two months."

"I didn't break the bubble."

"No, you didn't, but you were fortunate that an *esclave* found you," Fallon said. "They're programmed for personal protection, but their programming must be flawed because they put others in danger by breaking the bubble. I'm sure that will be addressed, and we will not discuss it."

Ever hesitated, but Fallon seemed like she would wait indefinitely, so Ever gritted her teeth and took off her underwear. Now, all her clothes were on the ground, and she covered herself with her hands in shame. She was miles away from the gate, at least where the gate used to be.

Fallon turned and motioned her to follow along. They marched with the *esclave* troupe behind them until they reached a reservoir with a hydrant and hose. At intervals, irrigation stations pumped clean water into the fields the same way they were set up in the Control Group. She knew immediately what would happen before Fallon picked up the end of the hose and opened the valve.

When the cold water hit her, she wanted to turn and flee. The air was hot and humid, but the water was freezing cold. She danced around as the jet seemed to hit her from all sides.

"Stand still. We have to get as much as we can off you."

"What's on me?" she cried harder now as her teeth chattered, but she resolved not to move until Fallon was done. Fallon circled around her mercilessly with the jet of water.

"A toxic nerve agent," Fallon said. "Those plants were designed to capture the chemicals in the soil and move them into their leaves so they can be recovered safely and disposed of. You're very lucky. If you had attempted to cross over any further down the road, Albie would've been carrying you out, and you would have spent the next week puking up blood."

At the mention of Ailbe, her shame rapidly piled on guilt. She dragged him into this. While she was complaining, she didn't know what happened to him.

Fallon sensed the change. "He's already in the hospital, and they are administering an antidote. Fortunately for him, we know exactly what you two have been into. His recovery will not be quick." Fallon's hard eyes scoured her worse than the cold water. "You will visit him every day until his recovery is complete."

"Of course," she agreed, relieved and not daring to ask why he was so much sicker than she was.

"And after you visit Ailbe, you will be in your room studying every plant we have out here, their purpose, and why they are dangerous."

She nodded in agreement, not risking a response that might be interpreted as an objection. She liked the farm equipment, but she hated botany. However, right now, her mother made perfect sense. After she was thoroughly hosed down, she walked back with their mother. True to Fallon's statement, she saw people rushing between the houses using the transparent tubes that bridged the buildings, but they were too busy to glance her way.

# 6. GRANDFATHER

Ever adapted quickly to her new schedule and the new reality of spending most of her time inside under her mother's watchful gaze.

When the bubble burst, the outside air contaminated the purified air in this section of the outer rim but not the whole outer rim. Apparently, when the bubble started losing integrity, an inner barrier segmented this part of Dill from the rest.

The window in her room revealed less after the damage. The humidity fogged over the glass in the morning. The street outside was desolate. *Esclaves* moved freely through the contaminated air, but bicycle traffic declined, and the cowl-covered pedestrians with their masks and filters were difficult to recognize. Her mother wasn't popular with their immediate neighbors, which wasn't to say they didn't trust her. They listened closely when she spoke but seldom invited Fallon and, by extension, Ever to a social activity.

When foot traffic on the sidewalks diminished, everyone used the bridges connecting houses to move in and out of the rim. Instead of looking out the window, she found herself watching the viewscreen by the lift as unfamiliar people crossed the sky bridge, walking between houses to get to a terminal.

Although it was common knowledge that *esclaves* broke the bubble to rescue two children in danger, she wasn't sure if anyone other than her immediate neighbors knew who the children were, and her mother told her not to speak of it again, but the guilt gnawed at her until she approached her mother at the table in the morning.

"Aren't the peacekeepers going to come for me?" she asked her mother. She imagined a small army of blue *flics* at her door. Their squared-off bodies could extend to block doors or cage miscreants. She rarely saw the machines but knew their function.

"Why would they do that?" Fallon asked. "The *esclaves* caused the damage, a fault in their programming."

"But I was the one they saved."

"Very few people know that. Right now, you are a child, and your privacy is protected—no pictures or streams. That won't be the case when you grow up. Everything, and I mean everything, is recorded if you know how to ask the question."

"I just need a bag."

"Why?"

"To pack for jail. I'll be living there from now on."

"You can pack a bag if you want, but you won't leave here. I'm glad you feel responsible. You share responsibility. You violated curfew. You ignored multiple warnings. Disobeyed me —all for a look outside."

Fallon got up from the table and left, presumably for her workroom. Ever knew she left out Ailbe. He was recovering faster than expected, but her mother seemed more concerned with Ever's new botanical studies and the state of her room than his well-being.

*Esclaves* worked on the new gate behind her house every day. The new gate was much larger than the old one. When complete, the new gate would be large enough for *deplacers*, and the bubble would be reloaded with inert particles.

In the meantime, massive air filters rolled into the streets to clean the air. Her mother seemed to think the effort was a waste of energy, but she rarely mentioned her thoughts to others, only to Ever when the noise from the giant turbines rattled the walls.

She continued to watch her neighbors roam through the tubes and houses for the next few weeks without complaint. The feelings of shame and worry diminished until she mentioned to her mother how pained she felt that the *esclaves* were so poorly programmed that they put everyone at risk. The bald assertion with a direct stare, followed shortly by a deep sigh.

The days were long again and she preferred people interacting over people watching. The people she usually met in the Control Group used *esclaves* to visit the farm, and she wasn't allowed outside the house. At school, she had viewscreens, but at home, the only viewscreen was embedded into the lift, forcing her into the hallway.

Most of the time, she used the screen to watch people commute, but that was boring until she thought of attaching stories to the people. She broke out her figures from confinement and started changing them to match the people on the screen.

The figures turned into caricatures, an unfamiliar term that came to her as she built a story. The story became elaborate until her mother found her playing at the lift.

Fallon took the altered figurines, examining each one. Some were missing arms or legs or made out to be young or old. They were all dressed in scraps she found in the recycling and dyed with food coloring. They were in a battle, and each side had its own color. She named each one after people she'd seen and told her mother the names.

Fallon listened gravely to the detail, giving no hint of recognition, although she was sure her mother must recognize the names.

"Ever do you understand what an eimai is?" Fallon asked. "I

thought they would have explained this in school."

"Ailbe claims I don't have one," she said, annoyed. "But I think he just doesn't know how to look."

"Some people keep their eimai closer than others," Fallon said. "We keep our eimai in here." Fallon pointed at her heart. "But most people keep their eimai out, visible to everyone." Fallon raised her hands, pointing out to the sky.

"That's why I know things when I look at them," Ever said. "People don't know who I am?"

"They do," Fallon said, "but they don't know much since we hold it so close. It's not uncommon in the Union, but it is uncommon in Dill."

"Then why don't we put our eimai out there?" she asked. She wasn't sure where there was, but she figured it was all around if she couldn't see it.

"That's part of who we are, but the important thing to remember is that everyone takes eimai seriously. Although most of that eimai is emotional and intellectual, part of it is physical too."

"My figures are like miniature people with their own eimai," she said.

"But they are also copies of people you know—poor copies. How would you like it if someone made a poor copy of you?"

She thought about that one for a moment, not liking the comparison.

"I guess I wouldn't like it, but it's not like I'm harming them. No one knows about it but me."

"That's not completely true, but even if it were, you would still limit yourself to believing what you created was real. You need to be careful with how you use eimai, especially physical attributes. The hallmark of civilized society is recognizing different but equal."

Fallon took the figures she modified to the first floor, where she dumped them into the grinder. She begged her not to, but her mother activated the grinder as she stomped to her room.

*How can she be so stupid?* She knew they weren't real

people. The more she thought about it, the more ridiculous her mother sounded.

The tension lasted through the day but dissipated to boredom going into the next. She avoided the lift viewscreen. Until the lift activated, sending her a mental chime. That was unusual, and she jumped from her bed to get a look at the guest at her lift door.

The streets were not used yet, and the guest had come through the corridors connecting the houses along the rim. The only access to the living space was from the lift shaft. When an unfamiliar person triggered the lift to descend, the system automatically sent a query to the occupants.

She peered through the viewscreen. For a moment, the screen showed no one. She tried switching the angles. The screen flashed, and a person appeared at the lift door.

It was an old man with wavy grey-brown hair and short grey whiskers. He was of medium build and wore a worn, frayed single suit, a color somewhere between brown and rust. The many pockets created bulges all over his body. The backpack he wore was a solid black metallic shell fitted to his suit. There was a green canvas bag at his side. He had big boots buckled to the suit but his gloves seemed to be missing.

She did not know who he was, and as the old man looked directly at the camera, she tried to identify him. The response was only one word. "Jorge". She focused on the query and tried to dig deeper, but nothing new came up.

A bubble popped on the screen from her mother.

"You can let him in."

She thought she heard her mother's voice in her mind, but getting confirmation from the screen was good. She pressed the button to allow entrance to the living space, and the lift descended.

The lift doors opened to reveal the old man taller than Fallon and much taller than Ever, who only came up to Fallon's shoulder.

"You've grown so much," Jorge said.

She found his familiarity immediately off-putting. No one commented directly on her physical appearance, and her mother just said such comments were uncivilized. *I can one-up his rudeness.*

"Who are you?" she demanded. There was no hostility, but good manners dictated letting the person in, showing them to a chair and asking them if they wanted something to drink. She stood in his way, holding the lift doors open with a wide stance, and pretended she was a *flic*. This door was impassable.

"Your grandfather, of course," Jorge said with a grin. "You're a lot like your mother." The old man stepped neatly around her, swiveling with deft steps. As she stood there stunned, he retreated around the corner to the living room.

She knew she had a grandfather but didn't know who his grandfather was. She asked her mother many questions about her family growing up—about her father. Most of the time, the answers were simple and unrevealing, such as "He left." The answers were pointed and delivered with steady don't ask for more expression, making her give up.

The few things she knew about her grandfather directly corresponded to how improved her mother was as a parent. She had the impression that her grandfather was meticulous and demanding in organization and hygiene. The description didn't match the disheveled, sweaty old man who smelled distinctly of the worst parts of outdoor living.

As she rounded the corner into the living room, she found Jorge rearranging the furniture. He moved the chair directly in front of the couch, sat down on the couch, put his feet up on the chair, and motioned for Ever to sit on her own couch.

"How's it been?" Jorge said. "News of you seems to get around."

"Fine," she said cautiously, "What news?"

"Why the bubble, of course," Jorge said. "It's probably been fifty years since Dill had a failure. The Free People are laughing from here to Oastin. They say the Oastinish are smirking under their wide brimmed hats, but I doubt that. Whenever the Oastinish hear about a bubble failure, they spend all their time looking at old weather reports."

"I thought they didn't release my name," she said, stung.

"Naturally not, but who else could it be?" he grinned. "Our family has a history of troublemaking. You're starting at an early age."

How Jorge said family seemed different. She had often heard of "a" family or "the" family, but he took possession of the concept.

He also took possession of the couch and attempted to soften the pillows that supported his back.

"I don't know when hard couches came into style," he said. "There was a time when you could sit on a couch as if you were sitting on a cloud. Now everyone has to be industrious all the time, and no one can sit comfortably."

Fallon's workroom door opened, and she stepped out.

"What are you doing here, old man?" Fallon asked. Her mother's tone was accusatory.

"I came for moral support," he said. "What has it been three or four years?"

"More like fifteen or twenty," Fallon said. "Don't you have a place you need to be?"

"That job can take care of itself for a while. Sometimes, it's good to step away and get a big-picture perspective. You are part of the picture. It sounds like you could use the help."

"I'm doing just fine," she said.

"There's no doubt about that. I was talking to Ever here, and I can tell she's quick—so quick that I think maybe it's time for her to go on a little trip and see the countryside."

"That sounds like a reward. She has responsibilities."

"Nothing that can't wait for a day or two."

"An overnight trip?" Her mother's eyebrows arched in surprise. Ever couldn't understand what she was hearing. Her mother was usually involved with every decision and place she went to. Now, the grandfather she never met was proposing a trip, and Fallon seemed to consider it. *Am I being sent away?*

"Only one night. I have friends outside the city we can stay with."

"Free People," Fallon said flatly.

"Good people," Jorge responded. "An excellent family, allies, by the way."

"I doubt they even know what they are supporting," Fallon said. "I'm sure they spend most of their time digging holes, looking for clean water."

"It's not so bad in the country, Fallon," the old man said reprovingly. "They live about a day's walk north of the city, not that far. They have a horse."

"Really?" Fallon asked, surprised. "How did they manage that?"

"They keep it completely separated from other horses," Jorge said. "The whole family spends time with the animal. I think they have it convinced they are horses. It's perfectly safe."

"That's incredible. Okay, you've convinced me, old man, you can have your two days." Fallon looked at her. She seemed to be mentally sizing her. "I've got an exosuit for Ever in storage. You can take care of the rest?"

Jorge nodded while Ever stood stunned. She was being entrusted with a strange old man for two days.

# 7. THE TRIP

Ever wasn't sure what to pack. Her mother and the old man sounded at odds. He insisted she didn't need to bring anything, while her mother wanted to be prepared for everything.

Fallon opened one of her storage rooms and returned with an exosuit in burgundy similar to the one the old man was wearing but folded and clean. She even brought out a set of boots, but this was where Jorge stopped her.

"Her shoes will be good enough," Jorge said. "We can loosen them up to fit over the suit, and it's not far. Perfectly safe."

Her mother's expression was flinty. "I'll not have you put her in danger, old man. You don't know what might get stirred up in the dust."

Ever's fear of traveling with a stranger had switched to enthusiasm, but these arguments usually prevented her from doing anything fun. She held her breath and watched. She learned long ago that interfering with positive or negative input would make it worse.

"How long has it been since you've crossed open country?" Jorge asked.

Fallon paused. "It has been a while," she admitted.

"Then take advice from a traveler. There's nothing

dangerous this close to the city. Right now, the biggest danger is blisters, and I don't want to carry her back. This is heavy enough." He pointed at the backpack he wore.

"That's your responsibility, old man."

"You don't have to remind me," he said. "I've been carrying it a long time. The suit will work fine with the shoes. It's bad enough that you have her wearing a full exosuit. Climate protection would be sufficient. Does she know how much it weighs?"

"She'll be fine," Fallon said. "It might slow her down so you can keep up."

The old man huffed, but then he grinned, and everything was okay. This left Ever in her bedroom with her school bag. She knew nothing about the family they were staying with and very little about horses. She recalled learning in school that they were dangerous and roamed the plains in the northwest.

At first, Ever planned to bring her figurines, but they wouldn't all fit in the bag, and then she realized with horror she made them from plant husks. From what little she recalled, horses ate plants. One crisis narrowly averted, and that eliminated almost every craft she could bring from her room.

She decided to bring at least two sets of clothes in case she got lost. She also went to the kitchen and took utensils. *How can I eat without my favorite spoon?*

One of her favorite toys was a set of small historical animals carved from rock. The animals were heavy, and the bag was bulging from the clothes, but she had to bring them.

Last, with effort, she slid in two of her favorite books. Most reading was done on a screen in school, and she could recall any story she'd ever heard, but it was possible to get printed books, and these were some of the most expensive possessions she owned. Compared to Ailbe, she had almost no possessions at all, and this was a rare opportunity. The books would have to be shown off.

The following morning, she felt mostly prepared, but the old man looked skeptically at the bag.

"Can you even pick it up?" he asked.

"Of course I can," she said. She bent down and put one strap around her shoulder to show him just how light the bag was. She grunted as she stood and tottered off balance for a minute, but she managed to get both straps over her shoulders with an effort.

The old man looked at her gravely. "Have you tried on the exosuit yet?"

"I was just going to do that." She slowly removed the straps and sat her bag down with an audible thunk.

The suit required some effort to get into. It went over her clothes, leaving only her hands free. There were buckles on the legs and arms for heavy boots and gloves, but she didn't mind missing those. She could move more freely with her shoes and preferred her hands free.

There were also buckles around her neck and shoulders for a cowl and mask. Ever saw masks worn outside, and the teachers' ceremonial robes had cowls draped across their backs. Most of the clothing in Dill suggested where a cowl might be fitted even if it was missing.

The exosuit was heavy but also cool to the touch. Every motion she made seemed to be magnified slightly, as if the fabric strained with her to complete the movement. Experimentally, she tried running around in the suit, jumping up on the couch, back to the floor, and quickly sprinting around the lift. There was a distinct smell, like cleaning chemicals, but the suit felt cool, and she had a free range of motion.

"That's enough of that," Fallon said. "Can you still carry your bag?"

She went over to her bag and lifted it. "No problem," She wiped at her face. *Is that water on my face?*

"You wanted to take her." Her mother shrugged at the old man dismissively.

He gave her a mocking salute with a grin. "It's a worthwhile lesson."

They set out a little bit later in the morning. The sun was still behind the buildings on the east side of the bubble, but as soon as it rose, the light refracted, giving the bubble a warm, scintillating glow.

Jorge pulled two hats from his canvas bag and set one on her head. The oversized hat had floppy sides.

"Not a perfect fit," he said, "but it's extra protection."

They left through the upper floor corridors, joining the morning foot traffic on the bridges, but before long, they took a public lift to the ground floor.

They were north of her house but still in the Control Group. As they exited the lift, she could hear the massive air filters in the street drowning out all the other sounds until they reached the wall.

She didn't question why they were using a gate from the farm. Jorge must have his reasons. Perhaps this was the fastest way to go. Walking or riding bicycles was encouraged in the bubble, and infrastructure was designed for it, but Dill was far too large for manual transportation. A series of hypertubes connected the city at public junctions spread around each ring road. Unlike spokes in a wheel, the transportation hub was in the city's north section, where the intercontinental hypertubes pushed commerce to other territories in the Union.

Before they walked too close to the gate to be heard, the old man stopped and raised his hand, fist closed.

"Open Sesame." Jorge extended his fingers dramatically, wiggling them in the air. The gate blinked to life, lights flashing. The doors slid open to reveal the inner lock. She was not impressed.

"You had Mother open the gate for you," she accused the old man.

Jorge looked a little hurt. "I have a few tricks of my own," he said, eyes twinkling.

They exited the lock and walked the gravel roads between the fields. This was all stuff she'd seen before, making it patently uninteresting and dull, but the air smelled fresh of growing plants today.

As they walked, Jorge quickly pointed out the roads' organization. The gravel roads made a labyrinth, but if you were willing to take an indirect route, you could stay on the road and leave the city without cutting across furrows.

Each field was marked with signs showing what type of plants were cultivated and included added environmental variables. Some farm plots were walled and glassed, but most were open.

Jorge delighted in pointing out every sign to her, and he would often stop for a second or two and either shake his head in dissatisfaction or nod approvingly.

She couldn't care less. Her eyes were on the road, and it wasn't until almost noon when he stopped by yet another sign. His burgundy suit was covered in pockets with plastic zippers and flaps, each one stuffed with something from their pantry. He had a canvas bag on his shoulder and a backpack he always kept on. Overall, he resembled a weathered conch shell she had seen in a biology class on the ancient ocean.

He put down his canvas bag and fished out a bottle of water and two cups.

"This is it, the city limit."

Ever looked back at Dill. From this far away, the curvature was slightly visible, including a new wall, partly constructed. The new outer ring expanded the city into the northwest. There was a massive complex of tubes on the north side of the bubble. A transit center ran underground and above ground in all directions, but she was miles away from discerning any pods traveling the tubes. The bubble glistened under the direct sunlight.

She should have been overheating from the climate as most people stayed indoors in the middle of the day, even in the bubble, but her suit was cool if still heavy. She'd gotten used to the extra weight. The exosuit spread the weight across her entire body with an ingenious set of internal straps that assisted her movement.

Jorge had long since given her gloves to protect her hands, and the big floppy hat repelled the sunlight, although the reflection off the ground left her squinting from the brightness.

She looked past the city, and there was nothing but grass and wildflowers. The road made faint elevations and descents, but it was not rolling, just boring. The field grass wasn't even tall, although there was a distinct smell of recent growth, and she could tell that enormous sections of the grass had been cut.

"There's nothing here," she said with disappointment.

"At least for a while, this is all grass," he said. "They send out *esclaves* occasionally to keep it cut. It will be another four or five hours before we reach the tree line."

She immediately perked up.

"There's a small group of the Free Folk who trade with the city to the north, northwest of us. They've built a semi-permanent encampment there."

"Free Folk?"

"Free People your mom might have called them. Folk is an old term, but they've always existed. In ancient texts, there are always Free People. Sometimes, they are called folks, sometimes even free men. The words get changed around, but they often like to travel and always live away from the city. I doubt your mother had anything good to say about them."

*That was certainly true.* The few times Fallon had mentioned the Free People, she looked angry. She asked Jorge why.

"That's an old story, but the important part is that she isn't really angry with them. She just wants them to be safe. They're a hard group to convince."

"But you said it was safe out here."

"Yes, this is close to the city it's safe. We could get help almost immediately. How many *esclaves* do you see?"

At first, she thought he was joking. There were so many *esclaves* in the bubble, either flying or walking, that they quickly became part of the background. The field was empty, devoid of machines, but she paused to count. She could see an *apiculteur* trundle around the field surrounded by a swarm of buzzbees. There were flying *esclaves* that moved so quickly she couldn't identify them. They headed into the city or away from it, far from her, but quite a number. There were a few *cultivers* in the grasslands. She spotted a few holes in the ground and she expected there were *esclaves* underground aerating the soil.

She stopped counting. These machines were all pretty limited in intelligence, but there were still hundreds.

"But these are dumb machines," she said.

"Dumb, but still connected to the net and still an *esclave*."

"You mean my mother is watching us right now?" she said.

"Well, your mother is in charge of the farm *esclaves,* so technically she wouldn't have access to these," Jorge said solemnly, but then he winked. "Knowing your mother, I'm sure she's found a way."

Ever waved her arms around in every direction.

"What are you doing?"

"Waving at Mother!"

# 8. THE WOODS

They walked for several more hours before Ever saw even one tree. Her school bag pulled at her shoulders, and the weight became increasingly uncomfortable. She shrugged, shifting the position of the backpack and ultimately finding the easiest recourse was to drag the bag behind her. She tried that for only a short time before Jorge wordlessly picked up the bag, tossing it easily over a shoulder.

During that time, he introduced her to what he called "field rations." These were reconstituted blocks of plant matter shaped into cubes, stamped with a date and a code, and then dried into bricks. She sniffed at the block, tentatively searching for a recognizable odor, and detected nothing but the faint smell of dried wood.

After a tiny nibble, she determined the brick was overall tasteless, and she refused to eat it. He kept prodding her to at least keep nibbling on the plant brick. Her refusal got so far that he threatened to set down her bag, at which point she agreed to hold the ration and try some now and then.

After a few miles, Dill dwindled from sight, and she encountered her first natural tree. The geography she learned from aerial photographs in school was full of straight lines, but in person, the tree line was not straight. Everything under the bubble was constructed with perfect angles and calculated arcs, leveled, centered, flat, and dull, but not natural.

The road was relatively flat, and while she could see pretty far into the distance, the first tree she saw stood alone near the road.

It wasn't a tall tree, and she recognized the species from the farm. The green leaves at the top sprouted from a twisted and stunted frame. The tree provided very little shade and no reason to stop. The farm had plots of trees, grasses, and flowers, but the area around Dill lacked variety, so she asked Jorge.

"They don't encourage growth this near the bubble," Jorge said. "They don't discourage it either, but very little survives without active soil management. Years ago, when you planted a seed, it would grow. That's not the case."

"I'm not sure about that," she said. "I've seen seeds grow. In school, we grew lima beans, and for some of those plants, we took away light and water, but they all still tried to grow."

"I'm sure the soil you used was prepared for the experiment," he said. "Out here, if you plant a seed, it will die quickly. This grass will help repair the soil, but even this has to be actively maintained."

"Who maintains the grass?"

"The *esclaves* do the work, but people measure the soil. Don't worry. In a few more miles, you will be in the largest contiguous forest in the world with a variety of plant life."

After that first twisted tree, more trees dotted the landscape. She squinted at the road ahead and thought she could see a dark line at the edges of her vision. She wasn't sure if that line was in her imagination, but it got bigger with every step. She noticed that the trees spontaneously appearing in the landscape were taller, less twisted, and had darker green leaves.

As they walked further away from Dill. The size of the trees and the size of the leaves continued to grow. Many leaves had fallen on the ground, and a few had blown across the road. She picked one up, studying the veins and points. It was almost four times the size of her hand, larger than her head, and larger than any of the tree leaves on the farm.

She traced the veins of the leaf before dropping it. The trees were large enough to tower and cast a pool of darkness, but instead of random growth, they were spaced out almost mathematically, and she could see bright green *esclaves* moving in the woods.

These *esclaves* were not humanoid and would not fit through most doors. They were about twice the size of an adult and had six legs with ridges on the inside of each leg. As they scuttled about, she realized they could move in any direction. The eyes and antenna of the *esclave* rotated on a turret set at the top for a 360-degree view of their surroundings.

The *esclave* stopped by fallen tree branches, and she saw that each of the legs on the hexapede was equipped with different cutting tools. They carried a net on one side of their back and what looked like a giant stinger on the other. The esclave went from tree to tree, collecting sticks. Occasionally, they would climb straight up a tree and cut down branches, returning with limbs.

This was the first time she had seen an operation like this, and she had a lot of questions. Most of the time, her mother berated her for not finding the answers on her own, but the old man's good nature seemed like credit she could use instead of listening to the droning voice in her head whenever she sent a question to the net.

"Where do all the branches go?" she asked him.

"The *araignee* is one of your mother's favorite *esclaves*. She had some personal input into their design. They are collecting branches that will go back to Dill. Most of them will be ground down and shaped into particle board."

"What are those stingers for?"

"Those aren't stingers. They are collapsed solar panels. These *esclaves* are small and need to work independently for a long time. They can recharge their batteries sitting in a field or even hanging from trees."

"How many are there?"

Jorge laughed and said, "How many people live in the bubble?"

"Millions." Ever said but thought again. Jorge seemed to enjoy turning an answer into a question. *Or maybe he wants to laugh at me.* "They aren't all directeurs."

"No, they're not," Jorge said cheerfully, "There are hundreds of millions of people in Dill, not counting the other major territories that use this forest as a resource, and millions of *esclaves* maintain the forest, but every *esclave* doesn't need individual attention all the time."

He stopped considering for a moment while she attempted to rally another question. Since he was willing to answer, she wasn't above smiling and looking extra interested, but there was something about the trees that didn't make sense.

"There are probably as many kinds of *esclaves* as plants and animals now," Jorge mused.

That was when she noticed a pattern that bothered her.

"All the trees are the same," she said. Not just the same kind of tree. While she saw subtle differences in growth patterns, there were too many similarities.

"Yes," he said. "They are all clones. The ecology requires different species of trees in the forest to support livestock, but every plant in the forest is a clone. I'm sure you recognize these as oak trees. This tree was designed for this environment. The environment changed, but we don't need to make a new tree if we actively maintain the PH levels and regularly infuse the soil with bacteria."

"Creating new kinds of life is illegal." She knew the law very well. This was a law emphasized in school. It was a precept of the Union, and while she had a loose sense of justice for concepts like ownership or privacy, she was committed to fairness.

"Genetic engineering is regulated," Jorge said, unconcerned

with her posturing. "So is cloning, just like fusion reactors and weapons. Every tool has to be guaranteed to work without putting lives at risk. Territories like Dill are careful with tools that can break the Peace. That's a good way to get the attention of the Guardians. People who get their attention disappear.

# 9. THE FREE PEOPLE

The trees shouldered the road, blocking Ever's view, but she immediately noticed the shade's effect on her face. At least the giant trees held the oppressive heat from the sun above the forest floor. Sparse ferns grew under the canopy, increasing in density as the large leaves created cover from the direct sunlight.

Eventually, she neared the limit of walking she could endure. Her suit was cool, but she was sweaty and tired. The farther she walked, the heavier the exosuit became. The old man told her stories he said came from ancient texts—stories where exosuits could process sweat into drinkable water. The fantasy was hard to believe, and the old man admitted the technology seemed impossible. The gaps in her exosuit near her collar smelled funny, and her skin felt raw.

Jorge stopped to drink water again, passing a collapsible cup to Ever.

"Almost there," he said. After the brief respite, he picked up the pace as if he knew she wouldn't last much longer. The road continued to run through the forest, but it inclined slightly for a hillock. He seemed indefatigable, carrying three loads, while she trudged behind him, counting each footfall.

Before they reached the top of the hill, he turned sharply to the left and started walking off the road between trees and down a beaten path. The path was not wide, and the thick underbrush poked at her from each side, threatening her footing. Although the oak trees were the only tall trees, there was a low palm with spikey fronds and a fern that grew several feet off the ground. A few small wildflowers with pink and orange blossoms on vine-like stems curled around the taller plants.

The tracks of heavy boots stomped into the turf, creating a narrow corridor and forcing her to follow behind Jorge. Not that she had the strength to run ahead. The ferns grew above her waist, and she walked some time down the path before it turned back around the hillock and wound to a dugout into the hillside.

Several buildings, all made of local oak, stood beside the dugout. The structures were made of rough-cut timbers and boards, hidden by trees.

"This is the most southern trading post for the Free People," Jorge said, "and one of a loose collection of houses, but we are at the right place."

Through the lined and craggy trunks, she could see a glint. The thick finish on wooden slats gleamed in the low light on the wood-framed outbuildings. The sun was invisible, but in the summer months, the days were long, and she studied her surroundings.

They thatched the outbuildings with dried, woven fronds that were a foot thick at the top and bushy at the edges. She wanted to feel the texture but didn't see a convenient way to reach the eaves of the peaked roof.

Between the wood frame structures stood a large fire pit with half-burnt logs still smoldering. The distinct smell of smoke hung in the air, permeating the area. A tall pile of split wood logs stacked beside the fire with a hatchet embedded into the split wood marked recent activity. That seemed like a strange archaic tool to Ever, but maybe they had an *esclave* do the work.

Before they reached the house, a young woman came around the corner of one outbuilding. She carried a long-barreled, scoped weapon over her shoulders. It looked very heavy and had a tripod with a gimbal folded into the base. The barrel and tripod were metallic with a deep grey finish, but the stock was wooden and slotted with small tools embedded in the holes.

She was wearing an exosuit constructed the same as Jorge's and Ever's, but instead of a solid burgundy color, her suit shifted patterns into forest colors, and everything but her face and hands disappeared into the background when she stopped. She recognized Jorge immediately, but he held up his hand.

"Father," she yelled back to the door in the mound. After just a moment, the door opened to a large, bearded man. The door seemed of average size, but he had to duck his head and turn sideways to get through the frame.

When Jorge saw him, a strange ceremony started. Jorge went down on one knee and held up a hand expectedly.

"Dia San," Jorge said, waiting.

The tall stranger strode forward and gripped his hand, pulling Jorge up.

"Dia San I, Jorge," the stranger said. "Have I gone back in time? The last time I heard that, my grandfather was still alive. You bring back the last war before The Peace."

"There's no such thing as time travel, Richard, but it's good for the young to appreciate the past. That wasn't the first war. Until the Union, there was only war, and we celebrated pockets of peace as if they'd last for eternity." Jorge motioned to Ever, who stepped forward with trepidation. "This is my grandchild, Ever."

At the mention of her name, Richard looked sharply at Jorge, but he just shrugged.

"This *is* a good time for ceremony." Richard crouched to her height. His massive face dominated her vision, and his beard touched with a hint of gray, reached to her waist. "Hello, little one."

Normally, she would have been put off by his reference to her size, which was demeaning and uncivilized, and by his condescending tone. Still, Richard was so incredibly large she realized that everything must appear small to him. Even on his knees, he towered above her like a massive boulder.

Richard held out his hand. Easily large enough to engulf her arm, she took the gesture to mean something. Finally, she took the hand and squeezed it firmly. Size would not intimidate her.

"This is a mighty child you have," Richard said to Jorge, then turned back to Ever. "I also have strong children," Richard said, motioning to the young woman. The resemblance was unmistakable, but she was slight by any measure except for her arms. Unlike most women in Dill, she had shoulder-length hair tied back. "This is Riley, and Reign is in our stable."

"They both begin with R," Ever said.

"Yes, my wife was very pleased with me for some reason." Richard laughed. "She named both children after me."

"Where is your wife?" she asked without thinking.

"She died a long time ago. She fell into a rabbit warren and was killed instantly. Rabbits are vicious. You must always watch your step."

"I'm sorry." She shouldn't have brought up old memories. It was impolite to ask, but she found remembering her manners in unfamiliar situations hard.

"Don't be sorry. The highest honor we can pay to those we lost is to remember their success and learn from their mistakes. Even when it's difficult to do so. Always watch where you are going. Danger is only one step away." Richard looked back at Jorge as he returned to his feet. "Word of this must reach the others, but I will be here two months before the buyer of my horse arrives."

"That's not a concern. There's no rush and a lot of work to be done."

Richard lifted his eyebrows. They were big and shaggy, like

lifting two combs full of hair.

"There's been visitors recently," Richard said. "Missionary travelers moving overland and by tube. Their numbers are growing. Haven't you seen them on the road?"

"No, I've been away. Business to attend to in the west. I came back south by tube just the day before."

"You missed them by a little over a week. They are recruiting for the cause, although it's unclear what the cause is for. They keep the Peace but claim that true peace is found in the aether. The priest spent several days here until all the other families left and then branded a follower with the Third Eye."

"Branding?" the old man asked. "That's difficult to do."

"The priest worked himself up to it for over an hour, chanting before he applied the brand, and then he branded his own arm with the Eye. The priest claimed he could see through the Eye."

"Impossible," Jorge said flatly. "Their fearless leader makes claims while he hides in the shadows. I'm sure he would like nothing more than to turn people into *esclaves*. He's nothing more than a husk of what he used to be."

Richard shrugged, seemingly unconcerned by Jorge's sudden turn to bitterness. "The priest's arm was covered in hundreds of brands."

Jorge considered this carefully. "We need to talk more on this, Richard, but Ever would like to meet your horse. Could we let Riley make the introduction?"

# 10. THE SIBLING

Riley and Ever parted for the stable, leaving Jorge and Richard. She wanted to stay and hear more, but Riley kept her moving, guiding her by the arm. Riley's hold was unfamiliar and surprising. Usually, she was the one dragging Ailbe along, and in a momentary flash of chagrin, she realized her school, neighbors, in fact, everyone in Dill shared a concept of personal space she'd resisted all along.

The stable was a small building not far away but far enough that she couldn't hear what was being said. The building itself didn't seem any different from the other outbuildings that dotted the forest with wooden slats and a tufted thatched roof. A faint resinous odor caused her nose to itch, almost like pine. She hadn't seen any pine trees but knew several varieties existed on the farm.

"My father thinks this is the first stable since the beginning of the Peace," Riley said.

"Really?" She was unfamiliar with what a stable was, but like so many unfamiliar words, when she thought about it, she knew the definition.

"Yeah, I'm not sure. There aren't any records of domesticating livestock, but it would surprise me if this is the first or only attempt."

The stable had a newly expanded broad door and a small window on each side. Inside was a brown four-legged animal behind a half-height wall with two ropes securely tied to both sides of the frame. The ropes had a little slack, and she didn't think the horse could turn around, but otherwise, it seemed happy and focused on chewing.

She looked into the deep brown eyes, expecting to see malevolence buried beneath the surface, but the horse looked back at her with a dull-eyed expression of indifference.

Riley's sibling was feeding the animal by holding a bucket up to the horse's mouth. The horse didn't seem fully grown, and she struggled to find the word for a horse child until it came to her. It was a colt.

"Hey Reign," Riley said, "This is Ever. She arrived with Jorge."

Reign stiffened for a moment and then turned around. Ever realized then that he was blind.

Being blind was not an unusual condition. She knew many blind students in school. Most of them had an acute sense of vision, but not through their eyes. There were cameras and sensors all around Dill, and with them, a blind person could see clearly. Much more acute than a seeing person because they could see around corners and through objects. Some of them said they could see words spoken from a distance.

Since the technology was available, she'd tried testing this with Ailbe by having each of them sit in a separate room. They held up their hands with a different number of fingers extended, closed their eyes, and tried to get a picture of what the other person was doing. He claimed to have seen nothing.

She thought she saw a picture of Peanut, but no sooner did she see the black cat than Fallon came out of her workroom and told her that not only was she doing it wrong, and she was not allowed to "park in the handicap zone." She wasn't sure what that meant. Unlike all the other words and phrases her implant automatically provided, sometimes her mother used terms she didn't understand. Her mother made certain she stopped, and she hadn't tried again.

"That's a nice horse," Ever said by way of greeting.

"Obviously. We'll see if it lasts," Reign said. His tone was uncomfortably dismissive for an initial greeting. She could tell he was older than she was, older than Ailbe, but that was no reason to be impolite. "No one has tamed a horse before. There are ancient records of riding horses, but animals that we altered seem to hate us. I don't blame them for it. They all taste good." He laughed.

The horse continued chewing, otherwise oblivious to its likely outcome as a food source, but she couldn't help but feel a little sad for the beast.

Most of the protein in the city was plant-based from vertical farms, but there was also meat protein grown in vats and harvested from the countryside. The most costly meat was livestock harvested by *chasseur*. *Chasseurs* had four arms. Otherwise, they weren't that much different from the *cultivers*. The two arms in the back carried the carcass while the rest of the *esclave* mimicked human performance.

Some people enjoyed hunting by *chasseur*, and she'd heard of people paying for the experience and recording their kills. She hadn't realized the Free People were also hunters. Many people liked to watch the hunts, and she wouldn't be surprised if Riley sold her hunting expeditions, although she was too polite to ask.

Meat was not something that she enjoyed, although her mother would often make processed steak or goat for dinner. Even Ailbe seemed to have a taste for it. Sometimes she wondered if he didn't get his taste for meat from Peanut.

Riley leaned her gun against the wall carefully. The long barrel was balanced against a large moderator with blinking status lights, a large scope with a digital display. The double-sided view screen neatly folded into the frame. Cameras and other sensors in the moderator guaranteed every plasma bolt discharged was legal and safe.

"I had a run-in with a herd of goats this morning," Riley said. Her brother looked concerned, and she quickly added. "They were still far away, over four miles, but they turned in my direction, and the wind was against my favor. I was about thirty feet up in a tree when I spotted them. I was looking for stragglers. They must have caught my scent. An *araignee* warned me off."

"What could they do if you were in a tree?" Ever asked curiously.

"I'd probably have to yell for help." Riley shrugged. "It's never happened to me, but a large enough herd will chew down a tree to get to a person. They don't look very smart with their shifty square irises, but you have to respect the herd."

"Four miles." Reign snickered. "Sounds like you were going for a record."

"Their grandfather bulls-eyed goats and bear from over five miles away," the gun said from against the wall. "In fact, his last kill was 5.3 miles from peak to peak." The small speaker on the stock gave the gun a high-pitched nasal voice she found immediately annoying. The gun wanted to continue, but Reign interrupted.

"I don't want to hear that old story again, Varmint. You make it sound like he climbed both sides of the mountain for that kill and then hauled the carcass back after gutting the animal with his teeth."

"But he did!" Varmint exclaimed.

"Varmint?" she asked, surprised.

"It gave itself the name Varmint Slayer," Reign said tiredly, "and we haven't figured out how to fix it. I call it Varmint because that's what it is."

"He climbed both sides." The gun interjected. "The west side and the north side."

"No more," Reign commanded with finality, and the gun shut up, chastened.

"It's been in our family a long time." Riley grinned. "But Reign doesn't like it much. Especially since it passed to me."

"Maybe if you took him hunting with it?" Ever asked. When possible, she liked to play peacemaker, and she could sense a growing discord. Emotions between the two siblings changed direction quickly.

"I have chores to do." Reign grabbed a stick, set the bucket against the stable wall, and stalked out.

Riley shrugged an apology at her but waited for a moment until Reign was away.

"Reign can't see, so he can't hunt," Riley said.

That didn't make sense to Ever.

"I'm sure the gun could send him the picture if he practiced."

"The gun is not the problem."

That was when Ever noticed. She always knew where other people were, even if she didn't scout out information about their eimai. Even now, she had a feeling about where her grandfather was, but as soon as Reign left the room, he disappeared. She had no location sense about Riley or her father.

"You aren't connected?" She hadn't heard of this before. She didn't want to make it sound like an accusation.

"Very few of us are. Those who choose this lifestyle rarely get implants."

"Then Reign isn't allowed to see?" She knew her sense of justice was getting the better of her.

"Not at all," Riley said. "Father and I have encouraged him to get the implant, but Reign…" She seemed at a loss for words. "Reign's uncertain."

The sun was falling, and she wanted to learn more about the horse. Riley was glad to switch topics.

So Ever could see the animal better, Riley turned on push lights mounted on the walls. This gave the stable a warm glow. There were bags of grain that she inspected, along with shovels and drying grass under a hot lamp. Riley used a long rake to turn over the grass.

The horse defecated, and she was amazed at the size of

the growing pile of waste under the animal, although Riley reassured her the stall was cleaned out every day.

"How did you catch him?"

"It was not so much of a catch than a find. We were out west where the marsh meets the plains. There are herds of Mustang that travel from the north to the south during the rainy season."

"This one must have been separated from his heard early on," Riley continued, "because we found him wandering alone. He was weak, practically a newborn, but we fed him milk, and he didn't seem aggressive. We were able to find a buyer quickly, and we brought him here."

Ever continued to ask questions about the horse, and eventually, the last slivers of sunlight turned into evening. Riley needed to close the stable. Ever wanted to help, so they moved the horse to a separate stall, and Riley showed her how to shovel the manure and matted hay into a bucket to add it to a compost heap behind the building.

Riley closed all the windows and inspected the seals. She activated an air filter and inspected the cartridge. Finally, she inspected the batteries that powered all the systems in the stable.

Examining the arrangement, Ever realized almost everything was portable, even the windows and doors. She expected that if the Free People left, the only things that would remain were the walls and roof.

They retreated to the house under the hill when twilight turned to darkness. She had some concerns about leaving the horse, but Riley reassured her that only under the worst conditions would they need to bring the animal inside.

"The animal is adapted to outdoor living," Riley said. "We shouldn't have a problem. There's been no sign of lions this far south, and we keep the fire burning. They have no reason to travel this far, but my father says there is no reason to risk such an expensive commodity."

The mound house was not big inside, but it was a modern

shelter, well insulated, unlike the rough-shaped outbuildings around it. There was a viewscreen near the entrance with the weather, indoor and outdoor air quality, and travel guidance.

The ceilings were low if convex. She had a lot of room. Richard's hair nearly brushed the ceiling when he stood up from the table. There was one central dining room with a fireplace, a kitchenette, and four separate bedrooms around it. Each room was half a sphere, like a shipping pod cut in half and buried below ground.

There was also the soft, comforting purr of air conditioning, and she took off her outdoor wear and put the suit on a hook by the entrance. In contrast to city living, that was where all the modern comforts ended.

The facilities included an emergency bucket if you couldn't reach the outhouse, and she firmly resolved to hold it all night if necessary.

Overall, the house was disappointing and normal to her, except for the fireplace. Fire was carefully controlled in Dill, and the most she'd seen were the burners on her hydrogen stove at home. The dancing flames on burning logs immediately distracted her with the light and heat radiating through the glass. Perhaps Jorge had known this because he saved her a seat on the end of the table close to the fire and motioned for her to sit there.

Richard must have spread the table beforehand because all the plates and utensils were there, with a serving plate full of crusty biscuits and a stew in salty broth loaded with vegetables. She suspected the protein was a goat, but she didn't ask.

Richard stopped talking with Jorge long enough to serve. "No customs here," he said. "Dig in."

After the long walk with only a stale plant brick to chew on, her stomach rumbled before she could even take a bite. The food was both familiar and good. She had a warm and filled sensation that she rarely got when it was just herself and Fallon.

They ate silently, except for a few friendly jabs between Riley and Reign. Reign's mood improved, and he moved around the house so easily that she forgot he couldn't see.

Afterward, she helped clear the table and move the dishes to a small sink in the kitchenette on the wall, where Riley and Reign scrubbed and dried the plates and spoons by hand.

She offered to help with the scrubbing, but Richard kindly let her know it was their chore. This left her with little to do except admire the pictures on the wall. Compared to houses in Dill, there were many pictures.

Varmint Slayer hung over the mantle, and when she looked that way, the gun's scope lit up, but she quickly turned away, not wanting to engage the gregarious machine in conversation. Instead, she looked at the pictures on the wall. They were all static images of family that seemed to go way back. A wooden tool she didn't recognize hung on the wall.

"That's a guitar," Richard said, noticing her interest. "It would make sound from strings tightened across the box like an echo chamber." With Richard's direction, she noticed where strings could be tightened across the curved wood. "It was my mother's guitar. I can still remember her playing it a little. It made strange sounds. I'm not sure if she knew how to play it. No one has played music in a long time, but I still remember some verses. 'A clever string signed into bone will be the key to bring us home.'" Richard stated. "I've often wondered if the missing strings would make sounds in keys. Music was said to have keys."

She yawned loudly, unable to help herself, and Richard shrugged.

"We get up early here too, before the sunrise," he said a little sadly, "And there's still more to do before the night is over." Richard turned to Jorge. "We have one extra room." He was asking a question she gathered.

"Let's put Ever out here on the floor by the fire," Jorge said. "We can slide the table out of the way."

They moved the table out of the way and brought blankets

and pillows. While Jorge and Ever were arranging the space, she heard an argument in Reign's room. It ended quickly, but as Richard left the room, the door closed forcefully, rattling the frame, and Richard winced.

"I'm sending a message to the buyer," Richard said to Jorge. "If he wants the horse, he must get it in the next two days. We will head north after that."

Jorge nodded in agreement, and Richard continued, "This may be the last time I see you for a while, old friend. Riley and I will be up early hunting. We need fresh meat before we leave."

Jorge clasped Richard's hand.

"Good journey."

"And to you, old friend."

Ever slept late the following morning. The room was cool, and the fire died down in the fireplace to ashes. Richard and Riley were gone. They left to go hunting in the early hours. She had the faint memory of the door opening and closing but little else from their departure.

The old man was up, dressed, and putting his pack on the table. Surprisingly so was Reign, both up and carrying a canvas bag almost as big as he was.

"You're coming with us?" she asked, surprised.

"Obviously. Apparently, I'm needed in the city."

"That's not a bad way to look at it," Jorge said, "but try to keep an open mind, and you might be surprised at what you can learn."

"Where are you going to live?" she asked.

"That's also obvious," Reign said. "With you."

# 11. THE BEST PLACE

After a long day of walking, Ever, Reign, and Jorge returned to the bubble. While they were out, Fallon converted one of her storage rooms into a bedroom. Reign arrived to a bedroom complete with furniture but little else. Both children ate voraciously and then went to bed early after the walk.

Fallon and Jorge sat at the table. Jorge finished raiding the refrigerator and the pantry and built a fair-sized pile with several plates, bowls, and boxes. While he crunched through a feast for two, boxes and canned goods disappeared into the canvas bag sitting on the floor beside him. Fallon sat forward pensively in her chair. Her elbows were on the table, and her hands were steepled.

"There was a time when you would have observed more of the niceties before raiding my pantry," she said.

"I guess that's the benefit of familiarity," Jorge said with a grin.

"They say familiarity breeds contempt. But putting that aside, at least for now, it's refreshing to see a blatant rascal in action."

"Ever doesn't provide you with enough entertainment?" Jorge asked.

"Ever definitely keeps me on my toes. You can't believe half of what she does and almost everything she says. Ever's good at heart, though. Then, of course, there's you."

The old man laughed. He didn't seem to take the slur with

offense.

"That's why we need these brief visits. The world, outside and inside, is changing."

"For the worse?" Fallon asked.

"I can't be sure," responded Jorge thoughtfully. "It could be outside manipulation. In Dill, it seems like we lost a lot, but if you get far enough out into the countryside, you can still find the 'niceties' you're missing."

"I don't know if we are talking about the same thing, old man."

"They have customs, traditions, and even some strange behaviors in the densely populated areas, but they don't know why they repeat the same patterns like beats in a story. If you get far enough away from the city, you can connect with the why. Where the Peace is thinner, I can judge the changes."

"I think you are spending too much time with the Free People," Fallon said, disgusted. "They spend their brief lives killing and hiding and, on occasion, pontificating."

"It's their choice, and it's getting better, Fallon," Jorge said. "Their lives are not as short. The cleanup efforts are helping, but the actual point is they understand the value of the old traditions. Of course, when you get a few people together, the herd mentality washes out critical judgment. We solved the who, but the how and why remain elusive. Maybe that's why they stay away. At some level, the Free People must recognize what they are losing even if they can't understand it."

"I'm not sure if that's a good thing," Fallon remarked. "What we had nearly destroyed us."

"And protecting the Union might destroy us, but the Union needs allies," Jorge said. "Sometimes the best ally is an old enemy. I'll try to make more frequent visits. There are too many listeners on the net. We need to stick to the old protocols for communication."

"Exit strategy?"

"It's too early. This is still the best place to be." Jorge glanced off toward Ever's room. "She's still so young."

"Age takes time, old man. You should be a specialist of time at your age. She is at a wonderful age for changes."

"Not that kind of change."

"Don't underestimate Ever. I've noticed a lot of time spent sneaking around behind closed doors and a definite penchant for lying, but what I see the most is the ability for independent action."

"That's not hereditary."

# 12. THE DREAM

"I don't understand why you won't go," Ever told her mother. Fallon stood near the dining room table. A simple rectangular wood table, unremarkable except that the transparent finish on the boards repelled Ever's every attempt to scratch the surface over the years.

Her school robes lay in a heap on the table, right beside Reign's, with the exception that his were neatly folded over a chair. Fallon circled him with a pair of shears. The antique hair trimmers buzzed with an annoying sound, and she'd already changed the battery twice. Cameras on the shears created a three-dimensional model of your head, and you could select a style with a thought.

Technically, he should have been able to do this on his own, but he had little faith in the shears, even though this was the only day where style didn't matter. Her hair was already cut a half inch from her scalp. It was a warm day, and the cold draft around the back of her neck felt amazing. She wondered if tomorrow she'd miss the locks that went past her shoulders.

"I don't need to go," Fallon said. "I already know who you are. I don't need the University's categorization theory to give me a label."

"It's not just a label. It represents how everyone sees you and how you see yourself," Ever explained for the umpteenth time.

"Fallon's right," Reign said. "The Free People don't use labels."

"The *Free* People?" Ever asked, putting sarcasm on the word free. "You can't even say the word 'people' without adding a label."

"Obviously we have to distinguish ourselves, but just one label is enough."

"Why didn't you protest the ceremony?"

"I considered it, but then I would have to take extra tests for any class I was interested in. One and done is better than that. There's not much left for me here, anyway."

"You need to give school a chance," Fallon said. "You've barely scratched the surface of the skills you can learn. Speaking of which," she paused and looked hard at Ever. "Stop trying to scratch the table."

Lost in thought, Ever had seized one of the extra blades for the shears and was scraping its edge against the tabletop. She promptly placed the blade on the table. There were no visible marks on the surface, but she thought her fingers felt an imperfection—time to hastily change the subject to her mother's deficient parenting.

"If you aren't there, how will I get an accurate placement?" she complained. "The test is supposed to consider how other people see me." She thought of an old rhyme that went with the classis. "One to love and One to hate, Two for friends to make your fate."

"We don't hate anyone in the Union," Fallon said. "We rehabilitate. My attendance won't make a difference. It might even hurt your chances."

Reign nodded in agreement. His eyes were closed. After much dithering, he got an implant. Cameras built into the walls and ceilings gave him perfect vision, regardless of his eyelids.

"You know I'm going to get into Divinus," Ever said. "I have the highest marks at school, and every teacher tells me I can do anything."

"I think you're just interested in the job opportunities you get from being selected first in Divinus," Reign said. "It's more than the label. It's the rank that makes the difference to the University."

"Of course, I'll be the highest rank. Ailbe made the highest rank."

"In Anima," Reign added.

"Ailbe's a unique talent," Fallon added. "I remember a time when we had over four classis. The classis used to mean something. Then it became popular to divide people into groups of four, and people made silly rhymes."

"The four classis have been the standard in the West since the Union," Reign said, puzzled. "Just like the East uses caste. It's just easier to change classis in the West."

"That's an oversimplification. Not all the territories in the West use classis, and not every territory in the East uses caste. Four classis is hardly a measure for anyone. The effort is a waste of time."

"There's really only three classis," Ever mused. "Just Divinus, Persona and Anima."

"If you want to live in a city like Dill," Reign admitted. "I bet you already have a list of professions."

She had a list of professions she'd been thinking about for a while, but she didn't want to share them with him. He would make fun of her decisions, and her mother would only be disappointed if she changed her mind later. Still, it was worth throwing a few thoughts out there to see what they thought about her options.

"I've been watching the construction of the new rim road," she began, but he interrupted.

"You want to go into construction?"

"No, at least not personally. I want to make sure it's built to the right standards."

"Civil Architecture," Fallon said thoughtfully. Ever watched her expressions actively looking for any hint of praise or dissatisfaction, but Fallon was inscrutable. What she really wanted to go into was government. The government of Dill was run by the University, and only the highest-ranking academics in political science attained any actual status.

Fallon finished cutting Reign's hair, trimmed short like hers but faded in from the sides. Reign inspected the results and thanked Fallon. He didn't need a mirror.

Ever and Reign dressed in their school robes, pulling the ceremonial cowl over their heads. The cowls were too short to give more than the appearance of coverage, which helped. Many of the antiquated school systems still relied solely on facial recognition.

This wasn't a typical school day. Every territory in the Union that subscribed to the classis had a window of activity they could use for the selection process. Their school was not well funded, so they met in the middle of the night on a weekend.

For one brief instant, the Union AI, the most powerful intelligence in the world, would focus on her. In that instant, that massive intelligence would evaluate every thought she had and every thought about her and determine her destiny with a single word.

# 13. THE AI

Ever and Reign walked to school together, taking the sky tube across the outer rim to a public intersection and east to Third Rim Road. The school was one of the first buildings to dominate the landscape, easily the tallest.

She decided she was lucky to have his company. In the last two years, he'd completed a challenging schedule of condensed learning to match Dill's education standards. He was much older than she was, not that placement was determined by age, but despite his roughly average marks, she was a little envious of how quickly he sponged material. He was nearly finished with general education. Near her thirteenth year, she still had the chance to pick specialized courses. Ailbe told her everything would change when she turned thirteen. She didn't understand why, but she knew he came home shaken on his birthday.

A fortunate coincidence placed Reign with her for the categorization ceremony.

When they arrived at school, they took a lift from the public entrance to their section of the building. They couldn't go directly to their floor. They had to climb stairs the rest of the way. As usual, she was sweating, and he was muttering under his breath by the time they scaled the eight flights to their homeroom.

If going to school in the middle of the night could be considered normal, that was where normal ended.

"All the desks are gone," she said. A black-robed teacher immediately hushed her. The teacher's cowl was pulled down all the way, hiding her eyes but revealing her frown. Names sprang to Ever's lips, but following instructions, she said nothing as she was escorted around the room.

All the students were lined in a circle, incomplete because Ever and Reign were still early. Behind each student, family and friends gathered to watch the event. A teacher greeted each student who walked through the door, hushed them to silence, and then arranged them in order. Ever was more than a little disappointed when she looked at the empty space behind herself and Reign.

With practiced ease, the teacher drew back Ever's cowl and placed a headset over her freshly shaved head. A rigid frame of wires spiked into her scalp. It wasn't painful, but it wasn't pleasant.

She wondered why they couldn't do this with the implant for the hundredth time this week, not realizing she'd voiced her complaint aloud until the teacher touched her lips with a finger.

"The implant enhances the eimai, interpreting rational thought from the brain's logic centers. The AI will read every thought, conscious and unconscious, before deciding."

The teacher whispered her response with practiced, placating ease before moving on to adjust the headset on Reign's head. That freed Ever to look around, and she realized that not only was the furniture gone—there were no *esclaves* in the room. There were at least twenty teachers, the first time she had seen so many gathered physically in a single place, and she expected the circle to hold at least five hundred students.

Ever almost said something, but a firm look from the teacher silenced her and, as a new group walked by, ready to be placed in the circle, she decided that she could wait patiently if she had to.

There was nothing special about her homeroom. Recessed lighting, off-white paint, and rolled flooring decorated with false tiles made the space more "room" than "home." The vents blasted freezing air that did nothing for the smell of sweat and chemicals that pervaded the school.

Today, the lights were dim, but after sundown, they always dimmed to conserve power. She thought little of it, except that it lent an extra air of ceremony to the categorization.

In short order, the circle was complete. The teachers found spaces at intervals inside the circle. Throwing back their own cowls, they placed the same headsets on themselves. Everyone waited expectantly. There seemed to be some disagreement about who would speak, and she shifted from foot to foot until the principal arrived, parting the circle to reach the center.

The principal was a spare man with a short, well-trimmed beard. She had never met him, but she imagined running up and down the stairs all day would encourage a lean frame. He must have run from his last engagement because he was breathing hard, gasping, while attempting to project his voice to the other students.

"Today is your Categorization Day," the principal began huffing. "In five, no, make that four minutes, the Union will provide you with insight into your strengths and weaknesses. When humankind created AI, we realized a gift and a curse. For the first time, we knew an intelligence greater than our own, and for the first time, we were judged by our own creation. Today is the day you will be judged, but remember that no matter what you learn today, you are still human, capable of change, both for the better and the worse. Smarter hence the honor."

"Smarter hence the honor." Everyone intoned the words of Dill.

"You already know the classis. From this point forward, your schedule will be based on your rank and categorization.

One at a time, you will be called by name, step forward, and be examined. Your categorization and rank will be announced. You will step back in the circle."

The instructions were simple. The Union AI would have only seconds for an evaluation before moving to the next student. *How was it possible to make a judgment in that time? Could the Union AI really read the minds of everyone here in seconds?* She looked at the lattice of wires artfully stabbing skulls around the room and concluded that, despite what the teacher said, it couldn't.

The Union AI wasn't reading minds, but it had access to every record on the net. That was the actual source of information. The skull cap was just for show. Possibly, the rudimentary device let the AI confirm its own results.

Satisfied with her conclusion, she sat back on her heels, prepared to wait. Even a few seconds per student meant this was going to take hours. The principal left the circle. She didn't have to wait long before a name was called over the audio system.

"Reign." The voice was utterly platonic in a smooth baritone.

"I guess I'm starting this fiasco," Reign said, too low for anyone besides her to hear. He stepped forward into the circle. Did the lights flicker? Her scalp tingled for a second, but then it was gone.

"Quattuordecim Persona," the voice intoned. Reign stepped back into the circle. She tried to congratulate him, but he shrugged in forced nonchalance. He wasn't in the top ten, but the rank wasn't anything to scoff at. She quietly watched to see if he was secretly pleased with the outcome.

Persona was the most common classis, but it wasn't uncommon for higher-ranked Persona to move to Divinus. Of course, the same could be said for lower-ranked Divinus, but she didn't want to think about that. Divinus opened doors into the University for intellectual pursuits, but she appreciated that everyone had a place.

She watched as a loud-mouthed classmate who usually harassed her with unwanted commentary stepped forward.

"Finally, a reckoning," she said to Reign. She felt a now familiar tingle. She wanted to say more like, "I hope he spends his days rolling rocks uphill.", but she knew Reign wouldn't appreciate the comment.

"I hope he gets help," he said. He frowned at Ever.

"Novem Umbra," the voice intoned.

"Shadow classis," she crowed triumphantly. "Welcome to mandatory reeducation. I'm going to send him a self-help book."

"You will not," Reign said.

"No, but I'm going to think about it."

"Shadow classis is not a destination. By graduation, he will have moved on."

"Ever," the voice intoned, reverberating from the recessed speakers above their heads.

"Wish me luck," she said, stepping forward. The light was a little brighter in the middle of the room. She didn't go far. Like the rest of the students, a few steps was enough.

She felt a familiar tingle, and the lights dimmed. She waited. Usually, this was over by now. Then she heard a voice in her head. It was coming from her implant. A voice only she could hear.

"What are you?"

If the Union AI was going to ask, she was going to give it the right answer. Maybe this was how it worked.

"Divinus," she thought. She sent the category into the net. Next, she would tell it about her rank.

"No, you are not Divinus." The lights dimmed further, going almost completely dark, and everyone in the circle was looking around. There were emergency exit signs, but there was no reason to believe there was a problem unless they turned on. The tingle in her scalp turned sharp, almost painful. Through her implant, she felt a presence in the room. It didn't have a physical location. It was part of the net. The presence probed at her implant for a history. Every query she sent, every answer she received, every conscious thought she had was like a pool of knowledge its hands dipped into, but each time, the memories dissolved and fell away before they could be extricated. The hand dipped a thousand times into the pool but came back with nothing. She could sense the frustration in the AI which was worrying.

Time slowed to a crawl. Everyone around her reached to their face, moving in slow motion. She ignored the discomfort. She was not about to give up on her dreams just because of an *esclave,* even a smart one like the AI.

"I am Divinus." She directed the command through the net at the AI. Whenever she directed an *esclave*, it responded, and she felt the confirmation. Sometimes the *esclaves* resisted. What she asked could not be done, or they did not understand it. Her command to the AI went over the net and divided a million times. Each response was a blow of resistance, scattering her attempt to force the change like a million voices shivering in response to the truth she offered.

"You are a rebel. An outlaw," the singular voice echoed back to her implant.

"I am Divinus," she said. She put all her effort into the command, pushing back the resistance. People around her grabbed at their temples in slow motion. The command fractured, multiplying back negation at her. The closest ones reached her first, coming not from the AI but from the people around her.

She didn't feel any pain, but she looked at Reign. He'd fallen to one knee and clutched his head in both hands.

"Am I doing this?" she asked the Union AI.

"You can't change who you are with a lie."

"How do I make it stop?"

"Acceptance."

Her face sagged in defeat. Time returned to normal. The circle of her peers and teachers pulled off the headsets, looking stunned. Power resumed, turning the lights to full brightness, and the emergency exit lights turned on, sending a soft message for a disciplined exit.

"Unus Umbra," the voice intoned over the speakers. There was a gasp from a teacher, but Ever noticed some of her classmates nodded. To her knowledge there had never been an Unus Umbra. The words were almost a dichotomy.

The principal pushed his way into the circle, projecting his voice. He explained that the school had experienced a power surge. They would complete all remaining categorizations later after the source of the event was discovered.

She heard the words, but she knew the truth. The source would never be discovered. Reign nodded at her knowingly but without judging.

*Am I in Umbra because the Union AI wouldn't do what I say or because no one else would accept I am Divinus?* She had to accept what they believed, but she didn't believe it was the truth. *I will show them I'm Divinus.* Words weren't enough. She would have to use actions.

# 14. THE IMPLANT

When Reign arrived at Dill, he outright refused an implant. To his surprise, his resistance was not met in turn. He didn't expect anyone to tell him he had to get an implant. That was not the way the Union worked, but he expected passive insistence.

His father always supported his decisions. He did it even when he contradicted his father's philosophy. There was never a time when he asked for help and didn't get it, but he felt like his father was storing those disagreements for a later date.

Until Richard sent him off to the city.

The city, any city, had a poor reputation with the Free People. As a people, they stayed out of the cities and licensed property from the Union. That wasn't enough to survive. They still depended on commerce from the territories. He didn't like to think too closely about the contradiction. He didn't ascribe any particular feelings other than pity to people living in their hives under the rule of endless regulation.

Living with Fallon forced him to reevaluate his suppositions. He expected obstacles, gentle reminders, and limitations about his abilities. What he found was accommodation. He thought navigation would be a problem, but there was always a person or *maison* to guide him. He thought going to school would be a problem, but there were teachers dedicated to his instruction.

His condition was unusual but not unheard of. Some people living in the city couldn't take an implant. If he decided not to get one, someone would help him, but their patience wore him down until not getting an implant felt silly, almost a mockery of people who had no choice.

The only person who questioned his reluctance was Ever. She pestered him constantly about getting an implant. Her complaints seemed selfish and focused on knowing where he was and not having to knock on the bathroom door before entering. His resolve would've broken faster if not for her prodding.

Consequently, he waited almost a year before approaching Fallon about the medical procedure. He found her in her workroom with the door open. She posed as was her custom, holding strange positions on the padded floor. He didn't want to interrupt, but she waved him in. Exercise was important, but what was the point of flashing your fists and kicking your feet into the air?

"I've been thinking about the implant and how I could see again, but I don't know if I want to depend on technology."

"Most Free People share your misgivings," she said. "But most, when they have the option, still restore their senses. I think there's something about the implant that bothers you beyond technology dependence."

"I've heard my father talk about how the implant changes people. That people with implants aren't the same anymore."

"Did he say how?"

"No. I asked him about it. He didn't go into it further, but he sounded scared, and my father never sounds afraid. He still asked me to think about getting one."

Fallon frowned, considering for a moment.

"I know something about the history of implants with

your father. The implant is a communication tool that can be used to profound effect. It won't change who you are. Like any tool, it can magnify your achievements and mistakes. Who you are in success and failure might surprise you, but without those opportunities, you won't grow into what you can be."

"Is that true, though? What about Ailbe?"

"Ailbe is an unusual case. He intuitively manages his implant, and as a result, he feels much closer to it than most people do for years, if ever. I'm not sure if that makes sense to you, but I can virtually guarantee your experience will be different."

He left with answers, but he still wasn't sure if he knew the right questions. *What about implants scares my father?*

Regardless, he decided to get implanted. His father cut him out of the Free People. He needed to find a future for himself in Dill without his father's gilders. Fallon wasn't quick to act on the decision, perhaps sensing his internal reticence. He spent weeks waiting before admission to the hospital for the routine operation.

The procedure was uneventful.

The *infirmier* anesthetized him using a third arm equipped with a rotating hand of spring-loaded syringes. *Infirmiers* were one of the few three-armed *esclaves*. There was always a directeur cast into an *infirmier*, watching out from the cameras and talking through the voice box.

The directeur was not only skilled with *esclaves* but also a certified doctor. Even so, the remote presence wasn't much of a comfort. He would never trust his life to a machine, even for a routine procedure. The *infirmier* painlessly implanted the small hybrid organic silicon device into the back of his neck. There were no scars but a sore feeling for several days.

He was older than most for the operation, but his situation was not unheard of. In Dill, they usually connected newborns right after birth, but some parents held off on the implant until later years.

He knew the implant would build organic pathways to

different parts of his brain and that, eventually, he would see from the network of cameras and *esclaves* in Dill.

Sometimes, he thought he could remember sight. For a brief time, he could see, but a genetic disorder narrowed and stopped his vision entirely. What little he remembered of sight was unclear, but he thought he could remember what his mother looked like.

The procedure did not offer vision immediately. He'd been warned about this, but he'd been hopeful. The first thing he felt was a sense of presence.

He could tell who was in the room with him. What followed was a spatial awareness that kept him from running into walls. Soon after, he could determine shapes, but it was a year before he had a sense of color.

He found that the accessibility net interpreted the surroundings into a constructed perspective that looked out from his unseeing eyes. That felt very natural as he turned his head at who he was addressing.

During this time, he became good friends with Ailbe, and he and Ever negotiated an all-important truce over bathroom rights. His vision continued to improve well beyond traditional sight in both acuity and perspective.

While Ailbe didn't show interest, Ever frequently liked to test herself against him.

The competition started with simple gestures. He found he could cast his eimai to an *esclave*, and she wasn't satisfied until she could do the same. He could change his perspective in a room with the cameras embedded into the walls and ceiling.

She could do this, too, but the method she used was different. He looked through a camera by moving forward physically or moving his perspective forward by pushing it outward, but she could only see through cameras she gave a name.

He thought she had a name for every *esclave* and camera in the outer rim. He and Ailbe found her personification of objects more than a little disturbing, but on Fallon's advice, they mentioned it to no one.

Like most Free People, he'd received an education at home. That didn't match the class schedule at Dill, but he cruised through basic education.

Most of the training seemed worthless to him. Advanced math was the province of machines, and he had no interest in design, manufacturing, or programming. He struggled with most subjects, while Ever seemed to pass every test with the highest marks.

By the time he reached her education level, he believed prospects for University were not worth pursuing. Dill had only one University. A mega institution that governed the territory. They were always looking for new recruits, but joining the status quo was against everything he believed.

Fallon cautioned him against judgment and pulled him aside on a day Ever dragged a morose Ailbe out to the inner city. Reign was attempting to put together lunch when Fallon interrupted him.

"Categorization day isn't far away," she said.

"I was thinking about abstaining," he said. "It's not required. Another label isn't going to help me pass."

"It's not required, but it can be useful. Ever has her hopes pinned on Divinus."

He snorted. "She has the marks. Why anyone would want to be in a classis is beyond me."

"I would like you to go with her."

He knew enough about his marks to have a good idea of where he would fall during categorization. Only the brightest and most dedicated intellectual thinkers got into Divinus. The largest classis was Persona, followed by Anima. Ailbe was first in Anima. Unsurprising given his talent. Reign hadn't talked with him much about his plans for the future because it was a foregone conclusion. Ailbe loved working with animals, and his parents already had him interning at the University.

Few professions in Anima rivaled the status of Divinus, but he was sure to find one. Divinus might run the territory, but the doctors and scientists who created the implant made modern life possible.

Categorization in Persona was the most likely outcome for Reign, but it didn't seem useful. He respected Fallon, but he didn't understand her career choice. Everyone remarked on how talented she was at handling multiple *cultivers*, but she worked on the farm doing menial labor.

"Why?" he asked Fallon. Ever didn't even need him. While they generally got along, he wasn't interested in going to celebrate her marks.

"I'm not going. She needs someone to be there."

"Why don't you go?" That was unexpected. Fallon wasn't inattentive. Enigmatic, definitely. Perplexing, obviously. But she always made an appearance.

"I'm not going to legitimize the system. I think it's important for Ever to know that. Especially afterward."

"You sound like you know something I don't."

"It will not go well. I'd like you to be there."

Categorization day came, and somehow, Fallon knew in advance. A teacher approached Ever afterward and hugged her while she stood there with a forced smile, unsteady. Families congratulated their children or consoled the disappointed. He wasn't sure how to help, so he walked beside her on the way home. He could work with fourteen, but her face was a pale mask of unshed tears. In Umbra, she'd spend her free hours in education on ethics and virtue, supposedly common knowledge in the Union. In one night, her dreams had vanished, and he wasn't sure what she would replace them with.

# 15. CASTING

Reign wasn't sure how to use his prospects in Persona until he was tested for casting aptitude.

Casting tests were performed independently. A room was set aside for them in school, forty floors above the ground. He didn't appreciate all the stairs. There were few lifts for student transportation, and they didn't ascend to specific floors, forcing him to trudge along until he came to a mostly empty room.

The testing room was too large for the single desk and chair in the center, but the emptiness was welcoming. No matter how much time he spent in Dill, he would never get used to all the crowding, and the school was no different. The room seemed almost wasteful, and he added the thought into a log of school improvements he kept for future use.

It was a standard school desk with a height-adjustable solid wood top and a sturdy metal frame. The vents in the walls poured out air conditioning, and he was chilled to the bone. The air was cold, and the seat was cold. The faint smell of fresh paint permeated the room, and he sat in the chair and felt like the chemicals were being blown directly into his face. *Another architectural flaw.*

His loneliness at the emptiness surprised him, and he surveyed his surroundings with false interest. Two *esclaves* and no people, he thought, but then corrected himself. Only one *esclave* was in the room, and another was in the viewscreen's picture. The large viewscreen covered the entire wall in front of the desk.

Most viewscreens responded to him. They sent a picture directly to his implant. This one did not, but he could clearly see what was on the screen from the cameras behind him.

The screen was a mirror image. The walls were painted the same color, an indistinct beige, with the same lone desk sitting directly in the center. A sighted person might have lost perspective, imagining the room was twice as large or confusing the viewscreen for a mirror.

He was quick to learn visual tricks. When he entered the room, he automatically shifted his perspective. With a little effort, he could construct a three-dimensional picture, but this had an unnerving effect, as if he were outside his body, looking down at himself. *That might be an advantage.*

The *esclaves* were identical—a mirror image standing in salute. The machines were humanoid in function, with two arms and two legs, but not in form. They were distinctively recognizable as appliances with metal skeletons, pneumatic muscle fibers, and the low hum of an electric motor supplying continuous pressure to the system. These were archaic *esclaves* —the flimsy models used for testing.

While he waited impatiently, the *esclaves* released built-up pressure in a pitch Ailbe and Ever would have found hilarious but only increased his melancholy. Was this his future in Dill? Listening to *esclaves* fart?

A woman entered the room behind him, wearing the traditional black robes of a teacher trimmed in gold and green. The robes hung almost to the ground and included the suggestion of a black cowl, but the cowl was not big enough to be pulled over the face to make a mask, and the fabric was too thin for protection.

Everything in the city was for show without function. Dill was worse than most. The academics had a strange fascination with flaunting their knowledge using esoteric stripes and symbols for the higher orders of "enlightenment."

At Third Rim West, in a group of students and teachers, teachers were easily identifiable by the black robes. Underneath the robes, the teachers wore the same thing as the students: grey pants and cream shirts. Recycled fabrics without dye, clothing unadorned, and fabric uniform except for the dark band around the neckline, the cuffs, and the waist.

Only the University professors boasted more colors, and he'd seen Ailbe's parents parade around in getups that hurt his eyes.

Although it was in poor taste for academic underachievers to wear excessively bright clothes, he always looked forward to ditching his school greys for forest patterns he grew up wearing.

"Here for your casting test?" she asked. "It's Reign, right?"

"That's right," he said tiredly and slumped down in the chair, leaning his school bag on the floor against the desk. Without a doubt, the teacher had a school picture of him, including the phonetic pronunciation of his name, but there was a familiar pattern to these conversations.

"Have you ever taken a casting test before, Reign?"

Obviously, she should know this from his file, but he would once again follow the pattern, even though he felt forced to appreciate the necessity.

"No." The response was terse, so he continued. "I'm ready to give it a try."

She smiled approvingly. "I can see from your file your caregiver is a directeur. Have you ever tried to control an *esclave*?"

"Yes. Fallon passed control of an *esclave* over to me, and I could move it around."

"That's excellent!" she exclaimed. He thought she was too

excited about a mundane achievement.

"What I would like you to do is try to control the *ausbildung* in the room with us," she said, and before she even completed the sentence, the *ausbildung* lifted its arm and waved at her.

"That's great!" she boomed. He didn't want to, but he smiled anyway. Her obvious enthusiasm was infectious.

"What else would you like me to have it do?"

"This part is going to get a little harder. I want you to look through the *ausbildung* and wave its arms, but also move your eimai into the *ausbildung*. When you feel your physical senses disappear, you will have cast into the *ausbildung*."

He was familiar with this, having had many conversations with Ailbe on what it was like to move your eimai. When Ailbe was being Peanut, he was the cat, but when Reign moved his eimai into an *esclave*, he wasn't the machine. If anything, he was more himself when he used an *esclave*. Most *esclaves* were pretty stupid.

He cast his eimai to the *ausbildung* and allowed the *esclave* to replace his physical senses. Surprisingly, he felt like his consciousness was emptying into a bottomless bucket. He could feel the air whisper around his open frame and smell the room. He could hear the teacher, and there was a faint echo. He realized the echo was coming from his own ears.

"You'll notice this *ausbildung* is different," she said. "It's been upgraded to mimic and augment your senses, not just accept commands. It may look old, but it's smarter than a *maison* or *cultiver*. With the *ausbildung,* we are going to measure how far you can go into the cast."

He felt like something was attached to his back. He reached with it experimentally, and a third arm unfolded from behind. He waved this at the teacher.

"And you've found the third arm! Great work! The more dissimilar an *esclave* is from the human body, the more difficult it is to merge eimai. You've completed this part of the test, but there's one more part. Put the arm back and break the cast. You can return your perspective to your body by focusing on your physical senses."

"What's next?" This was the first time he was excited about school in a long time, and he knew how to take a win.

"Your next test is over here," a man said as he walked onto the screen. He was wearing teachers' robes trimmed in gold and red. *He must be from a different school.*

"This *ausbildung* is identical to the one you have been working with. Your next test is to control this *esclave*."

"Where is it?" he asked, puzzled. He'd never tried to control an *esclave* out of his vicinity. He tried to find its location through the viewscreen, but the screen didn't reply.

"Don't worry about where it is. The net will guide you to the *esclave* with its public identifier. You can think of it as the machine equivalent of an eimai but remember *esclaves* are not alive. Just pretend the *ausbildung* is right beside you." He seemed very confident, probably because he wasn't taking the test.

Reign held back a sigh. The only thing he could do was try.

Rather than attempt to make it wave at the teacher, he cast his eimai into the machine. There was a tenuous connection at first. He was split between two distances, but as the *ausbildung* body became more familiar, his human body grew indistinct until he was whole, standing beside this new teacher.

"That's great," the teacher said. "Your eimai cannot be in two places at the same time. Few people can span the distance on their first try." Teachers were full of all kinds of superlatives.

The teacher produced a little tiny doll-like *ausbildung*, a complete replica of Reign, and handed it to him. He took it from the teacher, the metal hands carefully gripping the plush doll.

"You just passed the first part. You could take the doll from my hand. Now, I'm going to ask you to manipulate the doll. Can you make its hands clap?"

He put his hands on its little arms and made them clap. The teacher asked him to move the doll around in different ways.

Overall, he wanted to find this demeaning, but the teacher offered so much encouragement at every step that he couldn't help but soak up the wins.

"You can break the cast," the teacher said, finally finished.

The two teachers then had a technical conversation until he was dismissed. They were excited about the results. Terms like latency, effective utilization, and situational awareness were floated around. The actual numbers meant nothing to him, but when the teacher said he would have training on using this talent, he thought there might be more for him at school.

# 16. THE UNKNOWN

Reign hated early testing. For some ridiculous reason, all the placement tests started at the same time in Dill—first thing in the morning. The schedule disadvantaged late sleepers, particularly Free People who synchronized their circadian rhythm with the rising sun. He grudgingly admitted the Free People adjusted their schedule for game, but nature dictated those circumstances, not the whim of bureaucrats.

He considered starting an activist group in school to change the schedule, but there were already too many groups since activism was an approved activity. The school seemed to balance the groups against each other so that nothing was really accomplished.

He waited feigning patience. The auditorium was stacked, and cameras scrutinized the students. Few teachers circulated in the rows, most present only as *esclaves*—more cameras. He should be appreciative, but without a doubt, the footage would be reviewed and analyzed.

Out of the data would come interesting facts. From those facts, questions would be asked to fine-tune his misery. How much did he sweat over each question? Where did his focus increase or falter? Can we rearrange the words to make the answer less obvious? The analytics would feed inquiring administrators who needed presentation points on academic statistics. He couldn't imagine a worse fate than being another cog in the machine, but he did appreciate the sheer momentum of nonsense.

The school he shared with Ever and Ailbe had a name, but everyone called it Third Ring West as if all the signs didn't matter. It wasn't tall or wealthy compared to the inner-ring schools. Three auditorium floors were spaced around the building, and the *maisons* must have been up all night moving desks to accommodate testing. They spaced the desks out so that no one was close to touching, all to prevent cheating.

His body language contributed to statistics gathered by camera, but he used the accessibility net for testing. While the other students had a screen to look at fastened to their desks, he completed the examination in his head. Net activity was suppressed for everyone else in all the typical bands. The only person he could send a message to was Ever. For some reason, he could always get a message to her. They knew each other too well.

Instead of notepads and calculators represented as visual objects on a flat screen, he used resources from the net. At first, this seemed like a disadvantage. Unlike building a calculator on the net, a calculator on a screen didn't require much attention. Later, he realized how much further he could advance using his implant.

Usually, the net was available to everyone, but it required mental dexterity, alertness, and discipline. He closed his eyes, relaxed, and appeared almost asleep. The chairs were adjustable but hard, and he shifted position to find the right spot to release the tension from his back.

He couldn't help but notice his neighbors bent glumly over their screens. He didn't want to annoy anyone with his slouched, inattentive posture, but sometimes he felt the pressure for conformity suffocating his need to be intolerable.

Placement testing always started with a lot of chatter. Ever was at the center of the local noise forecast. She had exceptionally high marks, and other students would bring her questions, circling her desk like prehistoric buzzards until the test started. They didn't care about her classis in Umbra, and she gave the answers freely. That might be why she was in Umbra. He wasn't sure how to explain to her she was subverting the system.

Her popularity didn't bother him, but the noise bounced around the high ceilings and irritated him. He'd used his implant to see for several years now, but his ears were still sensitive. He was annoyed enough to get a few digs in before the test started.

"Name three rivers that operate as major trade routes for the Union." He sent the message directly to her, and he saw her pause the conversation momentarily before firing back a response.

"The Swansong, the Gloaming, and the Calm," Ever said, obviously irritated. "You know I know them."

Fallon spent half the night going over geography with Ever. Ever didn't seem to know the answers when Fallon was around, but he concluded that if Fallon had been his teacher, he might have forgotten the answers under her demanding gaze.

A frigid breeze swept from the ceiling above him. Massive ducts ran across the ceiling, with giant circular vents large enough to crawl through. The chilled air was unwelcome. After a childhood spent outside in the heat, he didn't adapt well to the cold air. He wished for a proper exosuit for the millionth time. An exosuit was life to a Free Person. *Somehow, I always end up under a vent.*

The timer started, and his implant buzzed him. The test was available. Over the years, he learned to appropriate resources, but they required his attention. Not that there was a finite limit for memory, but the more information he stored on the net, the more he had to keep track of. Whatever lost his attention for too long disappeared. The net archived the information away—lost and forgotten unless he remembered how to recall it.

A tedious process called cataloging was supposed to improve recall, but he seldom made the effort.

Until the test was engaged, the buzz was a low hum that only he could hear, complete with a visual reminder. He quickly activated the test with a thought and began scrolling the SAQs and giving rapid answers as they appeared before him.

Most of the short answer questions were easy, but some LAQs required him to store thoughts on the net. He had to combine thoughts and try to find an answer.

He immersed himself into the net until a stranger walked by his desk over to Ever, jarring him back to his physical senses.

Reign expanded his view of the auditorium for a second. He expected an *enseignant* or perhaps a teacher, but nothing was there. He focused on the test. Geography, particularly eastern geography, came easily to him. He traveled extensively before making Dill his home. Combined with fact-based education, those memories gave him a command of location. His chances to score better than Ever made him secretly quite pleased.

The more he focused on the test, the more acutely he felt the presence. He realized whoever was ghosting around her desk didn't want to be noticed. He felt a particular glee that he usually suppressed when he discovered some mischief she was up to and reported it back to Fallon for her own good.

"I don't know who is helping you," he sent to Ever, "but you are going to get caught."

"No one is helping me. You hate to lose to someone younger than you."

One skill he developed was the ability to use his peripheral awareness. *Esclaves* came in many types, and the most advanced *esclaves* were specialized for their environments. Whether that was deep in the sea, underground, or in space, they were not humanoid. To direct a complex *esclave*, you needed to monitor pressure, stress, heat, and ambient vibrations. The implant mapped mechanical sensors more sensitive than any natural organs directly into the nervous system and protected his eimai from being overloaded by the details. Although his thoughts were consecutive, he could divide his attention into peripheral awareness.

While he took his test, he divided out a portion of his attention to access the sensors in the auditorium. As long as he checked up on them occasionally, those sensors joined his eimai.

His effort was met with disappointment. None of the sensors identified a person moving between the rows. The longer he watched, the more certain he was that this was a person. What was worse was that whoever it was spent a lot of time hovering around Ever's desk.

Regardless of what he said, he knew there was no competing with her at school, but she had a tough time fitting in any where else. Her first instinct almost always ended in a wrong decision. Ailbe mostly went along with it, but he felt responsible for providing resistance to obvious stupidity.

He divided his attention further from the test, trying to include as many sensors as possible in his eimai. He spent a long time learning the secrets of his implant, and he could recognize where responses came from on the net. Most of the nonvisual information that composed his eimai came from the public net, the source of identity and governance.

But when he was in a house, an auditorium, a park, or a even restaurant, some sensors were available to anyone who needed them for mobility and safety—the accessibility net.

He accessed these sensors using a protocol, a separate underlayment or framework that let him work with any screen or system. These protocols were private and allowed him to navigate inside buildings with confidence.

He attuned his senses to the information fed into the implant and an image emerged in his visual perspective.

Although the public net showed no image, he realized the accessibility net identified a person crouching beside her.

The stranger didn't wear clothes he recognized—dark pants, polished shoes, a white high-collared shirt, and a short robe that matched the pants. He had a hand at the back of Ever's neck. He was turned away from Reign and at eye level with Ever's hunched shoulders. Reign couldn't see what he was doing. He was completely invisible on the public net.

Involuntarily, Reign jerked backward, sitting straight. His unseeing gaze pointed straight at the ghost. He wasn't sure if it was the motion or if the stranger was aware, as the accessibility net in the room bled details on his position. He stood and turned in Reign's direction.

Reign could see him plainly now, but his face was missing. Hair and ears framed the flat expanse where a face should be before the figure disappeared.

Reign sat frozen, studying the sensors in the auditorium from every angle for the rest of the test. He did not know who or what that was. The public net identified people and carried their eimai to an observer. *Was that a program or an AI?*

The Union AI wouldn't allow another Artificial Intelligence on the net. As he thought about the experience, he wondered if what he saw wasn't a glitch in the net. The net was redundant but not infallible. Cameras failed, and sensors glitched.

*Maybe it's an illusion?* He supposed the object detection might have superimposed a figure onto his eimai.

# 17. THE GHOSTS

The ghosts did not stay away, and when they realized Reign wouldn't do anything about it, they dismissed his presence. He was certain there were multiple ghosts, and they would show up to spend time with Ever.

They appeared as different people but never simultaneously, as if each had an allotment of time. Their clothing could only be described as unique and nonfunctional. Pointy shoes with tall heels, heavy layered fabrics, or worse, flimsy garments exposing skin. Their bodies were perfectly formed, but their faces were missing.

More than likely, this was Ever's scheming, but there was also the possibility that something was wrong with his implant, and he decided to talk with Ailbe as soon as time was right. Ailbe would know what to do and the last thing he wanted was an extra trip to the doctor. Besides it wasn't like he was hurt.

The day came when Ailbe and Peanut were in his room on the third floor, looking at models of *esclaves* he'd collected. He wouldn't have let any other animal in his room, but Peanut was exceptionally well-behaved and usually rode around on Ailbe's shoulder or slept quietly on the bed.

Except for Ever and the tiny people she made from field scraps, most children had toys that reflected their interests in future occupations. For him, this was his extensive collection of specialized *esclaves*. While Ailbe wasn't that interested in directing *esclaves*, he was interested in the details of Reign's models. Ailbe stared at gears and screws as if something magical was hidden in the transfer and multiplication of force.

Reign thought of most animals as being identical. *After all, what separates one goat from another?* Ailbe claimed the differences were on the inside.

School days were short in the summer months, which was ironic because the heat outside kept everyone trapped indoors for the afternoon.

They were admiring a new deep-sea excavation *esclave* he'd acquired. It was an unmanned *merpelleteuse* with various retractable tools that could be extended from the submersible body. The entire model was made of carved wood and parted into two pieces to store all the attachments inside.

His father sent him to Fallon, but Richard also created an account he could draw on for purchases. Reign avoided even looking at the gilders most of the time. He didn't want to owe Richard anything. *Esclave* models were a special case. This might be his future. He needed something tactile he could feel with his hands.

"I refused to go with Ever today," Ailbe said, the tone indicating there was much more to follow.

"Why is that?" he asked. Most of his attention was on sorting out tools that fit on the model's prehensile arms.

"They've introduced birds onto the farm. Ever is determined to catch one, and she wants to use Peanut. The bird is way bigger than Peanut." Ailbe held up his hands to show the size. "I think they called it a pheasant. It's flightless. That's about as much as I know."

"What do you think her chances are of catching one?" He was always concerned about her schemes, and the ghosts had him on edge. He decided to ease into the conversation with Ailbe.

"Without Peanut? Close to zero. I've heard they are quite skittish."

"Have you noticed anything strange around Ever?"

"Around her? No. About Ever? All the time. There's nothing she does that isn't strange."

"I know that." He looked up from the model. He was sightless but he knew that sincerity was looking at the person you were talking to and he suddenly found that he needed Ailbe to take him seriously. "Lately, I've been seeing images around Ever."

"Images?" Ailbe asked, "Of what?"

"People. It looks like they are talking to her. Mostly when I see them, they disappear, but lately, they just come and go as they please."

This got Ailbe's complete attention. He set down the *merpelleteuse* carapace. "Have you talked to Fallon about it?"

"No," he replied. "Not yet."

"You should talk to Fallon right now. Ever can get in over her head quick." Ailbe gave him a mirthless grin and shook his head. "You don't want to get caught up in that. My neighbor's house is still broken, and it's been more than a year."

They descended one level on the lift and went to Fallon's workroom. The door was closed, but they could faintly hear sounds. The sounds made little sense. There was a pattern, but the words didn't have meanings.

Reign knocked on the door politely, and the sound stopped. The door opened to reveal Fallon. She wasn't very tall. In the last few years, he and Ailbe grew feet taller, topping Fallon by head and shoulders, but they both felt dwarfed whenever she stared them down.

Today was no exception, but he stuttered the story he told Ailbe. He didn't get the reaction that he feared. Fallon seemed quizzical but not angry. She walked over to the chair in the living room and sat, motioning for them to sit on the couch.

He always found this couch uncomfortably firm. They were forced to perch upright while Fallon was relaxed in a soft, squishy chair.

Fallon addressed Reign first. "I'm sure you've spoken with your father and have some ideas about my family's business."

He nodded. "I know he's spending a lot of time meeting with leaders of the Free People. We haven't been able to talk much, but I know there is a new movement called the Third Eye."

"It's not new. It's just another rehash of the same ideas. It's a waste of time, but every so often someone gets revolutionary, and they romanticize mysticism. The Third Eye is little different, but they are interested in ancient technology. That makes them dangerous."

"Don't the Guardians protect us from that?" Reign asked, and Ailbe winced.

"The Guardians protect people," Fallon agreed "Their protection comes at a cost."

Reign nodded. "They aren't especially nice to Free People looking for working old tech."

"Some old technologies still exist on the net but are harmless unless we give them power," Fallon said. "The ghosts you are seeing are like that. They are, most times, harmless."

That was a relief to him, and he could see that Ailbe was physically relieved, but Ailbe had more to say.

"I've heard some of the forbidden technologies can change people, strengthen them, and even heal them," Ailbe said. He made the statement conversationally, but it hung in the air while Fallon studied him.

"That's true. I'm sure you learned in school that they had cures for genetic diseases like Reign's blindness. What we have now is even better. He can see, and we have the Peace. There are already too many engineered people. This entire farm's sole purpose is to diversify what little nature we have left. That's why those tools are forbidden. I would make it a rule to keep forbidden conversations to just the three of us."

Fallon wasn't asking a question, but he nodded, and after a quick pause, Ailbe jerked a stiff, late nod, too, but Reign didn't think he was going to give up so easily.

# 18. SNEAKING AROUND

Ever woke to darkness—not an unusual occurrence. School started well before the sun was up, and she slept until the last minute, unwilling to get out of bed until she absolutely had to.

She was a deep sleeper, but a sound woke her. The house was silent at night. Lucas kept a watchful eye on the *cultivers* in the fields doing routine tasks since he never slept, but sleep was best for health, and people performed only the most essential nighttime tasks in Dill.

Ever thought she heard a voice.

She listened intently, hearing noises in the ventilation ducts. The cool, filtered air purred from the vent and smelled over-purified, carrying the faint scent of hydrogen peroxide. Sounds were coming from downstairs. They were muffled, but the lift shaft carried noise, and she could distinctly discern voices.

More curious than scared, she slipped from bed and walked out of her room to the lift as quietly as possible.

Normally, the lift would activate if it sensed people

approaching, but she had long ago learned how to sneak around the sensor. She recognized the voices, an exchange between Fallon and Jorge. If she could go downstairs unnoticed, this might be the best opportunity she had to find out what was happening.

There was a service entrance beside the lift shaft. It was a small, hinged door with a catching mechanism to keep it closed without an *esclave* key. The fitment wasn't too tight for her fingers, and although it was nominally locked, she pushed downward on the door panel and pried the door away from the locking pin.

The entrance was more than wide enough for her, and when she slipped in, she could use the rungs to move freely between any level in the house. To her left was the metal frame supporting the lift, and to her right, grey conduit and bundles of tightly wrapped wires snaked their way from the house's base up the core to the top of the tower.

Carefully, she climbed down the ladder until she reached the first floor. The first floor had the most shared spaces— a table for eating, the kitchen, and the bathroom. She could tell she moved silently, but the floors and the ceiling amplified even the smallest sounds. She thought the conversation was coming from the pantry, but the source walked around, moving to the kitchen table.

She couldn't see them from where she was hidden in the service chute. The lights were on downstairs, and the cracks in the panel glowed, ruining her night vision. She gritted her teeth. Her door was pointed away from the action, so she closed her eyes and tried to listen to the conversation.

She couldn't be sure, but it sounded like her mother was threatening her grandfather's life.

"Few people sneak up on me without learning to regret it, old man," Fallon said.

"Just one benefit that comes with being me," Jorge said. There was a hint of mischievousness in his voice, and Ever relaxed. She could picture his usual dissembling posture and there was no doubt he was going to lay on his pitch thick. Usually, this was some kind of request, and most of the time, it benefited her.

"What have you been up to, old man?"

"A little of this, a little of that. Right now, I'm raiding your refrigerator. After I finish eating all your food, I'll probably carry away as much of it as I can."

"I've never seen it out of your sight before." There was an edge to Fallon's voice that Ever could only interpret as worry, but she had never heard that before from her mother.

"Don't worry. It's safe." Jorge seemed to be eating at the table, and she heard his sentences between crunching sounds. *Is he eating my cereal?* "I don't like leaving it behind, but this visit was necessary, and I can't risk getting it too close to certain people without explanations, and I'd prefer to have a working arrangement first. He's not far behind."

"Just who have you brought to us, old man?" Fallon's voice went from worry to ice.

"No one if you leave right now," he said cheerfully.

"You know I can't do that."

"Then I guess you are going to meet him, and I think he's going to stick by you."

"You're just full of answers today. Who is he, and why would he do that?"

"Well, to get to me, of course. He seems to have made it his personal mission to catch me. He has that 'find the truth at all costs' mentality. Witnesses can be very persistent. I think the last one followed me around for almost a decade."

Fallon let out a breath like someone had punched her in the stomach. "You led your monster straight to Ever."

"They aren't monsters," Jorge said carefully. "They're people just like us. Some people would call us monsters."

"They've been augmented to the point they're barely human. The best thing we have now is respect for life—Human life. They're no longer needed."

"I know I will not change your mind on this, Fallon. If you

want to get rid of him, certainly you can handle one Witness. Just make him disappear."

There was silence for a moment. "I'm not sure I can," Fallon said, and it sounded like a humbling admission.

"Has it gone that far?" Jorge sounded surprised.

"The distraction is bad enough. I can barely control the *cultivers* on the farm."

"It's always worse at the end of a cycle," Jorge said. "But motivation makes a difference."

"I'm not sure I could kill him," Fallon said, and Ever's heart started pounding hard in their chest. The words seemed to ring in their mind. Kill him. Was her mother a murderer?

Jorge fished around in his possessions. He usually traveled with a heavy canvas bag, and Ever was sure he was looking through it. A moment later, he started again.

"I know you know how to use it," Jorge said as he turned over the item to Fallon. Unfortunately, the effect is quite temporary."

"That depends on what you think of as fortunate," Fallon said. "It's a step closer to your Witness."

"Even Witnesses know the Peace," Jorge said, "but in this case, it's worse than that. Our new peace is not so easily defeated by electronics. The more you use it, the more you need to use it, and the less effective it will be."

"I didn't know that," Fallon said.

"I didn't think you remembered. Sometimes I take for granted that I have an uncommon experience with recent changes to our physiology," Jorge said.

"A thousand years is recent?" Fallon asked. "You've been carrying around too many thoughts."

"In terms of human evolution, that might as well be yesterday. I don't want to pile on the bad news, but how soon can you be ready to leave?"

"I should be able to put plans in motion for tomorrow afternoon. With a little finessing, I can alter a hypertube manifest to arrange for our transport anonymously."

"Hypertube's are out. I'm afraid the Third Eye is watching all our exits. They've moved into the city like locusts. They've reached the point where they are demanding resources from the Chancellor."

"That would take thousands, even tens of thousands of people, father. Certainly they haven't moved their entire organization into Dill."

"No, somehow they've managed to get new converts, and I'm not sure from where. That's just one of the things I'm looking into. I've heard rumors a molting friend of ours might be involved."

"You can't be serious," Fallon exclaimed.

"Yes, there are rumors they have a new Eye with a scaley skin condition."

"Him I could kill," Fallon said.

"Don't get ahead of yourself. I might find him first," Jorge said, crunching through the last of her cereal. "So that's the complete situation report."

"Surrounded with no friends," Fallon said.

"Not at all," Jorge said, "Head north. I'll prepare the way, and you can catch up with me at the Union City."

There was further discussion but Ever was numb to the conversation. They discussed old roads and past sights. All the questions were about how quickly Fallon could travel and what tools she would take. Ever listened. Little of it made sense, and when Jorge left toward the backdoor, she silently climbed the rungs.

She made only one mistake as she exited the service hatch. She tripped the motion sensor on the lift, causing the door to open. Her heart was racing again, but realizing no one was coming out the door, she soft-footed it back to her room.

Opening and closing the bedroom door gently, she got back in bed. It wasn't until a long time later that Fallon opened the door and checked inside to find her fast asleep.

# 19. TOO INTERESTING

Ever woke late to scraping sounds from the upper floor. She dressed quickly, putting a cursory effort into personal hygiene, then scrambled to the next floor using the lift and an exceptional display of patience. The storage rooms were open, and she could hear Fallon and Reign talking.

Of course he would be awake. He lived on this floor. A loud clamor and glass shattered as if something stacked precariously had found its way to the floor at high velocity.

She heard him apologize and imagined her mother's withering reply, but she didn't interrupt. She wasn't good with secrets, and her first confidant was Ailbe, then Reign, followed by everyone else she met. Secrets were meant to be shared. Most people found the trait endearing, but not her mother, who answered every question with the fewest possible words.

She left Reign and Fallon undisturbed and returned to the lift as four *cultivers* stepped onto the floor. The lift was barely large enough for all four of them, and she skirted around behind the *esclaves* as they exited,. She signaled the lift for the ground floor.

Fallon rarely let her into her storage room, but she knew many boxes were too heavy for a single person. She also knew she might be missing the chance of a lifetime, but she needed to tell Ailbe.

She left, shouldering the front door, unintentionally slamming the thick wood door against the frame seal, and ran down Rim Road to Ailbe's house. Her house was narrow, and she couldn't reach full speed before dashing into his front door.

Fortunately, the lock recognized her and released the seal, avoiding a painful collision. He was at the table, finishing breakfast with his school bag ready.

"We're leaving!" She spluttered out the words nonsensically. He was used to this from her and gave her a quick glance before returning to his repast. She made it just in time. His cup was empty, morning green juice drunk.

"You're going to be late again," he said. "Did you know your shirt is on backward, and where's your bag?"

"No," she said, still panting from the run. She attempted to breathe deeply. Fallon said that she had a touch of asthma. Nothing to be concerned about, but she had her do breathing exercises—focused training on breathing into her mouth and out her nose whenever she got too excited. She took a few breaths while he dutifully waited. "We're leaving Dill."

Ailbe's eyes widened with surprise.

"Where are you going?" he asked.

"I'm not sure," she said, "but we're traveling overland."

"Wait," he said, "Start from the beginning. What did you hear?"

She filled him in on the details she heard last night, leaving out the part where Mother said she would kill someone. That was too horrific to repeat, but she included what Fallon and Reign were doing this morning. He didn't have questions about the Third Eye, but he was very interested in what her grandfather said.

"What do you think he left behind?" he asked.

"I don't know," she responded. "I couldn't see them from the service shaft."

"Some piece of ancient tech, I would guess. Your family seems to be involved with that."

"Maybe," she said, "but it sounds like there's a cult after us."

Ailbe shrugged. "They could be dangerous, but they won't break the Peace, and I think your mother has connections."

"What kind of connections?" she asked belatedly.

"I'm not sure. But you three live alone in that house, and a *cultiver* directeur doesn't make that kind of money."

"My mother works all the time," she protested.

"It still doesn't add up. Thirteen people live here, and it's considered a luxury. Besides, my parents are scientists recognized by the University."

She wasn't going to try to refute his logic once he locked on to a "fact." He was just too stubborn. He retrieved his schoolbag from the floor.

"Looks like I'm not going to school today. I need to get ready."

"What?" It was her turn to be surprised, but she caught on quickly. "You can't go!"

"Of course I can," he said matter-of-factly. "If Fallon is letting Reign go, then she'll let me go. Besides, I've spent more time outside than either of you."

Ailbe spent quite a bit of time outside of Dill. His particular skill with animals put him in specialized training courses, and she knew he worked with a team of biologists trying to create a habitat for panthers. Panthers were one of the few large cats that were not augmented, and their historic hunting techniques were unsuccessful in the modern environment. She had to admit that he was probably the most prepared.

"Okay. I couldn't leave without you." Ever knew that was true. While Ailbe and Reign made other friends and always seemed to fit in, she leaned heavily on their support.

"The only thing that doesn't add up is the Third Eye," he said. "If they were blocking the transit, the Chancellor would send *flics* to move them aside. Your mother doesn't want the government to know wherever we're going."

"What about the Witness?"

"They're record keepers. They usually officiate weddings. At least the high-profile ones. Your grandfather isn't trying to marry off Fallon, is he?" Ailbe laughed, and she gave him an icy stare.

"I'm sorry about that. I went too far."

"How long will it take you to get ready?"

"I'm already packed for an expedition. I just need to suit up."

He dumped his school bag in his room and suited for a trip outside. He already had an expedition bag prepared. It was full of emergency gear, medical supplies, and a water bottle, but he also had a few electronics designed to locate and track panthers. She was envious of how neat his pack was set up.

The backpack's dark grey and black stitching matched Ailbe's exosuit and adhered to the back of his suit. The backpack and exosuit had patches of gold and green with the motto in bold black lettering. Internal elastic smart straps spread the weight of the backpack across his shoulders while his cowl lifted automatically by silent command.

The smart fabric cowl was more advanced than her suit and as it settled onto his face it created a transparent shield that molded into a mask complete with a respiration filter. When he pulled the cowl aside the fabric returned to normal. Her burgundy exosuit was manual, something her mother approved of. Fallon said the extra electronic frills broke when you needed them.

Peanut jumped onto his shoulders and used the backpack as a shelf to lie on. Her black fur blended nicely into the exosuit.

"What are you going to tell your parents when they find out you're not here?"

"The truth," he replied. "I'm going to tell them I am on an expedition with Fallon. They trust her for some reason." He shrugged.

They returned to her house to find the usually well-organized living space stacked with boxes. A strange sight, *cultivers* were in the house moving up and down the lift carrying boxes, two or four at a time. Most of the boxes were made of flexible synthetic material. Ailbe peeked into a box on the dining room table.

"Hermetically sealed water," he said and looked at the box lid, studying the label stamped on the inside. "Expensive."

Ever looked into another box and grimaced.

"Plant bricks," she said, wincing. "I hope these are just for emergencies. Maybe I should try to hide them."

"And go hungry?" He snagged the box of rations and held them close to his chest. "I'll be taking care of these. A little vegetable oil can solve a lot of problems."

Ailbe carried the plant bricks like his life depended on it while they looked through the stack. Most of the items were depressingly recognizable if in a travel size, like air filters and range extenders. Some electronics looked similar to what kept the bubble suspended above Dill, but most of the equipment was esoteric, like a triangle that unfolded to look like a plate.

They were still browsing when a *cultiver* told them to come out the back door. They found Fallon and Reign loading equipment on two large pallets. Reign was already dressed in an exosuit of Free People design in camo. The pattern-shifting colors didn't cause him to disappear in Dill, but in the wild, the colors would slowly match the background.

On closer inspection of the pallets, Ever realized they were made of *cultivers*, folded and clamped to each other's limbs to make a large cargo box. Other *cultivers* were loading the containers under Fallon's watchful eye.

"I see you've found Ailbe," Fallon said, "And by the looks of things, he wants to come with us."

"I can help," he said. "I've been outside Dill on several expeditions. I'm not afraid of the dangers."

"A few rough nights outside are the least of our dangers. If I told you to stay, would you?"

"I'm staying with Ever."

"What if one of these *cultivers* held you here until we left?"

"As soon as it lets me go, I'll catch up."

"But what if it never let you go?" Fallon's voice grew remarkably harder. "What if it took you to a quiet place and kept you there?"

"It wouldn't let me starve, and as soon as I got out, I would find you."

"It won't starve you. It'll feed you and water you. It will talk to you if you get bored, but you'll never leave." Two of the *cultivers* shouldered their way beside him. Ever tried to push one away. Usually, *esclaves* would move out of the way, but these two didn't budge.

"Do you understand the risks, Ailbe?" Fallon said. "There are worse things that can happen, more than you realize."

"I'm still going," he said, deflated, but Ever was amazed at his persistence. Usually, he was the first to buckle under her mother's questioning.

"Very well then," Fallon said cooly and smiled. "I thought you would say that, and for what it's worth, there's a reward for every risk. If you live to see it." The two *cultivers* at his shoulders melted away to do their jobs, but she wasn't finished with him yet. "I have one condition. Peanut has to stay here. This isn't a trip for house cats."

Ailbe nodded numbly. Peanut was the one consistent friend he had since he'd been removed from his mother, and losing the cat was the real test. Peanut would be well cared for. Cats were welcomed everywhere inside the bubble to take care of pests. Even Reign seemed stunned by the dialog, but he was the first to shake it off.

"If you are planning on stealing these *cultivers*, we are going to need a power source," Reign said, and Ever decided it was time to chime in while her mother was still weighing her options.

"We can take Lucas," she said. "He has his own power

source and he is really smart."

"The *maitre* series was designed for a certain amount of independent action, but he doesn't have a cab or a seat." Fallon pointed out.

"We could tie a mattress on top. And then use them to sleep on."

"The foam should repel water for a while."

Her mother considered the idea. Although she'd been forbidden to use her mattress outside, this might be her opportunity.

"Even the *esclaves* with a cab only hold one or two people," Reign added. "We would have to take more equipment. We would be more noticeable."

"That's not a problem," Fallon said. "There's only one person who is going to notice we're missing. Unfortunately, he's getting closer, so we have to decide soon."

"The Witness?" Ailbe asked. Fallon seemed unsurprised that Ailbe knew, but she gave Ever a long look.

"Listening at closed doors again, are we?" Fallon asked her.

"The sound carries to my room."

Fallon looked at each member of the group in turn. "My father left him an information trail straight to us in public records. I could have obscured those, but eventually, the Witness would sort it out. I would much prefer to meet him here than on the road in the middle of the night. Don't let him get close to you. My father thinks the Witness could be useful, but I would prefer if he just kept going."

They settled on taking Lucas, but Fallon required them to always keep their gloves and cowls strapped to the exosuits. When pulled over her face, the cowl bent and folded into a convex mask, creating a transparent mask with a filter. Some of the Free People's cowls even had a heads-up display, but the shade from her cowl was not nearly as good as her hat.

After Fallon was satisfied with the contents, more *cultivers* mounted on top and enclosed the containers with their bodies. They strapped mattresses on Lucas and the cargo boxes. Using synthetic rope, they fashioned several handholds on top of the machines. She fetched her favorite pillow, and belatedly, so did Ailbe while Reign shook his head. He didn't understand preferences, but his head toss was more than the casual disdain he typically exhibited for her choices. He was concerned.

Several hundred *cultivers* from across the farm converged on the area behind her house, but no one noticed, or if they noticed, they said nothing. Fallon gathered the group together, keeping a hand on Ever right beside her. *Cultivers* formed protective lines around them. Fallon left a clear opening to their right. When Ailbe asked why, Fallon told him to always leave your enemy an escape.

"He's here," Fallon said. A small group of *cultivers* entered the house through the back door. Ever presumed to meet the stranger. "I'm going to let him in. Remember, he's looking for my father. He has no reason to stay here."

"Unless he's interested in the small army of *esclaves*," Reign said, and Fallon's head snapped up from concentration to look at him.

"I've played right into his hands," Fallon said.

"Whose?" Ever asked, looking around frantically.

"My fathers," she said. Before she could explain, the *cultivers* walked the Witness out the back door, two in front walking backward, their chest cameras fixed on his white exosuit.

# 20. THE WITNESS

It was unusual to see a *cultiver* walk backward. They had the general configuration of a person but no head since their sensory equipment was on their chest. The directeur looked out of the *cultiver* from the front. These two focused on the Witness, walking in front of him like a thin green line. The Witness's head almost brushed the door frame.

He was still much shorter than Richard, who had to duck to fit through a door, but he was lean with a full head of hair on an almost skeletal frame. Ever knew little about Witnesses, but she expected him to wear white robes.

When officials worked in an official capacity, they wore uniforms of office. Peacekeepers wore blue. Teachers and judges wore black. Stewards and representatives of the Union wore a deep purple or gold. Those were all elected from the population, but she knew that Witnesses were not elected. They were chosen.

She didn't expect armor. His head was unprotected, the cowl thrown back across his shoulders, merging into a reflective silvered cape that bunched at his shoulders and brushed the ground. He wore a bright white exosuit, but over top of the fabric, a burnished breastplate. The breastplate had distinctive markings etched on the surface. On the right over his heart was a vertical line with concentric arcs and, on his left, a parallelogram bisected into triangles. Metallic cords webbed from underneath the plate around his body, adhering to his suit and running down his arms to soft gloves and down his legs into black thick-soled and steel-toed boots.

Behind the Witness walked an *esclave* unlike any she'd seen. The *esclave* did duck through the door, was taller than Richard, and was just as thick-bodied. Where Richard would have turned sideways, this *esclave's* arms folded backward as it navigated the door frame and extended outward again past the threshold.

"An *Amplus Facere*," Reign whispered, shocked. "That's a very rare *esclave* assigned only to Witnesses."

The *Facere* had eight arms and was not humanoid. It lacked a head, and any discernible sensing equipment was hidden in the body. There were no exposed wires, and like the Witness, the esclave's extremities were armored with thick, overlapping plates.

"It provides him nourishment," Fallon said. "A Witness cannot travel far without their *Facere*." He was at least twenty feet away when Fallon called out. "That's far enough." She projected her voice across the distance.

The stranger stopped, and Fallon's escort circled around him and stepped back until a clear opening appeared. Reign started to say something, maybe ask the stranger a question, but Fallon motioned him to silence. They all scrutinized the stranger. This close, Ever could easily read his eimai, although she suspected Fallon already knew the public record.

Paul. His name was Paul. She could trace back his family tree and even had coordinates for a residence that was far to the north in Bragg. He had a service history as a public servant. She glossed over all the public details of his life in a heartbeat. His eimai didn't seem interesting, but the net flashed a warning. Paul was not human. The admission made her wonder what a human was, but the net didn't have a definition. His countenance was not displeasing or deformed. If anything, he was too symmetric, and his eyes were large for his narrow face.

"What is your purpose here?" Fallon asked.

"I'm chasing a ghost and think I've found another."

"There are no ghosts here, but if you mean to catch my father, chase him. He left through that gate yesterday."

Paul nodded. "He went into this house, which is registered to no one, and through a gate. I've followed him, and every door and gate he's opened none have recorded his passage until now."

"Perhaps he would like to show you something, and he's afraid you will get lost. If you hurry, you can catch him and ask."

"Or maybe he is showing me something already." There was no emotion in the conversation. Everything that Fallon and the Witness said was simply a statement. The Witness did not even seem to look directly at Fallon.

"I see many *cultivers*. Far more than a single person can direct. They are all listening to you."

"I'm a licensed directeur with a strong eimai. But if you are looking for answers about *esclaves*, talk to my father. He knows many things about *esclaves*. I'm sure he can answer your questions."

The Witness nodded once again.

"This is a strange organization for *cultivers* to take," Paul said.

"The children are learning a new configuration for *cultivers*," Fallon said. Ever wouldn't have caught it if she hadn't spent her entire childhood hanging on her mother's words. Fallon sounded confident, but the response was too quick and certain. This was the voice Fallon used with her when she wanted to end a conversation that could lead to something more interesting. She could tell the Witness sensed the change immediately, and he had a visible transformation. His posture shifted, and his eyes focused on Fallon.

"These are containers for travel?" Paul asked. Fallon didn't answer, but the two closest *cultivers* jerked forward and grabbed the Witness's right arm and shoulders. Paul's *Amplus Facere* moved toward the *cultivers*, but Paul waved it off with a slight nod of his head.

He used his free arm to brush at the hands constraining him. The movement was accompanied by a sickening sharp sound of crackling fiberglass, frayed wire, and springs stretched to breaking, but in a moment, the Witness stood free while the *cultivers* held mangled hands bent at the wrist and forearm.

"I'm coming with you," Paul said.

"Why? Your answer is close."

"You may have the answer, or you will lead me to him. I suspect that my *Amplus Facere* will be useless against you."

"A truce then? If you travel with us, you must do as I say at all times without question."

"No, I could easily follow behind you without restriction."

"Are you certain, though? I can move quickly when I want to."

There was a long moment, and Fallon seemed content to draw it out. Ever thought the Witness appeared to be puzzled.

"Perhaps a lesser arrangement then," Fallon said when they seemed to be at an impasse. "You will do as I say while we travel together, but if what I ask conflicts with your objective, you will wait for one day before pursuing us. With this agreement, you lose nothing."

The Witness paused only for a second before nodding. "I agree to those terms."

Immediately, the *cultivers* lost their ranks and assembled into a new pattern around the cargo boxes. Fallon seemed relieved and went to Paul. Ever followed close behind.

"Then we have agreement," Fallon said, as if completing a pattern. "You and your *Facere* will ride with Reign on this." Fallon pointed to one of the mattress-covered containers.

"I can ride my *Facere*."

"Already forgetting the agreement." Fallon smiled scornfully.

"If this is what you require, then I will comply. However, the *Facere* travels quickly." Paul was unfocused again. His eyes and face seemed to move in different directions as if roving, and they rarely met Fallon's gaze.

"Not fast enough, Paul," Fallon said personably, if condescending. "We aren't taking a direct route, and I will need long legs."

As Fallon spoke, *cultivers* on all sides of the containers joined, three making each base and then two interlocking into a pattern above. The *cultivers* climbed over each other, adding height to the construct to make legs twenty feet tall. The legs curled down from the air as hydraulic muscles compressed to reach the container and join with it.

Reign and Paul took a seat on the container using the rope as straps. Each container had six legs that could stand taller than Lucas, but flexed in a gentle arc. They lifted upwards, ascending to the height of the second floor of her house. While she watched, the massive hexapede crawled toward the gate two legs at a time. The *Amplus Facere* followed behind. It would easily fit on the platform, but it was apparent Paul's resistance wasn't over.

"Are you sure he will be okay?" she asked Fallon. Ailbe was mesmerized, watching the mechanized hexapede plod toward the gate.

"A Witness would not lie overtly when negotiating a cease-fire, and Paul even less so. I can keep him from contacting anyone else. There aren't nearly as many of them as there used to be. All I have to do is keep him contained."

"I mean about Reign. You put Reign up there with him."

"That was his choice. He's interested in the *Facere*. There aren't many *esclaves* in service left from before the Union, but Witnesses have them."

Fallon gave Ailbe a gentle tug on the arm to get his attention.

"You and Ever are going to ride on this one." Fallon motioned to the second hexapede.

"I wanted to ride on Lucas," Ever said. "We can all fit up there."

"We can," Fallon agreed, "but right now, I'm going to ride on Lucas in the center, and you two will be in the rear." Ever wanted to complain further, but Fallon's tone was no-nonsense. Ailbe said nothing. He obeyed as instructed and clamored onto the mattress, grabbing a rope handhold. She climbed beside him. There was plenty of room for them both to face forward.

The ascent was unnerving. She'd taken lifts and pods all her life, but those were fully enclosed. Suddenly, she was hoisted above the first floor with a simple rope handhold. Whose idea was this? She thought until she remembered. *It was mine.*

She could see through the fire escape window into her living room. From this vantage, the Control Group spread before her, right to the wall and gate.

One of her hexapede's front legs made a platform for her mother, lifting Fallon onto Lucas's back. She sat in the middle of the mattress, eyes closed. Ever realized her mother must be looking out through the hundreds of *cultiver* cameras all around them as they struck out to the gate.

The low-frequency hum of the bubble was irritating, and she pulled up and sealed her cowl over her hat, flattening the broad brim but blocking some of the noise as she neared the bubble.

The new gate was an impressive rebuild, big enough for even the largest farm *esclave* to enter or exit, although Reign had models of *esclaves* larger still. Lucas didn't have to crawl anymore, and the lock was spacious enough for all three hexapedes to enter together. The locking mechanism was not unduly long even for a gate of this size, and in short order, they were on the west road, and she could pull back her cowl.

As the hexapedes picked up speed, the wind rushed past

her, pulling at her hatstrings. She held on to the ropes, and Ailbe studied the road, cowl covering his face to protect his head from the sun beating down on them. The sun was always stronger outside the bubble. Unprotected skin felt immediately prickly, and sunburn was a certainty after just a few minutes of exposure.

She was surprised at how cool and protected the exosuit kept her, but she wondered what they really could do if all that energy wasn't spent on just staying alive. She couldn't say how hot it was right now, although she was sure Lucas knew. She didn't want to ask while her mother was controlling the *maitre*. There was an ugly effect on *esclaves* if two people tried to control the same *esclave* at the same time and gave countermanding directions.

"This is impossible," Ailbe shouted to her over the noise and returned to squinting ahead at the road while they galloped along on their *esclaves*. She didn't understand what he meant. But then he clarified, sensing her confusion. "*Esclaves* can't do this. You can't pile more *esclaves* on top of each other to make a new one. Their governance depends on strict parameters."

Ever shrugged, unsure what to say. He would know better than she about governance. Reign studied *esclaves*, but Ailbe was in Anima. The implant augmented the eimai to direct *esclaves*. Maybe he misunderstood what he learned at school. She didn't dwell on the statement.

"What are you looking for?" she asked him. She bent close to his ear, preferring to talk rather than shout or send the question.

"The road north," he said. "At this speed, we aren't that far away from it."

"How do you know we are going north?"

He rewarded her with a perplexed look.

"Really," she said. "How do you know?"

"It's the only way we can go. The only roads are north. To the east, west, and south you would run into the ocean."

"We could be going to the ocean." He liked to make assumptions, and she liked to question those assumptions.

"I don't think so," he said with confidence. "We didn't pack anything for the ocean, and your mother is, if anything, prepared. She doesn't travel light. I've gone on expeditions with ten people with less than this."

"Or maybe we'll be gone for a long time."

He looked startled at her pronouncement, but when he saw the road ahead, he quickly pointed it out.

"See, we are turning north," he said, shouting over the wind. He had the right to be surprised. Hypertubes connected every territory in the Union. In a few hours, they could cross the continent. Only the Free People used slower means of travel, and it was hard to imagine not getting where they were going in a few hours.

When they turned north, she thought about their group and leaving Dill, the only real home she'd known. Her house was full of too many secrets.

Across the farm, there were thousands of *cultivers,* but her mother was effectively taking almost every *cultiver* within her section, and she wondered if they would be noticed and stopped when they left. There were no visible alarms, and she wasn't sure what to ask without telegraphing their activity on the net, so she remained silent.

Anyone could ask the net a question and receive an answer, but you had to know the question to ask to make any progress. She found the system annoying and tried to ignore it. The net didn't have any of the answers she needed. *Who is my father? Where did I come from?* The net had almost nothing about her family, but her ability to find answers seemed to impress her teachers, so her advanced studies had focused on the organization of terms and logical hierarchies.

School geography didn't help her sense of scale.

Dill was so large that the wall seemed completely straight unless you were miles away. They headed north at speed, and in no time, they'd covered those miles and almost made the tree line.

She looked over her shoulder at Dill. The flat grassland gently rose enough to reveal the transit tubes connecting Dill to the rest of the world.

The transit hub stood hundreds of stories tall and extended like a wedge all the way into the center of the city. Everything that came and went in Dill passed through that hub of tubes. She had few possessions, but most of them had a mark of origin outside of the territory. While goods traveled freely, transit by tube was harder for people. A good part of the transit hub was devoted to temporary accommodations.

She was too far away from Fallon to yell a question, so she focused on her implant to send a message.

"Will we stop at the trading post?" she sent.

"No," Fallon said. "Too close and too well known."

Ever thought she recognized the hillock as they passed the trading post on the road, and they continued down the north forest road for what seemed like hours until they turned on a new road heading east.

Fallon allowed brief stops on the all-day ride. Ever threw a few snacks from the pantry into her school bag, now repurposed for travel. She offered to share with Ailbe, but he declined. He stuffed his pack full of the tasteless plant bricks and enjoyed waving them around and making a show of gnawing on the blocks.

When the forest roads became boring, she laid back on the mattress. Although her perch was level, the thrust of acceleration required them to tie themselves down or risk rolling off the hexapede.

She woke from a reverie when the motion changed. The cargo box lowered to the ground with a firm thunk. She pulled back the cowl and her bent hat. The sun had moved into late afternoon. Its weakening light was less oppressive, but all the heat captured during the day hung in the humid air.

Fallon was still mounted on Lucas, but he was lowering his belly into the flattened grass between the other two hexapedes.

As soon as they touched the ground, the legs sprang apart into *cultivers* and wandered through tall grass to create a perimeter.

"Where are we?" Ever asked. The forest was at their back, a dark outline against the afternoon sun. High ferns and tall grass surrounded them, but *cultivers* flattened the ground around their rest stop with padded feet. Ever could see a few twisted trees and an old broken building in the distance.

"The leading edge of the old world," Fallon said. "Where civilization ends."

# PART 2—IN THE CRACKS

Grey trim stare, unblinking eyes
swollen veins and silent cries
Where bodies lie around the road
and reapers laugh at what we sowed.

The fences fell, bent to the ground
Melted steel, wind whistling sound.
That pierces deep into the night
Calling ghouls to their delight.

To feast upon the dreams of home,
lost to those that roamed alone.
Their midnight searches never cease
Without a grave, to rest in peace.

"Laments of the Catastrophe" by Unknown
Recovered from digital archives of the Federation
circa 2149, Western Common Metric

# 21. THE AXIS

Ever felt slightly off balance even after she stopped moving. There was a pattern to organic biology. The stretch and constriction of back muscles. The send-off of a sprinter on a run. Those rhythmic patterns of biology that a self-programmed machine with six legs didn't need to follow. The surface was uneven, and the hexapede stayed level, but the legs worked independently in an unrecognizable cadence.

She realized that level to an *esclave* resulted from an average—the average of all the degrees off-level over time. The result of that average was an unrestful experience. The further she traveled on the back of the hexapede, the more the machine took liberties with that average, causing her to wonder if they didn't stop, would the math allow the *esclave* to throw them off a cliff to get from point "a" to point "b?"

The hexapede was not one *esclave* it was Fallon's construction. Just how far did her mother go to put in failsafes?

The hexapede body stayed mostly together even as the legs and top disassembled themselves into individual *cultivers*. Most *cultivers* set out in all directions, wading through the tall grass, while several others went close to Lucas for recharging.

She was sure her mother would have the *cultivers* rotate into proximity of the *maitre de terrain* to restore their batteries. They didn't need to touch Lucas physically, but they needed to be in his immediate vicinity daily.

The *cultivers* were farm equipment, and they were sturdier construction than their indoor counterparts, the *maisons*. That made them heavier. To compensate, they were built with large batteries but consumed power more quickly. Their bright yellow and green painted exteriors clashed wildly with the surrounding vegetation, rapidly getting stamped into a flat circle from the activity.

Fallon extended Lucas's middle legs to drag two heavy tents off the ground in a vertical position so they could be unfolded for the night. Reign and Ailbe sought the few trees to make their contribution to nature, and she thought this might be her only alone time with her mother, so she dared a few questions.

"I'm surprised you didn't stop Reign and Ailbe from coming with us. If this is dangerous, why bring them along?" she tried to keep Ailbe from coming, but that was with mixed emotions. She was glad he was here.

Fallon didn't immediately turn to look at her, focused as she was on expanding the tents. "They can be useful, and they are here to support you."

"That's true. Ailbe said he came for me," she said, remembering his insistence. "But I don't think that was the only reason. I think you promised him something. I know he wouldn't leave his parents with just a message. There's not enough evil in his nature." She smiled innocently while probing for more information. He was her best friend, but he grew more distant in the last few years. For a while, it seemed like his internal struggles had resolved themselves, and it felt like almost a betrayal that he should trust her mother with something this important.

Fallon laughed. "You're right." She became more serious. "He has his own reasons, and as long as they align with our mission, we can use his help. They are both taking serious risks. I'm going to keep us as safe as I can, even if that means an indirect route, but the dangers are real. We are taking a route in between the old world and the new, but predators move with their prey, and we can't be certain none are out here. We also have to worry about contaminants. While this area has been marked clear for a long time, there are toxic chemicals that move with the wind. Keep your suit on. We will wipe down when we go in and out of the tents. Reign and Ailbe already know the process. They have experienced outdoor living."

The tents were heavy enough that Fallon had *cultivers* help her expand them into position. Lucas moved his head around to inspect the operation, and Fallon patted his signal lights. Her mother was rarely affectionate, but after the ordeal at the farm, even she appreciated Lucas.

"One benefit to Lucas," Fallon said. "We won't need a center pole for support. That gives us more room to move around in the tent."

"Why are these so heavy?" Ever asked.

"They are lead-lined. While we could get them together by ourselves, each shelter weighs over a hundred pounds. They can be quite useful for several reasons."

Fallon's eyes darted over to the Witness. He was walking around the perimeter of the camp. A ways away, there was a ruined structure. From this distance, Ever could tell the concrete had crumbled away. It had a partial roof and square-cut holes for windows but little else.

"It's a post office," Paul said. The Witness chuckled, staring off into the ruins.

"I thought you might approve," Fallon said. Although Paul always seemed to look in a different direction, he nodded. "Tomorrow, you can inspect it. We might be here for a day or two."

The Witness looked at Fallon, finally meeting her gaze. "What's the reason for the delay?"

"We are waiting here for someone. If they can meet us in

time. We are also waiting to see if we are being followed."

He nodded slowly, and she continued. "We may need to leave quickly. I need you to stay prepared and to stay fully fueled."

"I can go several days before feeding."

"Regardless, this is an opportunity we might not get in the future, and the sun is almost down. I have *cultivers* circulating around the perimeter. You will be the first one to know if they find something."

He shrugged stiffly. He didn't seem as concerned as he was offended, but he didn't push back. Ailbe and Reign returned, and they watched the Witness mount stirrups on his *Facere* outside the camp center.

The *Facere* enfolded the Witness, each arm bending forward until the Witness was cradled with his cape in a cocoon. The *esclave's* chest cavity opened, and prehensile tubules snaked inside the cocoon, out of sight but not hearing, as there was a distinct wet click when the tubules attached to their target. As the machine bent over, a back cavity opened, and a dish unfolded. It scouted the sky for a moment before settling into position.

"Can he hear us?" Reign asked.

"Not while he is trying to connect," Fallon said. "It's a limitation in their design, and I don't think he'll have much success tonight." Four *cultivers* sprang into action as soon as the Witness bonded with his *Facere*. They pulled a large tent from storage and unceremoniously draped the mass of fabric over the Witness and his *esclave*. "He'll figure that out tomorrow, but I'll claim innocence." The turn of her lips indicated almost feline satisfaction. "He'll know I'm lying, of course, but that will give us one more day that he can't report our activities."

"Can't he just send a message?" Ailbe asked. "I can still feel my parents. I'm surprised they haven't contacted me."

"I asked them not to," Fallon told him. "Witnesses don't communicate over the public net. They use an older technology before the Peace. Everything they hear and say ultimately ends up in Bragg. He has to connect directly through satellites overhead. It's like a primitive version of a *sentinelle* but deeper in space. From now on, avoid using the public net." Fallon turned to look directly at Ever as she delivered the last statement.

"Of course," Ever agreed glibly.

"I can see where Ever gets her tricks," Reign commented.

"I didn't want to bring him with us, but we weren't given much choice. We are going to wait here and see how sophisticated we are being tracked. As you know," Fallon said, with a faint touch of annoyance in Ever's direction, "I'm being pursued. If they leave the city, I will know. If they take a tube, I will know."

"How will you know?" Reign asked, but Fallon ignored the question and continued to lob commands.

"The sun has set. Grab your gear and bed down. Ever and I will share this tent while you two take the other one," Fallon finished, and the look she gave them brooked no argument.

The procedure for getting into the tent was elaborate. Fallon had her wipe her exosuit front and back and even the bottom of her boots. After entering the tent, she peeled off the suit, but Fallon had her immediately fold it inside out and wipe down the inside of the suit before she changed into new clothing. Fallon took all the old clothes and put them in a bag. She put a small pod from a sealed container into the bag and shook it vigorously.

"In a few minutes, that will clean the clothes. They can be folded and stored."

The tent was a hexahedron, made of triangles and internally lit with light strips across the seams. There was no light leakage through the fabric and no windows. Some external vents were connected to various electronics. The climate control and air filter inside the unit quietly pumped out clean, deodorized air. Rings were built into the ceiling to break off the tent into sections, and a box expanded into facilities for separating waste and reclaiming water. Ever decided she would go thirsty before using that one.

She was tired from travel and unexpectedly sore in a few places where she held on to the ropes, but it was early enough that she didn't want to go to bed. She tried asking a question instead.

"How do you control so many *cultivers* at the same time?" she asked.

This wasn't the first time she'd asked, but usually, these questions didn't get answered, or Fallon answered them with chores. Unfortunately, it was a popular opinion that children were better at chores than *maisons*. Simple chores left undone like "sort the recycling" and "wash the dishes" seemed to get prioritized over answers.

Today was different, and Fallon considered. She motioned Ever to sit beside her.

"Controlling multiple *cultivers* is simple. But stray thoughts and emotions can be dangerous. They can engage the eimai, create turbulence where you need to have calm. Remember the techniques we used at home for meditation? Prepare your eimai by clearing out stray thoughts. The eimai is consciousness, identity, and perspective enhanced by your implant. You need to create an Axis."

"What's an Axis?" Ever interrupted. She thought she understood the word, but her mother used it in a different way.

"The school should have taught you an Axis in math. An Axis is a dimensional boundary. Here, it's a boundary in your eimai. Some people need to visualize a map, but that's unnecessary and can be limiting. Reign is very good at controlling *esclaves* because the prejudice of sight does not limit him."

Ever focused on creating the Axis and she shared the construct with Fallon. The construct was more than words and more than a visualization. With the implant, it was possible to share a mental state that was more complicated than the verbal thoughts that existed in serial logic.

The construct was closer to an emotion in complexity, which could be shared and felt but more complete than an intuition that connected two disparate thoughts with a nonconsecutive leap.

Like an emotion, the construct needed to be experienced to be understood, although it was possible to focus on different parts of the construct. Without context, the construct had almost no meaning, but the implant could retain a more complex logical construct in her eimai than she could.

"Is this right?" she asked, and Fallon experienced the construct before she responded.

"You need to make sure that you are not in the Axis, Ever. This is most important, especially for us. It's a shortcut for others, but you need to keep people out of the Axis unless they have a role. To the degree that you can do this, the more you will experience and the better a directeur you will be. You will see how the esclaves see, hear what they hear, and feel what they feel without empathizing with the machines. You can command an army. If you can remember the music from home, try to bury your emotions into that and keep them separate from your eimai."

That was a struggle. Without realizing it, she'd placed a third-person version of herself in the center of the Axis and constructed the boundary outward from there. She struggled to dismiss herself from the Axis, removing stray thoughts for herself outside the boundary.

"That's a good first step," Fallon said approvingly.

The thoughts didn't want to stay, and Ever tried to recall the unique sounds she heard in the workroom. She queried the net, but the response she received was unintelligible.

"You won't get help there," Fallon said. "You need to remember on your own."

The memories were distant. Most of the time, Fallon insisted on meditation Ever spent scheming. The music was generated from many sources. Fallon called them instruments. Ever remember that. Each instrument had a distinct sound and together carried on a complex medley. With an effort, she focused on the memory of that medley, trying to bury her stray thoughts into the music while keeping the construct of the Axis in her eimai.

"That's good enough," Fallon said. "Music can influence your thoughts and emotions. That can translate into bad decisions, but it's also a useful tool when starting, particularly because it uses different parts of your brain to process information. People don't multitask very well, but if you want to control many *esclaves*, you need to trust yourself to work on several tasks at the same time. You have to leave your eimai open to the experiences from the *esclaves* without trying to control each one.."

Ever heard the words, she labored to stay in the melody.

"You have to trust yourself, the net, and most importantly, you have to trust the *cultivers*," Fallon continued. "Listen to what you are receiving from the net. It can respond to your queries with words, pictures, scents, tastes, and textures, but you must be open to the feeling."

Within the Axis Ever created, several distinct points appeared. They had a distance between them, but there was no sense of scale. She recognized that the points were *cultivers*.

"How do I move them?" she asked.

"Where would you move them to?" Fallon answered with a gentle laugh. "Right now, your Axis isn't tied to a physical location.

Experimentally, she tried to move one point, and she could tell that it moved some distance, but then it stopped. She tried to push the point in her mind further, but it wouldn't budge, although she felt the resistance weaken.

"If it moves any further, the *cultiver* will walk over Reign and Ailbe," Fallon warned, "The *cultivers* are programmed to protect people. They will resist commands to run them over."

Ever cast into the point opened into her eimai and she tried to see what the *cultiver* was seeing. She caught the image of the tent dark against the night sky. The *cultiver* had one leg in the air outstretched over the structure, but all she could do was back away. She tried to regain her perspective from the *cultiver*, but she let the Axis collapse. She was left in the tent without a connection to the *esclaves*. She opened her eyes.

"That was very good for a first try," Fallon said encouragingly.

"What if I placed Ailbe and Reign in the Axis?" she asked, "Then I can walk around them."

"You could do that," Fallon said, "but what if there were hundreds of people?"

"That would be too many people to keep track of in the Axis," Ever said with a hint of a question in their voice.

"Too many for you, but not too many for the net," Fallon said. "This last part is probably the most important for you. Trust the *esclaves* and keep people out of the Axis. To do that, suppress your sense of others, no matter how you feel."

"You might think of this sense as empathy, but it's the Peace," Fallon continued. "You will find that it encroaches on your thinking more and more with time, but this separates people who can juggle control of a few *esclaves* and those who can command thousands."

Ever struggled to put the Axis together a few more times but was foiled by anticipation of what she would do once she had it in place. Fallon watched patiently but eventually told her it was time to rest. As she fell asleep, her last sense was the cluster of *esclaves* ranging miles around them under Lucas's watchful eye.

# 22. SENT

Ever wasn't sure when she fell asleep, but it must have been late. The insulated tents blacked out the light but were far from soundproof. All night, she woke at the slightest noise, filled with nervous energy. Every *cultiver* treading the grass in the campsite might have been a mountain lion or night bear on the prowl.

She directed no more *cultivers*, fearing that would wake her mother. Fallon seemed to put herself to sleep at will. Ever wasn't sure if that was a technique she needed to learn, but in the middle of the night, with nothing to do, she envied her mother's peaceful repose and steady breathing.

As a result, she woke late in the morning. She could hear conversations in the camp and pulled on the exosuit groggily, worming into the leg and arm holes before stumbling through the narrow door flap that didn't quite unzip to the ground. She spotted Ailbe, Reign, and Fallon sitting on folded stools beside a portable oven. A *cultiver* cooked with a long spatula under Fallon's attentive gaze.

"I didn't think that was possible," Ailbe told her.

"I'm pretty sure it won't seal that way," Reign commented.

Fallon looked up and gave her an irritated glance that

ended in a sigh and a firm command.

"Go back and put it on the right way. Make sure you follow the cleansing procedure."

Ever stared back at them blankly.

"You have the exosuit on backward," Ailbe said. That was when she realized the cowl was draped across her chest. The cowl, paired with the suit, found the right position. *My exosuit is on backward.*

She could feel the heat rising to her cheeks, and she darted back to the tent, but remembering Fallon's irritation, she performed the whole cleansing process if a bit quickly before suiting up correctly to join the others.

"Come over here and have some breakfast," her mother said. Fallon crouched by a portable burner and oven. She'd never been much of a cook, breakfast being the exception, and Ever wasn't sure if that wasn't because she woke up hungry and demanding every morning.

When they were home, breakfast was high-protein. An assortment of different meats was grown fresh, extruded into shape, and delivered regularly. Eggs were always on the menu, although the treatment of fowl in the harvesting chambers made her sick.

If she made it out of bed on time, there would be sausage or bacon, eggs, toast, and green juice. She usually managed a thick slice of the toast and green juice, if nothing else. The green juice was faintly sweet and, according to her mother, a natural source of all the vitamins and minerals she needed— dehydrated into a powder until mixed with water.

She wasn't sure what to expect while traveling. A fried plant brick was out of the question. She was pleasantly surprised to find that breakfast was much the same as at home.

The portable oven toasted bread on a tray, and she separated the crust from the warm, soft interior. Her monther preferred her bacon chewy, while she preferred bacon crispy with all the fat melted off. The bacon sizzled on a pan under Fallon's watchful eye, and the pan turned down the burner after frying the bacon to a crumbly strip. That was when Ever knew this would be a good day.

They didn't have camp chairs. Fallon preferred to use stools made from folded *cultivers*. *Cultiver* stools gathered in a circle around the stove, their arms and legs bent to create a flat seat on their backs. It was firm but not uncomfortable, and with a thought, Ever lowered her chair slightly so her feet settled flat on the ground. Sending a command to an *esclave* right in front of her was simple. It didn't require an Axis or even forethought.

When they finished eating, Fallon stood, and several *cultivers* removed the portable stove. They were left with their plates and utensils while Fallon brought out cleaning supplies so they could wash their own dishes. Ever attempted to have a *cultiver* wash her plate, but she only succeeded in waving it around in the air until it almost smacked Reign.

"Watch where you're going with that thing," he said. She took the plate away from the *cultiver*. They both knew the *cultiver* couldn't hit him, but he enjoyed being irrational whenever she tried something new.

During breakfast, Paul sat patiently. The Witness didn't sit on a stool, although she saw there was one for him. Instead, he sat on his strange *esclave,* which had a saddle on its back.

When he stood up, so did the *esclave,* and the saddle disappeared. The *Amplus Facere* towered over the smaller *cultivers.* She was familiar with *esclaves,* and while almost all of them were taller than she was, she had never thought of them as looming until now. Where the Witness walked, his *Facere* stalked closely behind.

"How long will we be here?" he asked Fallon.

"At least one day, and it's going to take a while to reorganize what we brought. We didn't have time yesterday to prepare, and I'll break down the beds today. We are going to use the foam to make padded chairs."

"I thought we were riding on the beds," Ever said.

She didn't like losing her bed. Even sharing her bed last

night on the ground was better than sleeping on the floor.

"That works okay for traveling on flat ground, but soon we're going to be climbing boulders and jumping between peaks. The beds are made of waterproof foam that can be cut and shaped to make seats. Unless you're held down, you will fly off. Unless those seats are padded, we'll all be bruised. We can use inflatable beds for sleeping."

Her mother's plan sounded like a lot of work, but Fallon had plenty of *esclaves* for the menial activities.

"Okay, so what are we supposed to do?" she asked, hoping she wouldn't be outlining foam all day.

"I'm sending you to the Post Office."

# 23. THE POST OFFICE

Ever had completely forgotten about the ruins, which was surprising since they camped only a few hundred yards from the collapsed building. But she was doubly surprised when Fallon, with some insistence, sent her, along with Ailbe, Reign, and Paul, to look at what was left of the dilapidated facility.

A pair of *cultivers* occupied with a fraction of Fallon's attention walked beside them, but she felt a nervous expectation of sudden action that conflicted with her mother's laissez-faire change of heart. She noticed that Reign stayed close to the *cultivers*, and she realized he was using the cameras on the *esclaves* for vision. They were out in the wild, and he couldn't see without them.

The Witness's *Facere* stayed behind, watching Fallon direct *cultivers* to cut the beds with short blades. Fallon pulled out a transparent wrap from one of her storage containers to pad the *cultivers* with foam.

Dill's inner ring contained wide buildings that were also thousands of feet tall, and tunnels and sky tubes between them made it difficult to distinguish one structure from the next.

The post office was wide but not very tall. She enjoyed the clear sky, but the building seemed too simple. It took up too much space in the landscape to justify its existence.

She studied history in school. While records from the age of technology were incomplete, this was clearly from the prime of the Federation. It was common knowledge that the higher the level of technology, the more sophisticated and taller the construction. The squat ruins belied that point, proving the ancients were either less adept at technology or woefully primitive in culture.

According to Ever's education, the ancients lived in an age of unfettered technology. Most of the building was exposed to the weather, but enough of the roof was left for her to perceive the dimensions. Even where the walls were intact, massive door frames left gaping holes.

The foundations were solid despite the structure's apparent age, but most of the brick facade had crumbled away, leaving cement blocks exposed. The blocks crept into each other, but she could find the lines and even completely hollow cavities that went right through the building.

As she approached, she couldn't help but vocalize her objection to the dimensions, resisting the impulse to ask the net for answers.

"Wheeled vehicles would roll up to the doors and take packages for delivery," Paul said. "They had so many packages to deliver, and everyone was so spread out they built these distribution centers as quickly as possible. Most fell apart, wasting building materials and injuring the inhabitants."

"They had many languages back then, and everything had to be printed in a different language," Reign said.

"That's true," Paul agreed, "but language was not a barrier to efficiency. They had machines that could speak every language, and many people spoke two or three. In the beginning, before stockpiling, they used technology to build and ship what they needed right before they delivered it."

They entered the building through what might have been

the front door, but it was now just a hollowed-out opening. Some roof was still left, and remnants of a counter stretched hundreds of feet across the front entrance.

The Witness turned around to look at the broken windows. There was no evidence of the glass, just a half wall with a gaping opening to the outside. The building was slightly elevated from the camp, but if there were steps or a ramp, they were long since buried under the dirt, which swept right up to the opening.

The Witness pointed out to the camp. "They would have driven personal vehicles and placed them in lines around the building where the grass is now."

She tried to picture the process in her mind and was startled to realize there were square miles of flat grasslands around them.

"How many do you think?" Ailbe asked.

"Tens of thousands at a time," the Witness said in his usual disconnected fashion to the open air. Paul didn't seem to have difficulty holding a conversation, but most times, he wouldn't look right at you, just beside or around you. At first, she felt disconnected, but the more time she spent with Paul, the easier it became. "More vehicles called trams would bring them in by group to the distribution center, where they would wait in long lines."

"What were they waiting for?" Reign asked.

"In the beginning, for things they bought, but in the end, mostly food," Paul said. "Before the Union and the Peace, the cycle of violence repeated over decades and centuries. The Federation was the stabilizing force in the West."

There were granite tiles where the floor remained intact, but so much dirt and debris had blown through the windows that Ever wasn't sure of their coloration. They found a place to walk around the long counter. Even the slightest touch turned the laminated wood into crackling dust. A sharp reminder came from Fallon through the nearby *cultiver*. *Look with your eyes and not with your fingers.*

Behind the counter was a wall with many low openings, like crawl spaces. The wall was mostly blocks of bare concrete cracked and flaking, but there were plastic signs, warped and weathered with age. Most of the signs were unreadable and had fallen to the floor, but one sign still held to the wall, driven in by a pin, caught her eye.

The sign had a symbol similar to the symbol embossed on the Witnesses' breastplate. The breastplate was silver over his white exosuit and would catch the sun's rays through the roof with flashes of light. On the right side of his breastplate, the parallelogram was bisected into triangles. She pointed that out to Paul.

"That is a symbol of the Witness. I think she knew I would come here, if for no other reason than to see."

"What does it mean?" Ailbe asked.

"It represents the people who chose the life of a Witness. At the end of the age of technology, truth could be twisted into lies. They used machines to make people and had those people say and do whatever they wanted."

"*Esclaves* made into people," Reign sounded disgusted.

"Not just *esclaves*, but images and sounds. The network was insecure, and they tried to rebuild it many times. Eventually, the Western Federation turned to civil servants to become part of the network. From those volunteers, they created Witnesses. They guaranteed veracity and were dispatched to the military and civilian population, although before the Peace, there was minor distinction between the two. As war changed, the Witnesses became the military."

Ever crouched and walked through one of the low crawlspaces in the wall that separated the service desk from the warehouse. Reign chose a different opening and studied the inside framing.

"There was a tube or conveyor system here. But the metal is gone. It could have corroded away, but I don't see any signs of rust, and the wall is damaged."

"It was probably recycled," Ailbe said. "Giant *esclaves* forage for metal and concrete all the time. I've seen them when I was out on expeditions. They're massive." Ailbe turned to Reign. "Don't you have a model of the one that turns old concrete into aggregate?"

Reign nodded. "There are several specialized *esclaves* for dismantling old world structures, but nothing small enough to get into here and pull rails away from a wall. For some reason, they must have used smaller *esclaves*, something like a *maison* or *cultiver*, to keep the building intact."

The warehouse floor was covered in dirt and debris, with clumps of weeds and grass growing through cracks in the floor. There was no ceiling, but as her grandfather explained before, little grew in the soil without help, and the few plants that she saw looked sickly.

Reign and Ailbe attempted to scrape some of the dirt to see if they could find any mounting points for a shute. There were places in the concrete that gave evidence of a subfloor but no entrance. They debated on how similar this would operate to the tubes used today to create a distribution network while Paul filled in what little he knew.

In Dill, most people walked to retrieve their groceries. Sometimes, entire houses or floors would go together. Ever's mother wasn't much of a shopper and would often send a *maison*, but Ailbe's house shopped together, and she frequently went with them. It was considered a social event that happened several times a week. From what she gathered, this ancient process was unrecognizably different and seemed to involve either standing and waiting or sitting and waiting.

She was patient enough with the conversation but eventually dragged Ailbe and Reign through a gaping distribution gate outside the warehouse floor.

Paul wanted to linger at every service desk and look for workrooms, but she wanted to make a full loop around the building. The *cultivers* shadowing their footsteps split between the two groups, and Ever, Ailbe, and Reign left Paul.

The morning started cool, but the heat increased

dramatically closer to midday. She unfolded her hat from a pocket in her exosuit. The hat sprung into the right shape regardless of how she stored it. Ailbe and Reign lifted their cowls to block the sun from their eyes but remained unmasked. She noticed they rarely masked all the way, and despite her mother's warnings, Fallon rarely sealed her exosuit. *Do as I say, not as I do.*

Although the exosuits kept them cool in the damp heat, she underestimated the distance. After about half an hour, another *cultiver* came running behind them with water and snacks. After transferring its cargo, the *cultiver* returned. Reign was doing calculations on the length of their walk.

"If this building is one mile on the side and we are traveling four miles an hour, we should be back in one hour," he said.

"Except we aren't traveling four miles an hour," Ailbe said. "We're also spending time going up and down."

*Ailbe is right. This is going to take all day.* The ground around the building wasn't flat. Each gate was about twenty feet apart, and little valleys were in front of each entrance. While the wall had partly collapsed in the middle, the valleys on the outside remained, and for every few steps forward, they were taking one step up or down.

There was very little grass close to the building, just dirt, rocks and occasionally dried out leaves that must have blown in from the forest. Those would crunch under their boots, but the leaves decayed slowly as even the tiniest pieces were embedded in the soil, which Ever reflected was mostly dry dust. More dust rose with every step they took, but Fallon didn't seem concerned.

"If we walk on the inside, it's flatter," Reign offered.

"But we might miss something," she said.

"What's to miss?" Ailbe asked. "All I see is dirt and grass for miles. It's hard to believe all of this was parking?"

"If they lined up all the vehicles, they might have made a decent tube," Reign replied thoughtfully.

"Not really." The *cultiver* spoke with Fallon's voice, startling

Ever. For a while, she forgot that her mother was listening in. Normally, she was busy enough directing the *cultivers* that Ever spoke freely, but now Ever realized she might have to pay attention to what her mother was doing.

"They had cities where they used tubes. But out in the country, they used camion to deliver to houses until those systems broke down, and then they used cars, a smaller type of personal conveyance like a pod with wheels, until they ran out of parts to fix the cars. Some cars are still used today."

"Then what did they do?" Ever asked.

"Eventually, they had to get closer together. Much of the countryside was abandoned. It was the right decision. By then, it wasn't hospitable for life, anyway."

"Why did we stop here if there is nothing to see?" she complained.

"There's a lot to see here," Fallon said, speaking from the *cultiver*. "And just as importantly, we are keeping him busy."

"You mean the Witness," Reign said.

"Yes, this is something he would be drawn to. Not just because of its historical significance but because a Witness doesn't like to leave unanswered questions. Facts are an integral part of their nature. They carry around a lot of information, but they can't carry everything, and I've prevented him from connecting to get more details. Naturally, he's going to spend some time investigating. He almost can't avoid following his reconnaissance programming." Ever noted that Fallon was quite smug with her response.

"Why is it still here?" Ailbe asked Fallon. "I'm surprised the foundation and walls haven't been recycled."

"That's part of its historical significance. This was the last post office before the Peace, and they made it into a national monument. They designated the land as protected in public systems. Most of the Federation's underlying operating systems still exist today. The Union was born after the Peace, but building new systems from scratch would have been difficult, if not impossible, so they built on top of what was left.

Witnesses predate the Union. They have an extensive history all the way back into the information age even before the Catestrophe."

"How did this place get so damaged if it's a monument?" Reign asked Fallon.

"Public *esclaves* controlled by the Union will avoid this area during recycling expeditions. That doesn't apply to private endeavors. Even after the Peace, many people looked upon places like this with anger. The fact that so much remains is surprising. As you saw, all the metal is missing. They must have brought in small *esclaves* to recycle the package handling system and even the doors and roof, but we shouldn't see any concrete recycling or earth movers here."

The *cultiver* tapped on the exterior wall experimentally, causing it to chip. "Even back then, we had pretty good self-healing cement, but this area has been irradiated so many times it's completely dead," Fallon mused. "It's been a long time. There are no signs of radiation now, and most of those tactical missiles had a short half-life.

"What will we see if we walk around the entire building?" Ailbe asked Fallon. Not the first time he undermined her exploratory efforts, but she held on to the walk by determination more than interest.

"Nothing, but you will get some exercise. You can continue around or come directly back to camp. I'm busy with the chairs. I'm leaving the *cultiver* to follow you, Reign."

It came down to a vote. Ailbe didn't want to miss lunch, and Reign claimed to have slept poorly. She was outvoted two to one to return.

# 24. ROBOTS

Obviously, turning around and walking back was duller than the hike around the Post Office. Ailbe and Ever chatted almost nonstop, but Reign had to focus on keeping from falling over on the uneven surface between each gate. The *cultiver* was a wonderful machine, and because of the accessibility net, he didn't really have to think to see. The *esclave* hung in the back, its eyes a set of cameras looking forward, creating a reference for eimai.

The *cultiver*'s mind wasn't particularly strong, and Reign only had two choices: He could extrapolate perspective from the *cultiver*'s position that helped his sense of balance, or he could look at everything the *cultiver* saw. He chose the latter, adding the sense to his eimai.

Everyone else saw with just two eyes, and he thought he might have an advantage if he could see from a different perspective. He tried to walk confidently, but each footfall was an act of will as he watched himself walk.

To his amazement, after about half an hour, his mind bridged the disconnect. *Or is it my implant?* Regardless, he diverted more of his attention from walking up and down the small hills between each gate to paying attention to the surroundings.

The walls stood, but the gates were so wide that he had an unobstructed view of the interior through wide-angled lenses on the *cultiver*. Most of the attached warehouse was empty space open to the sky. A few interior walls remained closer to the front of the building, and the *cultiver* could see those, but they were at the far range of the *esclave*'s focused vision and well out of range for human eyes.

He was studying those interior walls when he saw a shape skitter in ruins behind broken walls.

At first, he thought he saw the Witness, but the shape was the wrong color. The Witness wore white and silver. *Maybe the Facere came after the Witness?* The *Facere* was in darker colors, deep blacks, and dark grays.

That didn't match either. The *cultivers* and the *maitre* were all in green and yellow, very distinguishable. The pattern of movement didn't match an *esclave*. It was organic, like a person or animal, and white on the top and black on the bottom.

Like one of the faceless, but they only existed on the net. He was conscious of the net, and, per Fallon's admonishment, he stayed away from those resources. With the net, he might identify what those pixels in the distance were.

"I wonder who is out there?" he said aloud. He wasn't following Ailbe's and Ever's conversation.

"Do you see something?" Ever asked. "We should investigate."

"Your mother said that we should come directly back," Ailbe said. "I don't think she wants us wandering around."

"Directly back is through the Post Office. If there were anything dangerous here, she wouldn't have let me go in the first place. What did you see?"

"I'm not sure." Reign frowned. "It was probably nothing. It reminded me of something I'd seen before."

"What?" Ever asked.

"I can't remember." He gave Ailbe a knowing look, which Ailbe was slow to notice. "But I recall Fallon told me it was harmless."

"I guess it's okay," Ailbe said belatedly.

"Are you two keeping something from me?" Ever asked.

"Fallon says a lot of strange things. Cutting across will get us back faster. I'm tired of walking. If this keeps up, I'm going to have the *cultiver* carry me."

Ailbe continued to complain at Reign while Ever took the victory. They went through a gate, walking over the broken floor. Reign extended his vision as far as the *cultiver* could see, taking advantage of all the cameras and sensors on the machine, but the ghost was gone—disappeared in the remains of the low walls.

While they walked, Ever kicked at the dirt to reveal the concrete slabs underneath. The slabs were long and wide. Wider than a house, they melted together into the cracks where some other long-gone material was used for expansion and contraction.

Rare stalks of grass grew in corners where one slab met the next in repeating patterns until they neared the front of the building. They were only minutes from the laminated counter when he belatedly realized all the grass was gone. There was no ceiling. The sunlight hit the dirt floor, and the breeze carried the same odor, but the smell was different, almost metallic.

He stopped to examine their surroundings while Ever, and Ailbe moved on until, without warning, the ground fell away.

He didn't have a particularly firm sense of balance. Some part of the implant and *cultiver* was working on his vision, and that combination kept him upright in free fall. He landed on his feet, knees flexing, but it wasn't enough.

A flash of pain traveled like lightning up his heels to his knees, and he fell on his back, stunned. The feeling lasted only seconds before he realized he'd fallen ten feet to a subfloor. The *cultiver* landed without incident, but they were not alone.

Misshapen *esclaves* scrambled around the room. They were on all fours, but most had only two or three working legs as they circled him and the *cultiver*, dragging mangled parts. It was a dark room except for the sunlight that came down from the top, but the *cultiver* had vision beyond human senses, and Reign could see a workshop of sorts. There were machines, ancient like these. quadrupeds tossed in piles.

Pieces of the quadrupeds were dissected on tables. Many of them had tools fastened to their frames—long barrels and sharpened stakes. They were covered in a course, leathery material, dried out and fragmented with tufts of fur. Each one had a mouthful of teeth, a dirty white attachment on mechanical jaws.

"You've stumbled on something that should not be here," Fallon's voice came from the *cultiver*. The fall must have alerted her. Or maybe Ever and Ailbe, they called from the top as the *esclaves* circled. The *cultiver* tracked their movements adroitly, sidestepping around Reign, who regained his feet.

"What are they?" Reign asked.

"Robots from an old war. They must have been gathered and tossed here. Someone reactivated them."

"Why aren't they attacking?"

"I don't know, but we aren't waiting to find out." The *cultiver* turned around, grabbing him by his exosuit at the waist. Its engine revved, emitting a high-frequency whine and building pressure. Dropping lower, the cylindrical muscle strands contracted arms and legs while its fingers tightened on his suit. The weight of the *cultiver* pulled him down until it grabbed his collar. Roughly, the *cultiver* hoisted him into the air like a bag of fertilizer with no appearance of effort.

He tried to grab the *cultiver* for balance, but before he could, the machine straightened, hurling him directly upward over the ceiling and back onto the ground by Ever and Ailbe. He gasped and coughed as he landed roughly on his stomach, but he still saw through the *cultiver's* cameras.

The robots dashed at the *cultiver* coming from all sides. The action would have been fatal for a human, but the *cultiver* caught two of the robots and used the momentum of the catch to swing them in a circle, pounding the other circling robots and sending debris across the room. Jaws gnashed at the *esclave's* arms, and there was a sharp retort of breaking fiberglass. The *cultiver* lifted the robots and slammed them against the floor until they were silent.

Still more red eyes glared back from corners around the workroom, hiding behind whatever rubbish they could find. Fallon methodically went around the room, destroying the remnants, until she stopped by a control panel with wires splayed in all directions. The *cultiver* pounded on the panel with a steel fist, and doors on the ceiling closed much more slowly than they opened. At the last second, the *cultiver* jumped, grabbed the edge, and spun itself to the surface.

Surprisingly, although the dirt was disturbed on these panels, not all of it fell away when the trapdoors opened, leaving a slight depression that would fill in quickly with the wind and rain. There were gouges all over the *cultiver*, but it looked functional.

"I thought robots were dangerous," Ailbe said. "They didn't put up much of a fight."

"You didn't see them from up close," Reign said. "They were old, really old and damaged."

"Still, all it took was one *cultiver*."

"A *cultiver* wouldn't be a match for even one robot under normal circumstances," Fallon interrupted from the machine. "They're farm equipment. What's disturbing is they had the advantage of surprise, but they didn't use it. We can't stay here long. We need to move faster."

# 25. INVENTORY

Paul eventually returned to camp a few hours later, looking troubled. Whatever his concerns, he didn't share them, and he considered Fallon's modifications to their new chair *cultivers* with skepticism.

Each *cultiver* serving as a chair had a thick layer of foam tightly wrapped around its body. Fallon had been careful to expose the sensors at the top of the chest, but she thoroughly padded the legs and arms.

As she demonstrated, when a *cultiver* became a chair, you could sit on its legs and use the body as a backrest. One *cultiver* arm would wrap around your waist or chest for support while the other *cultiver* arm positioned itself as a headrest. Because the chair was an intelligent machine, it moved with the motion of the hexapede, flexing to soften falls and adjusting for expected impacts. With the hydraulic muscle strands, they had their own personal shock absorbers.

*Cultivers* were not very tall, and neither was Fallon. The perch seemed extremely comfortable for her, but when Paul tried, his legs were nearly doubled over to get into the seat.

"I can ride the *Facere*, and it will hold the back of the hexapede."

She reluctantly agreed.

"Just be sure to strap yourself down or have it hold you down thoroughly. We can place you on your own hexapede."

Paul's normally unfocused eyes centered back on Fallon. "I will ride with you or the children."

"Ideally, we should balance out the weight between hexapedes. As part of our arrangement to travel together, you agreed to follow my directions as long as they did not conflict with your mission. I believe your goals are still being met?"

"Yes."

"Then we are at an agreement. You will ride on the hexapede, and you and your *Facere* will cover our back."

Paul didn't seem to agree with Fallon, and the more she attempted to get a commitment out of him, the more distracted and unfocused he became until Fallon accused him of grey-rocking her and gave up.

She called in *cultivers* to test the arrangement with one cargo box converted into a tall hexapede. She claimed traveling without testing your equipment was the worst kind of folly and muttered about laws made by Murphy without explanation, confusing Ever and causing Paul to blink.

Her morose responses didn't build confidence with Reign and Ailbe, while Ever jumped at the opportunity to test the hexapede.

Although losing her bed felt like severing another thread connecting Ever to home, the force of the legs through the carapace translated to a roiling back-and-forth motion that made her afraid of falling off. The chairs were an enormous improvement.

The new seat was firmly anchored. The *cultiver's* hands and feet made effective clamps. The *cultiver's* right arm snugged around her midsection, almost chest high, giving her support to hold her arms around, while the headrest and body of the *cultiver* gave her something to push against when the entire hexapede shifted upward precariously.

Experimentally, she pushed against the deck of the

hexapede and let go, rebounding in the chair. The *cultiver* rocked as if the legs were springs moving against her effort and absorbing the shock. Fallon gave her a moment to settle in before putting the form through its paces with Ever and Reign on the back of the beast.

"I'm going to tilt the front and then jump it forward," Fallon said with confidence.

Reign sat beside Ever with a white knuckle grip on the restraints, and she couldn't understand what he was afraid of. They'd ridden *esclaves* before. The only difference was he wasn't in control.

No sooner did Fallon say it than the front two arms of the hexapede lifted high in the air in front of them. Ever titled backward as the back legs compressed, and she raised off the ground at a severe angle as the middle legs extended.

"I don't think this is a good idea," he whispered to her. "Just a moment ago, your mother said everything that could go wrong would. I don't think they designed *cultivers* for this kind of operation."

"Nonsense," Fallon said, overhearing Reign despite his hushed tones. "The load is well within their specification. Put your head on the headrest Ever."

"I think I'm better off like this." She clutched at the arm of her chair, leaning forward and straining to hold on. Reign's fear was catching. When the *esclave* tilted she had the sudden realization of how high off the ground she was.

"Lean back. You need to relax and let the *cultiver* support you. If you try to hold yourself up, you will end up with torn muscles and pulled ligaments."

She complied and leaned into the seat. No sooner did she relax than the center arms of the hexapede sprang upward, heaving the carapace backward in an almost vertical position. Gravity pushed her into the padding, and the rear legs contracted, balancing the hexapede on two legs, leaving her stomach somewhere above her in the open air.

The *cultivers* had hydraulic muscle strand bundles that

could compress and expand quickly in a range of motion. When they switched directions under load, those artificial muscles gave a perceptible grunt as they locked into position and the pressure built to release.

She heard a series of grunts, each one louder than the next, as the rear legs took all the weight of the hexapede shortly before a sense of overwhelming pressure triggered an explosive force, speeding her forward.

Ever shot into the open sky. She sat on the front of the hexapede, and all she could see were the two front legs flailing in the open air. *Are those legs keeping balance or grasping at an invisible lifeline?* The sensation seemed to go on indeterminably, but she quickly reached the top of the arc and plummeted rapidly in what she was certain was an uncontrolled fall.

The rear legs hit the ground first, acting to absorb the shock. For a moment, she thought they would fall backward and the weight of the *cultivers* would crush them, but the hexapede settled forward on the middle legs and front legs until they returned level to the ground.

"That was fifty percent power," Fallon remarked to Ailbe. He watched the test with undisguised glee, but when Ever turned her head to frown at him, a wave of nausea almost made her throw up.

"How far up did they go?" he asked Fallon.

"Over forty feet. That should be far enough." Her mother's analytical approach to problem-solving was distinctly unnerving when Ever was stuck in a chair.

"What if we doubled the power?" he asked.

Ever was stuck in disbelief, but Reign was quick to respond.

"She said that was far enough."

"It wouldn't be twice as high," Fallon told Ailbe. She ignored Reign. "There's diminished return with the power to mass ratio."

"But how high would it be?" Ailbe persisted.

"The only way to know for certain would be to test it,"

Fallon said, considering his question.

"I think we should do that, just in case."

"We've tested it enough," Ever called down. "Get me off of this thing." The *cultiver* arm that held her did not reach around her completely, and she could work her way around the obstacle and out of the chair. Ailbe snickered at them, but Fallon lowered the hexapede to the ground. Reign and Ever disembarked on shaky knees.

"Are you sure that's safe?" Reign asked.

"You can check for yourself," Fallon said, "but each of the *cultivers* has a lifting capacity equal to the load, and I've it split up between four *cultivers*."

As Fallon talked, one of the cultivers came over for their inspection. Its green and yellow paint was still clean after a day of road dust. The nanocoating resisted all but the worst dirt.

"Most *esclaves* are built to be as light and energy efficient as possible. Although these *cultivers* have the same fundamental design, they have a solid steel frame stiffened and braced where the leg and arm joints meet. The internals of this *cultiver* are as well constructed as that beast over there." Fallon pointed at the *Facere*, standing in silent observance not that far away.

"But exposed," Reign said. There were uncovered conduits exposed below the fiberglass shell, and cylinders that powered the hydraulic muscle strands were easily identifiable on the frame, unlike the *Facere*, whose body comprised a set of overlapping plates that silently shifted position with every motion.

"Each part is designed to be field replaceable," Fallon said. With a motion, another *cultiver* came forward. There was a series of quick popping sounds as pressurized valves disconnected, but in less than a minute, the two *cultivers* exchanged right arms. "And because both the hands and feet can clamp on to mounting points, we can make larger functional constructs."

"I guess that's what bothers me," Reign said. "I've studied lots of *esclaves,* but I've never seen anyone put them together in a configuration they were not designed for."

"Most load-bearing *esclaves* are hexapedes. The net knows how a hexapede works. How to make it walk, run, and jump. All you have to do is tell it to."

Reign seemed troubled about the idea, but it made sense to Ever. She had been asking the net for answers before she even knew what it was, and it always came back with an answer. You just had to know the right question. There was a nagging thought in the back of her mind, though. For a moment, Ever thought she might fall backward. An *esclave* couldn't hurt a person, but when they were put together in a form, there wasn't a single mind governing their performance. By acting together, could they break the moral code built into the *esclave* programming?

They spent the rest of the day unpacking and repacking the storage boxes. What she thought had been deliberate leave-taking the day before was not the case, according to Fallon.

"Look at this. All these spars are broken," Fallon said. She was holding up a pole that went to one of their tents. The tents were lead-lined and very heavy. The poles were embedded in a series of pockets in the tent.

Not all the tents were put together. Fallon stored two tents collapsed in separate boxes. They had surreptitiously used one on the Witness last night. Ever noticed that the tent had been folded and placed back into its box this morning. *Maybe Fallon retrieved it before the Witness woke?* She saw that some joints on the spars were broken.

"The poles are strong and flexible, but the joints have to move in the groove. They are always the first thing to break. I don't have enough spare spars to fix this."

"I found lights," Reign said triumphantly, holding up a box. "These are adhesive lights." He took a small flat light about the size of his hand and pressed it to the front of the suit. The light glowed brightly even in full daylight, drawing power from the internal wiring.

As Fallon methodically inventoried her equipment, she

realized how unprepared they were. As the sun went down, at least a quarter of what they brought was in a growing junk pile.

"Shouldn't we recycle this?" Ailbe asked, looking down at an air filtration system Fallon said was too old to be repaired. She had tossed it into the pile of junk with particular malevolence.

"I think I might have worse problems than a fine for littering," Fallon said. "I borrowed about two hundred *cultivers*, not to mention one of them is fusion-powered and large enough to require regular Union inspection. I'm not carrying extra weight around the continent."

She wasn't sure if her mother was satisfied, but by the time the sun settled in the western horizon, everything was repacked except for the tents and bedding they were using and a portable stove that doubled as a fire pit. There was a stiff, damp breeze moving from the east, carrying the odor of waste. The smell was concentrated, and she wrinkled her nose. Ailbe and Reign attempted to cover their faces with masks, although Fallon and Paul seemed unaffected.

"We are closer to the Pannish channel," Fallon said. "The bacterial blooms can be quite strong. If we are lucky tonight, we might see a StarFall."

Ever looked at Fallon blankly, but Reign was quick to chime in enthusiastically. "I've been studying how we harvest StarFalls from the channel in school, but they don't say much about how they get into the channel."

"You aren't missing much," Ailbe commented. "They are definitely bright, but it's just a light that travels down to the horizon. You would have to be on the water to feel the impact."

"What is a StarFall?" Ever asked. Normally, she could do a quick query on the net, but she remembered Fallon's prohibition on net inquiries.

"Ancient technology," Fallon said. "One of the few joint efforts between the Federation and the Empire still operating today. They used robots to section off metallic asteroids and then shape the fragments to land in the ocean."

"Like the machines we saw today?" Ailbe asked. *"Esclaves* land the StarFall."

"Even older and more primitive. They don't have the quantum circuitry to interface with an eimai. They follow pre-programmed directives. The Union retrieves the StarFall from the robots and *esclaves* land it into the ocean."

# 26. ESCAPE

As the sky darkened, *sentinelles* brightened the night. The pale twinkling reminded Ever of the watchful eyes of the Union. Regardless of what Fallon feared, the Union stood for peace. With *sentinelles* watching, what could go wrong?

Fallon used the stove to prepare a simple meal from what they brought from the refrigerator at home. The Witness did not eat. He didn't seem to require regular food, and what was left was split between the four people, and she was nervous about how long it would last. They had a lot of canned and dry goods from the pantry, but most of her favorites were already gone.

"What's happening up there?" she asked, pointing at a patch of lights flashing and weaving in the northern hemisphere.

There were many *sentinelles*. Sometimes, they formed patterns in their slow march across the sky. She'd looked at the night sky outside the bubble and was familiar with the patterns, but this was different. Even though most of the lights seemed distant, these lights were closer, brighter, and moving quickly, dodging and weaving.

"An old Federation robot must have descended too

low," Fallon said, and she moved closer to Ever and pointed at the lights. "Look for the triangular pattern of lights. That's the Federation robot. The other lights are Union *streiters*. They are engaged in a battle."

This sounded dangerous and made her distinctly nervous. "Who will win?"

"The *streiters* will, eventually. There's more of them. The Federation robot probably descended because it was damaged or malfunctioning. They are ancient technology, but they're still dangerous. Some of them are controlled by AI, and AI from back then can get pretty nasty. The *streiters* are operated by directeurs. Even this close, there is a bit of a time lag on reflexive communications. That gives the AI an advantage, but when technology is equivalent, numbers usually win a battle."

After dinner, they sat around the fire. Fallon said there was something special about fire when you were traveling overland. Fire was not unfamiliar to Ever. They used a hydrogen gas-burning stove at home, but what little heating was required in the winter months was forced air from an electric heat pump.

The cold light from the *sentinelles* didn't offer any real illumination, and they obscured what little light came from the disc-shaped moon as their darkened shapes passed over, blocking the light.

The fire pushed back the darkness that closed in around the campsite. The tents were black domes framing the western night sky. Inside, they were brightly lit, but the many layers of fabric kept the interior wholly hidden.

"Even the most dangerous animals still fear fire," Ailbe said to the fire, and Reign nodded.

"It's the one thing that makes living outside really possible."

"How long will we be here?" Ever asked Fallon. Paul was inspecting his *Facere*, but as soon as she asked Fallon, his normally distracted gaze focused on her.

"Not long. I thought at least one more night, but she's close to us now. Something's not right."

"Who is she?" Paul asked, but Fallon ignored him.

"It's your sister, Reign. We were supposed to meet your sister and father at the south trading post, but they weren't there."

"Where's my father? Can I try to contact him?"

"No. I don't know. Don't try anything yet. Whatever you did would not be secure. Your sister has been running for a long time. I have two *cultivers* supporting her, but she's exhausted."

The news brought everyone to attention, and Ever's eyes squinted into the darkness. There was a flurry of activity in the darkness as more *cultivers* wandered into the camp from the periphery and Lucas's face brightened as his scanners probed the night.

During the day, the *esclave's* bright yellow and green bodies were reassuring, but at night, they moved like ghosts around them. The faint red circles of light glowing from their infrared sensors did not reflect the firelight, and she couldn't help but feel the night transforming their friendly servants into demons.

Demons that were always in motion except for the Witness's *Facere* that sat in silence away from camp but observing with four bright red lights like two sets of eyes stacked in an unblinking stare.

She hadn't physically seen Riley in several years, although she communed through the net a few times, tagging along behind Reign. Riley didn't have an implant, but she had other options. Riley's gun Varmint Slayer was connected to the net and had cameras and a viewfinder.

Riley made a substantial income by posting content to the net. She had a growing fan base on Riley's Kills. Ailbe and Reign watched fervently, although Reign's observations were almost always critical. He said he had to keep her humble. Hunting didn't appeal to Ever, but she listened to him about organizing hunting parties and setting clever traps. A trap was much like a trick, and a well-timed trick was worth a laugh or two. He rarely talked about the things he missed from the Free People, but she sensed one was the community effort to farm the herds.

The woman the two *cultivers* half dragged and half carried into camp was not the one she remembered. Riley's face was covered in dirt, hardly recognizable. Her hair was tangled, and her exosuit was ripped, revealing the clothing beneath. The *cultivers* held her upright, supporting both shoulders, and one of them had Varmint Slayer strapped to its back. Ever was surprised Riley still had the heavy gun, but without it, she would be disconnected.

Riley's boots were more destroyed than the rest of her outfit. The soles were completely missing. The bottom half of her suit below the knees was just fragments of the heavy fabric tied to her ankles, exposing feet that were not that different from a *cultiver*. Instead of green and yellow, these were stainless metallic appendages.

Even as the *cultivers* holding her stopped, Riley's legs kept trying to walk, but she started awake and stopped the motion. Reign leapt to her side and shouldered a *cultiver* out of the way to take her arm.

"Made it," Riley said. She leaned heavily on her brother.

"You're safe here," he said.

"Let's get her over by the fire." Fallon had a first aid kit in hand, and she put a sensor on Riley's wrist. "She's seriously dehydrated, but her vital signs are good."

When Riley was seated, Fallon mixed a restorative directly from the first aid kit into water and pressed a collapsible travel cup into Riley's hands. She drank, downing the liquid, and Fallon refilled the cup.

"What did you put in this?" Riley asked her, wondering at the liquid. She already looked more animated. "It tastes like water."

"It's flavorless. A long time ago, it was used on the battlefield. It's perfectly safe, at least in small quantities. You need to avoid exerting yourself like that for the next few days. The effects will wear off in about eight hours, but until then, you will feel awake."

"A few minutes ago, I thought I was going to collapse on the ground. Now I feel like I could run for miles."

"I'd prefer to let you sleep if I could, but right now, I need to know what you know. Where's your father?"

"I left him."

# 27. THE CAPTURE

"It's going to be okay," Fallon said in a rare moment of comfort. "I know if you left him, you had good reason. I want you to start from the beginning, but before we start, I need to know if you think you were followed?"

Reign stiffened. Riley was startled at the suggestion but thought for a moment before speaking.

"No, I'm sure I caught them by surprise. Only Varmint knew where you were, and they didn't have him for long."

"Where's father?" Reign asked. Riley started to answer, but Fallon motioned her to silence.

"It will not help me if I get bits and pieces out of order. I need you to remember details. I need to know where you were and what you were doing."

"About a week ago, we were coming back from the plains when we got a message from Jorge to meet you at the trading post," Riley said. "There are fairly good roads between Oastin and Dill. They don't travel straight as a hypertube, but we usually make good time. That must not have been fast enough because father rented a camion in Oastin, and we left most of our belongings in a Wayfair."

"What's a Wayfair?" Ever interrupted.

"It's a permanent structure used by the Free People on a temporary basis," Reign explained quickly.

"Like the trading post?" she asked.

"That was once a Wayfair, but it's visited so often it's grown into a small village," Reign said, but his attention was focused on Riley. "What happened?"

"Before we reached the trading post, the camion stopped. I'm not exactly sure where we were or when it stopped. We were in bunks in the back. When I woke up, it was completely dark."

"Were there any readings on the instrumentation?" Fallon asked. "Even a weather report would help."

"Everything turned off," Riley continued. "We couldn't turn it back on. The power was completely dead. We had other gear with us, and Father tried to boost the power by plugging it into a battery port, but nothing would turn on. Even our air filtration system, which has its own battery, wouldn't start."

"What about your gun, Varmint?" Fallon asked, and Riley flushed.

"We didn't think to try him. I stored him in a safe under my bunk because he wouldn't stop talking," Riley said. "My father thought we must have been misrouted to a Deadzone."

"What's a Deadzone?" Ever asked, interrupting again.

"Places where electronics won't work," Reign said sharply. "Obviously, that wasn't the case. You could still walk."

"It seemed plausible," Riley said. "My legs are shielded better than most equipment, and I was still in the camion. He told me to stay inside. But when he opened the cab, they jumped him. I heard yells, and I wanted to get behind them. I went for the top hatch, but they were waiting with catch poles and dropped a noose around my neck."

Riley's hand went to her neck, and Ever noticed a welt beneath the dirt. It still looked sore.

"Did you get a closer look at them?" Fallon asked.

"Not then. It was dark. We were under a canopy of trees but still on the road. I could see their robes by the way they moved, and they were wearing night vision goggles."

"Robes?" Fallon asked, and Riley confirmed with a nod. Not many cultures wear robes unless they are for a ceremony or position. Did you get a closer look at them? How many were there?"

"Not until later. Most of them were on my father. I would guess there must have been at least twenty, maybe more, waiting on the road for us. They dragged me to the ground. They had catch poles around my father's neck and arms. He was struggling, rolling around. They fell all over each other, but I couldn't see much in the dark."

"Richard has a form of giantism and would not go down easily."

"No, he kept struggling. But then they threatened me."

"They threatened to harm you?" Fallon asked, surprised.

"They told him they would make me one of them. After that, he complied, at least for a while. They forced us into a march for several miles off the road, where they had a camp set up with a big fire. They dumped everything we had in the camion on the ground."

"Did you see their robes?"

"Yes, they were wearing them loosely over the exosuit. They were red and not like anything I've seen in Dill."

"Ajat Maata, maybe. But what would they be doing in a western territory? I know your mother came from one of the eastern territories. Did your father ever mention any details about that?"

"No," Riley said, looking at Reign, who nodded. "We knew he traveled to the eastern continent, but they never said much." Riley appeared to remember something else. "There was a silver band around their neck, overtop the exosuit."

"That's just like an implant. They have a longer range because there is less infrastructure in the rural areas of the eastern territories."

"Do you think this has something to do with our mother?" Reign asked Fallon.

"That's hard to say for certain. People immigrate back and forth between the territories. That is not unusual, but most people won't leave their families. Others have jobs or causes that align with specific industries or local politics. How did you escape?"

"They tied us to a tree. They had other people tied to the trees—Free People. A man wore a short white coat, and a surgical table was tilted up near the fire and about waist high at the base. They were forcing people onto the table. Tying them down to the rails and clamping their heads to the frame. He took a long rod, it seemed sharp, and jammed it into their eye."

"Describe the rod. How long was it? Was it solid? Was it serrated like a knife?"

"No. The end of it seemed flexible. It was very thin. He held it almost like a stylus."

"What was he doing?" Ailbe asked.

"It sounds like a lobotomy," Fallon mused. "But why, I don't know. What happened to them afterward?"

"I saw it twice," Riley said. "One of the red robes led them off. They didn't run away. They weren't tied."

"Completely docile, almost like a drugged animal?" Ailbe asked.

"Drugs would have been a lot easier," Fallon said. "Although the effects would have been short-term. They must hope for something more permanent."

"Test subjects?" Ailbe asked.

"Maybe," Fallon said.

"Did that happen to our father?" Reign's voice was thick, and Ever put an arm around his shoulder in support.

"I'm not sure," Riley said bleakly. "Probably. When they went to get Father, they didn't remember how strong he was. He threw them back and yelled at me to run. He knew all along that I could break the ropes."

Riley lifted one leg, showing off the metallic foot. There was a semblance of toes and heel, but with a motion, she flexed them together into a clamp in a way a physical foot could not do, making her artificial appendages into a second set of hands.

"I dropped to the ground and used my feet to break the ropes. I grabbed Varmint from the pile and ran while they tried to hold him down."

"That is a lie," Paul said. The Witness stood quietly in the background. So quietly, Ever forgot he was there, always watching with his shifty eyes.

Fallon turned and looked at Paul, who responded to the gaze.

"She believes everything she saw and did until this point, but she did not run."

Fallon looked at Riley, and so did Reign.

"What happened?" Reign asked Riley.

"I was angry, so angry, but when I grabbed Varmint, I knew I should run. Father was yelling at me to run. With Varmint, I knew I could get away. His fusion cell lets me run farther and faster than I can by myself."

"You shot them?" Ever was aghast.

"A gun can't shoot a person," Ailbe said. "The moderator on the gun won't let a person come to harm."

"Let her talk," Fallon said.

"No, I didn't shoot them. I almost wish I'd tried. I slung Varmint behind my back with the shoulder strap. When the first one reached for me, I grabbed her arm. I'm not sure how, but I turned her wrist, and then I kicked her."

"I'm sure it will be okay," Reign said.

"I felt her insides break," Riley said, eyes downcast. "When she dropped to the ground, I realized what I did. That's when I ran."

"This is her truth," the Witness said.

# 28. BREAKING CAMP

Riley slumped in her seat. All the energy she had before drained out of her. Shock painted Ailbe's and Reign's faces, but Ever wasn't sure why. *They must understand the circumstances.* Breaking the Peace was unusual, but not unheard of, and every city had *flics* and peacekeepers. Most crimes were crimes of ignorance, but there were always a few who hurt others deliberately, usually to get what they wanted, and they had to be jailed until they could be re-educated.

"Let's go back to our doctor," Fallon said. "I need you to give me the best description you can." The question made the others uncomfortable.

"He was wearing a white coat and dark pants," Riley stammered.

"Did he have any markings on his clothing?"

"Yes, there was a golden eye on the back of his coat."

"Two arcs with a shaded circle in the middle?" Fallon said, and Riley nodded in confirmation. "That's a priest of the Third Eye, maybe a high priest. The Third Eye operates in the West. It doesn't make sense for them to be engaged with an Eastern organization. They aren't welcome in the East."

"The skin on his face and hands..." Riley seemed to trail off.

"What about his face?"

"It was rough, mottled in shades of green and purple," Riley said with effort.

As soon as she heard the words, Fallon jerked to her feet.

"Murdoch," she cursed.

"Who is Murdoch?" Ever asked.

Fallon hesitated for a moment before answering. Ever knew that she was not just finding the right words but figuring out how much she could omit, and she wondered when her mother would trust them with a full explanation.

"He's an enemy of our family, and I mean that in the most literal way. He has an abiding hatred for us. Your grandfather, most especially, but you and I are included under that umbrella. If he's with the Third Eye, then they report to him. It's a made-up cult to violate the Peace."

"Why don't the authorities break up the cult?" Reign asked.

"It's spread out and hard to find. It's also not remarkably successful. There are always a few malcontents, and the Third Eye has accomplished little except to gather in the whiners. They spend most of their time pontificating. This is something new. With Murdoch in charge, they will be a force to be reckoned with."

"How dangerous is he, really?" Ailbe asked.

"We are leaving right now," Fallon decided, catching everyone off guard. There was a sudden flurry of *cultiver* activity as their silent servants standing around the camp surged for the tents. Lucas lowered his legs, dropping the ceilings as *cultivers* carried out equipment. More *cultivers* appeared to fold and pack.

"Riley needs to rest," Reign said to Fallon, still at his sister's side.

"We can't afford to wait. He's too close already."

While Fallon talked, the *cultivers* continued with their tasks. As everyone stood, chairs became workers, and workers joined together, clamping arms to legs until they created flexible towers that reached into the night.

"They must have splintered the net to stop the camion. That would take a lot more than twenty or thirty of the Ajat Maata."

"Divide the net into pieces?" Ailbe asked.

"Not divided. Splintered. The net is an amalgamation of many systems. If you want to think of it as levels in a hierarchy, Union law is encoded at the highest level. Laws aren't the same for all territories, but the net is the same—a logical construct of the East and West. If enough people from one territory are physically located together, they can enforce their own laws. On a map, this is part of Dill. But the forest is owned by the people. No one can own land where they cannot provide ongoing ecological support. That's an underlying tenant of the Union."

"They created a territory within a territory?" Ever asked.

"Effectively. Once they controlled the geography, they turned off the net for unauthorized activity. It won't last for long without a challenge. It's ingenious." Fallon smiled grimly. "But it was also foolish to use so early on."

The tower of *cultivers* bent, seeming to defy gravity as they extended metallic hands to clamp onto the main rectangular body. The padded *cultivers* fashioned as seats climbed on top of those oddly shaped cargo containers. The carapace lifted slightly away from the flattened grass, and hundreds of red eyes looked outward in all directions from the physical construct.

The night air was hot and humid, and the breeze coming in from the east smelled like an open sewer. The temperature-regulated exosuit kept her cool, but the day's exertions made her feel grimy, and she wondered what it would be like going for days in the exosuit without bathing. Although the others seemed content to follow orders, she wasn't beyond complaining.

"Why don't we contact the peacekeepers?" Ever asked her mother.

"We could contact them. We are outside Dill, but they

would be here almost instantly. Of course, they would take us in for questioning, and we would be detained, probably for a long time, while they completed an investigation."

"How long?" she asked.

"Months. Then there is the case of the borrowed *cultivers*. That won't look good, even if I can talk our way out of it."

"But we have a Witness," Ever said, looking over to Paul. "He can confirm we are being chased."

"Ever," Fallon said patiently, and Ever hated it when Fallon used her name like that, "The only thing Paul can confirm is that a girl told a story she believes. He's seen nothing."

"So we take them to the problem and make them see."

"They would know we were coming before we got there. If we remained in the custody of the peacekeepers, we could end up surrounded. Not that I would let that happen."

"We have to run again?"

"I don't like to think of it as running. Try to think of it as repositioning assets."

"What about my father?" Riley said. She was standing on her own, although Reign still held her arm protectively.

"I can't go back for him," Fallon said. "We aren't prepared for a confrontation."

"What if we filed a missing person report?" Reign asked.

"You could do that, but then they would know where we are," Fallon said. "There's a chance they know already. I wouldn't put it past Murdoch to let Riley escape so that he could track her to us."

"You have hundreds of *esclaves*," he said.

"Hundreds of *cultivers*. There could be thousands of them out there," Fallon said, gesturing into the darkness around camp.

As Ever looked out into the darkness, the area lit by fire seemed to shrink, growing smaller and smaller. Unconsciously, they all grouped closer to the light. Even the Witness's *Facere* moved to a closer vantage point, although both stood observing a few paces away as if they were a separate group unto themselves.

Ever had only felt genuine fear a few times. According to Ailbe and Reign, she had a disconcerting ability to ignore posted warning signs. She also had a propensity for climbing into small spaces and a strong desire to use electrical cables as ropes. All of those activities were exciting, but she felt genuine fear when she endangered her friends. Nothing was worse than the fear she felt when she lost Ailbe outside the bubble. She felt a growing sense of certainty that what was happening to her friends was her fault.

"There's very little we can do right now for Richard—accept hope the damage can be undone," Fallon said. "To undo it later, we need to escape right now."

Fallon turned on her exosuit light, and one of the few remaining *cultivers* turned off and packed the camp stove. Soundlessly, the *Facere* crouched down, its long body exposing the saddle on its back. The Witness, dressed in his white burnished exosuit, glowed in the artificial light, but the *Facere's* dark hands looked like part of the night as the esclave effortlessly lifted the Witness onto the saddle.

Several of the *cultivers* clamored on top of Lucas. They clamped down on mounting points to create a platform with two chairs. Lucas moved deeper into the night with a low rumble, stopping far away from the camp as the hexapedes formed a line behind him. The Witness followed in a loping motion until the *Facere* made a surprising leap onto Lucas's back, using its many arms to secure a purchase.

All this happened effortlessly as Fallon talked, and Ever continued to be amazed. Was her mother really tracking all these *cultivers*?

"And I still have to deal with that," Fallon said, looking at the Witness. Reign and Riley wanted to ride together and climbed onto the nearest of the hexapedes, leaving Ailbe, Fallon, and Ever.

"Is he going to help us?" Ever asked.

"I don't know," Fallon said. "I had a conversation with his

*Facere* while you were out this morning, and I don't think we need to be worried about him reporting on us for a while."

"How long are we going to run?"

"We're going to head north to Galt. We have friends there, and the Third Eye isn't welcome. Trade lords run the territory. Their government is largely based on financial influence."

"That's not far. Even traveling this slowly, that's less than a day from here," Ailbe said.

"Only if you go directly," Fallon told him.

# 29. SIGHT BEYOND SIGHT

Reign was not easily motion sick. That simple fact gave him confidence in physical challenges, but tonight, his confidence was shaken. The nausea burning the back of his throat gave evidence something was wrong.

*Esclave* racing was uncommon, and the way Ever liked to race *cultivers* by sitting on top of their shoulders was unconventional at best, illegal at worst, and dangerous most of the time. None of that stopped her and she couldn't leave his competence untested—inevitably, a challenge would be issued.

She had some unusual talents with *cultivers*, but her attempts were cumbersome and sloppy, whereas he was deft and precise. She didn't have casting training, and he had a distinct advantage. He put his eimai into the *cultiver*. When the *cultiver* ran, it was like him running. He could cast into an *esclave* more quickly than anyone he knew.

He wasn't sure if this was a natural ability or something to do with his childhood. Even when the net built vision from his physical perspective by extrapolating the surroundings from multiple angles, he preferred looking out from an *esclave's* perspective when he could. The Free People preferred their own feet but were more likely to use a manually driven camion than an *esclave*. He'd grown up racing around the forest while listening to his father organize hunting parties. He knew how to commit to action without hesitation.

When he raced Ever, rather than going around obstacles, he moved through them, inches away from a high-speed collision with buildings. Sometimes, he put so much of his eimai into the *esclave* he forgot he had a human body. The mundane awareness of that body rarely interrupted him.

This was not the case tonight, and he let out a belch as his stomach cramped into a hard ball before attempting flip-flops in the chair. *What's wrong with me?*

They left the road before camp, but until then, they'd traveled mostly on flat land. Although the forest was dense in the center, the outside edges left plenty of room for the hexapedes to navigate between the trees.

Where there was life, there was the Union and protection, but they left the forest, the grasslands, and any semblance of life behind when Fallon pushed east. He surmised they were on an old highway system. The Free People were nomadic but didn't travel to either coast. The remnants of the old world contained too many contaminants.

This was beyond his experience. Only fools or foolish fortune hunters searched the remains of the old world.

He'd traveled through the central part of the continent, but he had few memories of roads before he lost his sight. The roads of the Free People tread were carved out of the landscape, but only where necessary. The Free People preferred to travel over the land in its rawest form. It was disgraceful to use a hypertube. A camion could be tolerated if the need was sufficient, but casual use was a sign of poor judgment. The Union did not build the roads, but they built bridges across canals and hypertubes to villages with a stable population.

They were traveling at night, and *sentinelles* twinkled. The accompanying silver disc of moonlight was too little light to see in the normal spectrum. Everyone else was effectively blind except for him and probably Fallon. Reign could see clearly, although the infrared cameras skewed the colors.

He didn't like what he saw.

The road was a compact foundation of gravel and broken concrete where it wasn't washed away to sand. Galt was to the north, but they were traveling northeast into the mountains and the coast. Originally, the road must have cut through these mountains, but landslides blocked off access for wheeled vehicles.

Unlike the mountains on the west coast, these mountains were dead. There were no trees, only boulders, sand, and gravel. Many peaks had flat tops, and the land was pockmarked with craters.

Fallon was taking them directly into the old world.

He had hundreds of cameras to choose from. The hexapede made from *cultivers* had hundreds of eyes looking in every direction. He looked forward, following the natural sense of movement, and tried to ease his queasiness by dumping his awareness into a *cultiver*, but the net didn't respond.

"I can't contact the peacekeepers," Riley yelled, giving him a start. She'd pulled back her cowl. The fabric whipped back and forth in the wind, and he did the same.

"Fallon told us not to," he said to Riley. Each footfall from the hexapede was a thud, and the sound of the wind, as they rushed forward, forced him to talk louder, if not quite a shout, even though Riley sat right beside him.

"I know, but I had to try."

He sent out an inquiry on the net but did not receive a reply. He tried half a dozen queries, but none were answered. He could still sense all the surrounding sensors. They were feeding data into the accessibility net, ready to give him their eyes, automatically numbered and prioritized. However, the resources he usually felt when he worked with *cultivers* were missing.

"Is this what happened to you before?" he asked.

"No." She was looking at the viewfinder on Varmint. The shoulder strap looped across her back, and she had the weapon in front of her on the padded armrest made from a *cultiver* arm. "At least, I don't think so."

"Then it's Fallon. The *cultivers*, the net. They all worked oddly around her."

He wasn't sure what else to say.

"Father said to trust her," Riley said, but even over the wind, he knew she said that for her own reassurance. The Free People were less trusting than most.

"You can trust her." He tried to sound reassuring. Riley nodded, but he wondered. *I lived with her for years, but do I trust her?*

The *cultivers* moved at a fraction of the speed of a hypertube, and they weren't even traveling in a straight line as the road curved more to the northeast. Nights were almost as hot as days, but the eastern direction put the hot, stinking wind into his face.

When the road leveled briefly, he reached for his cowl, completely masking his face, and adhered the smart fabric to the suit, creating a sealed mask. The top of the mask in front of his eyes became transparent, and the outside of the suit shed dust and water, but inside, it collected humidity.

They traveled for another hour, on and off the road. Fallon kept them from going over any ridges, so they crossed back and forth between the foothills. She aimed for a tall peak. A road snaked up the mountain, carved into the rock face.

"I want to look back, and we will have a good vantage point up ahead," Fallon sent them. "Make sure you keep your suit lights off."

"The net seems to work for her," Riley said, but he only nodded.

They climbed the mountain when they reached the cliff face rather than cut back and forth across the switchbacks. His chair tilted precariously backward as the forearms of the hexapede reached up onto the ledge and levered the body.

Each hexapede forearm had a foot made of *cultivers*, evenly dispersing the weight and providing grasping hands that sunk deep into the ledge. The hexapede folded them into wedges and struck the surface, turning the hands into pitons.

Reign clutched the support, but soon, he realized pushing his body back deeper into the chair was easier. The center legs came up next, grasping the edge, and then there was a wild see-saw motion as they swung forward hard.

At first, rushing up the cliff was death-defying. At one point, he lost vision entirely as he focused on holding on to the restraints, but with each ledge, he focused on relaxing bunched muscles until he accepted his fate—one moment at a time.

He found himself on the top of the escarpment, sweating inside his damp suit, but instead of being terrified, he was exhilarated by the climb. They lined up on their hexapedes, sitting about the same height, although Lucas stood above the shorter hexapedes. Lucas raised his legs to the maximum height as Fallon studied their former campsite and the great forest that ran to the edge of the clearing.

He wasn't sure how far upward they traveled, but he felt a distinct pressure in his ears. The air seemed both dry and clean. There was little dust on the rock face, and he surmised the wind blew the mountains clean of debris since there was no vegetation to hold a substrate to the surface of the rocks.

During the climb, Fallon turned off the infrared lights on the *esclaves*, leaving him with only light in the visible spectrum. Organic eyes had limitations. He controlled the shutter speed, aperture size, and focus as he probed the sky above and the ground below, wishing he had access to an *esclave* with a long-range thermographic camera.

*Sentinelles* littered the sky and clustered in distinct patterns. Searching for light sources in the darkness below was confusing. Even faint lights reflected off bodies of water, but he dismissed stationary lights and lights with an unchanging vector. There was nothing visible in the grasslands. To the east, broken towers darkened the sky, but there was no movement—no light.

He turned his attention to the west and the forest. Trying to follow the presumed path they had taken through the trees. Far beyond the forest, a faint haze of light in the distance from the Dill bubble momentarily distracted him until he caught flashes of light moving in and out of the woods.

He repurposed distinct images from the *cultiver* crew to create a composite image. Tracking movement at this distance with accuracy was difficult, and when he tried to leverage the net to triangulate the distance from multiple perspectives, he failed again.

"Use Lucas," Fallon sent to him. Apparently, she noticed what he was doing.

With a thought, he cast his eimai to the *maitre de terrain* and was surprised by his intelligence. Lucas was far more intelligent than the *cultivers* he monitored, and Reign felt a kinship. He dismissed the feeling—*esclaves* were not human.

Comparing the images, Lucas discerned which flickers of light were unique. Reign spread the virtual map before him, plotting all the lights in the forest as Lucas identified each unique point.

"There are thousands," he whispered. He passed the composition to Fallon, and an audible gasp from the others followed the message.

She rose, standing on top of Lucas, her *cultiver* restraints melted away as she stretched. Paul, mounted on his *Facere*, sat behind Fallon, and she turned to him.

"What do you make of it?" she asked him.

"They are following us. They are taking the same general route, although they are spread out amongst the trees. They don't know exactly where we are."

"Unusual, wouldn't you say?" she pointed out to Paul.

"Unusual but not illegal. It doesn't verify Riley's story, but it supports the claim. More vectored light sources exist than the peacekeeping force at Dill."

"But Dill has millions of people," Ever said.

"Very few people break the Peace," Ailbe said, as if in explanation.

Paul waved his arm across the expanse below them in a rare moment of focused clarity. "There is no reason to believe the Peace is broken."

"I know what I saw," Riley said to him. "There are people down there coming for us who aren't friendly. What do you think is going on here?"

"The truth doesn't require rationalization to draw conclusions. It simply is, and until it's discovered, it cannot be understood."

"Let's hope we don't *discover* the truth today," Fallon said. "They aren't leaving us with many choices. If we keep going through the mountains, we risk being seen, possibly surrounded. We aren't in a good position right now. They might bring support from the north. We can head east and north to the coast, but we will go through the old world. They won't follow us, but we run a distinct set of risks, and eventually, we will have to turn west again to get to Galt."

"What kind of risks?" Ever asked before she finished, but Reign already knew. There was a reason the Free People didn't travel to either coast. The dense population centers on the coast used the sea to transport goods. Before the Federation succumbed to the Union, they suffered the most during the East-West War.

He knew people were different before the Peace, savage and creative. They cared little for each other and used their imagination to create destruction. From microscopic nanomachines to engines to reshape the continent. Under the rubble and ruin along the coast, ancient weapons lay dormant.

The Free People had stories and even a few traditions that survived the endless fighting, but every few years, a group of would-be adventurers would go missing in the old world.

Only the Union, with its vast collective resources, could

afford to send *esclaves* into the old world to recover or recycle what was lost, and even those *esclaves* were highly mobile.

"Robots," Fallon said. "I don't plan on digging for lost treasure, but we will likely encounter a few damaged machines still running. The Union has *esclaves* digging in the ruins. Sometimes, that can cause problems. With Paul, we might have an advantage."

"That's not the whole truth," Paul sounded almost defensive.

"The whole truth would take too long to get into," Fallon told him sardonically. "The truth we need right now is that Witnesses played an integral part in the Federation, and even a broken robot will pay attention to you if you were to ward it off. You are one of the few old military organizations that still have a face in the new world."

"We are the gatekeepers of the Immutable Records. Not snow, rain, ash, or blood shall keep a Witness from their service." He pronounced the words like he was reading from a history lesson, but she didn't seem to notice or care.

"Exactly. You were designed to wade through war unharmed, like crossing a stream. You're practically indestructible, but even robots bent on destruction will probably avoid you."

Reign watched the map of lights he created while she spoke. Although the light was faint from this distance, it was discernable and recordable until it wasn't.

"All the lights are gone," he said.

"They know we're here," she said. "Sound carries too well in these mountains. If they've locked on to us, finding our location is a simple formula."

"Do they know where we are going?" Ever asked.

"It won't matter. I think our decision is made for us. The old world is the one place I know Murdoch won't go."

# 30. SAFETY

The way back down the peak was much worse than climbing up the ledges and switchbacks. Fallon insisted they travel in reverse. They turned around in the darkness, facing backward. Ever could only see the night sky as the hexapede skittered down cliffs.

When Fallon learned they were being tracked, she picked up speed, relying on her *cultiver* constructs to catch the weight as they dropped off ledges into the open night air.

Each drop brought them a little further down into the valley, a little further down the remnants of old highways, and a little closer to flat land. Each drop was unexpected, and gravity forced her deeper into the padded foam *cultiver* chair as the ground rushed to meet her after a sudden free fall. She felt like she left her stomach somewhere on top of the mountain, and she tasted bile.

They started the journey down the mountain on the south slope, but Fallon steadily rotated east around the mountain. Every motion that wasn't a drop to a lower elevation moved them further from pursuit. When they reached the bottom of the switchbacks, the hexapedes turned around and joined a line with Fallon on Lucas, leading the way.

Ever missed the thin air. She was used to the humidity, but the sour odor of decay permeated the lowlands. Her first instinct was to close her hood, but the filter wouldn't remove the smell, and the hood trapped the humidity inside her cowl. Her exosuit was already damp.

Even though they traveled at speed, the long legs of her hexapede split off into individual *cultivers*. Like falling down a ladder one rung at a time, she gripped the armrest while she jolted and tottered to the ground level as the legs and arms of the hexapede lost knees and elbows.

Ever and Ailbe were left with individual *cultivers* holding their platform. The *cultivers'* legs pumped, and their infrared lights glowed as they ran. Without warning, there was a jolt from behind. She looked and saw that Reign and Riley's hexapede join theirs, two of the *cultivers* locking together horizontally to become a hitch.

"We are like pods in a tube," Ailbe said. He yelled over the noise of the wind.

Lucas led the way, lowered to the ground, becoming a giant buzzbeetle on his belly just a few feet above the road. His rear rubber tracks folded down onto the ground. No longer technically a hexapede, he picked up speed, and their *cultiver*-driven pods matched his velocity.

She watched with fascination as the same hitching activity happened up front. Two *cultivers* climbed on top of their container. Their bodies momentarily whistled in the wind and blocked her view. The *cultivers* stretched out their arms and clamped down their feet as they reached their hands out to Lucas and used a mount point built into the body of the *maitre de terrain*. Lucas's head extended on his motorized neck and looped around his body, looking back at them. She couldn't help but wave at him, and he tilted his head back and forth as if to reply.

They increased speed again. The surplus *cultivers* from the hexapede made a vanguard around them. Running on two legs, they dropped to all fours, steel limbs mimicking the motions of a giant cat. Their front and rear legs moved together and crossed between each other so that each motion covered maximum distance. The *esclaves* did not have flexible backs like a cat. Their arms and legs forced locomotion, biting repurposed hands into the soft ground as they scrambled forward with inhuman speed..

A vibration built in their pod, rattling her teeth. Her chair shook. The harder she gripped the armrest, the more violent the shaking until, with another burst of acceleration from Lucas, the shudder stopped.

The wind beat at her face so hard she had to use two hands to pull at her cowl, but with the hood on, the wind split around the smooth and reflective fabric, and she parted the air easily. The *cultivers* holding the container had changed their strategy again. No longer running, each *esclave* operated as a separate leg attached to the pods. She wasn't sure how, but they struck the ground like pistons, perfectly timed with their neighbors.

The vanguard of *cultivers* was now behind them. She wasn't sure why until she saw rocks and debris shoot out beside them into the darkness. The road wasn't flat or maintained if this could still be called a road. Lucas' forearms folded into an inclined frame in front of him, and whatever obstacles too large to go over were ejected out of the way by the plow, and the combined mass of the *esclaves* linked together like a rod made of thousands of pounds of steel pushing through the dirt.

She was curious about her surroundings and nervous about being caught, but eventually, the repetitive motion left her tired. She found herself leaning over the armrest in a daze until the chair folded backward against the pod. She didn't resist. The cultiver held her in place, and she stared into the darkness, relieved by tiny points of light. For a while, she watched the *sentinelles* dance in the night sky, imagining the millions of eyes staring down at her before she fell asleep.

Ever woke inside a tent on an air mattress still in her damp exosuit. She recalled stopping during the night or in the morning. No one was in the tent, but she could hear voices softly over the ventilation system. She found a set of clothes laid out for her, cleaning towels, and a waste composting machine for the morning necessities.

She wanted to rush outside, but she put aside the feeling so she could go through the motions. She cleansed the outside of her exosuit and then removed the suit completely. Her clothes underneath were a damp and wrinkled mess. Those went into a bag with detergent. Then she washed out the inside of the suit before toweling down and putting on new, fresh clothes after washing her face, brushing her teeth, and combing her hair. She resigned herself to the fact this would always be tedious. There was a gentle tap at the tent flap.

"I'm getting ready," she whispered.

"You don't need to whisper," Reign said. "We are having breakfast, or maybe it's lunch."

Her stomach growled, and she wondered about the time. Before realizing what she was doing, she sent a query to the net and received a response. The response was oddly formatted, but the message was understandable, and it was already afternoon, late even for lunch.

She exited the tent, trying not to slip while crossing the raised threshold. She stood on granite floor tiles bathed in a pool of light from the missing ceiling far above her.

She couldn't count the floors or the balconies facing inward to the courtyard where they made camp. Some columns supporting the structure were cracked, but overall, the building seemed solid. The balconies had no railings. Spaced at intervals around all four walls, gaping holes where lifts once stood appeared to be the only access to the levels above her. All the metal and glass was removed. *A Federation building.* She recognized style elements from the Post Office. This was from the same bygone era in time.

A stairway behind the tent went down several floors and led to what she assumed was the front of the building and an open atrium. The stairway was almost as wide as the wall and spread even further into the atrium below. There were no handrails, but evidence from holes in the floors and walls showed someone had ripped the handrails out. Even broken, the grandiose design was emblematic of the time. Very few interior spaces in the Union were wasted on something as nonfunctional as this display.

*Cultivers* stood at every opening, looking out past corners. Their bodies were more or less square and rigid. They attempted to stay in the shadows behind columns and tilt those brightly finished green and yellow frames around corners, but the attempt was more comical than subtle.

Fallon came up beside her just as a *cultiver*, ducking behind a corner, mis-stepped and clattered unceremoniously to the floor. The *cultiver* immediately scrambled to its feet, hugging the wall. Ever laughed.

"I'm going to have to talk with Lucas about staying out of sight," Fallon said. "I'm not sure how it happened, but someone gave him strange ideas about subterfuge."

Ever decided to change the subject. "Where are we?"

"I think this was a bank, but more to the point, we are further east than Murdoch will go. Our lookouts aren't for him. We aren't far from Union *esclaves,* and we really don't want to be noticed by Federation robots, either."

"When are we going to leave?" she asked, and her stomach rumbled audibly.

"First breakfast, and then we will decide."

# 31. TRAINING

It was midday, but Ailbe put together a breakfast on their portable stove worthy of home. He pulled out the plates and utensils and served everyone. Ever watched as he portioned out the eggs and used the last of their oil to fry vegetables for an omelet. He stared at the empty bottle. If there was one thing he liked, it was food, and she knew she would hear about rations today.

She didn't see the Witness, but knowing that he fed off his *Facere,* she wasn't concerned about eating without him. She took a plate from Ailbe.

"That's the last of the perishables," he said. He'd taken it upon himself to inventory all the food. "We probably have a month's supply of the dried food as long as we can keep it sealed. We have the water pouches and purifier, assuming we can find water." Left unsaid was a ready source of water none of them relished using, even Reign. He said that the Free People found water sources.

"Food and water aren't a concern," Fallon said. "We aren't going to hole up in a mountain. Let's start by getting a look at our surroundings. I plan to climb this tower. It's been a long time since I've been this far east, and the landscape has changed."

"How are we going to get up there?" Reign asked.

"*Cultiver* elevator." She walked below a balcony as a group of cultivers marched into their temporary camp. They clamored on top of each other, creating a wall of *esclaves*. One lay on the floor in front of the wall, and she stepped neatly on its chest. The arms raised, and she held the *cultiver's* hand to balance herself as the legs hoisted the body off the ground.

Using its partners like a ladder, the *cultiver* effortlessly lifted her to the next level. More *cultivers* lay on the floor, waiting expectantly.

"Are you coming?" Fallon asked.

"I think I'll make it on my own," Riley said. Her suit was still torn at the bottom, but rather than replace the boots, the suit was sealed against her prosthetic calves. She gripped the *cultiver* wall with her feet, climbing to the next level at a run while Ever, Ailbe, and Reign waited for the *esclaves* to lift them to the top.

"This isn't as fast as the hexapede," Reign said.

"It's more civilized," Fallon said, laughing. "I don't play hard indoors."

"I could get used to servants all the time," Ailbe said.

"I didn't borrow these *cultivers* for chores. If you're curious, your parents had a *maison* before they adopted you."

"What happened to it?" he asked.

"I asked them to get rid of it. Chores build character. Don't expect these *cultivers* to wash the dishes."

Ever had tried to do just that, but if Fallon noticed she didn't mention it. Perhaps this was her mother's way of saying not again and she sighed. When was she going to get an opportunity to train with *esclaves*?

They progressed one level at a time until they were on the top floor of the building. The towers in Dill dwarfed this structure, but as they rode the elevator, the top floors made her giddy. The *cultiver* held her hand firmly, but a few inches of metal didn't seem like security. Even a casual glance at the floor caused the ground to shake until she realized it was her knees. Ailbe, Reign, and Riley seemed unaffected by the heights, but she felt like something was wrong with her legs.

Fallon noticed and talked to her quietly.

"Don't look down," Fallon said. "Look at me."

"I'm going to fall," she said, wobbling, but her mother forced her to meet her gaze even as the *esclaves* lifted them upward. Every inch felt like a new opportunity, as if the ground below called her to jump. Not that she wanted to jump, but she had to end the painful expectation of the inevitable fall into dead space.

"I had problems with heights. But you can't shut down or freeze because your perspective changes."

"How did you get over the fear?" she asked.

"Training, exposure, and focus on what I wanted. Focus on how you want to be at the top."

Her knees shook the entire way up the tower, and her mother extended the width of *esclave* elevator so they could stand together. She asked Fallon to send her back a few times, but her mother would not relent and told her she could do it herself if she wanted to.

Just one look into the open air, and she lost all semblance of *esclave* control. She feared the *esclaves* would fall and voiced her concerns.

"Ridiculous. Watch."

Before she could stop her mother, Fallon motioned with her hand as if selecting a target. The unlucky *cultiver* she landed on made a running leap off the balcony and dropped like a rock hundreds of feet. The *cultiver* extended both arms and legs in the air and landed with an audible crack as the tiles below shattered. After jumping up from the crawling position, the *esclave* joined the others at the bottom.

"You could have destroyed him," Ever accused her.

"It's a machine. I knew it would be fine. I need every *cultiver* I brought, but if I had to, I could destroy them all. Don't personify your tools."

"Do you think a person could survive the fall?" Reign asked. He saw the distance through the *cultiver's* eyes, but a *cultiver* lacked the sensory experience of more sophisticated *esclaves*.

"No. With some exceptions. Most of us would splatter, and the others would probably die slowly from massive bodily damage unless they stuck the landing perfectly," Fallon said, glancing at Riley. "Don't get any ideas."

"I know my limits." Riley looked down over the balcony. "I've jumped off trees maybe a quarter this height."

From the top floor, they could see the coast. The murky grey waters occasionally flashed green. There was a steady, salty breeze, and Ever thought she smelled the faintest hint of sulfur.

"It doesn't smell as bad as I thought last night," Ailbe told Fallon.

"You've been in the stink all day. You're nose blind. If we stay here long enough, everything we open will need to be washed."

All the tall buildings dotting the coastline surprised Ever, many as tall as this one or taller. They were spread out, not clustered like Dill, and entire blocks were missing. Dirt and debris buried whatever roads were left. There were no signposts or light posts.

Rocks and broken concrete dotted the shoreline. A gray film covered the rocks except where the water struck them. Outside of a flash of green from those waves, the landscape was colorless, with no signs of life.

She moved to the western side of the tower, and Fallon followed her. She saw more buildings like their tower, and a few blocks away, something worse.

"Robots," she yelled. Her excitement at the spectacle overwhelmed her caution, but the anticipation of the danger wasn't far behind in her feelings.

In the distance, a monstrous construct of legs and arms appeared to feast on the side of a building. The machine was easily several hundred feet tall. Arms pivoted around the machine, each with multiple articulation points and a giant toothed bucket that gouged out concrete. The shovel dumped the broken concrete into the base of the machine. An icy tingle went down her back.

"Concrete recycling," Reign said indifferently, pointing to an *esclave* further back. "The interesting one is behind it, the *concasseur*. That one crushes the concrete into a reusable aggregate."

"Do you see it back there, Ever?" Ailbe asked. "It has all the belts, just like the model in his room."

Suffering momentarily chagrin, she realized these machines were the same as the models in Reign's room, if on an epic scale. She hadn't been particularly interested in his models, but she knew each one of these *esclaves* had hundreds of directeurs monitoring operations. Giant *esclaves* required multiple operators. She wasn't sure why.

"It's the other *esclaves* I'm not familiar with," Reign said, puzzled, and she realized that she had become so distracted by the bigger machinery she overlooked the smaller *esclaves* shaped remarkably similar to a *cultiver* or even the Witnesses *Facere*. These *esclaves* were larger, maybe twenty feet tall, and bipedal—almost human-shaped but headless and armored. The sensory equipment was placed in the center of the body, but the arms ended in a cluster of long barrels.

"*Beruhigen*," Fallon said. "They are a modern, squad version of a *combattant*. They are military *esclaves* sent to protect the equipment. They have a directeur for each arm and specialized weapons."

"For the robots?" she asked. She didn't care about how many directeurs it took to operate a machine if a robot attack was imminent.

"Will we see any fighting?" Reign asked over the top of her. Something changed in him since his father was taken. He normally held her back, but he seemed more excited about the prospects of a fight than she was.

"Most likely not," Fallon said. "Sometimes there are rogue

Federation robots, and occasionally the Union will stumble on an old hive, but the Union doesn't engage with the Federation except in low orbit."

"Who would win if they did fight?" Ailbe asked.

"Out here, it depends on the forces. The Federation buried machine factories underground. Most of the hives are nonfunctional and out of resources. Sometimes, the Union will stumble on one while excavating. Usually, the *esclaves* can move off and wait for the robots to run out of power. It's always better to avoid a fight if you can. The Union wouldn't commit to a battle unless it's surrounded."

"Has anyone seen Paul this morning?" Ever asked.

"Last night, he went to check and see if we were being followed," Fallon said.

"I think I see him right now," Reign said. "I wonder if an ordinary person can ride a *Facere*."

From this height, Ever could see far onto the mainland. The coast rose, turning into a ridge of broken concrete and rubble. With sudden certainty, she realized the landscape looked like a tsunami pushed the city back away from the shore like shoveling sand away with a tide.

For a moment, Ever and Ailbe couldn't see anything where Reign pointed except for a faint cloud of dust over the ridge. Then, the gleam of white and silver resolved itself into the Witness riding his *Facere* east over the ridge to the tower.

"He's going fast," Ailbe said.

"But not toward us," Reign pointed out. "He's heading to the Union."

That interrupted whatever quiet contemplation Fallon had fallen into, and she cursed softly under her breath as she studied the situation. Abruptly, an alarm note trumpeted from the Union *esclave*—the brassy sounds quickly reaching the top of the tower. After the alarm, the Union *esclaves* began a retreat as the ground imploded to the north of their excavation, dropping away into a massive sinkhole. The remaining section of the building collapsed into rubble, leaving a cloud of dust, but Ever stared at the new dark hole in the ground.

From out of that dark hole, a swarm of flying robots emerged. Each robot was a fraction of the size of the *beruhigen*, but they darted around using propellers. The swarm was dense enough to create a shadow on the ground, and the high-pitched hum of their propellers vibrated through the air blocks away. She tried to count but quickly lost track of their numbers.

"There are hundreds," Ailbe said, frightened. "Should we get out of here?"

"They're not interested in us," Fallon said.

The swarm launched directly for the Union *esclaves*, still in full retreat. The Witness was caught in the middle of a pitched battle as *beruhigen*, armed with energy weapons, distorted the sky with waves of heat and fire. Some of the swarm exploded midair, while other robots left burning trails through the sky.

At first, Paul was trapped in the center of battle, but his *Facere* deftly navigated the flurry of activity. While two *Facere* arms kept the Witness firmly in his seat, the others warded off debris, catching spinning rotors in the air and slamming burnt-out husks into the ground.

The *Facere* headed east to their tower even as the Union, in full retreat, departed over the ridge, the swarm following close behind.

"I think we've learned all we can here," Fallon said.

The *cultiver* descender ride was uneventful, although Fallon kept coaching her on how to deal with her fear of heights. By the time they reached the ground, it was late afternoon.

Paul was waiting for them when they got there. His brightly finished exosuit was still stained with smoke and char, but before he could speak, Fallon asked him a question forcefully, setting him back.

"Were we followed?" Fallon asked.

"No. They stopped in the mountains. I followed them, but they had camion designed for the overland trails. They headed north."

"They are trying to get ahead of us, but I don't think they will find the welcome in Galt they are looking for. Galt has a history of strong leadership. Did you get a closer look at them?"

"From a distance, but there were no robes, only exosuits frozen in the green and browns of the Free People," Paul said, then hesitated. "They had unusual tools for the Free People and kept their faces uncovered."

"What kind of tools?"

"Constabulary. Restraining equipment."

Fallon nodded thoughtfully. "That's antithetical to the Free People."

"For some reason, I've been unable to communicate with my leadership." Paul's eyes locked on Fallon. "My *Facere* cannot negotiate a handshake, and when I went to the Union, the Federation attacked."

"Your presence probably triggered the robots. I'm sure they didn't attack you personally."

"No, but that is not the whole truth," Paul said grimly.

"I guess if you want more truth, you're going to have to keep up, and remember, you promised to follow my directions."

Paul didn't reply and turned his back on her, stalking off with his *Facere* close in tow. Fallon watched him leave before turning back to the others.

"We'll stay here today and tomorrow. It's already late, and we need the rest. This is the safest place we can be."

For the first time, Ever noticed the circles under Fallon's eyes and realized that while everyone else could rest during the ride, her mother had been up all night. She shuddered at the concentration necessary to control the *cultivers* hour after hour.

"I'll break into the field rations," Ailbe said quickly, and Fallon smiled.

"I don't think that's necessary, Ailbe. We still have enough food from the pantry. As long as the jars are intact, I can make spaghetti."

Reign and Riley laughed, and Ever felt a fleeting jealousy at their connection. She forcefully dismissed the feeling. Sometimes, she forgot that Reign and Riley were siblings, and she knew that the fear of losing their father had them on edge. He attempted to explain their levity.

"There's an old family myth that we worshipped spaghetti," he said. "While we're in the old world, maybe we should start pastafaria."

They retreated to their tents early that night. Instead of foam mattresses, they used air mattresses and chairs that inflated and deflated in seconds with a burst of compressed air. Unlike the solid mattress, they made the tents functional, as both a bedroom and a living space. She still missed her bed, and the smell of self-healing vinyl furniture left a lot to be desired, but she appreciated having a chair, even if it was squishy and sank to the ground when she sat on it.

Before going to bed, Fallon made her assemble an Axis. Instead of just *cultivers*, Fallon asked her to add landscape elements.

"What should I add to the Axis?" she asked.

"Let's start with something simple. Do you remember the buildings around this one?"

"Not perfectly," she said, trying to draw a mental picture of the buildings on the Axis.

"You don't need to remember them perfectly. You don't even need to remember what they look like. The net knows that already. Just think about them on the Axis. The simpler you make it, the better, but you must be consistent with your shapes. You could use a circle or a square, but consistency will let you organize data faster and decide more quickly."

She placed a circle representing this building, and other circles appeared on her Axis. She realized she could move the Axis like scrolling around a map on a screen. Mentally, she tried to zoom out and place her perspective further away from the Axis to see more circles, but everything disappeared.

"It went away," she said, confused, describing her mental image.

"Your Axis collapsed because it was two-dimensional, and you tried to create a third dimension without a frame of context," Fallon said. "Try not to add dimensions while you are controlling *esclaves*. The results can be unpredictable."

"How many dimensions can I add?" she asked.

"Let's keep it to three for now, and we can work on the others later," Fallon said. When you construct your Axis, consider height when you create your point of reference. Start from the beginning."

"How do I know how tall things are?"

"The net knows. Keep practicing."

# 32. NEW TOOLS

The next morning, Ever woke to scraping and crashing sounds outside of her tent. Her mother had already dressed and left. Her mother always started the day early while she was a late sleeper unless late-night planning went into the next day. She vaguely remembered being told to get up, but she couldn't tell how long ago that was, and even the net didn't have a response to the query, so she must not have been fully conscious.

She made a cursory attempt at the morning rituals before sliding out of the tent and then went through her own mental checklist: Was her hair brushed? No, but she had a hat for that. Fully clothed and exosuit on in the right direction? Absolutely. Teeth and tongue brushed and exuding minty delight. Positively.

Fallon was with Lucas and Reign. Four *cultivers* dragged two of the flying robots into camp. They were bigger than the *cultivers,* with twelve double-bladed rotors extending from the body. A turret was on the bottom, and they sat awkwardly tilted with no apparent landing gear. Reign was examining the turret when Ailbe came up behind her.

"There's leftover spaghetti for breakfast," Ailbe told Ever.

Cold spaghetti was better than a field ration. She'd noticed the field rations had flavors in small print on the foil wrapping, and most of them were vegetable protein combinations.

"What are they doing with that?" she asked, pointing at the unresponsive robot. Reign attempted to move the machines to get a better view, but they were too heavy and fell in a heap from one side to the other.

"He thinks we can use them. I don't know what for. He is taking off the turret. I guess it doesn't work, anyway."

"The turret fires bullets," Fallon said, looking back at them. "None of those have been made in a long time, but the designs for Federation robots included ballistic weapons."

"The robot looks like new," Ever said.

"It probably is new. Without outside influence, the Hive will keep building the same robot to specification, even if it doesn't have gunpowder to create bullets or ammunition to arm the robot. These cause enough damage to the Union by crashing into *esclaves* at high velocity."

"What are we going to use them for?" she asked.

"Aerial surveillance," Reign said. "Eyes in the sky."

"Fallon calls them 'hummers,'" Ailbe put in. "Because the blades make a humming sound you can hear from far away."

"It's a good idea," Fallon said. "You could all use practice working with *esclaves* in three dimensions. Right now, Lucas is the only one I can depend on to manage the *esclaves* when I'm busy."

Apparently, the Witness didn't count, or maybe he couldn't direct an *esclave* other than his own?

By weight, a lot of what Fallon brought was tools, and many of them attached to a *cultiver*, creating a versatile set of powered equipment. Reign was mechanically adept, and he got on his hands and knees, guiding the *cultivers* to lift the hummer while he examined the turret. He unbolted the gun and wiring that went to the sighting mechanism.

With Fallon's help, he took apart a *cultiver*. The cameras and processing were part of the central body, and he moved the processing into the interior of the robot and routed the smart connections to an access port. Using a soft weld stick, they stuck the *esclave's* cameras in position around the hummer's body.

"I'm not sure how the *esclave* will interface with the robot's programming," he said to Fallon, worried.

"That's not an issue," she replied. "Fundamentally, the logic systems are all built on the same Federation framework. You will control the robot if you try to access the *esclave*."

"I haven't been able to query the net since yesterday. I can still see from the accessibility net, but nothing else works."

"And you shouldn't try," she said quickly. "We don't want to reveal our position. Keep to local resources. I'm not surprised you are having trouble. The net is unreliable out here. Radiation plumes interfere with the *sentinelles*. The accessibility net is just one part of an *esclave*. You can control one *esclave* at a time without the net if you are close enough and you cast your eimai."

Ailbe, Reign, and even Riley believed her mother completely, but Ever didn't have any problem with the net, and Fallon's response sounded a bit too much like the trite answers she spit out whenever Ever had an important question. Answers like "clean your room", "do the dishes" or "he left". She kept her thoughts to herself. This was not the time.

Reign bolted on the body plate from the *cultiver*, including the arms and legs, in the gun's place to give their hummer landing gear. The last thing he did was replace the molten salt battery on the hummer with the modern battery pack from the *cultiver*. Reign was concerned about the difference in battery packs, but Fallon reassured him that modern cultivers had much higher density energy storage and a built-in power regulator.

When Fallon attempted to start the hummer, an alarm sounded. Painfully loud, they fled to the other side of the building.

"Crowd control," she yelled over the top of the noise, and

after a few seconds, the sound stopped. The rotors twitched and spun, and the hummer lifted from the ground, blowing dust and debris.

Since they were inside a building, they didn't stake the tents down. Ever's tent blew over, rolling through camp before the hummer settled on its new *cultiver* legs and turned off.

"It worked," Reign said, ignoring the cacophony and disarray. He sounded halfway between surprise and excitement. "Let's get the next one."

"We'll start the next one in the atrium," Fallon said. She rummaged through Ever's upside-down tent and pulled out the air filtration system. "I don't want to lose equipment. Fortunately, they built this to take a tumble."

Ever, Ailbe and Riley were on cleanup duty while Reign built the second hummer. The Witness was once again missing, but Fallon assured her he was nearby, scouting the trail ahead.

"He's anxious to be on our way, but we need the day," she said. "Murdoch won't chase us up the coast."

After Reign completed the second hummer, Fallon had Ever and Reign fly them around the building. Ailbe enjoyed watching the *esclaves* do aerial tricks, and Fallon pestered him to try at least once or twice.

"I enjoy watching," he said, wincing under the onslaught. "But casting into machines is uncomfortable for me."

"You can think of it like a vulture if that helps. They don't hover and are much smaller, but at least you get the perspective."

While he struggled with the hummer, Ever and Reign compared notes. She tried to control the hummer using the Axis. The process was tedious while his hummer swooped around hers doing choreography. She attempted to show him how to set up an Axis, but Fallon cautioned her to stop.

"You can master both techniques in time. But right now, if you try to juggle the two, you'll accomplish nothing at best. You both need to stretch the talent you have."

"At worst?" Ever asked.

"You could get someone hurt."

# 33. THE POWER OF THOUGHT

They camped out for the night, woke before dawn, and started at first light. The *cultivers* could see perfectly in the dark, but Fallon preferred the light. She said there were too many potential dangers from robots. The Witness listened to her words with unmistakable skepticism only Ever appreciated.

Her mother formed the *cultivers* into pods, linking them to make a train, with Lucas serving as the engine. In the dark, with the wind and excitement, the ride had seemed fast. During the day, she realized they were traveling at only a fraction of the speed of a hypertube.

The coastline was to her right, but they stayed far enough away from the coast that she only caught glimpses of crashing waves in between broken buildings. They left a trail of dust behind them, and the east shore breeze caught the dust. Her nose was numb to the smell of the coast, but an overpowering smell of ozone came and left suddenly as they moved through the wreckage.

Occasionally, she saw Union *esclaves* from a distance demolishing buildings, scooping up their concrete bones and crushing them into aggregate. Then she saw a camion. Massive black tires dominated the yellow frame, carrying a load of aggregate away, and she assumed the eventual destination was Dill or Galt. Those were the only two territories close to the coast. Whatever roads the camions used, her mother stayed far away from them.

The midday heat kept increasing, and she sealed her hood and mask. This was the dry season with no clouds to block the sun. Even the exosuit felt warm. Before noon, Fallon stopped their train in the middle of the road.

"The heat wave is overwhelming the suits," Fallon told them. "We have to walk."

Ever realized she was sweating and not just a little. When she stood, the moisture pooled to her feet. She and Ailbe removed their shoes and unzipped their suit, turning their pants' legs inside out and letting the drops disappear into the rocks and sand.

"Disgusting," he said. "I'm completely soaked."

Fallon handed out sealed pouches of water and watched them drink. She followed the water with a tangy tablet that was supposed to help them deal with the heat, but Ever felt nothing after chewing the salty wafer.

"The suits convert motion and light to energy and uses that energy to stay cool," Fallon said.

"What if we find shade?" Reign asked. They all wore different colors, but all the suits reacted the same way, except his Free People color-shifting exosuit stopped changing color when it ran low on power and faded to a dull olive green and brown pattern.

"That wouldn't do any good," she said. "A high-pressure system moved in. It's not just the sun. If we stop moving, we will bake in the heat until we die."

After a brief respite, they started walking, and nearly immediately, she felt her suit cool. She had to keep her cowl and mask on to seal the suit against the heat reflecting from the rocks and sand and distorting the air.

Fallon launched the two hummers perched on Lucas, and they took turns looking at the landscape from above, although she kept them low to avoid discovery.

Only the Witness seemed unconcerned about the weather. Paul rode his *Facere* and rushed down the road only to reappear from either side, scrambling over rocks.

The masks muffled everyone's voice, but that didn't stop them from talking. The net seemed to work okay for Fallon and Ever, but Ailbe and Reign couldn't query the net. Riley tried Varmint, even climbing a pile of rocks and waving him in the air, but still no signal.

The gun volunteered to regale them with stories of Riley and Reign's grandfather. Ever and Ailbe were interested, but Reign shut that down immediately until the gun offered to show them where they were.

"How can you do that?" he asked.

"I've been here before," Varmint said glibly. "All I have to do is superimpose the visual over the landscape in my viewfinder."

Riley looked at the viewfinder, and Fallon sent a com. The commune expanded to include them linking their implants, and they shared the visual—the vision superimposed over the reality. They walked through rows of short hillocks that turned into the foundations of houses until the houses appeared, row upon row. Most were brick and covered in a white blanket.

"Is that ice on the roof?" Ever asked.

"Snow," Riley said. "I heard the temperature could drop low enough for snow in the old days. Ice and snow were a nuisance back then, worse than the heat waves. Now you only find snow in the northern territories."

"We had *esclaves* in the ice belt that brought back ice for water," Reign said.

"Is that better than filtered water?" Ever asked. She

remembered trying a bottle of glacial water at Ailbe's house. Other than being bottled, she couldn't tell the difference. Before Ailbe could chime in, Reign responded.

"I don't know about the bottled variety. I remember a trip when our mother was alive. We went into the mountains in the ice belt. There was a mountain stream, clear and cold. That was the best water I've ever had."

"I'm surprised you remember that," Riley said. "You were a toddler."

They walked in silence. No one wanted to interrupt his reverie until Fallon called them to remount the *cultivers*.

"We can ride until the suits are drained. I'm not walking all the way to Galt. When we turn west, the altitude should cool things down."

All day, they kept the sequence of walking and riding until Fallon turned them west. Before they left the coast, they stopped and made camp in another abandoned building, far smaller than the bank but still big enough for all the *cultiver*.

There wasn't an entrance large enough for Lucas, but after Fallon examined the structure, she had him back through a wall, sending a small cloud of dust into the night sky.

Once again, they secured their tents inside. There were no doors or windows, and they used the bottom floor. The heat wave turned into a raging wind, but what was left of the walls acted as a windbreak. Even with the walls, Fallon still wanted the tents staked with foot-long steel pins.

She made Ever and Reign direct the *cultivers* to pin the tents into the concrete floor, but they fought over control of the *esclaves* as her mother watched impatiently. When Ever placed the *cultivers* in her Axis, he couldn't control them unless she got distracted. Then, the circles would disappear until he released control.

The *cultivers* did not resist running into each other, and

they ended up with a twisted pile of scraped arms and legs. The contoured fiberglass body panels that accentuated the machine's squared-off shape broke and had to be swept clear before Fallon reset the position of the *esclaves* for her and Reign to try again.

Lucas inventoried the damage to his *cultivers* with blinking lights Ever interpreted as disappointment, and Ailbe guffawed at the result until Fallon threatened to make him stake his own tent.

"What went wrong?" Fallon asked Ever.

"Every time I tried to direct the *cultivers*, he cut in, and I lost control of them," she complained.

"Obviously while you marched them around in circles, nothing was getting done," Reign said.

"Neither one of you came up with a plan," Fallon said. "There was no communication, rather than work to your strengths. You attempted to finish the job alone."

"You do this by yourself all the time," Ever told Fallon.

"That's the result of practice and technique. You don't have either, but what you have is two people. Both of you are gifted, but that's worthless if you don't learn to communicate. Each of you has the power to finish the job, and if you allied together, you might even be as fast as me."

"What if you move the *cultivers* into position around the tent, and when you are ready, I will take over and stake the tent?" Reign asked Ever.

He was always the first to sound reasonable whenever her mother called her out. That earned him a stern look, but she knew she could be the bigger person, and she would tell him exactly what they would do.

"That sounds like a good plan," Fallon said, approving the effort before Ever could respond. "The second thing you are doing wrong is holding on to the *cultivers* too intimately. When you create the Axis, Ever, you need to include Reign. He isn't a bystander. Reign, you are putting too much of yourself into the *cultiver*. You can't move quickly if you anchor your eimai. You need to be fast."

Their second attempt was much better. She moved the *cultivers* into place around the tent. She included Reign in the Axis, and she was startled when he appeared as a bright blue circle. She hadn't consciously chosen a color, and all the other circles in her Axis were green. When she considered the shape, more information was available, just like when she peered out of the *cultiver's* eyes.

She wasn't sure what that meant, but as he moved from *cultiver* to *cultiver* pining down the tent, the *esclaves* stayed in the Axis. By the time they finished the last tent, he was jumping in and out of the *cultivers* in a fraction of a second.

"I didn't know I could do that." He wiped the sweat from his brow, and she realized that she was sweating from the mental effort, too. He'd always been fast, but she was impressed at how quickly he switched *esclaves.*

"You are both improving. From now on, I'll have to think of different tasks for you to perform," Fallon said.

Ailbe worked on putting dinner together while Ever despaired over what little edible foodstuffs remained. They brought everything in the refrigerator and pantry but were essentially unprepared to spend days outside unless they started digging into the rations. Dinner was a small, frozen, personal cheese pizza, toast and bagels, and an assortment of rehydrated vegetables divided between five people. Plant bricks were always available, but she didn't even attempt gnawing on one of those.

After the paralyzing sun, they sat around the campfire, not speaking, until Fallon gave them the plan.

"We'll be at Galt by tomorrow afternoon. It's a quick trip through the mountains. Then we go around the city to the north entrance. Given what we've seen so far, I think it's important we get a message to the Lord Governor."

"You can do that?" Ailbe asked, surprised.

"I have quite a few friends in the city. One of them is the Lieutenant Governor. He can make an introduction for us."

"Is there anything he can do for my father?" Reign asked Fallon.

"That depends on how smart Murdoch is. Paul didn't see any of the Ajat Maata. Murdoch must be holding back high-value assets. I would be surprised if he doesn't keep your father close."

"What are we going to do then?" Riley asked.

"Eventually, he'll overreach. I know Murdoch quite well. We will get your father back when he overreaches and see if we can undo the damage." Fallon bit her lip. It was rare for Ever to see her mother struggle with an explanation. "We don't know how Richard will react." Fallon looked straight at Riley. "We might have to subdue him."

"How do we do that when he's as strong as ten people?" Ever asked.

"We could hit him on the head," Reign suggested. "I've seen Dad nearly knock himself out on a door frame."

"I don't think we need to add additional brain trauma," Fallon said, standing and rummaging through her storage containers. She produced four rods, each two feet long, with a rubberized perforated grip, an easy thumb toggle, and a silver ball on the end. The wands collapsed to no more than eight inches and would easily fit in a pocket. She showed the maneuver.

"*Taub machen* are illegal for Union citizens," Paul commented to the open air.

"But a significant protection when you need them. If you activate the stick and touch any part of their body with the silver ball, their implant will put them to sleep. They won't work on an eastern collar."

"What does it do if you don't have an implant?" Riley asked.

"Nothing," Fallon said. "But Richard has an implant, even if he refuses to use it."

"My father would never get one of those," Riley said furiously to Fallon.

"I think he regrets it. Unlike the collars used in most of

the eastern territories, once installed, the implant cannot be removed, just deactivated." Fallon held up the rod. "This will work on him."

She gave each of them one rod, but when Ever asked her what her mother would do, Fallon said she had other alternatives.

# 34. SECRET MOTIVATION

True to her word, Fallon made Ever and Reign coordinate their efforts to break down camp the following morning. The Witness was already gone, but he returned before they headed out. There were still no signs of life, but sharply peaked mountains framed the western sky.

The roads between those peaks were badly damaged, and Fallon reformed their ride into hexapedes. She rode with Ailbe, and Ever was disappointed to lose her friend on the ride. She liked to pass the time talking. Her mother monopolized Lucas's time. Instead, she was left with the Witness and his *Facere* clinging to the hexapede.

She knew her mother had a palpable dislike of the Witness, and when Paul talked, she suspected he was probing for information. Over the last few days as traveling companions, she lost her fear of the strange man. She told him this directly, and he laughed. His eyes were always roving, but she felt like he consumed every word.

"It's been a long time since Witnesses were feared," Paul

said. "There are very few of us left. The Immortal Records speak of battles we fought long ago. That was before the Peace."

"I saw the way you brushed off the *cultivers*."

The Witness held up his hand, wearing stiff leather gloves, and studied the appendage almost as if it were separate from himself. The gloves were clean, as was his whole suit. After the battle, he spent a painstaking amount of time cleaning his suit but never removed it.

"I was engineered for strength."

"Yeah, to find the truth." She couldn't help but deemphasize it. More often than not, when the Witness did speak, it was a long diatribe about the truth.

"Not to find it, to deliver the truth. After the Peace, my people lost their purpose. They engineered us from human stock with qualities that bred true. Some of us wanted to reverse the process."

"The Union heavily regulates genetic engineering and the study of genetic traits."

He nodded. "Still, we were designed for a purpose that no longer exists."

"People still lie," she said, thinking about this morning. Somehow, Reign's toothpaste ended up in her bag. She borrowed it because he had the flavor crystals she liked, but she'd thought she put it back in his bag. To cover the theft, she casually asked him to borrow the toothpaste. Reign checked his bags and thought he lost it, but tomorrow, it would turn up in Ailbe's bag. *Problem solved.*

"True," the Witness said, "but conflict is rare, and they wouldn't tell a lie of real consequence. After the Peace, the weight of social responsibility affected people profoundly. There was no need for Witnesses in the new social order."

"Why didn't the Witnesses join the peacekeepers?"

"That was considered," Paul said, "but Western territories prefer a division of governing powers, and there was a concern with how the executive branch would function if constabulary powers were uniform across the territories. A compromise was reached, and Witnesses kept their core values intact. The treaty granted us the right of passage."

"I think you got a lousy deal," she said. "Everyone can travel within the Union."

"No," he said. "Everyone has negative liberty to pursue their interests without interference, but only within their own capabilities and power. Only Witnesses have the positive liberty to go anywhere and open any door. The Union enables us to pursue the truth."

"Does that mean you will tell everyone I'm carrying this around?" she asked, holding out the stun stick.

Paul laughed again.

"Eventually, everything I know will be part of the Immutable Records, but before then, I have the flexibility to tell the truth I choose. The Union has little interest in local politics and local laws. A Witness is the same. We are not accountable to the Union, only to ourselves. I disagree with Fallon giving you these weapons or her insistence that you need to be here. Her disregard for children's welfare is against the Union's tenets to protect and value human life."

"If the Union is so disinterested, why are you following us?" she asked, looking back at the Witness.

He studied her for a moment. He frequently fought with Fallon over little things. He wanted to ride with Reign and Riley. Reign expressed a lot of interest in the *Facere*, but Fallon insisted Paul ride with Ever. When he wasn't scouting, he usually stood around camp watching them. That bothered Fallon, and she spent a lot of time ordering him out of the way.

She noticed that Paul had two verbal techniques he alternated when dealing with her mother. The first was an extensive appeal to logic and the "truth." It was a long-winded, completely one-sided dialog because Fallon dismissed arguments she disagreed with out of hand. Ever tried the technique a few times, and it hadn't worked for her either. The second technique he used was the grey rock. It wasn't an option for her, but the Witness was an expert.

Paul didn't use either of these techniques when talking to the children, and while he often seemed distracted, he was entirely sincere.

"I've followed Jorge from Flagg City through the western marshes across six territories. He didn't leave a hint of his trail in a public record until he came to your house."

"But why did you follow him?" she asked.

"He asked me to."

"You go wherever you're asked," she said. "I didn't think Witnesses worked that way. I know Witnesses perform weddings, but I thought they were paid for it."

"Witnesses perform weddings," Paul chuckled, not denying the truth, but then became serious. "We don't have to go wherever we are asked. When Jorge approached me and asked me to follow him. I asked why."

"What did he tell you?" she interrupted.

"He said nothing to me," Paul said. "He spoke to my *Facere*. He called him by name. My *Facere* held me captive while he walked away. Understand, only a Witness knows the true name of their *Facere*. On initiation, the *Facere* tells them their name. The name secures the network, and a Witness would die before revealing the name of their *Facere*."

# 35. THE BLASTED HILLS

They traveled on the ruins of old highways, strewn with rubble like a massive hand smashed the side of the mountain and tossed boulders the size of houses. The boulders sank into the road, collapsing the retaining walls and exposing underlayment.

Fallon called this land the Blasted Hills, but she didn't bother to explain what battle or war destroyed it. The name itself was ominous, and the fact that she spent so much time following the contours of the hills and mountains on these roads and avoiding ridges added to the tension.

Ever studied the mountains pitted with craters, some small, some as wide as a city block. Inside the craters, stagnant pools of dead water created glass-like surfaces reflecting the cloudless sky.

There were vents on the sides of the mountains. Most were inactive, but steam under pressure roiled from many of them, indicating movement deep below the ground. The steam disappeared in the dry air as quickly as it rose.

The craters exposed the mountain's layers. These weren't volcanic fissures. The mountains were formed of sedimentary layers folded from the crust. Studying the scenery, she reached a conclusion. She queried the net without meaningful results. *How could the Union ignore an obvious sign of Federation activity below the surface?*

She didn't see any life, but a gentle breeze from the west gave her hope. The breeze was fresh air that carried the unmistakable scent of growing things. Fallon was right. The altitude thinned and cooled the air. They didn't have to stop to recharge their suits, but she was sweat-soaked all the same from gripping the armrest as they alighted from the edges of cliffs.

They spent all morning climbing the Blasted Hills until they came to harvest land planted on a rolling green landscape. Unlike the transition from forest to grasslands in the south, this was abrupt. A sharp, straight line created the border between life and death.

The land wasn't flat, but the fields were organized in perfect squares dedicated to specific crops. *Apiculteurs* waddled, dropping buzzbeetles while buzzbees circled the rotund *esclaves*. *Cultivers* walked lines, maintaining the crop. She knew there were eyes behind those machines that couldn't help but note their passing, but no one stopped from their task.

The mountains trailed each other like *esclaves* wandering away from a gathering, each peak further away from the last. A hazy frame of peaks distorted her perception of distance. Fallon changed the configuration of their ride into a running formation, and they covered ground on the crushed gravel road faster as the sun inched toward afternoon.

Far off into the distance, behind the shadow of mountains sparkling in the sun, she could make out a bulbous tower like a black line with a dot painted on a horizon of blue.

"What is that?" she asked without even attempting a query. It was bad manners to ask obvious questions, but her internal monologue spilled over frequently, and after all, her mother kept reminding her to stay off the net.

"That is the Spire," Paul said. "It stands in the center of Galt. It's the tallest structure built in the Western territories. Built before the Peace. The Spire can project a curtain of energy in all directions to neutralize airborne contaminants."

As they rode closer to the Spire, the black line took on features. Concave lenses covered the base and traveled the full height of the tower to a distinct aperture at the top. They were past noonday, still miles from Galt, but she could see strobing light travel from the base hidden behind the dark outline to a lens three-quarters of the way up the Spire. Heat waves distorted the air in a pattern around the tower for almost a quarter of an hour before the lens went dark.

Ever was confused, but the Witness explained.

"The aperture at the top of the tower is commonly called the Spear of Sorrows," Paul said. "After the Peace, they used the Spear for the last time. There are no official records as to the reason, but first-hand accounts of Witnesses say it was used to stop a hurricane. The consequences for the city were severe."

"What happened?" Ever asked.

"You will see for yourself when we arrive, but the eastern side of the city was destroyed. The loss of life was tremendous, and there was debate over whether to disassemble the Spear, but it remains functional to this day."

The road ended in a cracked clay surface baked by the sun, miles from the city center shaded in the valley. Only the Spire rose above the strange peaks she imagined as broken teeth. Unlike the Blasted Hills, sharp edges and strange geometry emerged from the slopes. The Spire, while insignificant in girth compared to the crenelations around Galt, matched the coloration. Each lens on the tower spanned hundreds of feet and absorbed the sunlight, keeping the tower a solid black line against the otherwise blue horizon.

Beside the road, a column of concrete and steel sported warning signs and a green light at the top. When she looked at the column, her implant buzzed her with a warning and a countdown timer. The timer had over twenty-four hours left, plenty of time to get to the city.

Fallon stopped their train in front of the column. The Witness and his *Facere* leaped off the container while she dismounted, staring into the distance where Ever discerned a shape riding an open vehicular transport. He sped along the cracked clay toward them.

"The *esclaves* will remain here," Fallon said. "They would draw too much attention in the city. You don't need to bring much with you, personal toiletries and clothes."

"Do we need to bring anything formal?" Ailbe asked, and Fallon considered carefully.

"I usually don't make a stop at court, but what we have seen so far merits at least a warning. Did you bring your official school robes?"

"I always pack them when traveling, just in case."

"I'll send a message out to your mother. She's a Senior Fellow, and that translates to a title in Galt. They are very formal here. They have a unicameral system of government, and the two political parties don't get along well. That's uncommon in the Western territories. Their representatives are voted in by titled leaders in the recognized professions. Collectively, they refer to themselves as the Trade Lords, and even though other territories don't take their titles seriously, they are very serious about them here."

While Ever struggled to fit her clothes into her school backpack, she was a little envious of Reign and Ailbe. They stood patiently waiting with organized packs. She shut down the feeling when she saw Riley standing in her ripped suit with Varmint, basically everything she owned.

By the time Ever finished, the open-air car stopped, and a middle-aged man in short black robes trimmed in red with a large gold medallion of office stepped out. On immediate inspection, she perused his eimai in real time. His name was Dan, to be addressed officially as Lord Dan or Lieutenant Governor Dan. His children and family were obscured, but she had a general idea of his occupation.

"Lord Dan," Fallon said. She bowed briefly.

This startled Dan, but he answered with a mocking, youthful smile, clicked his heels, and raised his arm in salute with his knuckles to his forehead.

"Reporting for duty. I'm sorry I'm late. It's been so long since we opened the overland gate to the north I had to find the key."

Dan dropped the salute and went to shake Fallon's hand. His eyes seemed to take in her features momentarily before she met his greeting. While it was impolite to query the net during a greeting, Ever had the impression he was trying to recall something.

"You've changed since we last met."

"Time changes us all."

"Not your father. I still remember him from when I was a boy. He hasn't changed in the slightest. He was here less than a week ago and wanted to make sure I would be ready for you. You have quite specific requirements for accommodations."

"I'm afraid I've spent too much time in the south. I know the best accommodations in Galt are underground, but I've grown claustrophobic over the years. I trust you have us at the ground level, at the city's edge."

"Absolutely, my family has known your father for a long time. Even though my parents are retired, I wouldn't hear the end of it if I disappointed them. I think my mother would have herself rolled into court to complain to me personally."

"I remember your mother very well, and she would do that."

After the brief greeting, they loaded into Dan's ground car, a narrow-wheeled contraption with a low deck but ample room for everyone and their luggage. The *Facere* silently took the back row to itself, and the deck settled alarmingly from the added weight but self-leveled almost immediately. The electric engine was completely silent, and a windshield blocked most of the noise from the air rushing around them. Ever looked back at Lucas and the rest of the *cultivers*, concerned as they drove away.

"I gave him specific instructions," Fallon said, measuring her glance. "We might have put too much intelligence into that one. He seems to have acquired some habits, but he will operate to specification."

They covered the ground quickly on the cracked clay, passing by another cement column with more lights and signage. She read the signs and checked the timer.

"The Spire is activated on a schedule," Dan said. "Most of the city is underground, and it's been generations since contamination levels were high enough to justify its use. But we keep the schedule—the last defense of honor." He said the words as if expecting comprehension, confusing Ever. Fallon nodded, but the blank looks of the others seemed to deter him." Galt sits in a valley, and most airborne contaminants blow over or around us."

"You still need the laser below the mountains," Fallon said. "To treat the buildup of radioactive waste."

"There are billions of gallons buried below us, but the treatment process increases speed and efficiency every year," Dan said. "Redirecting all power to treatment would give us another boost."

The car ascended the slope on a gravel road that started shortly after the signpost and wound between the hills to a mountain pass. The pass was cut into the black rock and opened to the city of Galt.

She expected to see buildings similar to those in Dill. She spent little time studying their closest neighbor in the tropics. Northern cities buried under ice or the floating bridges of the East were a lot more interesting. She was unimpressed with the long, flat construction that rose from the blue valley in front of them until she realized it wasn't a blue lake but surfaced with glass reflecting the open sky.

The Spire was in the center, and to the east, a waterfall of obsidian flowed down a misshapen mountain into that blue surface, distorting what would have been a perfect circle.

"Most of the city is underground," Dan said. "You are seeing the tops of buildings pass through the barrier. The ceiling lets the light in. When Galt was built, they used powerful lights to replicate sunlight, but we found there is no substitution for the real thing, so the surface was recreated with glass."

"How far does it go down?" she said. She should have checked, but it was impolite to query during a conversation—questions needed to be performed before or after.

"Thousands of feet," he said. "In fact, we have a request in court to dig past the crust to the mantle to tap power sources at the core. The requestor, Earl Edgar, wanted to talk to your father about land rights below the crust."

"My family has held on to those rights since the beginning of the Union, and they will not be licensed," Fallon said.

"They are kind of worthless if no one can dig that deep," Dan said.

"You can tell the Earl that's a non-starter. If he wants to be an energy magnate, he can look in a different direction."

# UPPER GALT

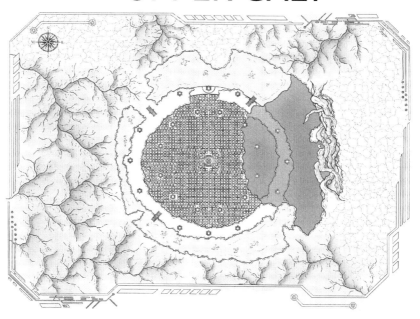

# 36. GALT

The ride into the city in the ground car was uneventful. The time spent pushed late afternoon into evening, and the upper city had light foot traffic. The walkers traveled in groups from building to building. The sounds of the city were familiar to Ever, and she realized she missed voices talking over each other. She even missed the obtrusive hum of commercial air filters fitted between the buildings, providing a gentle, cool breeze of electrostatically freshened air.

Dan boasted the only streetcar, part of a small fleet, and he gregariously explained that they forbid cars from the upper city except for government functions. Hypertubes below ground serviced communities, and unlike "fragile bubbles," the lower city was contaminant-free and had the highest birth rate in the Western territories.

Most walkers were tourists that came in by hypertube or the southern cavern complex, and they carried a variety of equipment similar to Reign and Riley.

"Why are there so many Free People? Riley asked.

"There's a vote on land use rights," Dan said. "I'm surprised your father didn't mention it to you."

"We've been out west the last few years. My father

forgets about the finer details of politics, and I'm part of the entertainment industry, so I don't get the inside information. What's the vote about?"

"Expanding free use licensing to conservation lands. Your father stands to make money if the law passes, and it has support from the Free People. They've been arriving all week to claim a stake. They are such a large voting block; they elected a representative to court."

"That's surprising," Riley said, puzzled. "The Free People always vote to protect conservation lands."

"It's a turn of events. The Free People usually vote with the Unionites, but they aligned with the Egalitarians on this issue."

"We need to know more about this," Fallon told Riley. "Do you have any contacts nearby?"

Riley took out Varmint and used his connection to make a query. Compared to the implant, it was painstakingly slow, and they all waited patiently for the results. Ever observed that Riley preferred to use devices, and the Free People were sensitive to modern technology to fix simple problems.

"I don't have any contacts, but I have followers close to us."

"That might be even better. Let's keep this subtle. You've booked us at the Vincenbilts?"

"The ground floor," Dan said. "I could have gotten you the penthouse suite, but my father insisted you would want the ground floor at The Vinny. I already checked you in using his name."

"Very good. He knows me well. We can walk from here."

Fallon asked him to pull the car over beside a group of people. As Paul and his *Facere* got out of the car, he touched Fallon's shoulder briefly to get her attention.

"I'm leaving. Bragg has an embassy in Galt. I assume our agreement stands if you inform me of your movements."

She hesitated. "Our agreement stands if you tell no one except your leaders we are here. I fully realize you cannot avoid that, but no one else."

The Witness nodded and departed, his long strides carrying him to the nearest hypertube station. Head and shoulders above the crowd, they parted for him and his *Facere* like a plasma cutter sheering through sheet metal.

Fallon wished Dan well and gave Riley general directions to the hostel so she could take the lead. They didn't have to wait long before someone flagged Riley, calling and waving furiously on the walkway. Ailbe and Reign walked close to Ever, and Reign turned to her.

"That's celebrity for you," he said. "If we stop for too long, she'll draw a crowd. It's a good thing we aren't tall like our father. She would never escape."

As Riley stopped, they caught up to her conversation. Fallon fell behind but was still close enough to hear, and she kept moving, her short frame disappearing into the group of people clustered around the pair who compared rifles.

Ever presumed he was a newbie hunter, and he was showing Riley his heavy weapon. Unlike Varmint's gun metal finish and wood stock, the chromed rifle painfully reflected the city lights. The gun had a deep baritone voice as it detailed its features, and a tripod ejected from its base after the owner grew too tired to hold it up.

The young man dressed in a color-shifting exosuit and crisp new backpack bled excitement, but Riley was more interested in his linked-steel collar than his weapon.

"Where did you get the neckpiece?" she asked.

"They're handing these out at the Durg consulate. Overproduction made them dirt cheap. With this collar, I can navigate around here without getting lost." The young man dropped his pack and pulled another collar out, offering the chain to Riley, who accepted it gravely.

"You can take these off easily," he said, unsnapping the collar from the back of his neck. He briefly held it up to her for inspection before putting it back on. "I don't understand why we don't use them."

"It looks well-constructed."

"And it matches my gun. Let me show you the viewfinder." He rotated the viewfinder toward her, but the image went dark. He tried a voice command and pressed buttons on the moderator, but it wouldn't respond.

"Some new models need to be calibrated first," she said. "Maybe you should take it in for service."

"Yeah, I'll do that," he said, still trying to get it to work. Riley gave him a shoulder squeeze to say farewell and pushed ahead. Ever, Reign, and Ailbe caught up, and Fallon reemerged from the crowd behind them.

"Did you do that?" Riley whispered harshly over her back. Ever was confused until Varmint spoke.

"It was full of bugs! Bad code practically begging to be exploited," the governor on Riley's rifle responded. The lights on the governor lit in a strange pattern, almost resembling a face as he talked. Varmint was no ordinary governor. He gave Ever a sly blinking wink from behind Riley's back.

"You can't keep doing that to every gun I look at," Riley complained.

"I also happened to download his interaction with the consulate," Varmint said.

"That could be useful," Fallon said, practically unseen behind Riley.

"Forwarded," Varmint replied.

"That's an invasion of privacy," Riley said.

"If you hadn't been examining his tripod so closely, you might have noticed."

It was a short walk to Vincenbilts. Riley stopped several times to greet her followers. Most of them sported the same collar, and while she received them cordially, it was apparent that keeping up the pretense for each visit was a strain.

Vincenbilts was on the city's western edge and less populated than the center of Galt. While walking down the empty street, Ever noticed the transparent floor. When the sun was up, the mountains reflected off the glass, making the surface opaque, but when the sun was behind the mountains, distant lights below the surface glowed, giving the impression she hovered above an overwhelming height.

She silently queried the net and knew the tiles could support tens of thousands of pounds, but as they crossed an expanse between buildings, she couldn't keep her eyes from scanning for supporting scaffolding or columns under the glass floor. Everything changed—her steps became hesitant, Ailbe's hand in hers became an insistent force pulling her across the road, and the road became as insubstantial as a cloud.

With palpable relief, she crossed the threshold to Vincenbilts. It was hard to rationalize the building's height. *Maybe I should measure it by depth?* She held on to the reasoning while stiffening her legs.

Regardless of its height, the visible structure had an impressive width—hundreds of yards long—and was built with solid granite bricks easily twice as tall and wide as she was. The outside was polished to bring out the natural earth colors, and the airlock was wide enough to handle crowds of entrants.

In contrast to the impressive exterior, the furnishings inside were spartan. *Maisons* staffed a counter, but the atrium wasn't particularly large and led directly to lifts. To the right of the counter, rectangular tables in long lines occupied most of the open space. Stone columns with geometric friezes relieved a room otherwise without ornamentation. A cafeteria-style buffet with specialized *esclaves* lined the far wall. Perhaps fifty people were eating, but there was room to seat hundreds. The smell was not unpleasant.

"No spa," Ailbe said mournfully. "Not even a pool."

"But there's good food," Reign said in return, beginning an exchange all too familiar.

"There's no plumbing in our bedrooms. Shared facilities at

the end of the corridors."

"And we have our pick of tables."

"We can't even control the thermostat."

"But there's good food."

"You already mentioned that one."

"I know, but you're bringing me down. All I need is something hot to eat and a soft bed. Yesterday, my bed deflated halfway into the night."

"Not to mention privacy and security," Fallon said. "This place reminds me of home. After you drop off your bags, you can peruse the mess. It's open 24/7. Our rooms are right beside each other. I splurged and rented each of us a room for the night. Don't stay up. We have an early morning."

Fallon looked directly at Reign, then sized up Riley. "I know you want to, but don't try to contact your father. In fact, you should keep your queries on the net at a minimum."

"But..." Reign started, and Fallon interrupted him.

"You won't succeed. And I don't want you to give away our position inadvertently. Murdoch knows we are coming here. He may even suspect where we are staying, but he won't act on suspicion."

Fallon left Ever at a nondescript door that opened to a sparsely furnished room. It was a solid door that recognized Ever's key by implant. The interior door frame had a physical lock and a swivel that she examined for a moment. The eight-by-ten room had a lamp sitting on a cubby, a bed with a brown coverlet, white sheets, and a terminal. There wasn't even a closet.

She'd never shared a room before this trip, and now the privacy of her own room felt like a luxury compared to the last few days of sleeping in a tent with her mother. She removed several figurines from her bag and arranged them under the lamp. Then she put the bag in the cubby and exited the room.

She found the bathrooms at the end of the corridor equally austere, with white porcelain tiles, round mirrors, and shallow sinks for simple grooming. Curtains separated the showers.

She took advantage of the facilities to remove and clean her exosuit and found that Ailbe and Reign were doing the same. After cleaning up, they left their exosuits in their rooms and returned to the mess.

The *cuisines* in the cafeteria were more specialized than your typical *maison*. Although they were still vaguely human-shaped, their appendages carried kitchen tools for serving and making food. From whisks to meat tenderizers. They used scoops, spatulas, forks, and knives to deliver exact portions.

She'd seen *maisons* use these tools before, but they used articulating fingers to grasp tools made for hands. They were generalized servants designed to operate safely with people. They performed basic tasks, usually slower than you could do them yourself, but they were still considered a luxury. Behind these counters, *cuisines* moved with the speed of thought, working in tandem. *I wonder if Reign and I could move that fast.*

She knew that *esclaves* could be programmed with routines that required observation and direction but not active attention. The attention required was, in principle, based on the freedom of the *esclave*, its intelligence, and its location. The *cuisines* were trapped behind the counter. One set of eyes might be behind these *esclaves*, observing the entire line. As she watched a *cuisine*, she realized the speed was for show.

Ailbe dropped in line behind her, followed by Reign. Behind the counter, the salad ran low. From the far side of the cafeteria, a *cuisine* threw a head of lettuce with perfect precision. Catching the lettuce in a webbed glove, another *cuisine* expertly sliced it with rotating blades while filling plates and moving trays down the line. Assorted vegetables received similar treatment. Cucumbers and carrots were launched like rockets and effortlessly plucked out of the air. Several *cuisines* worked on a side of meat, factory grown and easily weighing forty pounds. They juggled the meat between them, slicing and searing in midair.

Most onlookers ignored the display, but Ever and Ailbe were captivated. Reign nudged them in line.

"Impressed?" he asked.

"Only a little," Ailbe shrugged. "I should have known Vincenbilts would have *esclaves* on display. They have ties to mechanical engineering research and development that go way back. It doesn't make up for the pool."

They picked a table in the center of the dining room, but Fallon and Riley caught up with them, and she asked them to move farther to the outskirts of the room, close to the rear wall, where they talked quietly and ate.

"Tomorrow, you will be introduced to the Governor and the House of Lords. They are the legislative body for Galt." Fallon said.

"Can't we just stay here?" Reign asked.

"I considered it, but I want you all close to me. I'm not sure what Murdoch is up to." Fallon laid a hand on the wall in a show of familiarity. "I'm not sure if Vincenbilts can protect you. Your introduction will be informal. The legislature meets mid-morning before they go into session in the afternoon. You will not speak in session."

"All the lobbying happens in the morning," Ailbe said, and Reign grunted morosely.

"Yes, I can tell your parents gave you some education on politics."

"Only for Dill," Ailbe said, but apparently, he knew a lot about Galt. "Since my mother was a Senior Fellow, she was a potential candidate for an elected position, but in Dill, we have two assemblies."

Fallon nodded. "It's a bit different in Galt. They only have one assembly, the House of Lords. Titles are writs distributed to the recognized professions based on tax collection. These are, in turn, licensed to leaders in that profession. Those leaders are eligible for election. Technically, titles aren't hereditary, but since assets pass from generation to generation, most titles have stayed in families."

"But we're from Dill, so does it even matter?" Ever asked.

"Politics always matter," Riley said.

"It gets more complicated when foreigners are involved," Fallon said. "And even more complicated with the Free People. Just like the Lords of Galt, the Free People license land from the Union. While the licenses are tied to specific acreage, their rights are usable on any free land. Only the Union has financial assets sufficient to maintain large land masses, and they mark much of it inviolate for conservation."

"What does that have to do with Galt?" Reign asked.

"As a territory of the Union, Galt has administrative control of the surrounding lands," Fallon replied.

"The Free People license those lands." Reign said.

"Exactly, they are a recognized profession under Forestry, Fish and Game. They exerted that claim here. So many have staked a claim that they have an elected representative in the legislature. That's an unusual move by the Free People, and I'm sure Murdoch is influencing the election, but the representative hasn't appeared before the legislature."

# 37. READY FOR AN INTRODUCTION

Dan escorted them through the streets to a large administrative building the following morning. Ever was used to the concrete and steel jungle in the bubble where towers rose to dizzying heights of steel and glass. Galt was much squatter, taking up the entire valley, and the administrative building was wide. The front of the building lacked memorable features, except for the tubular lifts that resembled archaic columns spread uniformly across the front.

The lift doors opened every few seconds, spewing an unending stream of people in front of the glass doors. They looked like the fish farms in Dill at feeding time, and she couldn't help but get the impression they were gasping for air before taking the plunge inside the building or joining the march on the street in front of it.

At least two distinct groups of people were waving signs in front of the building. Everyone carried food and drinks as they meandered between the two parties. She read the signs. *Unionites don't know their rights!* And *Egalies love legalese!*

The rhetoric sounded harsh, but each party tried to draw in members from the other with grandiose oratory.

Reign and Ailbe were more interested in the building.

"I don't think it's twenty stories." Reign shrugged and adjusted a pair of glasses Fallon gave him last night. "Disappointing."

Ever and Ailbe agreed to try to keep him from depression by talking up the meeting. The plan was actually Ailbe's. He understood Reign's emotions better than she did, but his suggestion made perfect sense. He also told her the inevitable outcome. There was nothing here that was going to impress Reign, and he would be at highs and lows until the situation with his father worked itself out.

"Above ground," Dan replied. "Below ground, the building continues for thousands of feet."

"It's as wide as a city block," Ailbe said. "I don't think I can even see to the end." Ailbe was taller than Ever, and he stood on his tiptoes, trying to see past the rush of people moving in and out of the building.

"Just over one in ten people who live in Galt work in the administration building," Dan said. "The House of Lords meets at the top, but the commerce collectorate occupies the most space. The Union is always sending us new models."

The note of irritation in Dan's voice revealed his feelings for the Union's models, but everyone knew the Union AI monitored all trading so that the territories worked together fairly.

The crowds moved like a school of fish, but she hadn't realized how separated she would feel when everyone else seemed to know where to turn and dash. Fallon walked confidently, talking with Dan, while they followed along, trying not to get run over.

He led them straight past the lift tubes through the airlock into the atrium, where few people worked the counter, and countless others crowded in long lines waiting to see *esclaves* posted against the walls. Many internal doors opened to the atrium.

The corner where Dan led them was unpopulated compared to the rest of the floor, swarming with people pressed into the unfunctional airlock. Ever realized that her implant would guide her with alacrity regardless of where they were going. From the blank look on the faces of the surrounding people, she wondered if anyone knew where they were without continuous guidance. Were they really here if their attention was somewhere else? *A crowd of no one.*

Galt *esclaves* were humanoid. Although they didn't have faces, they were capable of expression from mid-mounted view screens. The *esclaves* were painted in black and gold with red trim around their dedicated screens. They had two arms, two legs, and articulated hands, which were useful for holding a warm beverage while users punched at the screen.

Unlike *maisons,* they had a robust frame capable of taking abuse, but they weren't as well built as *cultivers.* She was sure they had the basic programming for obstacle detection, and they doubtless knew the building well, but she guessed they weren't that smart.

A brief query told her these were *attendre,* usually painted in the colors of the territory. They were programmed with protocols for interfacing with people without implants with visual, auditory, and even touch aids.

The people waiting in front of the *attendres* asked the same questions repeatedly, sometimes raising their voices but most of the time waiting for a response from a person. Clusters of *attendres,* little more than kiosks, stood motionless and extended down the length of the lobby.

An angry woman slapped at the side of her *attendre,* trying to get the screen to refresh faster until a *flic* appeared. The giant boxy *esclave* nearly the size of the *Amplus Facere* escorted her away. Ever couldn't help skepticism of the system. In Dill, everything was vertically aligned, and while she hadn't been to the Chancellor's Office, her school functioned without pandemonium.

The human attendant at the counter recognized Dan and waved him forward with a knowing smile. They went through another set of double doors, wooden this time and carved in similar geometric patterns as the friezes at Vincenbilts. The granite tiles gave way to a close-cut, low-pile grey and burgundy carpet.

A slight earthy smell made her nose twitch as they went deeper into the building. The corridor was cool, and at each vent she saw the blue glow of ultraviolet lights behind the disperser and felt warm, dry air emerge into the hallway.

She was used to the closed-in spaces at school, but that was a comfort from familiarity. The depths made her feel claustrophobic, and the icy feeling in the pit of her stomach turned acidic. The lofty ceilings dropped when they entered the hallway, closing into normal height, and they could only walk two abreast.

She walked beside Reign behind Dan and Fallon while Ailbe and Riley, with Varmint strapped to her back, brought up the rear. Dan and Fallon continued to talk, now much more quietly. Reign's face was pointed straight ahead, and his steps seemed more timid, shorter together, and quick. She looked at him with an unvoiced question.

"I can't see much here," he said. "Once the walls closed in, I was cut out. These glasses help, but the net is suppressed. I'm sure you wouldn't understand."

She gave him a long look.

"No reason to be so serious," Ailbe cut in. "Strangers are chasing us, and we are in a strange city with a giant laser. What could go wrong?"

Before she could answer, they arrived at another door. Wooden and ornately carved with ivy and a thick waxed finish, this door was far older than the new doors with geometric patterns and looked out of place in the dull corridor. Inside, they were greeted with an antechamber with cathedral ceilings and hanging lights. Many doors opened into the chamber, and couches stood in the center facing each other.

There were pictures on the wall. She recognized the pictures as part of the founding of the Union when all people came together to create a single government.

They stopped in front of two massive doors with enough room for eight people to walk without touching each other's shoulders. Beside each one of those doors was a small, unadorned entryway blending into the wall.

As she watched, an *attendre* came out of the door behind them, moving swiftly past the group to the small doors. The *attendre* might have been carrying a tiny glass of water, but it moved so quickly she couldn't be certain.

After they were ushered into the antechamber, Dan stood close to a service door, listening and waiting for their turn. Ever wasn't sure why no one complained. Whenever she was caught listening, someone usually had something to say.

Ever, Ailbe, Reign, and Riley slouched on the couches. The seats were uncomfortably squishy and over-stuffed, and Reign started in a monologue about their poor design, but no one had the energy to listen. One good night's sleep hardly compensated for days of travel.

She was tired but full of nervous energy, and she expected everyone to be pretty much the same. Her mother separated herself from Dan and walked over to the couches.

"Ailbe, you will be introduced first, using your mother's title, followed by Reign, then Riley, and myself. On the other side of the door is the Hall of Economic Justice, and one of the Justices will announce you. There's a red carpet. Walk down it. Don't run. Just walk. There will be people eating and drinking in the hall. Try to stay to yourselves."

Fallon turned to Reign specifically. "You will use your father's title since he is indisposed. I've lodged a challenge with the Union against your father's mental competence." Fallon held up her hand to stop him from talking. "Until that inquiry is complete, as your guardian, I can assign his title to you. This will also protect your family's assets." Riley nodded in agreement. Ever wasn't sure if her mother had discussed this with her earlier, and she felt a little stung that conversations and decisions were happening without her.

The service doors were opening and closing all the time for *attendres* as they moved in and out, and one *attendre* emerged to talk with Dan.

Dan turned to the group. "They're ready for us."

# 38. UNEXPECTED GUESTS

The double doors swung open to reveal the red carpet leading into a wide and columned chamber with a vaulted ceiling. Indirect lighting lit the rafters of the Hall of Economic Justice. There was positive pressure in the room, and the warm air filled the antechamber with a delicate and floral scent as soon as the doors opened. Ever hadn't seen anything as ornate or ancient.

Inside, clusters of legislature representatives, lords in name, strutted in purple robes. They talked and laughed while *attendres* brought drinks and *cuisines,* worked at narrow tables, and prepared aperitifs on small plates. Most people wore loose robes of office, but she realized the partners and families of the legislature were also present and well-dressed. She spotted a few children younger than she was, but most of the crowd of socializers was far older.

A Justice in black robes with a dark cowl pulled ceremoniously low over the top of his head stood inside the door.

"Ailbe, Lord of Dill!" the Justice bellowed to the crowd. A few people looked up from their conversation, and Ailbe walked down the carpet. He wore his ceremonial black school robe trimmed in gold and green. *Only Ailbe would remember to bring his school robe.* After a significant pause, the Justice continued.

"Riley, Baroness of Union City!" the Justice said again. More people looked up for Riley as she walked down the carpet. She carried Varmint using two hands, with one hand on the pistol grip and the other on the hand guard pointed down. When she reached the bottom of the carpet, she moved with quick and precise skill to switch Varmint into a position strapped across her back in an elaborate flourish. No doubt Varmint was capturing the whole thing for the net.

"Reign, Earl of Marsh!" the Justice projected his voice, and everyone watched Reign in his camo as he made his way down the carpet. Ever was certain glassey-eyed stares meant queries were going out over the net. Whatever suppression Reign felt before wasn't in this informal gathering.

She knew Richard worked with her grandfather. She also had an inkling that he was well-known and probably wealthy, at least in the circles of the Free People. She sent out queries and realized that while the net didn't reveal private information, it revealed assets, licenses, and certifications. None of that mattered to her before, but the Lords of Galt, in their finery, watched them with measuring stares, and she wondered how she would fare.

Ailbe, Riley, and Reign branched off family trees with value chains extending from the beginning of the Union, but when she queried herself, the net returned next to nothing, only the relationship between herself, her mother, and her grandfather. The record listed Fallon's occupation as directeur and Jorge's as geometre. *What did he survey?* They worked for the same company, a management broker corporation.

She tore from her reverie and realized Fallon was arguing with the Justice, who wilted under the barrage.

"The House of Lords doesn't recognize archaic titles," he complained.

"They will recognize me. If you don't announce me soon, I'll move this venue outside into the Blasted Hills."

"You wouldn't," he said, paling visibly, his round red cheeks losing color.

"I'm considering it already. But I'm trying to spare you the walk. The justice provides the venue for the social, but you aren't part of the legislature."

"As hosts, we guarantee negotiations occur fairly within the law."

"But you aren't responsible for the guests of the legislature, and a title is not a negotiation. It's a statement of rank, whether recognized or not. Right now, you have an opportunity to pass this problem to the Lords. Or you can try to deal with it yourself—alone."

He hesitated only for a second before sucking in a deep breath. He had a barrel-like chest and announced in a deep baritone voice.

"Fallon, Field Marshall of the Federation," he intoned, quickly adding, "And child." Ever realized belatedly that she was the last-minute addition. Fallon motioned for her to follow, and she set a stately walk while Ever stumbled behind.

Ailbe wore his school robes in a way that matched the purple robes of the Lords and the black-robed Justices. Somehow, he managed to get his clothes pressed, and, just like the legislature under those ceremonial robes, he had fine clothing with sharp lines and shined shoes.

Riley and Reign each had a style that reflected the clothing of the Free People. Although they weren't wearing their exosuits with active camouflage, they wore camo clothing and dark black boots with a heavy tread.

For all her life, she was taught to ignore the differences between people, but she felt distinctly unacceptable. Her mother walked in confidently. Fallon dressed in everyday clothing that she wore around the house, a simple shirt and pants combination, except for the boots she wore with her exosuit. The boots gave her a lift, but like Ever, she was shorter than everyone else around her.

That didn't seem to matter to the crowd, which went from silent to angry muttering, although Ever could tell there was a division. The discontent was far louder and clustered to the back, but most in front looked on with approval and that gave her confidence. One older man actually smiled and waved gently at her. He had a thin face and bent back. The purple robes enveloped him like a tent and touched the floor behind him.

She walked behind Fallon, and Dan met them at the bottom of the carpet. He deftly snagged three drinks from an *attendre* and, keeping one for himself, passed the others to Fallon and Ever.

"That could have gone better. Why didn't you tell me you were going to dust off that old title?"

"The younger people need to be reminded. I've been content to lie low, but recent events changed my approach."

"Your father was always a bit more politic about how he presented himself."

"He's not invested in correcting foibles. I think he's entertained by them."

While Fallon talked to Dan, Ever joined her friends to sample the buffet, but she was separated by the older children, although Riley seemed to have gathered a crowd of young men and women.

Ever had a natural talent for working a crowd, but this morning, she didn't know what to expect and had eaten little. A *cuisine* handed her a small plate of neatly cubed but indiscernible protein decoratively painted with an orange sauce that framed the plate in a failed attempt at artistry. She ate several before realizing the surrounding crowd changed from vapid followers to would-be conversationalists.

"Are you from the old Federation?" a child asked. Glancing up, she identified him from the net, Alex—an adopted child.

His fathers were members of the legislature but from entirely different occupations. Although Alex stood at the same height as her, he was several years younger.

"No. I'm from Dill."

"You live in Dill," Alex said. "But your mother is from the old Federation. My father said they couldn't have children in the old world. Maybe you're a robot."

"I'm not a robot," she laughed. She showed him a scrape on her elbow she received when she tripped that morning. It was almost completely healed, but the abrasion was evident.

"I guess you're not a robot," he said, seeming disappointed. A few of the other children who came with Alex seemed equally unimpressed and wandered away, but Alex was undeterred.

"Do you know anything about the Federation?" he asked.

"When we traveled up the east coast, I saw the buildings of the old world," she said. "There weren't any people, a few old machines, but other than rocks and sand, not much."

Alex was gently shouldered out of the way by the older children. Their names and eimai flowed in from the net. Soojin, Remy, Quin, Hayden, and Gael surrounded her on all sides, but others seemed to wait in the wings.

She couldn't see between their shoulders, but remembering what her mother said, she didn't want to show signs of distress, so she buried the feelings deep while looking for a way out. Most questions were innocuous, but Hayden started asking pointed questions about her parentage.

"I've never met someone with so little on the net," Heydon said, and the others nodded. "You don't have a complete eimai."

"There isn't even a place for one," Gael said. She seemed to be performing a diagnostic analysis on Ever's net presence. "Maybe your implant is broken. How old are you?"

If Ever could make a hole in this group, she could follow it back out. She raised her hand to signal an *attendre* for refreshment, but she wasn't tall enough. Belatedly, she remembered the net, but instead of signaling an *esclave* with a message, she wanted to know how close it was. The situation was unbearable. As fast as she could tuck the feelings away, she watched the walls of bodies close in faster.

Drawing up a quavering Axis, the net responded with clear red dots for each *attendre* maneuvering through the crowd. She looked for her friends, and green dots appeared, representing Ailbe and Reign, her allies. They weren't far away, but she couldn't see them over the throng. Orange dots appeared all around her, and she realized these represented her band of interrogators.

Right then, she wanted them to leave her alone, and the thought slipped out with a sudden force that echoed off the net. *Go away!*

And then it happened. Gael stopped talking mid-sentence. The momentary silence released the pressure. She seemed distracted and unfocused. Heydon turned around aimlessly and started walking in a different direction. Within moments, that small area of the reception was clear except for Ailbe and Reign.

The old man who had waved at her earlier walked over. She was cultured enough to resist judgment based on physical traits she recognized in others, but although his movements were spry, his face was so lined, and his limbs so thin, she thought he might collapse at any moment, and instinctually, she tried to take his arm. The old man waved her attempt away.

"It's been years since I've seen your mother clear a crowd like that," he said with a dry chuckle.

"I didn't do anything," she said. "But I'm happy they left. It was getting crowded in this corner."

"I'm sure it won't stay that way long. You gave them a zap. The young ones haven't heard it before, so they're having little trouble distinguishing where it came from. They'll be back with more questions in a minute."

"I just wanted them to walk away."

The old man looked at her funny. "And they did, of their

own volition. The voice of command is like a shout inches away from your ear. It crowds out the net, and if you haven't heard it before, it can be quite startling."

"They will be okay?" she asked, concerned.

"They will be fine. It's not different from an amber or silver alert. Just more personal. You've heard a missing child alert?"

"I think I caused one." She remembered the sirens and lights when she and Ailbe got lost on the farm.

The old man cackled so hard she thought he might fall and turn into a pile of dried sticks. Fallon and Dan came over and gathered them up. She gave Ever a disappointed look.

"Getting in trouble already," Fallon said, exasperated.

"I didn't do anything," she said, but her mother ignored her.

"You might have more training to do with this one," the old man told Fallon.

"She is making progress, but recent events have interrupted us. I will speak to the legislature as soon as the session starts." She turned to the old man. "I trust I have your support."

"Always," he said but sighed. "Time is catching up with me, and there are far more active legislature members. My influence is limited. I've failed to pass on my leadership."

"They recognize and honor service. New leaders will emerge."

Fallon said more but was interrupted by the booming voice of the Justice. Ever realized the doors had opened to reveal a new guest.

# 39. THE REPRESENTATIVE

"Brother John, Lord of the Forest and Representative of the Free People," the Justice boomed.

Brother John wore brown priest's robes over simple clothes not dissimilar from what Ever was wearing except for the soft shoes. She tried not to stare at the brand decorating his forehead, the mark of the Third Eye. Two opposing arcs with a dot in the middle. She expected to see more brands. She heard each brand was self-inflicted, and leaders branded themselves and their followers to create a spiritual connection.

The brand reminded her of the icon etched into Paul's breastplate turned on its side. She should have asked him what it meant, but his icon had multiple arcs and a horizontal line in the center. In a way, Brother John's brand looked like a twisted version of the Witness's symbol.

"They elected someone outside of their profession," Dan said. "That's unheard of. I'm not sure if that's even legal."

"I'm sure it is," Fallon said. "Murdoch is a master of finding holes in systems and exploiting them for his purpose. With this move, he's taking the titles and controlling the vote of the Free People. What kind of effect will this have on an investigation?"

"He can't stop the hearings, but he can raise objections," Dan said. "As a representative, he can appeal the validity of unproven statements."

"Procedural powers can only slow down the process," she said. "I'm more concerned with his voting bloc. He seems to have convinced them of short-term gains, but in and of themselves, the Free People don't have enough votes to make changes to Galt unless they align with someone else."

A gentle trumpet call rose in volume as voices died in the reception.

"The session of the legislature is starting," Dan said. "Because I started this investigation, I recused myself from the proceedings."

Dan looked troubled, but he gathered Ever, Ailbe, Reign, and Riley with his eyes.

"You four will sit in the back row with me while Fallon addresses the Lord Governor."

Ever didn't like being separated from her mother but managed a nod to Dan. Another set of doors opened, presumably from the reception in the Hall of Justice to the chamber for the House of Lords. Fallon and the old man stepped forward, followed by Dan and the rest of the group.

The interior chamber was a vaulted rotunda, which made no sense to her because they were inside a rectangular building. Reign muttered something to the point, but a sharp look from Dan silenced him. Dan turned around to usher them into chairs set against the back wall. The old man separated from Fallon and moved to the front of the rotunda. He sat behind the governor's chair to the left. The chair to the right remained empty.

The net offered esoteric answers on political proceedings, so she asked Dan about the old man.

"Holden?" Dan responded. "He's the majority whip of the

Unionites. They've held legislative power for the last hundred years, but not by a supermajority, and they usually have to compromise with the Egalitarians to pass legislation."

The rows of chairs in the back of the rotunda were broken into two groups by the center aisle that proceeded toward the dais with four chairs where Holden sat.

The chair in the center was the largest and oldest. She assumed that was the governor's chair. The ornate carvings on the chair were a distinctive flower and leaf pattern unmatched by modern construction. A slightly smaller chair to the immediate right matched the design. She guessed the empty chair was Dan's chair. Beside those two chairs, modern chairs of geometric design matched the other chairs and benches in the rotunda. Brother John climbed the dais and seated himself to the right and in front of the governor, and Dan frowned.

"That position is reserved for the minority whip," he retorted. "That can't be changed without a party vote."

On each chair was a button to summon an *attendre*. Ailbe must already have pressed his because an *esclave* moved swiftly to his seat and asked him if he needed anything. Dan waved it off before Ailbe could ask. He was very intent on Fallon, who walked down the aisle to the center podium to address the governor.

"This session will now come to order," the Governor said. She sat in the center in the largest chair. Ever did a hasty query, gathering the basic details about the rule of order and the governor. Governor Keran had served eight years as governor and statistically supported the Unionites, which made sense to Ever since she had a brief term of service in the House of Lords in the Unionite party.

No one said anything outright, but it was clear to Ever this was a contest, and she felt an aggressive burst of competitive energy. Despite her attempts at persuasion, her school disapproved of competition as a learning tool, and she felt like she had a rare opportunity.

"Which party do we want to win?" she asked Dan.

He looked at her quizzically. "I want the best legislation to pass that represents the will of the people. Right now, your family is supporting the Unionite party, but that hasn't always been the case."

She tracked Dan's history and realized he was an active member of the Egalitarian Party. Why was her mother so confident in Dan if he endorsed a party she didn't support?

The room became noticeably quieter as Fallon stopped at the podium. The podium was a wooden structure of simple angles with a physical microphone mounted on a stalk on the top. She'd rarely seen such equipment as microphones were nearly invisible and embedded in the walls and floor.

"Citizen Fallon will address the House of Lords." The Justice announced loudly. Ever briefly wondered if that was his only job.

Governor Keran didn't seem happy about the visit. Her frown deepened until the creases in her face looked like jagged fangs, and she seemed quite agitated.

Fallon leaned forward to the microphone. "Correction. Field Marshal Fallon will address Lord Governor Keran."

"This office does not recognize the archaic military titles of fallen, destitute nations," Keran said. "Nor do we recognize the activities of you or your *father* as being in the interests of Galt."

Dan shook his head, muttering something about "confrontational." He didn't look displeased, only resigned. He must have known from the beginning what would happen. While half the House of Lords looked interested, the other half looked bored or angry.

"My activities are my own. If you look at my record, you will find I operate entirely within the boundaries of the law."

"I object," Brother John said, rising in his seat and forcing the governor to swivel in her chair. His brown robes clashed with the deep purple robes of office the lords wore. The inside edge of his robe was lined with reflective silver that caught the light when he moved.

"This isn't a judicial hearing," Keran said. "Citizen Fallon requested the right to address the legislature."

"This is unusual," Dan whispered to her. "All objections during the address should be passed to the governor's office."

"Still, I must object to untrue statements," he said. "This citizen broke the law of Dill, absconded with equipment funded by the taxpayers of Dill, and traveled overland by way of the old highway system.

"It's not illegal to travel overland," Fallon said. "The *esclaves* are leased to the government of Dill by my customer. The lease specifically states they can remove up to twenty percent of the *cultiver* workforce at any time for testing."

There was a chuckle from the sitting Lords, and the Governor guffawed loudly, but Ever couldn't tell if it was at Fallon or Brother John. Brother John thought he was the target, growing red-faced. His brand stood out sharply.

"Traveling through the remains of the old Federation is prohibited."

"But not in the legal province of Galt," Fallon said. "Neither is Dill."

"Why do you need to test *cultivers* in a wasteland?"

"I test equipment to endure the harshest environment. We are looking at new markets and plan to expand our brand with the Free People. We even solicited support from a prominent content maker to feature our products."

If her mother thought that would slow down Brother John, she was mistaken.

"Everyone knows you operate out of a shell company to hide assets converted from government-subsidized manufacturing."

"Stop the sparing," Keran said. "Brother John, sit down. Citizen Fallon, you are here to address the legislature. Do so, and let's be done with this fiasco. You and your father have inserted yourself into our politics too often, but I think your support in the House of Lords is over. Finish what you've come for and get out."

"I'm here with a warning for you. The countryside is

being ravaged, and the Third Eye threatens humanity." Fallon looked pointedly at Brother John. "You should mobilize your peacekeepers to the country land to protect the Free People and call on aid from the Union."

The governor took the news without surprise, and Ever realized that she either knew or suspected. Brother John looked entirely too satisfied.

"The representative of the Free People informed me moments ago that the Guardians of the Peace have been contacted and are coming here in force to investigate your role in subverting the Peace. They claim you and your father created a private militia."

The assemblage gasped audibly, followed by an immediate flurry of conversation. The governor attempted to quiet the crowd without success.

"The Guardians have never been welcomed in Galt," Dan whispered fiercely. "For them to come in force, they must have reason to believe that will change."

"Order!" A booming call from the Justice cut through the cacophony.

"Order!" The second call reached all ears, and by the third call, a semblance of quiet was restored.

Governor Keran was in full rage. Her face was flushed, and her hand was red from hitting her desk. Her anger was split between Brother John and Fallon.

"The Guardians have a strict interpretation of the Peace," Keran said. "Incompatible with the culture and industry of Galt. Until today, they had no interest in expanding their influence."

Fallon spoke into the microphone. "I came with a warning. What you do with it is up to you. If you are finished, let this audience be ended, and I will be on my way."

Governor Keran seemed to fall back in her chair deflated, but Brother John wasn't finished yet. He interrupted the Governor, standing again to address Fallon.

"No, this audience is not ended. You may think you

have the freedom to wander around creating havoc, but this assembly can detain you and whoever is traveling with you until an investigation is complete."

Ever, Ailbe, Reign, and Riley jumped to their feet. All Ever could think of was getting to her mother, and the rest of the group was right behind her. Dan tried to get them to sit back down, but they pushed around him and jumped on and over the chairs until they ran down the aisle to Fallon's side.

Fallon seemed nonplussed. "By whose authority?"

Brother John took in the lot of them and smiled a tight-lipped sneer at the sight of the children.

"For their safety, I am remanding these children to new families." He motioned to the *attendre* at his side, but it looked back blankly at him.

Ever noticed right then there was uncanny silence in the room. All this time, *attendres* had been answering calls, taking messages, and bringing food. There were hundreds of people in the assembly, more in the audience, and hundreds of *attendres* at their beck and call. Usually, they stood politely beside the wall waiting—able-bodied servants who answered without fail. Now, there was no movement. The *attendres* stopped mid-motion, and incomplete gestures made them into silent statues. They all seemed to turn slightly, their bodies rotating to look at Brother John.

"Are you sure that's what you want to do?" Fallon asked. "Your support staff doesn't seem to agree." Then, as one, all the *esclaves* stood straight, snapped their heels together, and saluted Fallon before falling into an at-ease stance with their hands at their sides. They were once again looking at Brother John. "I already have an army. I've never needed a militia." Instead of Brother John, this time, it was the governor who responded.

"Get out." Keran said, "Get out of my city."

"This isn't your city," Fallon said. "This is the people's city. I will leave here for now until I need to be here again. Thank you for your time."

And with that, her mother turned around and started walking up the aisle with Ever, Ailbe, Reign, and Riley close behind. Dan joined her. In a rush, all the *attendres* responded again, wordlessly resuming where they left off.

# PART 3—WANTED

As darkness spread across the skies,
The lies we told were monetized.
In the act of play, we froze in place,
concerned with others keeping pace.

The frost upon the window sill
froze the hearts and stilled the will.
A child laughed. A mother sighed.
The voices lost of those who died.

And now we count. Each crime read true.
We get our justice, take our due.
Shake our fists and call it straight
force our destiny, choose our fate.

"Laments of the Catastrophe" by Unknown
Recovered from digital archives of the Federation
circa 2149, Western Common Metric

# 40. ON THE RUN

"Back to the Vinny," Ailbe said. "Where the absence of luxury meets calculated precision."

"Obviously, Euclid would approve of each well-placed triangle," Reign said, referencing the pretechnological mathematician still the bane of geometry students everywhere, and Fallon gave them both a hard look. Her dark eyebrows seemed to have permanently settled lower on her face, and Ever tested with her finger to the bushy line on her face, wondering what the future might hold. She looked a lot like her mother, after all.

They were in Fallon's room. A space identical and no larger than their rooms, the five of them made a tight fit standing between the bed and the door. She followed her mother into the room, and the rest crowded behind her, looking for answers. Answers that were not forthcoming.

"Vincenbilts is the safest place we can be while Holden arranges us transport outside the city," Fallon said.

"Won't they find us if we try to use a hypertube?" Reign asked her.

"If we used a public hypertube, yes. If he can get himself a representative in the House, Murdoch has enough people to watch all the public exits."

"Shouldn't we be more concerned with Brother John?" Ever asked her mother.

"No. He's just a tool, and it's not that easy to detain someone without evidence of wrongdoing. I think we can all agree we aren't interested in Murdoch's made-up religion. *Brother* John is just a device of the cult. Right now, *John* is easier to go around than to fix. I expect the Lord Governor and the House of Lords will move against him anyway now that he's played his hand."

"What about that display at court?" she asked. "The entire assembly saw you direct the *attendres*. It's probably on the net already."

"Did they? I think there was a momentary hiccup in the net, causing the *attendres* to reset. I'm sure you noticed that net queries in court are filtered for the privacy of the proceedings."

She hadn't noticed any such thing, but Reign and Ailbe nodded in agreement.

"It was difficult to understand what was going on without net access," Reign said. "Regardless of John, I can't believe the Free People would ever align themselves with the Guardians."

"Unless the Free People are no longer free. I think we might find an answer in this." Fallon pulled out the stainless steel chain-linked collar that Riley had given her. "But I don't have the tools here to inspect it. It looks like the collars they use in the east, but you can't remove one of those so easily once you put it on. Just like the implants used in the West, children are usually provided a collar at an early age. The only difference is the implants grow with the user. The collars are fully functional, and the wearer is effectively integrated into their caste from birth. Don't be mistaken, though. Eastern territories are just as bound to the Peace as the West. They couldn't produce a collar that would hurt someone. Stay close tonight. Tomorrow morning, we are leaving."

Ever slept restlessly that night and woke before morning to a gentle tap and a silent message sent directly to her implant. She dressed quickly, packed her few belongings in her school backpack, and exited to the hallway. The lights were dim. After the daytime hours, the lights around the city dimmed the same way they did in Dill to conserve power. Fallon was there with Reign and Riley, and they waited only a moment for Ailbe to catch up.

As instructed by Fallon, they wore their exosuits with their bags strapped to their backs and hands free. Ever noted that Riley had a new suit and a backpack in Free People fashion, and she realized *maison* deliveries were happening to the hostel all the time. Admiring the many bulging pockets on Riley's gear, she internally set a reminder to ask her mother about a new backpack. The hallway was warm and damp compared to the rooms. The air vents spaced out much further, and the air carried the faint odor of ammonia cleaning products.

"Are we leaving Paul behind?" Reign whispered.

"He's going to meet us," Fallon spoke in a regular tone of voice. "There's no need to whisper. The walls are thick, and if there was a microphone, it could pick out your words, anyway."

"Before morning, we whisper," Ever whispered, and Fallon shrugged.

They went through the hallway and met Dan at the atrium. He was groomed and well-dressed in his ceremonial robe of office. He noticed her inspection.

"We start early. Not this early, but after I've taken you on a private tour, I'll be heading to the office."

They left Vincenbilts with Dan. He had a new domed car with bench seats waiting outside the building. The light mist hovering in the air coated her suit while the heat suffocated even early in the morning. She sat in the circle of benches inside the car, and when the doors closed, the air conditioning turned on, venting the heat and humidity.

The car had amber warning lights on all sides, but the light was barely visible through the heavily tinted windows. The seats felt like actual leather, either grown or harvested from longhorn. She rarely saw such luxury, and she noticed Ailbe opening a small cooler with a questioning expression to Dan.

"Feel free." He laughed but grew serious. "We usually use this vehicle for traveling dignitaries or investors, but I think this time it's serving a higher purpose."

Public lifts and pods in Dill jerk forward into motion, but there was almost no feeling of acceleration from the ground car. She watched the dim lights outside of the tinted windows and there was not even the hint of sunlight in the valley. With all other senses failing, she queried the net for her direction and realized they were heading west to the very outskirts of the city.

"Shouldn't we be heading north?" she asked her mother.

"We came in from the north side. They will expect us to leave that way. We are going a different way out."

"But they must know that you know what they expect, and then they will expect you to go a different way," Ailbe said. "Unless we go the way that we came, in which case they won't expect it because that is the way that you expect that they know." He puzzled over his own statements, confused.

"You are making it both too complex and too simple, Ailbe. There's always more than one way to do anything. The simplest option is to pick another route. Never confuse yourself into believing you can dictate the course of events by out-thinking your adversary's actions."

"Which way are we going?" Reign asked.

"I'm taking you to an old fission reactor on the northwest side of the city," Dan said. "It's off limits but should be safe. The fission reactors were replaced a long time ago with fusion power. Replacing the reactors was easy compared to cleaning up the radioactive waste. We'll avoid any hot zones and use the lifts to get to a lower floor."

# 41. FISSION POWER

After about half an hour, the car stopped on the outskirts of the city. Fewer buildings rose from the depths to break the glass surface. The building they stopped at was a nondescript concrete structure with warning signs and a serial number that meant nothing to Ever. When she looked at the steel-barred door, her implant flashed her with intense verbal and visual warnings that she quieted to a buzz.

Dan went first, and after a momentary pause, the door opened for him. The steel bars retracted into the wall silently. Fallon and Riley followed close behind Dan, but Reign, Ever, and Ailbe lagged until Fallon motioned them to hurry.

"This is the executive entrance. Most of the plant is below ground," Dan said.

"This would be prime real estate if it wasn't so close to a nuclear power plant," Ailbe said. "They have an open view of the sunset framed by the mountain tops." Ever remembered when he thought "Prime Real Estate" meant the biggest flat in the city. Over the years, he'd reevaluated the concept.

Dan nodded in agreement. "We've spent decades disassembling the plants and disposing of contaminated objects. There were twenty-four plants around the city to power the laser, and they were constructed hastily by the Federation. It's taken generations to get this far, but we are finally at the point where some independent organizations have bid to reconstruct the zone into private and commercial properties."

Fallon turned to Dan. "Should we expect anyone at this facility?"

"No, this property was recently acquired but hasn't been turned over yet. We may see a few *esclaves*, but they will be operated by Galt and will let us pass as long as I'm with you. This is the only plant on the west side that hasn't been released to the private sector."

Fallon looked at Dan. "The cooling intake for the reactors came from a pipeline on the east side that ran to the channel." Only her mother could pose a statement that was not a question and expected an answer.

"That infrastructure still exists, but it's been repurposed to process drinking water," Dan said.

"Carrying a fraction of the volume of seawater used to run the fission reactors."

Inside, Ever found a cored-out office building in much better shape than the abandoned ruins of the old world but still in a shamble. The floor was covered in broken tiles, exposing the concrete foundation. The walls were made of unpainted cement blocks with exposed holes for fasteners for an interior wall. There was no furniture, but the ceiling was still intact, and as they entered, the lights lit the entire floor to daytime brightness, momentarily blinding her.

They were in a corridor that dead-ended to a lift with mechanical switches and a sensor. Dan placed his finger on the sensor. There was a quick snap, and when he drew his hand away, she saw a dot of blood.

"These old systems verify users by their DNA. Most people won't come this way to avoid the process, and that's a shame. The executive lift opens onto the catwalk, where you can survey the operation of the whole plant. Seeing even the remains of one of these plants is quite a view."

They crowded into the lift. He assured them the ride was safe, but at each floor, the lift gave a little jerk. Instead of electromagnetics, the operation relied on a spool of cord that wound up and down like a grappling hook on one of Reign's models.

When the lift door opened, the heavy scent of ammonia and ozone smote her in the face like she was walking in a chemical bath. The lift opened directly to the catwalk, a steel bridge with rails wide enough for only one person at a time. As she walked down the catwalk, she kept both hands on the rails and looked down to the plant floor.

On the left side, about sixty feet below, the floor cut away into a deep pool of blue water with thousands of tubes formed into a rough, circular shape.

"There shouldn't be any water in here," Dan said, puzzled.

The source of the smell became obvious. On the right side of the catwalk, she saw a vat thirty feet wide on the floor billowing vapors. *Esclaves* moved in and out of the room, carrying armloads of discolored and tarnished rods that they stacked on the floor. Other *esclaves* severed the rods and drew out pellets that they processed into large barrels.

"Your eyes are bleeding," Reign said to her.

She touched her eyes, and her hand came away with blood. She looked at her mother. Her mother's eyes were bleeding, and streaks of blood-like tears ran down her face.

"Seal your exosuit," Fallon said, and they all quickly obliged, but Dan wasn't wearing a suit. They rushed him to the lift, but Fallon stopped there.

"We're going through the plant. It looks like they are trying to reprocess spent fuel rods for the appearance of a meltdown. I'm not going to be stuck in an investigation, so I'm leaving this to you."

Dan protested, but not for long, and she turned them around to take the lead while he disappeared in the lift.

"As long as we keep our exosuits sealed, we'll be okay for a short time," Fallon said.

The filter muffled her voice, but Ever discerned what she was saying. Blood from her eyes obscured the transparent shield, but the mask's nano-coating slowly pushed the smear into droplets and out of her view.

She crossed the catwalk following her mother, keeping both hands on the rails. They crossed at a jog. That in itself told her Fallon was concerned. Ever's senses heightened. She could feel her heart beating faster, pulsing in her fingertips. Even in the bulky exosuit, she felt lighter, and her limbs moved with unnatural speed. She forced herself to slow to match Fallon's controlled pace.

As they crossed, she saw the *esclaves* below her sitting on the factory floor, becoming motionless hulks. The wispy vapors that rose from the vat no longer billowed. Most *esclaves* were *chargeurs*, purpose-built with long forklike hands and heavy steel frames. Bright red signs on the *chargeurs* were a warning to stay away from machinery, and the yellow *esclaves* were burnt and discolored in places.

The catwalk ended at the far wall with a stair down to the plant floor. Fallon slowed and motioned to Riley.

"There's no one here, but I want you to take the rear just in case. Keep the children between us."

Riley's nod was almost imperceptible in the mask, but she immediately moved behind Reign and Ailbe as Fallon maneuvered down the stairs. Fallon kept one hand on the railing, and Ever did likewise. Their boots rang hollowly on the corrugated steps. The stairs shook, but the bolts embedded into the wall were solid. About every twenty feet, the stairs switched back until they were on the plant floor.

Fallon headed immediately across the floor to an enormous set of double doors, leaving little time for Ever to examine her surroundings. Massive piping ran in and out of the plant floor, and some tubing was missing, while pipes looked like someone had recently rerouted them to new destinations.

Fallon moved with confidence and breached the double doors. Ever thought her mother must be using directions from the net, but when she tried to call up a map, the esoteric plan she received was an indecipherable two-dimensional diagram rather than a modern wire frame.

Behind the double doors, they went down a hallway and turned left, stopping at an abrupt dead end. The same dull grey, off-white painted cement blocks encircled them, and Fallon hesitated, surprised.

"This shouldn't be here," she said, examining the wall and corners. Following her example, the others examined the dead-end wall.

"I think I've found a line," Riley said. She was looking at the hallway, and Fallon turned to examine her findings, feeling the almost invisible edge with her fingers.

"It's a paint line. You have remarkable vision to find this, Riley."

"When you spend a lot of time staring at a view screen, you learn to spot details." Riley shrugged.

Fallon found another line on the other side of the hallway to match the one that Riley found. At the same time, Ever heard the clamor of heavy footfalls, far too heavy for a person, and the yellow tarnished exterior of a *chargeur* with its long forks turned the corner into the shallow hallway. Everyone but Fallon lurched at the sight of the machine.

"I'm sorry," Fallon said. "I should have told you. We are going to use this *chargeur* to get through the wall. Let's back up around the corner."

They withdrew around the corner while Fallon positioned the *esclave* against the far wall.

"These *chargeurs* were made for lifting. Bipedal *chargeurs* walk slowly, but I can increase their speed temporarily."

Standing in the hallway behind the wall, Ever watched the *esclave* position its feet and raise its arms and hands into a wrecking ball. In a fraction of a second, the dull electronic whine built to a crescendo, and a warning sound piped from its speaker grill as the machine launched forward. On impact, a thunderous crash echoed down the hallway.

Fragments flew in all directions, but there was little dust. As Ever rounded the corner, she found the smoking remains of the *chargeur* lying motionless, crashed through two feet of concrete blocks. The displaced blocks created an easily navigable hole into a hallway with a set of lifts.

Fallon noticed her examine the smoking remnants of the *esclave*.

"You can usually push them past their limits, but the results are always the same. I'm sure they used the freight lifts to move waste rods from storage. This workers' entrance connects to an old public transport tunnel below ground."

They crowded into the first lift, which functioned normally for a relic. The further below ground they dropped, the more suffocated Ever felt. She knew what claustrophobia was, and she hadn't experienced the sensation before Galt.

The towers of Dill were so large, both wide and tall, that without ready navigation, you could get lost in them for days, but you were never alone. She felt closed in, and the low ceilings, cramped lift, and general lack of life pressed heavily.

She proceeded to remove her hood, and Fallon nodded. The air was stale, but the increased visibility helped, and Fallon handed her a moist cloth to wipe her face.

The lift jerked to a halt, and the doors slid open, collapsing to each side with a dampened squeak. The lights in the hallway turned on, activated by their presence, but most of the lights were broken, leaving a dimly lit corridor easily wide enough for them all to walk abreast.

Sensing equipment and old signage, showing traces of age, lined the corridor. The signs displayed pictographs of stick figures in motion describing how to walk and where to place your hands. The repetition of the same message bothered her. Even the unbroken floor tiles showed signs of wear, and tread marks were indelibly stained into the tile.

The corridor gently sloped to a dark and wet lobby with an

elevated ceiling. An open tunnel parted the lobby to the left and right. There was no sign of a framework to support a pod, and a damp breeze carried the scent of mildew in from the darkness.

Fallon turned right, and Ailbe inspected a crack dripping around the outer brickwork of the tunnel.

"Are you sure this is safe?" His voice carried down the tunnel, repeating his words endlessly.

"Yes," Fallon whispered. "This tunnel hasn't been in use for a long time, but it's been here for over a thousand years. It will not collapse today. It's drilled through solid bedrock."

"Now we whisper?" he whispered.

"Inside the tunnels, your voice will travel," Fallon whispered, turning on the light attached to her exosuit, exposing the inside of the tunnel. The tunnel wasn't round like a hypertube but hexagonal and easily over twenty feet on a side.

"You can see where the tube was attached to the tunnel wall," Fallon said, pointing to holes drilled into the floor, walls, and ceiling. "This loop ran around the entire city."

After the explanation, she waved them forward and picked up the pace. Ever jogged down the tunnel behind her for what felt like all day, but her internal chronometer betrayed her by stating a little over an hour had passed before they stopped by a ladder for a mechanized service entrance. The dull amber glow showed a sealed hatch and was the first artificial light she saw in absolute darkness.

The hatch opened with a negligent wave of Fallon's hand.

"Ostentatious?" Riley asked.

"A bad habit I picked up from my father," Fallon said, climbing the slippery rungs.

Dim lights lined the service entrance—a vertical shaft wide enough for Ever to climb with her backpack. It wasn't roomy, and after twenty feet, she felt sweat moisten the inside of her suit. Ailbe and Reign were breathing hard, although Riley, with her mechanical legs, was unaffected by the climb. She held to the back and didn't complain when they had to rest mid-climb.

In short order, they arrived at the top of the service entrance, and the hatch slid away for Fallon. Ever followed, climbing straight through the hatch that led to an alley between buildings. Immediately blinded, she squinted her eyes and looked around. Far in the distance, the glass ceiling reflected the light of the midmorning sun like a glowing dome, but the streetlights and surface lights on buildings transformed the darkness into incandescent daytime.

She helped pull Ailbe and Reign through the service hatch, and Riley followed, easily climbing the rungs, balancing with one foot on each rung, barely using her hands. Fallon gave them a moment for their eyes to adjust to the light. Then, the Witness moved out of the shadows in the alley.

# 42. TOMATO FARMER

Paul changed his garments dramatically from silver and white to black and dark grey. Ever looked closely at his breastplate and could still faintly see the etched lines of the insignia at each corner. The parallelogram over his heart directly opposed to the vertical line with its concentric arcs. Between those emblems, a star and two upside-down chevrons adorned his chest. That was new. The *Facere* stood close to him, a dark extension of his armor. Fallon didn't comment on his change of clothing. Instead, she gestured to the building.

"This building is one of several vertical farm companies in Galt owned by Holden. It reaches all the way to the top of the city, but what we are interested in is the hypertubes that connect this farm to the transcontinental system."

"Are we leaving the continent?" Reign asked.

"No, but Murdoch doesn't know that. A pod from here can take you anywhere in the world in a few hours. Right now, we are in a grey zone. There aren't any cameras in this alley, but we will be recognized as soon as we step out of it. There are steps I can take to obscure that, but eventually, Murdoch will find out we came through here."

"How do we get inside?" Ever asked.

"I can help with that," a stranger said, rounding the corner into the alley. The appearance of the short but broad-shouldered man with thick arm muscles startled Ever, but the net revealed his eimai, Alberto, but he preferred to be addressed as Al. Before Ever could react, Fallon reached out and clasped hands with Alberto. It was a gesture Ever hadn't seen before, but Al responded in kind, if hesitantly.

"The dock is near the center of the building," Al said. "Occasionally, I give tours to purchasing agents, and it's not unusual for the Free People to send representatives."

"Do you run this entire building?" Reign asked, impressed, and Al laughed.

"No, only a small farm I lease from Holden," Al said. "The product is perishable and fully organic. I move shipments out every fifteen minutes to maximize shelf life."

They followed Al around the corner, giving Ever a glimpse of the undercity of Galt. Few people were on the road at this level, but a lattice of transparent bridges and tubes extended to dizzying heights. Unlike the monolithic towers in Dill, they tapered the buildings at the top.

The same spheres Dill used to create a bubble hung from the bridges. She sent a query to the net and received a response regarding the uses of wave cancellation technology to prevent harmonic resonance.

The Spire rose in the city's center like a needle, and a wall of obsidian covered the east side, sparkling with a ghostly light even from miles away. The dark stone, like a frozen waterfall, dominated the entire city. A perpetual reminder. She stumbled while looking at the obsidian as they walked, and Al glanced back.

"Some people think the Spire is the landmark of Galt, but those that live here know that's not the case," Alberto said. "If you go to the city's east side, you will see buildings covered under a tidal wave of frozen obsidian stone—many with the bodies of victims still inside. There are efforts to drill through the rock, but it may take another five hundred years to free them all."

"A crime of inordinate magnitude," Paul said. "Potential loss of life is not justification for murder. This event mars the otherwise unspoiled history of the Peace."

Al nodded sadly. Ever couldn't find details on the net regarding the Spear, but the description of the atmospheric event precluding the weapon's firing and the associated justification seemed like sound logic. A massive weather event would have destroyed the continent.

They walked to a door marked as a service entry on what she thought of as the front of the building. The door recognized Al and opened, leading them into a warehouse of silos that rose a hundred feet in the air. On top of each silo, a funnel dilated open and close as a system of conveyor belts rotated around the warehouse. The conveyor system filled the warehouse with dull mechanical sound and deep vibration. The dry air sucked all the water out of her throat, and she had to swallow several times to create any moisture.

"The public entrance is above us," Al said, projecting his voice above the din. "There's a requirement to maintain a reserve of plant and animal calories in the city. The storage below the farm meets the requirement, but it has to be refreshed daily."

They took a freight lift to what Al called "Processing," an open-air floor with hundreds of wide columns and vertical plumbing supported by stainless steel frames. The columns stretched to the surface, each green and growing, with a *recolteuse* riding rails inspecting and picking fruit. The fruit was then deposited in a cargo container on the floor, where a wheeled chargeur picked it up and sped away.

She realized the entire building was hollow. Lifts traveled up and down the sides of the building, carrying both *esclaves* and people on an open internal framework of scaffolding that made her knees tingle. Bright lights mounted on the frame lit the entire building from the bottom to the top. A distant glow from a glass ceiling complemented the artificial light, but each plant had a set of LED lights customized to its growing needs.

Unlike the storage warehouse, the processing level was warm and humid, with tangible fresh produce smells. While Ever, Reign, and Ailbe gawked, Al motioned them forward. Lines on the floor separated foot traffic from *chargeur* traffic that sped up and down the rows, inches away. The wind from their passage buffeted her face, and she frequently looked over her shoulder for a madly careening *esclave* while she followed behind Ailbe across the farm floor.

After about fifteen minutes of walking, Al took a right, and they headed in between the stainless steel columns until he halted, briefly glancing at the leafy plants suspended on the framework. On the side of the column of vegetation, he punched at a control panel, expertly pressing a series of buttons.

"They hate it when I do this," Al said with a mischievous smile. "But it's important to show off the product."

Al's column was fifty feet wide and extended to the height of the ceiling, and the *recolteuse* that serviced his field dropped rapidly on its rails until it reached the last fifteen feet and then slowed its descent. Many arms sprouted from the *esclave's* bar-like body, and on each arm, a flexible hand with unnaturally long fingers, gripping pads, and clipping cutters. Cameras mounted in clusters on stalks across its wide but shallow body swiveled independently. The stalks seemed crab-like, and they gave Al a baleful stare as he interrupted their operation.

Al reached into a half-filled shipping container mounted on the side of the *esclave* and pulled out a handful of elongated red fruit on green stems. He handed them out before tasting his own. She didn't recognize the type, but the fruit smelled like a tomato, and when she bit down, it was both sweet and mild.

"There's nothing like a fresh Marzano," Al said. "I owed Holden for taking a risk, but he's been paid many times over from his share. What I am doing today is for myself."

"You understand the risk?" Fallon asked.

Alberto nodded. "Hopefully, having powerful friends will mitigate some of the risk."

"Powerful, but few. Keep close to confidants. The sooner we are away, the less risk there will be."

Al shook his head sadly. "No, I think the closer I am to you, the safer I am, but I won't leave my farm. There's too much change in the air. You have a reputation for surviving change, but people outside your immediate vicinity suffer collateral damage. Try to remember Galt and my family."

He gathered the remains of the Marzano fruits and put them in a waste receptacle for composting before they proceeded into the interior.

In the center of the farm stood a building in a building. A squat structure sixty feet tall, ringed with opened ports and an observation deck that wrapped around the circumference. The *chargeurs* deposited their cargo into the ports before speeding off.

Al brought them to a small lift to the observation deck, but he stopped there. The warning signs on the door buzzed Ever's implant. The visceral indications of danger flashed in her thoughts, competing with her vision. Death, severed limbs, and crushed bodies under shipping containers made her gag and sway.

Fallon momentarily gripped Ever and Ailbe, stabilizing their wobbling steps, while Reign staggered into Riley. Abruptly, the alarm stopped.

"The effect is worse for the children," Al said, puzzled, but looked speculatively at Fallon. "But the alarm seems to be disabled now. The shipping containers aren't closely monitored. The system is completely automated. When the pod enters the dock, I will override the order. You have fifteen seconds to get inside the pod before it's ejected into the tube. There are no safety procedures. If you are caught in the door or fall in the pod's path, you will die before I can stop the machine."

"Why does this sound like an incredibly bad idea?" Ailbe said perfunctorily.

"It's very simple," Fallon said. "You can easily step from one room to another in fifteen seconds. When Al disables the loader, we walk together onto the pod."

"What about the g forces?" he asked. "When we're shot into the tube?"

"If a tomato can survive, I'm sure you can," Reign said.

"You actually drop about a hundred feet before being inserted into the hypertube," Al said. "The air pressure cushions the fall. After you stop falling, you will feel acceleration, and the floor will gradually move from a horizontal to a vertical position to accommodate the increase in force."

"That sounds very similar to public hypertubes. The couches reverse during deceleration," Reign said.

"Couches with deep cushions," Ailbe said, but Fallon signaled Al to proceed.

Alberto opened the door, and the deafening sound triggered an alert from Ever's implant to find hearing protection. They crowded inside the door on a scaffolding with a control stalk and a stair with no rails that went down to a narrow ledge.

There was a hole in the ground where the floor should be and a framework of rails. As she watched, a pod shot up from the darkness. A sphere roughly thirty feet in diameter rose, magnetically suspended inches away from guiding rails. Unlike public transport, there were no windows, and the hatch fit so precisely that she couldn't find the door lines. Arms from the ceiling suctioned to the side of the sphere, quartering the transport to reveal an empty platform. A wide conveyor belt dropped like a bridge onto the platform and ejected storage containers, stacking them while a scanner read the coded destination.

While the platform was loaded, the sphere slowly moved from the right to the left over another hole in the floor. The sphere's sides clapped back together, and the rails holding the transport sprung apart, dropping the pod into darkness.

Al went to the control stalk and motioned them forward. Ailbe tried to go back out the door, but Fallon grabbed him by the arm and shouldered him forward down the stairs, where they waited on the narrow ledge.

She realized they were waiting for a particular shipment and watched Al's hands on the controls. Empty platforms passed Ever by, and she counted the seconds and prepared to step smoothly across the darkness over the railing and onto the platform.

Reign stood to her left, followed by Riley and Paul, with his *Facere* standing like a tall icon against the wall. She took Reign's hand in her own. The bulky suit gloves made it difficult to grip, but he didn't protest.

Alberto waved at them as the next capsule rose, and when the conveyor belt descended from the ceiling, he pulled a lever to halt the motion, causing a shrill alarm to cut the mechanical cacophony. The platform continued to move, and Fallon pushed Ailbe forward. He didn't budge. Ever wasn't sure what to do.

Fallon kicked the back of Ailbe's knee. While he collapsed, she twisted his arm under her shoulder and threw them both to flop on the platform. He landed flat on his chest, but somehow, she maneuvered to land on top of him. She shouted in his ear.

Ever couldn't make out the words as she focused on smoothly stepping forward with the others and walking carefully to the center of the platform. She knew that Ailbe delighted in complex mechanical operations, but his distress was almost palpable, and Reign immediately went over to help him.

Reign had little time before the arms clamped the pod walls onto the pod. There was abrupt darkness before Ever touched the light on her suit, and the platform tried to fall away, leaving her stomach in midair and causing her to sink to all fours.

"Stay down," Fallon said. She yelled, but the sound was muted, and Ever realized the noise had momentarily deafened her. Almost immediately, her hearing returned. Air whistled past the pod as it slowed, sending her another wave of nausea, and then they stopped with a jerk.

"We are in the vacuum chamber," Fallon said. She sat down by Ailbe, who flopped onto his side with Reign's help. He still seemed stunned, and the backpacks made getting up and down cumbersome. Fallon motioned Reign to sit. Riley, Paul, and his *Facere* all stood. They didn't seem to have trouble maintaining their balance.

"This is going to be a very short ride," Fallon said. "I don't think we will achieve full velocity."

"Where are we going?" Paul asked. He seemed unconcerned with the answer. He turned away from Fallon, and his roving eyes inspected the spartan capsule interior.

"A produce stand."

# 43. THE GUARDIANS

Ever sat behind the counter of the produce stand on a three-legged stool, waiting for her first customer of the day. The early morning sun touched the tarp on the stand, announcing midmorning, but she was already hot and moist from the humidity.

Tiny buzzbees from an errant *apiculteur* flew around her, and she practiced controlling them by forming an Axis and directing the miniature machines. They were not *esclaves* and did not have quantum encryption to connect to the net. Complicated commands failed immediately, but her implant managed them with swarm intelligence good at navigating around hanging obstacles.

She missed her exosuit. No matter the external temperature, she stayed cool as long as it had power. Fallon said the suits identified them, and they needed to blend into the Free People. Consequently, only Reign could scout out of their temporary residence wearing his suit.

Many of the Free People didn't wear exosuits all the time, especially if they were in their villages. This village was somewhere north of Galt, hundreds of miles away. Fortunately, Fallon had a contact, Ching-Yin, and a place to stay.

After Fallon went down on one knee to complete the greeting ritual, Ching-Yin invited them into her house. It was mostly subsurface, similar to Richard's house, but smaller with fewer subterranean domes.

Riley and Paul were too recognizable. Paul chaffed at the command, but he seemed unwilling or unable to take off his exosuit, so he stayed indoors. Ever had soundly suggested that if she removed her suit, she should be allowed out of the house. Her mother had taken the idea and proposed that Ever and Ailbe watch Ching-Yin's produce stand as repayment for their lodging.

Their job started before sunup: inspecting the produce. They threw anything showing signs of rot into a composting bin, which they sold back to the farms. Then, they stocked the shelves from the refrigerated containers. While she watched the counter, Ailbe faced the shelves.

At first, just one day in the heat drained her completely, and Fallon was forced to remind her that Ching-Yin managed the produce stand-alone.

"Why doesn't she use a *maison*?" Ailbe said, careful to voice his complaints when Ching-Yin was out. She was helping Fallon acquire various tools. Ever wasn't sure about the details, but Fallon spent most of her time analyzing the silvered steel chain-link collar at the wooden table in front of the small kitchenette.

"*Esclaves* are expensive," Fallon said, looking up from her work. She'd separated several of the links in the collar, exposing three-dimensional semiconductors layered into an oval mold. "Most Free People try to keep a low technology impact."

"How do they live this way?" he said, and Riley started with a sharp retort, but Fallon intervened, laughing to cut the tension.

"A day's hard work won't kill you. I disagree with their lifestyle, but I know they believe in it." Fallon passed an appreciative nod to Riley.

"Don't the Free People have child labor laws?"

"Not the same as Dill," Riley said. "We believe children should contribute directly to society. Children require a set of skills that usually means several apprenticeships. The entire community is responsible."

"I find it refreshing," Fallon said.

"How long are we going to be here?" Ever asked her mother.

"Until Lucas catches up with us. Taking the hypertubes is dangerous for us right now, but a *maitre* and his *cultivers* are barely worth notice. Few could make the journey alone, but Lucas is unusual. Reign and Ching-Yin can nose around and investigate the Third Eye. There doesn't seem to be much of a presence this far north. That's something we can be thankful for. As soon as Lucas gets here, we head further north to Union City. Hopefully, we'll meet your grandfather."

"I don't understand what we can do about all this," she said.

"Have you heard anything out of Galt?" Fallon asked.

"Well, no, what is that supposed to mean?" Ever asked.

"Exactly. In our case, hearing nothing is usually a success. We've already made a difference, but we can't treat the symptoms unless we know the disease." Fallon looked down at the collar with a heavy sigh. "I'm afraid this is beyond me. Pieces seem to be missing, and I can't break the encryption. It's much less effective than an implant but still capable of transmitting basic commands."

"I was beginning to believe there wasn't anything you couldn't do," Ailbe said, and Fallon gave him an exasperated look while replacing the links on the collar. She gave the collar to Ever.

"It's deactivated. For now, you can hold on to it."

Ever and Ailbe worked at the produce stand for the next several days. At first, the work was monotonous, but she appreciated the regular customers who shopped at the stand. To avoid spoilage, she received regular shipments by hypertube. Those went directly into refrigeration in the back. The Free People had a community, but most of the structures were small, at least partly underground, and their fresh stores often needed replenishment.

Her regular customers lived nearby, and Ailbe prepared larger orders for expeditions or families outside the village. Usually, *maisons* retrieved the order and delivered it at a cost to the purchaser. Ailbe sweated over the large orders while she worked the front of the produce stand. The *maisons* were meticulous in identifying missing items, and the delivery service charged back delays to the store, so he had to be fast on his feet.

As she spent more time in the village, she saw that the Free People produced a variety of goods, all of them made of materials they either scavenged from the surroundings or harvested from the forest. Their comparative wealth surprised her. As *esclaves* rolled out produce shipments, more *esclaves* reloaded the pods for return. There was a high demand for fresh meat in the city, and they loaded field-dressed carcasses from hunting parties and other popular goods like hand-carved models, quilts, and furniture.

Few of the Free People wore full exosuits in the village, but she still felt she stood out as part of the minority without smart clothing. The bubble reflected the ultraviolet light and much of the heat into the sky. Ever and Ailbe's clothes were designed for indoor and outdoor use in Dill.

Her clothes stayed dry in the humidity, but most of the Free People wore shirts and trousers of smart fabric that sealed together and created a ventilated envelope of air. They wore wide-brimmed hats like Ever's. Ailbe tried to buy a hat from the city, but Fallon stopped him. Purchases in the city were a matter of public record, and Fallon didn't want anyone to know where they were.

After the morning rush, the produce stand cleared out

except for one person lost in the aisle.

"How can I help you?" Ever asked. She peered at the stranger, but her implant revealed nothing. She might have been staring at a rock, and the stranger was dressed much like a rock in a grey exosuit with a matching cowl.

He had a neckpiece attached to the suit, also in grey, with a small transparent view screen that hovered under his eyes. She realized this was a substitute for an implant. She saw a reversed text on the screen with a basic description of her public eimai. It was a poor way to understand anyone because eimai wasn't serial, like language, but a host of competing ideas that had to be felt and considered. The more new people she met, the more she realized she'd only used the surface of the net.

The only other color on his suit was a single black stripe on each shoulder, but she'd never seen so many shades of gray. The suit had wires bound into the fabric and more mechanical components wrapping around his waist and shoulders than she had seen on other exosuits. The gray patterns were much darker than Ailbe's exosuit, so she didn't think he came from Dill.

He pulled back his cowl. Under the tarp, the stranger was joined by a companion who was similarly dressed but had three stripes.

While her public eimai was available for anyone to look at, having even a part of her eimai reflected felt distinctly demeaning and an invasion of privacy.

"My captain is looking for the custard apples," Single Stripe said.

She looked to the row where a crate of custard apples usually sat, but it was missing, and she realized Ailbe must be in the back getting a refill.

"It looks like we're out right now, but we should have them refilled in a moment," she said, sending Ailbe a quick message.

"You have an implant? That's unusual for the Free People," he said. A gauge on his display spiked when she sent the message.

"Free People have implants," she said, thinking of Reign and Richard. "My friend is blind, and he uses an implant to see."

"It's unfortunate so many Free People choose to suffer physical ailments. They oppose clean living and technology and burden society with their infirmities."

"It's a life choice." She felt the conscious need to defend Riley. "They choose to use only as much technology as they need to live independently."

"But they still go to the cities for medicine and healing," the stranger said.

"Only for the basics, and who wouldn't? They use smart clothing. I don't think they're against technology. It's just how it's used."

The stranger nodded as if confirming something. She wanted to get him out of the produce stand quickly, and Ailbe was taking too long, so she repeatedly sent messages for him to hurry despite the needle on the gauge.

Ailbe, dallying with the small crate of custard apples, reluctantly appeared. The fellow's companion questioned him regarding the apples before purchasing a few.

A few minutes after the gray-suited people left, Ailbe grabbed her shoulder and pulled her head close to whisper.

"Don't you know who that was?" he asked.

"I'm not sure, but he was quite rude," she said. His incredulous expression indicated that she should know, and he would tell her.

"They were Guardians. I think we're okay. They didn't seem interested in us. What did they talk to you about?"

"Just about the Free People," she said, and he mulled that over.

"Fallon said we should be on the lookout for the Third Eye. They're definitely not going to be here if the Guardians are around. The Guardians have a very strict interpretation of keeping the Peace. They can push around these villages, but the cities won't have them. This is probably good news as long as we stay out of their way."

"Does that mean you're ready to refill the Marzanos?" she asked.

"We're out again?"

"I've been pushing the product," she said. "It's the least we can do for Al."

Ailbe refilled the tomatoes and started to prepare a large order. She faced the few boxed goods, moving the boxes to the front, and answered customer questions until just before noon.

The one benefit of working at a produce stand, and there were few overall benefits, is that you had options for lunch. Ever and Ailbe didn't have a specific window for lunch breaks. The Free People operated a bit chaotically with scheduling, but there were windows of time when the stand was empty. The morning was busy, but midmorning and afternoon, the stand emptied, and they could find something to eat.

In the back of the building, they used an old methane stove running on a canister to fry tofu and vegetables on a rusty iron skillet. The stand carried many varieties of tofu in refrigerators in the back, and she was about to make a selection when a group of gray suits surrounded the stand. Their cowls were low, hiding their faces in shadow, but she recognized the stranger and their captain.

The produce stand wasn't very big. With a few quick steps, the stranger cleared the entrance and firmly held her arm. Two more of the Guardians brought Ailbe out from the back. They had both his arms, and he struggled to get away, in the process knocking over a table, but he was surrounded.

The captain turned and walked over to Ever. He provided a digital code that she took wordlessly.

"For the damages," the captain said and pointed to Ailbe. "This one isn't in compliance with keeping the Peace."

Ever tried to send a message to Fallon but found her access to the net was garbled, filled with strange terminology.

"We've suppressed net access," the captain said, noticing her blank expression. "It's a shame that Dill doesn't manage its citizens better."

"Where are you taking us?" Ever asked.

"We aren't taking you anywhere. You haven't broken the Peace. He doesn't comply, however," the captain said, motioning again to Ailbe. "If he'd been born in Ornia, he would have been taken into protective custody early on where he could learn to use his talents in service of the state. Dill is a backward society where citizens can break the Peace, and the state accepts the responsibility, but Dill is a long way from here."

"How did Ailbe break the Peace?" she asked. She struggled to create an Axis while talking to the captain. Despite what the captain said, the net was not unavailable. It spoke strangely, but she recognized the words. The Axis formed, and the iconography revealed *esclaves* around the village. There was almost nothing to work with close by. On the distant edges of the Axis, she sensed Lucas, but she had nothing to distract twenty of the gray suits from Ailbe.

"By himself, Ailbe probably wouldn't break the Peace," the captain admitted. She didn't like his familiarity. "But animals don't follow the Peace, and he has an association with them. Because of that association, he needs training and perpetual supervision, or he could be a danger to others. He isn't going to get that out here, but in Ornia, he will get the training he needs. In fact, being out here, close to the forest, is the most dangerous place for him."

Ailbe struggled and started yelling. Ever stepped forward to help, but a mechanical arm attached to the back of the captain's exosuit reached around and snatched her other forearm. He gripped her firmly and expertly twisted her arm behind her back so she couldn't move. Another Guardian dropped a noose on a long pole around Ailbe's neck.

When Ailbe continued to fight, the Guardian with the pole activated the noose with a trigger. A sharp electrical burst like a silent detonation dropped Ailbe. The released energy affected Ever's implant, and the Axis wavered. She realized that Ailbe's emblem disappeared from her awareness.

No sooner had Ailbe fallen than the Guardians scooped him up and rushed him out of the building. The captain shook his head.

"They always fight," the captain said and turned to Ever. "But once they get to Ornia and realize their responsibility, they are much happier."

"How can he be happy without friends and family?" she asked, and the captain sighed.

"When I was younger than you, I joined the Guardian's Youth Division," the captain said. "It seemed like the best way to get into the Guardians. In Ornia, you either join the youth division or get an implant. Most Guardians can't have an implant. On my first day, I asked my commanding officer why. He told me that a Guardian doesn't just have respect for life. They have respect for all lives, and that comes at a cost. Sometimes that cost is luxuries like an implant or personal happiness."

The unnamed Guardian holding her released her arms and left, but the captain remained. She wanted to run and get her mother, but she thought that would be a mistake. The captain could summon his troops and restrain her.

The practiced ease with which the Guardian had disabled her frightened her, and although she tried to stop it, tears rolled down her face, and she had to blink repeatedly to maintain her vision. Peacekeepers didn't resort to physical violence.

Although she didn't agree with him, she nodded mute understanding of the captain's words. The captain gave her another code.

"You can use this to contact me. Ailbe's implant will be suppressed, but I can relay messages to him until he is transferred to Ornia."

"How soon will that be?" she asked.

"Several weeks. The territories don't permit us to ride the hypertubes," the captain said and looked hard at Ever. The sincerity, false or not, disappeared from his face. "Don't think about freeing him. Our FangVolken is unassailable."

The captain left Ever, giving her an odd bow with two hands held horizontally against his chest. She wasted no time closing the shop or returning to the tiny house. She sent a quick message to her mother at priority, and the response to return was immediate. Fallon included Reign and Riley on the reply. She tried to send a com to her mother directly, but her mother did not accept. The walk back was a good fifteen minutes away, and she wasn't even sure if she was walking towards or away from Ailbe. *I can't leave him.*

The produce stand was one of several shops that were close enough together to warrant hard-packed dirt and gravel streets. Ever ran across the streets looking for the Guardians, but they disappeared, leaving her no choice but to follow instructions and return.

# 44. A NEW PLAN

When Ever returned to the house, she found Fallon, Riley, and Reign sitting at the long bench around the trestle table. Paul stood in front of an empty fireplace, ornamental in the summer. The fireplace was clean and unused. The animals stayed away from villages, and the tropical temperatures obviated the use of fire for heating. An empty cast-iron pot hung over a grate.

Ching-Yin went back to her shop. She offered Ever a sad hug and wiped her face before she left the house. Ever thought her eyes would remain dry while she stammered the story back to Fallon, but fresh tears welled. Her mother ignored them while considering her words. Her mouth was a hard line.

"Send me the code he gave you."

After Fallon received the code, her eyes glassed over in that familiar look of someone querying the net. "At least we know who we are dealing with. Captain Mateo has three children, all adults, and with different partners and twenty years in the Secuestrador."

"What does that mean?" Riley asked.

"His past tells me about what kind of man he is. He is determined and he is willing to sacrifice his family for the cause. He's also charismatic. Women believe him, and people follow him. I want to understand who I'm dealing with and find his chain of command. I have a history with the Guardians. If I can find a commanding officer I've worked with, I can get Ailbe released to us. The bad news is the Secuestrador are dedicated. Anyone serving in that branch for his entire career will be obstinate."

"What kind of history do you have with the Guardians?" Reign asked.

"There are some things even the Guardians won't do for the Peace. I think I have a name for us. It's a little complicated because they are divided into several distinct services. While I commune, remain perfectly silent. I don't want to be distracted, and there is always the possibility you could be overheard."

"Can I join?" Ever asked plaintively. "I won't say anything."

As soon as she asked, Riley and Reign both chimed in. Riley would have to watch on Varmint's viewscreen, but she could still be present. Fallon considered for a moment and then agreed to their request but left Paul out. She turned back to the others.

"You could be useful, but you must remain silent, even if he engages you in conversation," Fallon told them before turning to Paul. "I don't think he would interpret your presence favorably."

"How do you know he will respond?" Reign asked.

"He'll respond to me. Remember, you'll only see his avatar. The Secuestrador don't use implants, and the upper hierarch of the Guardians avoid them."

Ever wasn't sure how useful she would be if she wasn't allowed to talk, but she didn't voice her opinion. She needed to be part of anything that could help Ailbe. She was the reason he got caught by the Guardians. If she hadn't called him out, he would've gone unnoticed. Her mother sent her an invitation, and she focused on the com.

Her implant responded, and sensations of the kitchen in

the little house faded into the background until she was in a beige room, sitting on a bench not that dissimilar from the one she was sitting on in the physical world.

As long as she focused on the com, she stayed present, and her eimai joined with the others. Looking at her arms and hands, she was still transparent, and she attempted to solidify her presence. Unless she was cast into an *esclave*, her implant couldn't alter her eimai without active consent. Communing was a skill she used little, but she could see the benefits of a hybrid information landscape that she imagined her mother must live in all the time.

Fallon sat in an oversized, padded chair behind a burnished wooden desk at a right angle and in contrast to their simple bleached wood bench. The stain permeated the fine-grained wood, giving it a deep brown color, and it shone with layers of thick lacquer. Behind her mother's desk, two flags on brass poles hung nearly to the ground. She didn't recognize either of them, and she almost didn't recognize her mother. Fallon's appearance drastically changed. Her hair was cropped short, and she wore an olive dress suit of tightly woven fabric with pressed edges and brass buttons.

Reign joined them, and then Riley. Reign presented a solid projection of his eimai, but Riley was just a picture, complete with Free People color-shifting exosuit and a gun mounted onto a shoulder strap. Her body moved as she spoke but was otherwise a perfectly modeled reflection of the same angry expression she had in real life.

"Strategos Jackson," Fallon said to the open air. Her request went unanswered for a moment, then a Guardian appeared, not in a gray exosuit but a western-style dress suit in heavy grey fabric. On his left shoulder, badges of rank decorated the chest of his uniform, while on the right stood the symbol of the Guardians, a line-drawn figure sitting on top of the palm of the left hand while the right hand sheltered the tiny shape. When Captain Mateo bowed, he put his hands together in that shape. *He thinks he's protecting me, but what is he doing to Ailbe?*

The Strategos was sitting behind his own desk, or rather, a picture of him was sitting behind his own desk. The dueling desks faced off against each other.

"Fallon," Jackson replied congenially.

"I'm sure you realize this conversation cannot be traced."

"I know. You will forgive me for trying. We have our protocols. To what do I owe the pleasure of our conversation."

"An unfortunate incident. It seems one of your patrols has picked up a young friend of mine, Ailbe of Dill. Captain Mateo sequestered him while he was waiting for his parents."

Fallon raised her hand in the air, and a picture of Ailbe appeared in her hand with other documents. With a tossing motion, they flew by themselves to settle onto Jackson's desk. He studied them for a moment.

"This is unfortunate. Our young friend has some undesirable traits that would be better served in Ornia. Dill will protest. His parents are well connected—no doubt there will be an exchange. I'm sure in a year or so, he will be back in Dill with a healthy appreciation of the Peace, which begs the question. Why are you involved?"

"He is well connected. Beyond that, Ailbe is useful to my cause."

"But what cause is that really?" Jackson asked with apparent puzzlement that Ever didn't believe.

"The specifics don't matter, Jackson. What matters is that our causes align. You want to protect the Peace, and I'm sworn to defend the life and liberty of the West. There can be no liberty without peace."

"Some would say those two are at odds," Jackson said. "Indiscriminate individual liberty, imposing cost and pain on society, doesn't maintain the peace."

"Even so, but censure doesn't create peace, only rebellion," Fallon said and motioned to the bench. "Sometimes the tools to protect peace and liberty are the same ones that destroy it. I'm sure you've noticed that my father and I collect the tools I need."

Jackson glanced at the bench and turned to Fallon, but something caught his eye, and he turned back to stare at Ever, Reign, and Riley.

"You brought the Reaper?" he said, shaken.

"I'll use whatever tools I need."

Jackson must have been wringing his hands in real life. The gesture translated poorly into the commune, where imaging overlapped the pictures. Regardless, the essence came through. He talked, but not to Fallon. Maybe someone else was in another room. A muted but discernable slam of a door echoed in the com.

"We are alone now," Jackson said. "But I doubt we are secure. I'm sorry I can't help you with this. I would if I could. I'm sure Ailbe will be safe until he is released to his parents. We are making exchanges here faster than they are coming in. There have been leadership transitions in the Strategos, very recent changes, and they provided a new direction for the Guardians."

"What kind of direction?" Fallon asked.

"It's not clear yet, but they've added six new ranks to the top of the hierarchy. It's uncertain who is filling those ranks and what regions they will be responsible for. Right now, our orders are to bring in all potential peace breakers, and the numbers are managed from the top."

"This isn't negotiable for me."

"I understand. The only thing I ask is that you don't hurt anyone," Jackson said, breaking the connection. He disappeared from the commune immediately, but Fallon kept the invitation open. She stood. The desk disappeared, but she retained the uniform.

"Paul," Fallon said, and the Witness appeared. "I'm sure you overheard that."

"I did." Paul's roving eyes had nothing else to fix on except Fallon.

Fallon reached into the air, pulled out another poster-sized picture, and held it effortlessly above one hand. The picture was a two-dimensional representation of a large, wheeled, boxy transport.

Fallon studied the transport for a moment, and then she added a tiny image of herself to the picture for scale. She was half the height of one wheel. There were no windows on the transport, and they painted it a monotonous grey except for the black badging and Guardian symbolism of peace through protection.

If this is where the Guardians took Ailbe, Ever could not get inside. Ladders on the side were easily high enough that she would need to jump to catch the first rung. Those led to doors flush mounted on the body panels. The main entry and egress appeared to be a wide ramp on the back.

"This is where they took him. It's a Guardian FangVolken. Pretty much impenetrable. I don't suppose we could count on you to get us in?" Fallon asked Paul. "You could walk out with Ailbe."

"No. I observe and report. The children should be returned to Dill. The Guardians will not harm Ailbe."

"Somehow, I thought you would feel that way. That leaves us with two options. We can attempt to pry our way in. Lucas is close. I could use the *cultivers*. We outnumber them, but even their defensive weapons will be highly effective against *esclaves*."

"Can't we just sneak in?" Reign asked. "You could open the doors remotely and lock them in their rooms."

"Which brings us to our second option," Fallon said. "We can't sneak in. The Guardians have a good idea of what I can do, and they've always operated on the fringes of the law. All of their systems are air-gapped from the net."

"I could come in from the top," Riley suggested. "I'm sure Varmint could cut a hole through the roof."

"I don't think we need anything so dramatic," Fallon said. "They would know the minute you arrived. This is where they live and eat while on their peacekeeping expeditions. Because of its size, it's limited to specific roads, but its armor is thick enough to stop a herd of longhorns. Our best option is subterfuge."

"We trick them?" Reign asked. "How do we do that?"

"We already have. The captain warned Ever not to try to free Ailbe. Ever and I have very little presence on the net, and he didn't investigate far enough to figure out who we were. If we can get close enough to the systems operating the transport, I can lock them in their rooms, but I have to close the gap."

"How close do you have to be?" Riley asked.

"Inside the outer armor should be sufficient," Fallon said.

"How are you going to get them to take you in?" Ever asked, and Fallon looked at her curiously.

"I'm not," Fallon said. "I don't want to encourage the captain to investigate us further. You're going to get captured. Try not to fight too hard. Getting stunned is unpleasant."

# 45. BASIC TRAINING

"You are sending a child," Paul said emphatically. His eyes drilled into Fallon, but they didn't find what they sought from her mother, and Fallon deflected.

"That's perfectly fit for the job," Fallon said, closing the com. The snug shelter, with its long benches, trestle table, and miniature kitchenette, replaced the featureless room. "I can provide her implant instructions on how to override the system and close the internal doors while opening the external ones. Regardless of the outcome, we are leaving tonight."

While Paul brooded, Fallon's orders signaled them to pack. Over the past few days, Ever struggled to keep her things together and organized with little success. Her exosuit was hanging in the bathroom, her bag was in a bedroom, and the few items she brought were scattered around the house.

They took an hour to prepare, and around midafternoon, four *cultivers* arrived at the door. Their bright green exteriors gleamed still clean despite days of travel. The paint resisted dirt. The appearance of the *cultivers* was a reminder of home that made her long for Dill, but she worried for Ailbe. Wordlessly, the *cultivers* took away bags of fruit, vegetables, and a sundry of supplies Fallon purchased over the last few days in the village.

The produce stand closed at dusk, but they left before then. Ever sent a personal message of gratitude to Ching-Yin, and she expected everyone else did as well when they left. Fallon poured a glass of water from a bottle and placed both on the table. She said it was symbolic.

"How many people follow these old traditions?" Ever asked.

"I don't know. But you will find remnants of tradition in every culture. This is what the Free People still remember from the Catastrophe. It makes little sense, and it's not what I would have chosen. Some actions seem so deeply embedded in a people that no matter what happens, they carry it around and pass it down like it's written into their DNA."

"Maybe it is."

"Maybe. That's not something we need to worry about."

They headed north out of the village, walking down a trail surrounded by tall grass. Very few trees were this close to the village center, and the towering grass reached the top of Ever's head, so her visibility was limited. The ground they covered was beaten down by the feet of many *esclaves* over a long time. Fallon brought a few *cultivers*, but Lucas was nowhere to be seen.

Although she stayed cool in her exosuit, the air was a fetid soup. A long single-winged *planuer* dropped a mixture of chemicals and bacteria over the grasslands. She supposed this was to help the biological process break down the dead grass and to provide nutrients to new stalks of the sharp-bladed turf. The height of the grass had everyone but Fallon and Paul concerned.

Reign peered around with his glasses, and Riley was on high alert. Even the *cultivers* danced around extra, swiveling their bodies to get a better view.

"Are we close to the FangVolken?" she asked her mother. "I'm not sure why, but I feel like I'm being watched."

"No. We're going to stay pretty far away."

"It's the mountain lions," Riley said. "They like to hide in the tall grass."

"Now would be a good time to have Ailbe around," Reign said. Ailbe could find Peanut no matter where she was hiding, but she wondered why Reign thought he would know where the lions were.

After twists and turns and a few muddy holes filled with wet sand and crushed gravel, the trail closed into darkness under tall fronded trees, taller pole pines, and wide oaks that forced out the light below their thick canopies.

Reign and Riley peered at the boughs of the oak trees. In the darkness, his glasses mimicked the muted red lights of the *cultiver's* infrared cameras. The weight of the canopy, combined with the artificial darkness from the thick foliage, caused Ever to whisper.

"What are you looking for?" she asked, watching him study the treetops.

"Mountain lions climb the oaks and drop on top of you," Riley said.

"If they're big enough," Reign said.

"How big do they need to get to do that?" Ever asked, looking around at the oak boughs in the gloom.

"Most of these trees are still too small," he said, misunderstanding the question. "Even a newborn cub weighs over four hundred pounds."

"I meant the lions."

"Well," Reign considered. "I've heard the cubs are quite playful, so I guess it's possible they might try it, but I think at least six months to a year before their skills are adequately developed."

"There's nothing to be concerned about," Fallon told Ever. "We are on the wrong side of the canals for mountain lions."

"My father shot one close to here," Reign said.

"Sometimes an exile will cross, but it's unlikely. Their primary food source is on the plains. They have no interest in people. They were engineered to hate the taste of human blood and fear fire."

"Except for vengeance," Riley said. "I've seen their markings on the trees."

"How smart are they?" Ever asked.

"Nearly as intelligent as we are," Reign said. "Fallon's right. They were engineered for size, but they used human neurons to increase the feline brain's cognitive capacity."

"That's only a myth," Riley said.

"Maybe," Reign shrugged. "But I never eat the brain, just in case. That would be cannibalism."

"It's an animal created to keep the longhorns on the plain," Riley told Ever. "The herds travel with the rains on the plain, but it's another reason genetic engineering should never have been allowed."

The trail ended on a gravel road. The late afternoon sun broke into the canopy in places, transforming the dense jungle forest from night to day, but it took only a few seconds for Ever's eyes to adjust back to the light.

Fallon stopped and took her aside from the others, walking the hard-packed gravel out of sight. She took Ever's bag and sent her a message to commune directly. It was a strange request since they were standing together, but Ever accepted.

She stood in a room with Fallon identical to her mother's workroom in Dill. The walls reverberated softly with the music her mother listened to, bringing back memories of their time together in meditation. Before her mother could speak, she interrupted.

"You have a code for me to control the doors?" she asked.

"No. You don't need a code to control the doors. You could call that a useful metaphor for the others. You need training on how to use your implant on a system that doesn't operate on the net. As long as you can communicate, you will be recognized, and the doors will open or close on your command, just like the *esclaves*."

"That sounds complicated. Are you sure I can learn it in time?" She wanted to help Ailbe, but she didn't want to fail in the attempt. For better or worse, she would be with him, and that was important.

"It's actually very simple. You've seen the Free People build furniture, make pottery, sew, and weave. They use simple tools like hammers, saws, needles, and even their hands to create beautiful products. Simple tools can leverage effort into powerful results. Sometimes too powerful. The federation made weapons with tremendous potential and controlled them with a single button. That's something we wouldn't, couldn't do now."

"So how do I do it?" she asked. "I've felt nothing around locked doors before."

"The locked doors in our house are mechanical, with physical tumblers," Fallon said. "The doors in the FangVolken operate with computers. They are wired together with fiber optic connections. You understand how fiber optic connections work?"

"I've learned the basics in school. The signals are light pulses transmitted almost instantly."

"That's right," Fallon said. "You can't hack into a fiber optic cable unless you can reach the cable. You won't be able to reach those cables in the cell, and you won't have the tools to intercept and transmit light pulses. You need to reach a computer. Fortunately, they are all over the inside of the FangVolken. It's not exactly roomy in there. You need to be within five or six feet of the computer, closer if it's insulated from electromagnetic interference."

"What will they look like?" she asked Fallon.

"The door lock on your cell will be a computer, and so are switches that control the light and environment. Any of them will work to get you into the system, but the door lock will be faster."

"Then I could picture a lock in the Axis and ask it to open," Ever interrupted, and Fallon sighed.

"No, when you create an Axis, you are using resources from the net. You won't have access to the net. Their FangVolken is shielded. You understand how the net works? Wireless transmissions that operate at radio frequencies."

"Yes. But you said I won't have access to the net."

"The simple processors that operate doors and windows also operate at a frequency. Different from the net, but your implant will recognize them if you tell it to. If you are close enough, it can influence those frequencies and create your own access point into the system. Your implant already knows how to do this. The breadth of frequencies it can work with far exceed the usual implant, although the range is limited."

"How do I get it to make the connection?" Ever asked.

"You've practiced without knowing it. Close your eyes, listen to the music, and attune your implant to the frequency modulation. The implant is part of your eimai. Use your sense of hearing to correspond to its awareness of amplitude and wavelength."

She closed her eyes. At first, she found it difficult to stay communed with Fallon, but she focused on the music. In the physical world, she could feel a faint breeze, smell the deep green life of the forest, and even faint rustling in the background, threatening her connection.

With her eyes closed, the lack of visual input to her communion jeopardized the connection, but the music remained, waxing and waning with her attention until she focused on the sound.

It was repetitive, like waves crashing in the distance, but there was a corresponding depth to the music, and she pushed at her implant to connect to the depth until it synchronized, and she could feel another eimai beside her. Her implant-driven hearing understood the electromagnetic frequencies of other electronics, even other implants, and with a conscious thought, she tried to interpret that noise. A connection between them formed, and a wave of information stretched into an imponderable time until abruptly, the connection closed.

"You've got it figured out," Fallon said. "Once you feel the connection, you will be in the security system. Two more things."

Fallon fished a long kitchen knife out of her pack. She took Ever's clothes out of the bag, put the bare knife in there, and retrieved Ever's Taub machen.

"Just having this knife in your bag will be enough for them to hold you. Don't try to use it. You will still need to get their attention, and you can't let them push you out. The Taub machen will raise questions. I'll keep that for now. Have you ever punched anyone?"

Stunned, she shook her head no. Only peace breakers hurt people, and that was rare even in a city as large as Dill. Fallon sighed but continued.

"I thought you might have. Ailbe and Reign get annoying sometimes, and I thought you might fight back. I know they wouldn't say anything about it."

Fallon took Ever's hand, folded her fingers, and bent her thumb into a fist. She straightened Ever's wrist and put her fingers on Ever's knuckles.

"Strike with your knuckles and keep your wrist straight," Fallon said. "I'm afraid I neglected this part of your training, but it's not something I wanted noticed in Dill. If you get in close, bring your knee up into their groin."

Fallon demonstrated the strike and made her repeat the motions several times before remarking.

"They won't expect you to fight. When you do, they will take you and check your bag."

"Ailbe struggled," she said mutely.

"Most people will try to get away, but very few people fight," Fallon said. "The Strategos is afraid because there are psychopaths. People completely unaffected by the Peace who can kill without a qualm. Fortunately, they are an anomaly; most are smart enough to follow along and act like everyone else. The Guardians root out those who aren't so smart, but most people they take are just in the wrong place at the wrong time. They won't be expecting a fight. If you can hit one squarely on the nose, you may get by the first or the second before they catch you."

"I need them to capture me, and then I wait and open the doors?" Ever asked. In her mind, she visualized the struggle. She would sneak around the Guardians, and when they spotted her, she would scream and charge. After they dragged her into the cell, she would free Ailbe.

"Basically, and I didn't want to say this in front of Paul, but it would be better if they stunned you, so fight hard," Fallon said. "You don't want to be questioned, and you will recover from the stun faster than they expect. Ailbe may still be stunned. You don't need to open the main door. The holding cells are at the bottom level, and there are emergency exits. Suppress the security system, open your door, find Ailbe, and open the emergency exits. *Cultivers* will be waiting outside. You may need to drag him to the door."

"Okay, I'm ready," Ever said, shouldering her mostly empty school bag.

"If it helps," Fallon said seriously. "You are protecting them. There will be consequences if I have to go in there for Ailbe or you. Dire consequences."

# 46. HELLCAT

Ever walked on the gravel road alone. According to Fallon, she had several miles to walk before seeing the FangVolken. The boughs of the trees were neatly cut away from the road, and the sun setting in the western sky baked the red dirt and gravel, causing the heat to rise around her face. Her shadow stretched and distorted on the uneven surface. The road looked endless.

Fallon assured her she would see the FangVolken parked at the forest's edge. After about half an hour of walking, the trees and undergrowth thinned out, but she saw little until she stepped into an exposed meadow.

Hastily, she retreated behind the trees and studied the FangVolken in the clearing. Unlike the FangVolken in Fallon's image, the exterior of this one was beaten up. The paint was maintained and clean, but gouges in the armored exterior striped the emergency doors. Rungs were missing on the ladders, and the FangVolken had dents across the body large enough for her to stand in.

The sun had set, and it was dusk, but she was sure she'd been spotted. She expected an alarm or a rush of Guardians down the ramp to come for her, but there was no sign of activity.

Three Guardians strolled off a trail that most likely led to the village. They rounded the FangVolken, walking to the ramp. She realized they were going inside. *What would happen if the ramp went up before I tried to get in? Would I be locked out all night? What if the Guardians drove away while I banged futilely on the door?*

Necessity required action, but she didn't want a confrontation until the last possible moment. As the trio turned and climbed the ramp, she sprinted across the meadow to get behind them.

They heard her coming and turned around and waited on the ramp, foiling her attempt to get inside unnoticed. Her run slowed to an uncertain walk until she reached the base of the ramp, breathing hard.

"It's the child from the produce stand." A voice yelled from inside the FangVolken. The voice sounded unconcerned, and she was ashamed. All the blood in her body pumped into her face, leaving her legs weak and arms trembling. She gathered strength by remembering Ailbe.

"I'm getting Ailbe," she said, responding to the unseen voice.

Two of the Guardians stepped down the slope. They looked sadly at her, and their expressions almost dissolved her will to fight, even with Ailbe locked in the FangVolken. Let Fallon free Ailbe. She couldn't do it.

Ever recalled her mother's face for a moment, supplanting the pitying expressions. The penetrating eyes and unlined lips devoid of emotion, the statement that real psychopaths existed. Intellectual killers who could murder without a qualm and the warning if she failed, there would be consequences.

*I have to do this for the Guardians.* The realization gave her an unnatural calmness.

"I'm getting Ailbe," she said again, throwing herself at the closest Guardian. He was twice her size, but somehow, on the slope, their legs tangled. The Guardian fell, twisting to avoid landing on her, giving her the opportunity to straddle on top of his chest and strike at his face repeatedly.

Blood welled from the Guardian's nose at the blows before his hands caught her arms, but he seemed more angry than hurt. Another pair of arms grabbed her by the waist, lifting and hauling her into the air, but instinctively, she flung her elbows around, catching a Guardian on the side of her head. She dropped Ever roughly onto the ramp, and Ever landed off balance, falling into a roll.

She rebound from the ground at the base of the ramp with the quickness of youth and dashed into the FangVolken. More Guardians surrounded her, grabbing at her arms and legs as she threw herself to the floor. The longer she fought, the slower the Guardians seemed, and briefly, she thought she might maneuver around them and get to Ailbe.

"This one's a hellcat," a Guardian said.

She tried to use her size to slide between those ungainly legs but ended up getting kicked in the head, more on accident than on purpose. The impact stunned her momentarily, and she felt a rope drop around her neck. Hands pushed her to the ground.

She strained, expecting the crackle of energy to surge through her and the darkness of sleep. She once fell off a *cultiver* racing to beat Reign around a corner. She slammed into the side of a building and knocked herself out for several minutes, a cascade of sparks that faded to black. She tensed for the blackness.

A sharp electrical crackle and pinch vised the base of her neck. The energy channeled directly down into her bones and spread into her limbs in blue arcs.

The Guardians holding her stumbled away from her, shaking their hands. Her eyelids got heavy, and her vision narrowed and faded to darkness. Her arms and legs were numb and resisted command, but she was still awake and could hear.

"Did it touch the floor?" a Guardian asked.

"The floor should be grounded."

"Let's get her into a cell."

They lifted her, holding her limp body by her shoulders, and took her backpack away. Her head rocked, her chin falling and resting on her chest. Her eyes refused to open, and dull waves of numbness reverberated through her body. With an effort, a single Guardian picked her up, cradling her in his arms, and walked into the FangVolken. She lost track of the steps but felt the soft but firm padding as the Guardian repositioned her on a cot. She heard the door gently slide shut with a mechanical rasp and a clink of the lock engaging.

She lay on the cot motionless for what seemed like hours, mentally fading in and out. She tried to query her implant for the time, but there was no response. Each time she pulled herself out of the haze, the numbness subsided a bit more until she could move freely.

The cell was dark except for a small window in the door that glowed with dim light. The walls were a solid, flat grey, and she pulled herself into a sitting position. Sometime later, her implant responded, letting her know it was midnight.

Before she thought about it, she tried to activate her suit light, but it was gone along with her backpack. She stood on shaky legs, but after a few seconds, the feeling of strength returned. She was tall enough to look through the window in the door, but all she could see was another door across a narrow hallway. The hallway was empty and quiet. Beside the door was a panel, and she knew that her door had a similar panel.

*It's time to get this door open.* At first, exhilaration and expectation defeated her. She knew she needed to listen, really listen, but she couldn't keep her thoughts straight. What would happen when the door opened? She waited longer, listening and counting her breaths.

She wasn't sure when listening and counting changed her perception from outward to inward. The numbers didn't matter anymore. The sense of her surroundings was distant, but her implant felt close, and she harmonized the implant with the sound of her breathing.

The implant heard higher pitches, far beyond human hearing, but without a will to access those frequencies, it did nothing. Using the implant, she heard the strongest of them close by. She directed the implant to that frequency and was rewarded with an outpouring of information. The meditation broke as the network connected with her, but the connection remained solid. Cameras and sensors covered the inside of the FangVolken, and they returned a stream of information about motion, temperature, light, and humidity. Like an *esclave*, she could control this machine.

She found the Guardians, most of them in bunks on the upper level. The doors were closed, but she locked them to be on the safe side. There were two Guardians awake in a control room. They didn't seem to be paying attention, and she froze those controls and locked the door with a thought. Then she looked for Ailbe, going from camera to camera. There were people in most cells, and ultimately, after much internal debate, she decided not to free them into the night.

She found him in a nearby cell. She unlocked his cell and her own. Even though everyone appeared asleep or occupied, she ghosted down the hallway, each step a deliberate act of silence. Now that her link was established, she found she could move freely, like a cat jumping from branch to branch, her connection jumping from computer to computer.

She went into his cell and tried to wake him, but he didn't respond. She panicked momentarily, but she remembered what her mother said and listened to him breathe. She couldn't wake him, but otherwise, he seemed fine.

This started a complicated and embarrassing activity for the rescue. Ailbe was bigger and heavier than her. She pulled on an arm, but to get the rest of him off the bed, she had to brace herself against the wall under the cot and use her legs. She didn't want to roll him onto the floor. The raised cot was built into the wall and high enough off of the ground for serious damage.

She pulled him by both shoulders, and his head and body came off the bed, pining her underneath him on the cold floor. Again, she panicked, realizing she could not get free. After a combination of pushing and bracing herself against the narrow cell, she pried away from Ailbe, gasping from the effort.

She sweated profusely in her exosuit. Whatever cooling power the suit had must have discharged when the Guardians stunned her. She took both of Ailbe's arms and, gripping him by the wrists, dragged him out of the cell and down the narrow hallway to an emergency exit.

She stopped briefly to retrieve her backpack from a storage bin beside the hallway. Several backpacks, all superior to hers, lay in the bottom of the bin. Most were in the color-shifting camo of the Free People and nicer than her school backpack. She selected the best of the lot and raced to the exit. She commanded the doorway to unlock and pushed the heavy steel door open. The well-oiled hinges turned, and the door swung into the night while the hot and humid night air brought a new wave of sweat down her face.

The *sentinelles* in the sky brightened the meadow more than the recessed lighting in the dim hallway, but the trees were still a dark mass that rose from the west and north of the encampment. Red glowing eyes separated from that mass, clearing the meadow in seconds, and she immediately recognized the *cultivers*. The *esclaves* scaled the ladder on the FangVolken and drew out Ailbe's body.

"You've done well," a *cultiver* said in her mother's voice. Using one arm, the *cultiver* made a seat, and she gripped the *cultiver's* shoulders and sat down on the platform. Her body mostly obstructed the *esclaves* eyes, but the machine moved with agility, falling from the side of the FangVolken. At the same time, the legs flexed with the weight and sprang into a run beside the other *cultivers* carrying Ailbe's inert form.

The *cultivers* covered the distance she walked in a few minutes, then went further until they broke from the road into a game trail north. After half an hour, she wondered how far away the others were. The excitement and adrenaline that kept her engaged ran out abruptly, and she swayed in the arms of the *esclave*. Fallon must have noticed.

"Just a little farther," Fallon said. Her voice came out of the grill in the front of her chest.

They turned east and left the woods to a clearing of flattened grass. Lucas was there as well as his compliment of *cultivers*. The tents were set up around a low campfire on their multipurpose stove. There were few lights in the camp, mostly suit lights and the infrared lights of the *esclaves*.

Paul and his *Facere* stood on the outskirts of the camp, nearly as invisible as Reign and Riley, but his dark exosuit and *Facere* cut a shadow in the ambient light that she immediately recognized.

Fallon directed the *cultivers* holding Ailbe into a tent while Ever stepped away from her perch. She was unsteady but walked to a waiting chair by the fire. Reign put a bowl and spoon in her hands that smelled salty. The watery soup had vegetables with a few chunks of white meat, rice, and noodles.

Fallon came out of the tent and sealed the flap. She walked over to Ever and placed her hand on the back of her neck. She felt a raw, sore pinch on her neck and jerked, spilling some of her soup, and Fallon immediately moved her hand to her shoulder.

"You're okay, just dehydrated. Ailbe will be fine when he wakes up. Why don't you tell us how you got that bruise on your forehead?"

"I think by accident. I was trying to sneak between their legs, and I got kicked in the head."

"Go ahead and start from the beginning," Fallon said, and she nodded.

She started just after she found the FangVolken, going quickly over the fight but holding back her discussion with Fallon. Paul moved in closer to the conversation, and Reign gasped audibly when she described the blood coming out of the Guardian's nose.

"How many times did you hit him?" Reign asked.

"I'm not sure. It was several times, but I missed his face a few times too. He was really upset. When they zapped me, I almost blacked out."

"How did you stay awake?" Riley asked, puzzled.

"I don't know. They were holding me to the floor, and I got really tired. I wasn't awake, but I wasn't all the way asleep, either."

"That can happen sometimes if the stunner doesn't have full charge," Fallon said. "They stunned Ailbe."

Ever told the rest of the story, leaving out how she got stuck under Ailbe but describing how she locked and unlocked the doors.

"Did you unlock the doors before you left?"

"No. Why would I do that?"

"Good. I think the Guardians are in for a few long days. They won't be able to unlock those doors until someone notices they haven't responded and tries to contact them remotely. You didn't turn off the temperature or humidity regulator?"

"No," Ever stammered.

"They should be fine, then. They will probably be thirsty by the time a technician gets out here to override their security. I'm sure they'll have some bargaining to do with Galt. We're still in their territory."

# 47. FREED TO FOLLOW

Ailbe woke in the morning with a sore neck. He looked blankly at the exosuit hanging inside the familiar tent. He struggled to remember what happened yesterday. *I was held down. There was a rope around my neck. Was I captured?* But if so, he'd been released or maybe rescued. He wasn't sure what Fallon was capable of. Then he remembered the Guardians.

Even a vague memory of the Guardians was alarming, recalling memories of warnings from home. Before he left, he trained every school day, working with a team of scientists trying to reestablish tropical panthers to a natural habitat.

The panthers were unmodified from the original genetic stock. Much smaller than the big cats that roamed the northern forests and mountains, scientists in Dill hoped the panthers could fill an ecological niche and reduce the number of small prey animals.

Several small omnivorous animals survived and even diversified in the forest. Too small for mountain lions or night bears and dangerous in a colony. Colonies of varmints could chew down a meadow of new seedlings in a day or an unobservant person in a few minutes.

The panthers had the physical capabilities, but their instinctual approach to prey animals wouldn't work. Panthers could learn, and they taught their cubs. As part of the team, he worked on training young panthers on how to hunt a colony when you could be overwhelmed and outmatched in ferocity.

He frequently went on expeditions outside the bubble with the team. He took every precaution to make sure the University knew where he was because of the Guardians. The Guardians were a sect that manipulated governments, operated barely inside the precepts of the Union, and, above all else, threatened his freedom. Dill placed restrictions on the activities of the Guardians. Only a few at a time were allowed inside the bubble, and they were monitored.

He was outside of Dill, traveling between territories. Laws were sketched on a map but otherwise enforced solely through goodwill. In this lawless wilderness, he felt like the young panther. Nothing made sense.

He used a rinsing wipe to clean himself off. His hair was matted, but the wipe removed all traces of the previous day. He donned fresh clothing, picking out his favorite cat shirt and best pair of pants.

The exosuit went on next, and he was about to unseal the tent when the soft patter of rain started. Hastily, he pulled his cowl over his face and sealed the mask. Rain carried chemicals that could penetrate the skin. Where he and Ever grew up in Dill, the bubble would protect them from light rain, but on heavy rain days, everyone had to stay inside.

He emerged from the tent to find the camp in action. Everyone was fully suited. *Cultivers* rushed in, trampling the tall grass. Riley pushed a plant brick into his hands. Ailbe opened the foil around the ration and the unsealed the bottom of the mask carefully to get a bite. The cowl pushed the water away from his face so long as the rain was light, and he carefully cradled the ration under the hood away from the shower.

"What's happening?" he asked between bites that chipped shards off the ration.

"We're packing," Riley said. "Paul was gone this morning. As soon as Fallon found out, she loaded everything on the *esclaves*."

The equipment and supplies Fallon brought flattened the tall grass while the *cultivers* fitted on top of each other to form into six-legged hexapedes. Lucas spun around in the center of camp, his tracks cutting divots into the soft soil. Two *cultivers* mounted Lucas and froze into chairs, clamping on top of the *maitre de terrain*.

Ever and Reign emerged from the tents fully suited. They came over to Ailbe while the *cultivers*, their green bodies streaming rainwater, collapsed the tents.

"Mother doesn't like taking the tents down in the rain," Ever said, looking at Ailbe. "How are you feeling?"

"Still a little tingly, and my neck is sore. Next time, I think I'll go peacefully."

"Next time, fight harder. I had to go after you." She started to tell the story, but Reign interrupted her.

"Paul is back." He had a better view of the south side of camp where the Witness riding his *Facere* leapt through the tall brush. Rather than take a game trail, he must have traveled directly through the grass. The *Facere* folded into a bipedal position in a fluid motion, and Paul stepped away from his ride.

Ailbe wasn't sure about black-suited Paul. The Witness was usually a paragon of brevity, but his misfocused nature lent a childlike innocence. Since changing his uniform, Paul's brief focus seemed much more dangerous. *Or maybe I'm carrying emotions from yesterday, affecting my judgment.*

The *cultivers* collapsing the tents brought Ailbe his pack, neatly attaching it to the back of his exosuit, while he watched Fallon stalk across the camp to confront the Witness.

"Where have you been?" she asked. It was a question spoken as an accusation. Ailbe distinctly felt that she already knew the answer.

"I set the Guardians free. I couldn't leave their safety to the actions of a child, and Ever should not have to bear the responsibility of their confinement."

"Did they follow you?"

"I don't think so. Their transport is not disabled, but it's not made to travel through the forest."

Then, to Ailbe's surprise and even too quickly for the Witness to react, Fallon's hand flashed in a wide arc, slapping the Witness across the face.

"You've made it a race they can't win." She turned from Paul to address the group. "In half an hour, we'll have every Guardian south of Union City after us. They won't go into Union City territory. We're still hundreds of miles away, and we need to get there as soon as possible."

"If we stick to the forest, can we outrun them?" Riley asked.

"Using the roads, they could get ahead of us," Fallon said. "We can't take a direct route. We need to look like we are also heading east. Make them divide their efforts across forest roads."

"What if we take the old highways east?" Reign asked Fallon. "Those roads would slow them down."

"We still wouldn't be fast enough. Lucas is pretty quick on some of these roads, but he's farm equipment. They use wheeled FangVolken, and they have sensors and *esclaves* to pick the best route and choose a target. We are not the first to run from the Guardians. They are well prepared for a hunt."

"They've rounded up and relocated entire villages of the Free People if they thought they were too close to old-world technology," Riley said and shook her head. "They always bring overwhelming numbers, and they aren't afraid to destroy everything you own and pay restitution later."

As Riley finished, the group fell silent. In that silence, a distinct buzzing sound far in the distance circled closer, becoming louder. Ailbe looked over the tops of trees beyond the meadow. An *esclave* flew in a lazy arc. It cleared the meadow and made a sudden buzzbeeline south.

"They've spotted us for certain," Fallon said. "We'll have to stay ahead of them as best we can. If we are lucky, they won't have any more forces close to Union City. All we have to do is stay ahead of Captain Mateo by pushing east and north."

"If we are unlucky?" Reign asked Fallon.

"They beat us to the border."

"They don't seem to respect borders," Ailbe told Fallon.

"Union City is the birthplace of the Union, and the only city managed by the Union. If they don't respect that border, they could get sanctioned by the Union as a territory. Ornia might even be considered as a host to a terrorist organization breaking the Peace. They know what the cost is. I doubt you could compel them over the border. Ailbe, you are riding with me. We need to talk. Reign, get our hummers in the air. We need to know how far away they are."

Fallon turned back to the Witness, who stood quietly listening in.

"I suppose you're still coming with us," Fallon said. "Let me be perfectly clear. While you travel with me, there will be no side missions, regardless of your moral imperative."

Before Paul could answer, she turned, taking her pack from a *cultiver* and walking away while Ailbe scrambled to catch up.

# 48. THE SECUESTRADOR

Ailbe found riding on Lucas less pleasant than the hexapedes. The hexapedes were composed of many *cultivers* working together, pushing against the road and absorbing the shock of the impact. Lucas was a solid-framed *esclave*. His legs worked quickly and independently. His head swiveled from side to side, continuously scanning the terrain and making adjustments, but his body was not designed for high-speed travel, and he bounced and rocked in his seat.

Although Lucas worked tirelessly, Fallon was undoubtedly pushing the machine to the upward limits of speed. They skirted the forest's edge, an unmaintained landscape where fallen trees and dense brush continuously blocked their path. Lucas was high enough off the ground to pass over most of it, but branches scraped under his carapace.

Ailbe winced when they hit a large branch. The piercing sound of broken branches dragging against an all-metal shell hurt his ears, even through his cowl. Everything was wet, and leaves and plant debris coated the top of the Lucas and flew in his face.

He tried to push the leaves off his suit. The leaves stuck fast, glued with rainwater, and his gloves were too thick to pinch properly. He scraped away at the mask until it was clean enough for partial visibility.

The rain, in combination with the exosuit filter, cleared out most of the odor, leaving a fresh, if slightly acidic, scent in the air. He wondered if he was smelling ozone, but the overcast sky was bright under the mist and rain. Most downfalls were accompanied by lightning flashing across the upper atmosphere.

After Lucas tore another low-hanging branch, he had to say something.

"Isn't this slowing us down even more?" he asked Fallon.

"We have to find the road east. We are still in the range of their *esclave*, but there isn't much I can do about it."

He twisted in his chair and peered back into the sky. The mist obscured his vision, but he thought he could make out the dark spec of an *esclave*.

"You can't take control of it and send it back?" he asked Fallon. "Or maybe tell them we are going in the opposite direction?"

"The Guardians are very clever. They use few and stupid *esclaves*. Little more than drones, really. This one will have to report back to the FangVolken. If I time it right, I can change direction when the *esclave* returns. That will leave them in some doubt. That's why Reign is watching their *esclaves* with ours. Our hummers are connected to the net and have a much longer range. It's going to be close."

"If you need to leave me with them, I'll go," he said, considering her words. "I don't want anyone to get hurt. I'm pretty sure that my mothers and father wouldn't stop until I was free from the Guardians."

She turned to him, looking directly at him through her transparent mask. He knew Lucas controlled most of the *cultivers*, but he found it disconcerting to trust the machine without active direction.

"It's too late for that. Not that I ever considered that as an option. They might have written off a computer failure, but now that the Witness freed them, they know I'm involved. The Guardians have different factions under the Strategos Autokrator. Only the most determined Guardians join the Secuestrador. They operate out of FangVolken, usually in unwelcome territories, and they don't give up easily."

"Maybe we could convince them I'm not a threat to the Peace," he said.

"Why would they believe the lie?"

"Because I haven't hurt anyone," he said. Who did Fallon think he was? Sure, he had problems, but that didn't mean he would break the Peace.

"Last night, Ever went to the transport to rescue you, but she wasn't alone. I didn't want her to even think of the possibility, but mountain lions were circling the transport— more than one. Since you left Peanut behind, you've been calling out to them. Peanut was part of your eimai, and now she's missing."

He slumped, stunned worse than yesterday. The responsibility he felt fed back a replay of all his actions over the last few days, throwing his emotions into a tumult. There was only one lifeline out of the siege.

"No one was hurt," he said. It was both a question and a statement.

"Not yet, no," she said reassuringly. "The Free People know how to deal with lions, and it's not like you commanded them to attack. I'm not even sure if they would if you did. Cats are unreliable creatures."

"Why didn't you leave me with the Guardians?" he asked. "Or turn me over to the peacekeepers in Galt."

"You weren't attracting new friends in Galt," Fallon said. "Just like you didn't in Dill. Those cities are too big for your call to be heard. It's not really a problem unless we are in their domain, but what you're doing violates the Peace to the Guardians."

"Maybe I can block it or turn it off. The call comes from my implant, right?"

"I think you can with a conscious effort. But the cats are responding to you for a reason. I heard you had an affinity with the panther cubs. You've had more success than anyone else so far in training them."

"I think I had more patience, or maybe I practiced the training routine with them more frequently. Instinctively, they think that prey animals will respond with fear rather than aggression," he said. "But I can't talk with panthers with my implant. They aren't engineered."

"You didn't spend more time with the panthers. You spent considerably less. Until you started working with them, they didn't evaluate prey by the numbers. More often, they would complete a kill before taking to the trees, leaving them vulnerable for longer. Likely, the young panthers realized our training esclaves would not strike back lethally. Somehow, you conveyed a sense of danger to them. The panthers you worked with had a higher survival rate. How do you think you did that?"

Ailbe shook his head. The response was hardly visible in the deep cowl, but Fallon either saw the motion or the droplets that slid off in all directions.

"How much of the history of the implant did they teach you in school?" she asked.

"Well, I know the Western territories use an implant with biological and electronic components. The biological components form the connections to the nervous system while the electronic components do the processing."

"That's textbook, but it doesn't tell you the history. The technology we use in the Western territories is based on the Western Federation before the Peace and the Union."

"I knew that. I'm not sure why the Union didn't build new technology after the Peace."

"That would have been worse than building all new cities or all new hypertubes. Infrastructure and technology are one and the same. There was a time on this planet when life could survive without infrastructure, but if we attempted to start from scratch, everyone would die. The best approach was to build a bridge between the East and West. The Union is more than a political bridge. It's also the logical bridge between technologies. Beyond technology, city-states like Dill and Galt or even Ornia wouldn't be able to work together without the Union, and they are all Western territories."

"They could trade directly. Setup hypertubes and networks. We could exclude Ornia unless they called back the Guardians or made them agree to rules."

"Ornia can't survive without the Union. They would never think of trying, not just because of trade but also because only the Union can balance the ecology. To be fair, they desperately want to help."

"What does this have to do with my implant?"

"Everything," Fallon said. The smile touched her eyes behind her mask. "Before the Union, territories tried to balance the ecology on their own. Ultimately, the East and West came up with two completely different strategies. Each one created for their own benefit and worse, local politics unbalanced the systems with ridiculous rules."

"They must have noticed that it didn't work."

"That didn't stop them from trying to fix the problem themselves. In the West, they used the World Computer. The government rebuilt the World Computer as a source of truth. It wasn't designed to balance the ecology, but they tied every sensor they could think of to it. Not just sensors monitoring humans, but sensors for plants and animals that could read chemical responses, monitor and capture behavior, and learn the language of nature."

Fallon pointed to a tree on her left but further east in the direction they were heading. The gnarled oak tree grew out in all directions like a bush. Much smaller than the trees in the forest, they passed the boundary from the forest to grassland.

"What is that tree saying?" Fallon asked.

"I don't know," he said, puzzled.

"Let me know when you do. I've been curious what that must feel like. In any case, those Westerners used AI to make predictions. From the responses, AI built a new language and ultimately coded it back into the system. The implants we use today are based on that system, and a remnant of a remnant of that language lives inside our eimai."

"I'm not sure if it would talk in words," he said thoughtfully. "When you look at someone, you don't see just who they are. You feel their eimai."

"Maybe," Fallon said noncommittally, but he continued anyway. "Implants have existed and evolved for thousands of years. They've changed and so have the people using them."

"There's a depth to that feeling that's projected, and other emotions like stubbornness, uncertainty, and discomfort interact with the projection.

"The implant creates artificial synaptic chains that reach into the limbic system." She studied him, and he had the unpleasant sensation that more than his physical appearance was being observed, but her analysis seemed mechanical. "You may be sensitive enough to interpret the responses your implant is receiving more than just intellectually. You might even be more aware of the negative feedback than you are of the positive feedback."

"How does awareness give me control?" Ailbe asked her. "If I'm subconsciously calling out to the lions, how do I stop?"

"The conscious decision should be the start. Your implant is intelligent. It understands what you are thinking, and it's your voice it's magnifying."

"If it understands what I am thinking, can it change how I feel?" he asked, skirting around a forbidden realm in implant design. In Anima, his courses at Dill focused on implant technology. He knew far more than Ever and Reign about their operation, but Fallon did the impossible with *esclaves* as if the rules didn't apply.

Fallon shook her head visibly. "Not directly. They were created as a communication tool with specific safeguards. The Union controls the safeguards. The information the implant shows you can change how you feel, but the implant cannot do that directly. You can deactivate the implant by your own will, but once that's done, it might be difficult to find someone who can reactivate it."

"A last recourse?" he asked.

"No, and I don't want you to think about it that way. If you were to do something that foolish, I would reactivate it. That's something I can do."

"Why?" he asked, puzzled.

"I am not sure if you and those like you are an inevitable consequence, but you were born with a gift. Learn to use it, and you don't need to look outside to reinforce your eimai. You are adaptable. If you make a conscious effort to get what you want, you can change and be that person. Don't expect immediate results. The change will happen with each decision."

"And," Fallon said, her expression turning flinty. "You may need to call on the lions someday. There might be a time when you need violence to protect yourself or someone else. When that time comes, you need to consciously decide."

She turned away from him, her attention going far away, and they rode without speaking over the flat grasslands. The rain stopped, although the clouds overhead remained, blocking the sun. When they found a rough, rutted dirt road running east, she changed the configuration of the *esclaves* to increase speed.

"Their *esclave* is heading back," Reign sent the message, and he heard the words like a whisper in his ear.

"Bring in our hummers," Fallon said, sending the response.

Further down the road, Lucas braked, decelerating heavily, pushing Ailbe into the restraining arm. Lucas turned away from a road into the grasslands, and the rest of the *cultivers* followed behind him until he stopped. The *cultivers* dropped away from their positions as either legs or body parts and waited motionless until everyone disembarked. Fallon slipped off Lucas's back with the help of a *cultiver,* and he followed her lead.

"Why aren't we running?" Reign asked Fallon. "We were pulling ahead."

"It's not working." As Fallon spoke, the hexapedes broke down into individual *cultivers* except for the containers and ran into the tall grass. "They are too much faster than we are on the open roads. We have hundreds of miles to Union City territory, and there aren't any real obstacles between us and them."

The *cultivers* came back with armfuls of grass gathered from fields around them. They threw the grass on top of the containers.

"You can't expect this to fool them," Reign said. "The *esclaves* are equipped with more than just cameras."

"I'm counting on that," Fallon said. A *cultiver* brought Fallon a device from storage. Ailbe recognized it as a signal amplifier.

"That one might be broken," Reign said. "I tried to use that when we camped out in the old world, but I couldn't get it to work."

"That's because it's not a signal amplifier," she said, unconcerned. "It looks like one, but it's been reprogrammed as a repeater. This one will repeat our signal, mimicking the net activity of all of us and the *cultivers* until it runs out of power."

"How long will that last?" Riley asked, and Fallon handed the signal amplifier to a *cultiver.* She activated the device with a thought, and the *cultiver* ran away to the road. Once its feet touched gravel, it went into a three-legged gallop.

"The *cultiver* will run out of power before the signal amplifier. At that speed, probably less than a day."

Lucas brought his tracks down with a deep rumbling sound, digging them into the earth for traction. Ailbe and the others moved aside as Lucas angled his body in the dirt. Like a giant buzzbeetle, he pushed his forelegs and head into the soft earth, levering away the dirt with the blade-like extensions on his forelimbs.

The ground gave way, and Lucas formed a small hillock more quickly than Ailbe thought possible. The rooted grass and dirt blanked the *esclave* while *cultivers* filled in the gaps. Lifting his legs, he made room for chairs and the portable stove underneath his carapace. The *esclaves* rushed to set up camp in their new cave.

Ailbe and the others ducked under Lucas. Paul crouched to his knees while his *Facere* dropped to use all eight limbs as legs. Fallon and Ever walked around under Lucas freely.

The light in the cave grew dim as *cultivers* piled debris in front of the opening.

"When they are finished, I will spread out and deactivate the *cultivers*," Fallon said. "It's a risk, but we shouldn't have to wait long."

"How will you know if they took the bait?" Ailbe asked Fallon.

"I'll know. Don't access the net. The Guardians will look for the signal. They are very careful with net usage. It's a public system that will reveal their location as easily as ours. They will look for the signal, but they won't actually connect. That's one reason Guardians in the Secuestrador never have implants. That's also why our repeater will work to fool them."

# 49. BREAKING THE PEACE

Ailbe sat in the cave for what seemed like hours before Fallon confirmed the Guardians were following the *cultiver*. At intervals, she used a small plate she unfolded and thrust out of the cave through their debris shelter. A faint glow emerged from the cracks between her fingers when the plate activated in her hand.

Even more time passed, and he wasn't sure how much. He didn't query the net to find out, although he suspected that even if he tried, he would have failed. Fallon had a way to turn off the net, but for whatever reason, she cautioned everyone not to use it, regardless.

Ever spent the time playing simple games with Lucas. His head had a variety of sensors and flashing lights she equated to expressions. His motorized neck could extend bend and swivel even underneath his carapace, Ailbe realized Lucas was one of the few *esclaves* that could see his own butt.

Varmint, mounted on a shoulder strap affixed to Riley's

back, tried to tell them all a story of fighting the divine wind. The tale was supposedly from one of Riley's and Reign's ancestors, but they wouldn't have anything to do with it. Instead, Riley used the viewscreen to prepare A-roll.

Fallon alternated between the glassy-eyed look of someone on the net and giving the Witness instructions on what he was allowed and not allowed to do. For the most part, Paul ignored her. His eyes danced back and forth between his companions in the artificial light. His knees were tucked nearly to his chest as he sat on the *Facere*.

This left him and Reign. They distanced themselves as much as possible from the rest in their small cave to whisper together near the blanket of grass and debris that covered the opening. He hadn't heard the full story of his rescue, and Reign recalled the details of Ever's invasion. He sat in stunned silence when Reign described how she buffeted the Guardians.

"I think her gloves still have some blood on them," Reign told him.

"Fallon encouraged her?" he asked.

"Over Paul's objection. Fallon said Ever could open the doors, but she told me later that Fallon said she had to fight."

"To make it look as real as possible."

"I think it was real. Ever broke the Peace and not in an accidental way. She did it on purpose. I'm not sure if I could do that."

He nodded but remembered what Fallon had said about the mountain lions circling the transport. Lions hated people. They stayed far from fire, but even armed, a lion at a close distance had a size and weight advantage so extreme that people were like toys to them. If he knowingly called the big cats, he was guilty of breaking the Peace. *I will not call lions.* He hoped the implant understood his new mantra.

"Do you think Fallon is training us to break the Peace?" Ailbe asked. "She's hinted at it with me multiple times now that she would either break the Peace or expect me to do it."

Reign sat back on his heels thoughtfully. "She's definitely

hinted at it since the beginning, but she usually runs when she's confronted. We had to leave Dill because of the Third Eye and the Witness. She wouldn't return for my father, and we ran again because of the Third Eye. She says we are going after Ever's grandfather in Union City, but the Union doesn't get involved in territory disputes."

"We ran from Galt as soon as we saw the Third Eye," Ailbe said.

"And now we are being chased by the Guardians," Reign said, chuckling, "It's too bad the Guardians haven't run into the Third Eye. Those two groups don't get along."

"Except that Brother John called in the Guardians to Galt, remember," Ailbe said, considering the exchange. "I know Fallon doesn't like us to call him 'Brother' John, but that's his eimai."

"I'm not sure if I could fight, even if it was *John*," Reign said, emphatically removing the title. "Even if I knew he had my father. If we fight, then everyone fights. The principle of the Peace is the value of human life transcends our right to protect our own life. When we hold to that principle, we protect the Peace for everyone."

"Then we have to be clever," Ailbe said. "We can resist without breaking the Peace. We can still disable *esclaves* and equipment without hurting people. If we get to Union City, we'll be close to representatives from all territories. We can make our case there."

"We have lots of evidence. My sister has been reviewing footage from Varmint, and she found more details supporting their assault on the camion. We also have the captures from the nuclear power plant. Something was going on there."

"That should be more than enough to get the Union involved."

Reign sighed. "I'm more concerned about what you said."

"What do you mean?"

"That Fallon is training us. We need to resist her."

# 50. A PLAN FOR PEACE

The sky was growing dark by the time they left their artificial cave. Fallon manually reactivated the *cultivers*, a time-consuming process using a switch under a plate on the back of each *esclave*. Once activated, the *esclave* ran off to activate other *cultivers*, but *cultivers* were scattered around the campsite, hidden in the grass, and it took time to reach them all. Ever and the others helped by manually activating the *cultivers* closest to them. Everyone except Paul took part while he watched the sky.

As the sky darkened to evening, *sentinelles* brightened the night. They weren't moving in their usual arrangements, and she recognized Federation robots with their triangular patterns traveling across the horizon like a conveyor belt to the stars. At the end of that belt, lights danced and disappeared in a furious spectacle.

Suddenly feeling exposed, she looked for Ailbe, but he'd wandered off, perhaps still activating *cultivers*. Riley and Reign looked to be in deep conversation, leaving her with the

Witness. Since Ailbe came back from his brief confinement, he seemed different.

Reign and Ailbe spent a lot of time together, but she was always welcome. When she approached them in the cave, they went silent, and before they packed up camp, they were in a heated discussion about what the Peace meant.

There was no doubt in her mind this was her fault. She broke the Peace, and she would do it again to get Ailbe or Reign back. In retrospect, she felt almost nothing but excitement with each blow. Not empathy or even fear. *What's wrong with me?*

She couldn't help but gleefully imagine the captain's face when he got free and found out it was her. *Would he be disappointed? No, he would be angry.*

She laughed in the night air. The gentle breeze was clean but still fragrant and unpurified. She knew she shouldn't revel in the emotion, but she couldn't help but feel the condescending captain got what he deserved. He hurt her, and now he would get his due. They would escape, her mother would run circles around him until they made it to Union City, and she would laugh in his face at the border.

Paul studied her expressions. His eyes roamed as if mapping her face, a disconcerting trait she'd gotten used to. Experimentally, she reached to the ground, found two small stones, and tossed them to either side in front of the Witness.

Paul continued to look at her, and she sighed, disappointed.

"I wanted to know if your eyes could move independently in different directions," she said. Surprisingly, the Witness smiled one of his rare smiles. Each of his eyes darted in different directions, peering at the stones by his feet.

"Easily. But there is not much advantage in it. The *Facere* sees all the stones, and I see what the *Facere* sees."

Fallon formed the *cultivers* into hexapedes and kept Ailbe with her. Lucas was large enough to easily seat more, but Ever felt like she was intruding.

"Ride with me?" She asked the Witness, and Paul

nodded. She mounted the hexapede behind Lucas. Paul folded awkwardly in the short *cultiver* chair to sit beside her while his *Facere* rode in its usual place, clutched to the back of the *esclaves.*

Fallon spent no time heading down the road. Instead, she immediately cut north through the grasslands. The ground wasn't mountainous, but it was hilly. Even in the night, there was some *esclave* activity. The *apiculteurs* pulled all the tiny buzzbeetles and buzzbees into their bellies protectively at night, but a few *cultivers* were maintaining the fields. Some sections were cut back by *reduire* while others were left tall. *Balles* bundled the grass into giant wheels they left in the fields.

Most of the bundles sat organized, waiting, but some of them tilted precariously on the sides of hills or rolled into valleys. In the relative darkness, indistinct shapes of hexapedes many times the size of her ride dropped proboscis to the earth, sucking up the bundles into a large circular carapace. Inside, the *esclaves* shredded the grass into fine material and extruded the remains.

She looked on with wonder while Paul tried to explain.

"The *broyeur* separates the toxic elements from the plant matter and then returns the remains to fertilize the surface."

"Won't the rain bring in more chemicals," she asked, and Paul shrugged.

"Not all contaminants spread with rainwater. To protect life, we must capture and contain the threat wherever life is, large and small. The *broyeur* is small compared to the ocean *cueilleur*. They have fine filters to gather microplastics."

The breeze changed direction, blowing a cloud of dust across the path of their convoy before she could raise a mask. Involuntarily, she breathed in, gagged, and coughed out the finely shredded particles, eyes tearing up. She looked back to see that Reign and Riley were both caught off guard, but the Witness was unaffected.

"They don't seem to create an environment hospitable for life," she said. She couldn't use the exosuit sleeve to wipe her eyes, so she blinked furiously. The tears ran down her cheeks.

"The particulate is sprayed with bacteria to break down the remains," Paul said. "It's not toxic, but can irritate the lungs. Animals know to stay away from the *broyeur*."

"Unless they get caught in the cross breeze," she said, and Paul considered her words. The Witness seemed unusually distracted by something. While his eyes were always shifty, she watched him focus on the empty air several times in confusion.

"It's always possible to get caught in something greater than yourself," he said, and she thought Paul must be talking about himself. "And you might get crushed in the process. The footpads of the *broyeur* are twenty feet on a side. Each pad contains sensors, but *broyeur* does not stop moving for small animals."

"Why not?" she asked. A giant foot crushing a field mouse didn't sit well with her, even though mice were almost as notoriously mean-tempered as rabbits.

The Witness shrugged. "That would destabilize the *esclave*."

"So, for more life, we sacrifice life. That doesn't make sense."

"The positive impact of the effort is to restore nature, to improve life."

"Why don't we change nature, make a better one?" she asked.

The Witness grinned mirthlessly. "I am the result of changing nature, as many creatures now inhabiting this world. To protect the Peace, engineering is prohibited, but even if it was not, we have traveled across the land for weeks and covered only a tiny fraction of the world. Every *esclave* you have seen, every technology we have only addresses a sliver of the problem."

"You don't seem that different to me," she said. "You need your *Facere* to eat, but Riley uses artificial legs to walk. Reign uses cameras to see. Maybe you are stronger or faster, but you're still human."

The Witness seemed pained by her statement.

"The differences between us are extreme. You are only considering what makes me a Witness, but I was not born a Witness, although most of my people gravitate to the calling with time. Until we take up the mantle of our office, we remain separate. Before the Peace, we were *Homo Technologicus.* Our transformation was part of a service but also a promise of improvement. Now, we are called the *Malum.* Our freedom is compensation for our curse because the Union does not consider us human."

"But you are human." She exclaimed without considering Paul's words.

"No. Even if we share a semblance, the Peace recognizes the difference between us."

"But you follow the Peace," Ever said. "You freed the Guardians from the transport."

"The Union acts to restore nature for the people, not for nature," Paul said. "I protect the Peace for the Union because it protects my people." Paul grimaced. "When I returned to my order, I shared what I learned. About the Third Eye, Riley's story of Ajat Maata and later the sabotage in Galt. I did not tell our General about your grandfather. That is my concern and will be known in time."

"What did they say?" she asked.

"I will not tell you her words—the actions you can see for yourself. The General took my vestments of office and my ceremonial armor, and she gave me the armor of the Militia Dei —a relic of the past and a message that we will fight. But you cannot fight for peace. That is a contradiction."

"Do we really have to be peaceful to protect the Peace for others?" she asked, challenging the Witness. She understood he lived by a code, and she admired his persistence, but he would have left Ailbe with the Guardians. What about peace for Ailbe? What about justice?

"Without peace, there wouldn't be a world to protect,"

Paul said, pointing to the giant *broyeur*. "Destruction is easier than creation, and humans have become more powerful. Your thoughts can travel to any place instantly. You have tools that take metal from space and rearrange the ocean to create new territories."

"If we can sacrifice some life for more life, then maybe we can sacrifice some peace to have greater peace," she mused, searching for a middle ground.

The Witness seemed stunned but articulated. "The rationalist who created this world would agree with you. For them, there was always another reason for violence. You must look within yourself and understand if you believe in the Peace. The Peace was not part of the plan for this world. It was an unforeseen outcome that changed the genetic destiny of life."

The sincerity in his voice struck an emotional chord deep within her, resonating with words she buried under pride. She was in umbra, her free time spent in reeducation on ethics that mimicked Paul's message. She couldn't lie to herself and say she was unaffected.

"I'm not sure what I believe, but I know my mother believes in fighting for the Peace." Her mother was training her for a purpose, and Ever was determined to meet her expectations. So many times, she'd tried to be the person Fallon wanted her to be and this was the first time her mother had given her real responsibility, real decisions that mattered.

Paul's head turned, his eyes meeting her own.

"That woman is not your mother," he said. "I've tested both of your DNA. I've analyzed the familial response from your reactions. While you feel an instinctual closeness to Fallon, it's not reciprocated. I'm sorry. I wouldn't tell you this except that her influence on you is profoundly damaging."

Ever heard the words, and the finality of his statement left her dazed.

"Maybe you aren't human," she said, turning away from Paul.

# 51. FORDING

While Ever turned away from Paul as much as she could in the fixed chair, they approached a small tributary on her left. The river was sixty feet across with sandy banks. Shallow, fast-moving water rushed over a tumult of sharp rocks. Fallon turned the *esclaves* to plow through. The hexapede's feet sank into the riverbed, but the fast-running water wasn't deep enough to submerge the *cultivers*.

A dark spirit of grief sank behind her eyes. The weight of it was almost palpable. It wasn't tears, and it was spreading into her forehead. Her mother's voice dispelled the presence before it could spread.

"We're almost to the Swansong," Fallon said. "We'll stop for a break there."

The hexapedes climbed over a ridge and then into a deep gully. Deciduous trees of several types followed the ridgeline. Even in the dark, she could make out oak, maple, and catwood. *Araignee* hung in the oak trees, and the catwood trees were flowering, giving the air a pungent odor.

She'd watched a video of rivers in the southern territories that dwarfed the Swansong. She only remembered this river because Union City was built upstream, underneath the Falls and a curtain of crystal-like droplets that cleaned the air from impurities. Of all the territories, Union City was the most beautiful: A construction of the modern age where technologies of the West and East met to create a society in harmony with nature. It was the only city governed by the representatives of all territories working together. The Swansong was said to be the cleanest river in the Union, but that was far upstream. The river she saw was no cleaner than any other.

Fallon stopped the hexapedes and dismounted. Taking her queue, the rest of the group followed along. She went to Ailbe and fished a red apple she stored in his backpack. He seemed troubled, but when she inquired, he muttered enigmatically that he was 'working on controlling the voices' before he ambled away to talk to Reign and Riley. The two were increasingly distant to her, so she went over to stand by the waterline with her mother.

At the waterline, the river was a morass of thick mud and weeds. She surveyed the riverbed. The water was at least four or five feet below its peak. The rain kept the dirt moist. She took a step further, sank to her knee in the thick, oily mud, and tried to pull herself out. The Witness offered a hand, but she refused. She pulled at her leg, eventually losing her boot, but Ever's suit remained sealed around her foot.

A *cultiver* reached down and retrieved the boot in the mud using two hands. The boot followed with a sucking sound and a putrid stench.

A few feet past the waterline, she saw rocks and pieces of concrete in the river. The water rushed past the obstacles, sending out white waves, eddies, and whirls into the otherwise murky depths.

"A night crossing will be more dangerous," Paul said into the empty air.

"We need to put more distance between ourselves and the Guardians," Fallon said. "I wasn't planning to cross a river. The *cultivers* are water resistant, but they weren't designed to be submerged."

Idly Ever picked up a rock and threw it as far as she could. It fell well before the center of the river.

"We went through the last river okay," she told Fallon. "How deep is it?"

"The last river was little more than a stream. This could be twenty feet deep in the center and fast running water."

"We won't even get wet."

"It's not the depth. It's the speed of the water. Lucas sits pretty low. He will need to turn into the river and scuttle across the center. To keep the cargo containers above the water, we will have to break down two legs to increase the height."

Reign, Ailbe, and Riley joined them while Fallon laid out her plan. They had their suit lights on, and when the group stood together, the combined luminescence relieved the darkness but hid the details of the river that rushed behind them.

In the harsh light, Reign looked skeptical.

"The seals won't hold on the *cultivers*," Reign told Fallon. "Not the ones near the bottom."

"As long as we keep moving, they won't be near the bottom for long. Even if they fail, they should stay together."

"What about the pressure from the moving water?" he asked.

"We may lose a few. It's worth the risk. Our trick won't last for long. More than likely, Captain Mateo has already called for support. In a couple of days, this place will be clamoring with Guardians. Right now, this river separates us from the east coast. I prefer the coast to hiding in the forest if we can't make it to Union City. We have too many uninvited guests following us."

"Should we send up the hummers?" he asked, but Fallon shook her head.

"There's enough Federation technology moving around right now," she said, pointing upward toward the strange pattern of lights in the sky without looking. Let's not accidentally confuse anyone with even a weak signal."

They mounted the hexapedes, and Fallon transformed them from six legs to four taller legs, making them quadrupedes. The additional height, coupled with the loss of support, made the platforms unsteady.

Fallon went first, still riding Lucas with Ailbe, followed by Ever and Paul on the quadruped in the middle. Riley and Reign were on the last quadrupede, carrying the rear. Paul eschewed the seats this time and rode the *Facere* clutched to the container.

Ever's quadrupede tilted alarmingly as the first leg sank into the mud near the waterline. She clutched the arm of her *cultiver* chair and braced her feet in the pockets of the *esclave* cargo box to keep from sliding off. As each leg of the quadrupede moved into the surface of the dark water, she rocked violently in her chair.

Her light hid everything, but the immediate vicinity and she turned it off, sending the message to Ailbe and the others. Her eyes immediately adjusted to the dark, brightened only by *sentinelles* and a disc of moonlight.

As Lucas entered the river depths, he turned into the running water, dragging his belly in the current. He used each front leg like a spear, striking them into the bottom as the running water pushed him sideways and dragged him backward. His tracks spun on the rocks below the surface, sending vibrations into the water and air.

In short order, he was past the deepest point of the river, and Ever's quadrupede stumbled forward next, missing a step on a boulder below the surface but recovering. The quadrupede had no reason to turn into the river. Its long legs cut the water and carried the container just over the turbulence.

In the center of the river, the quadrupede stumbled again. The legs were at the limit of their height, and the container sagged alarmingly, one edge dipping into the current, spinning the *esclave* around until the quadrupede found purchase on the rocks. In moments, Ever and the Witness were on the other side in the shallows, beside Fallon and Ailbe.

Behind them, Reign and Riley crossed on their quadrupede, but it halted in the center of the river. The water rushing past the *cultivers* made a cacophony too loud for voices. Focusing on sending the verbal dialog at the same time, she queried her mother.

"Why aren't they moving?" she asked.

"The forward left leg is stuck under the water." Fallon included them all in the reply.

"Do I need to get out and push?" Reign asked with false levity.

"No," she said. "I'm attempting to shake it loose, but it's caught under a submerged boulder."

"Can you unclamp the stuck *cultivers*?" Ailbe asked Fallon.

"It's not responding. I think I'll take you up on your offer, Reign."

"I was just kidding. I really don't swim well."

"You don't need to swim. Just stand on the left of the platform and carefully jump up and down. I'll position your *cultiver* chair so you can hold on to it."

In the dark, Ever saw him slide out of his chair. The chair moved with him, turning back into a nicely padded and bipedal *cultiver* clamped to the platform with prehensile feet. Reign took the *cultiver*'s hands and carefully jumped on the edge of the container, where the leg met the body of the quadrupede.

"We're making progress. It's moving," Fallon said. Reign jumped hard, trying to shake the container.

"Not too hard," Ailbe cautioned him.

"I'm holding on to the *cultiver*," he replied.

"Just a little more," Fallon said.

As Reign jumped, the container tilted drastically, sending the corner into the water. He landed on his feet but slid off, landing partly in the current, still holding the *cultiver* with one hand. The other hand grabbed the *cultiver*'s wrist. The water pushed at the platform, but before the quadrupede flipped over, the rear right leg came up out of the water, balancing the quadrupede like a teeter-totter and shaking Reign completely off the platform into the river.

Ever watched helplessly as Fallon struggled to keep the quadrupede with Riley on it from being submerged. Paul and the *Facere* dove into the water. Paul broke free of the river a hundred feet downstream in seconds, powerful strokes carrying a coughing Reign.

Riley teetered on the quadrupede for only a moment before it steadied, and Fallon brought the stiff-legged *esclave* to shore. The bottom of the leg was missing, but the *Facere* held the remaining *cultivers*, extending the shorn-off leg to make up the missing height.

All the quadrupedes scrambled to the shore, where Fallon broke into the stores that she had in the cargo boxes. Turning on her suit light, she rummaged through supplies while *cultivers* threw themself out of her way. Everything she didn't need ended up tossed onto the ground until she emerged with a bottle.

Paul carried Reign across the rocks and jumped over the muddy shoreline, easily spanning the ten feet like he was hopping from one rock to the next.

"Thank you, but I think I can walk now," Reign said. His voice was a little wet, but he seemed otherwise fine, and Paul set him gently down.

Fallon pulled out a bottle from a container and motioned to Reign and Paul.

"Bring him over here," she said.

Reign walked on his own, but Paul was not far behind. "You need to drink this quickly."

"What will it do?" he asked Fallon.

"It will make you throw up. Right now. Drink it all." Fallon looked at Paul, who stepped forward, but Reign got the hint.

"I'll drink it," he said. Taking the bottle, he took a small drink. "It doesn't taste bad."

"Drink it all down. Right now."

Reign drank the rest of the bottle. Within seconds, he ran to the edge of the light, retching in the darkness. He heaved for a good ten minutes before returning.

"Now I feel like I'm dead," he told Fallon.

"Not yet," she said. She brought out eye drops, an inhaler, and a bottle with a transparent mask attached and made him breathe in the gas, causing him to cough. She wiped out his ears, mouth, and eyes before asking the direct question if the water got into the exosuit or into anything else.

"How bad is it?" Ailbe asked.

"The Swansong is one of the cleanest rivers," Fallon said, responding to Ailbe. "But it's still fatal if you drink the water. I'm pretty sure we got to him in time."

"Is all this really necessary?" Reign asked.

"You may feel a little queasy and probably tired for the next day, but if you feel anything else, tell me," Fallon said to Reign. "I wish we could wait and let you rest, but we need more distance. For now, I want you to use the inhaler every four hours."

"How many *cultivers* did we lose?" he asked Fallon. Reign's voice sounded rough.

"I think most of them will work once they've dried out. Eighteen of them are nonfunctional. The other *cultivers* can carry the load."

# 52. CROSS CAST

Fallon formed the *cultivers* into a train, linking the cargo boxes together and clamping them to a mounting point on Lucas. The boxes remained rigid while the flexible *cultiver* hitches flexed up and down and side to side.

After all the vomiting, Reign felt weak and nauseous. Even getting on to the platform looked insurmountable. Paul unceremoniously hoisted him on top, where Riley and Ailbe took his arms and got him to a chair.

The Witness turned to Fallon.

"I will take my *Facere* and scout ahead. North along the river?" Paul asked.

"A few miles ahead, you will find the remnants of a dock. There should be a road east and, after that, an intersection that turns north and winds around the river."

The Witness glanced at the densely packed *sentinelles* sailing in the night sky above them. Interrupting their dull cadence, a mass of triangular light patterns blinked on and off like a squadron of wedges—Federation robots in low orbit. Around the squadron, a growing number of *streiter* gathered.

"We are being watched tonight."

"That's nothing to be concerned about," Fallon said, following his gaze.

"Not from up there." Paul looked around in the darkness. "From right here."

Fallon frowned. In the darkness, lit only by exosuit lights, her face was a washed-out caricature.

"There's nothing we can do about that if we are."

Fallon mounted on Lucas, and Ever rode beside her, taking Ailbe's place. Paul mounted his *Facere* and galloped on the narrow trail beside the river leading north.

Reign wondered how Fallon would maneuver them on the tight trail until the *cultivers* picked them up, sloshing his stomach back and forth. The *esclaves* carried the load on their shoulders. With all the equipment, he was at least eight feet off the ground on a narrow platform. The roiling motion threw him left and right into the padded seat. Lucas was wider than the path, and his forearms acted like giant cudgels, knocking down the stunted, sickly trees.

He lost his glasses in the river, and he struggled to see as time passed. He rejected the composite image, and his perspective bounced from *cultiver* to *cultiver* while he labored to keep focus. Waves of fatigue crashed over him, and he found it difficult to keep his head upright. Hands pressed against him from both sides, and he realized Ailbe and Riley had moved closer, holding him in position.

"How are you feeling?" Ailbe asked, concerned.

"Tired." He stared at him with sightless eyes.

"Rest then," Riley said. "We will hold you."

He closed his eyes, but he couldn't sleep. *I'm more than tired.* He couldn't see, but the darkness spun around him. He tried to shut out the vertigo and sleep.

He went in and out of consciousness. Each time, he forgot where he was and was slower to remember what he was doing. He made queries to the net, asking for the time and place. The net returned answers, but they were meaningless to him.

In desperation and confusion, he pulled on the resources

from the net to cast his eimai. The closest smart *esclave* he could map his perceptions into was Lucas—a familiar target. He mapped every sensation until the perception of his body disappeared entirely and he delved as deeply into the cast as he could.

Lucas was the smartest *esclave* they had, but he was still an *esclave.* As consciousness sharpened, he realized that much of his eimai was on the net. As always, the sensation of two minds in one body was unusual. Ailbe sometimes spoke of a merger of minds, but Reign never felt a merger casting into an *esclave.*

His eimai was enormous compared with the *maitre,* and only the surface of his perceptions fit into the machine, but Lucas was undeniably present. Since categorization in Persona, he'd trained on *esclaves* of different magnitudes. The *ausbildung* he practiced with were less intelligent than Lucas, and oddly enough, Lucas thought of himself as him. He suspected Lucas' programming had been altered by his association with Ever and found thinking machines deeply disturbing. He brushed the emotion aside to focus on the sensations of his new body and understand without taking control.

The first sensation he felt was heat. The more he explored the sensation, the more depth the feeling had. Waves of fire burned inside him, releasing energy that electrified every system and burst out of him into the surrounding *cultivers.*

He realized he was feeling the fusion core. Carefully, he left, pushing away the sensation and focusing on hearing. He wasn't born blind, but after years of being blind, he prioritized hearing over sight.

"Why did the Guardian's FangVolken recognize me?" Ever asked. Reign realized he was listening to Fallon and Ever. He didn't want to listen in to a private conversation.

*How do I send a message as Lucas?* If he returned to his body, he would be lost again between unconsciousness and vertigo.

*Obviously, Fallon will realize I'm in Lucas.* But she had distractions of her own. He connected his vision to the cameras. Most of them were in the head, roving continuously around his body, but the motion was too extreme, so he put together a composite vision as if he was sitting on top of Lucas with Fallon and Ever.

Immediately, he realized he was not alone. Fallon was there, and so was Ever, but beside them sat a faceless man. Fallon did not seem to be aware of him. Out of a compartment in her suit, she pulled out a triangle. She unfolded it into a round plate and held it in her lap, pointing into the sky. Her hand glowed around the plate.

"All computers share the same common core logic." She seemed to search for something in the sky. "At least all computers in the West. Almost any technology here will recognize who you are."

"Who am I?" Ever asked.

"This isn't the time for an existential crisis," Fallon said, giving Ever a quick, sharp look before returning her gaze.

"That doesn't mean I can't have one." Ever's voice was more shrill than usual.

"You are part of a family that helps, and right now we are allied with the Union. Don't expect the Union to recognize us as allies," Fallon said. She sounded exasperated. "You are just like your grandfather and me."

"If we are helping, why didn't we stay in Galt?" Ever asked.

"There was no reason to. Holden has the situation well in hand. One thing you need to remember is to delegate. We can't afford to get caught in every squabble. There aren't that many of us."

"If we keep running, but we don't actually fix anything, when will it stop? When we're caught by John or the Guardians or Murdoch?"

Fallon sighed and refolded the plate, placing it into her exosuit.

"They aren't the problem. That's why we don't waste time trying to fix them. The Guardians are looking for people who break the Peace. Murdoch attracted a group of fawning malcontents and whiners who spend most of their time in self-flagellation. I already know what motivates them."

"If we aren't trying to stop them, why are we going to Union City?"

"There are two sources of power. One is a poor reflection of the other. The first is the public source of power, and that is in Union City. All territories have representation in the Union. That is where your grandfather is, or was the last I could contact him."

"He's missing?" Ever asked.

Reign hadn't met the old man in person in years, but Ever talked about him fondly. He'd imagined having a conversation with Jorge more than a few times. Whatever Jorge said to his father changed his life. He wasn't happy about that, and he belatedly realized it was happening again, but this time with Fallon.

"Missing, not dead," Fallon said mildly. "Almost nothing can kill the old man, at least completely, but if he's been captured, that could be a bigger problem."

"Why?" Ever asked tightly. "Another sacrifice for the cause?"

"Because of what he knows. What has you so wound up?"

"You almost killed Reign, and you don't even seem worried about it."

"I told you we got him out in time. There was nothing else we could do. The exosuit isn't made for submersion. Even his mask wouldn't have helped."

"If it wasn't for Paul, Reign would be dead."

"If Paul wasn't here, I would have taken a different route. I'm fully aware of what the Witness is capable of."

"If there is a safer route," she demanded, "why aren't we on it?"

"Safer but slower. This is already costing us. Look at the sky."

High in the sky, lights danced around each other as triangles and circles faced, bobbing and weaving. Reign's vision was much better than the naked eye. Lucas was equipped with a host of cameras and sensors.

Unlike simpler *esclaves*, Lucas had telescopic vision. To Reign, they were more than dancing lights. The lights were vessels, although they didn't seem to have a front or back as they swiveled in all directions. Apertures on all sides shot torrents of directed energy. Unseen explosions filled the thermosphere with particles.

"What's happening?" Ever asked Fallon.

"Something that shouldn't. The public powers are meeting the hidden powers."

"Why?" Ever asked, puzzled.

"To give me options. Unfortunately, it's not looking good for us. There's more than one or two FangVolken behind us. They must have been on their way since Galt to get here this fast. We've used up all our low-orbit resources for the time being."

"I have what I was looking for," the faceless man told Reign. Reign wasn't sure if the words were thoughts. They came to his senses like spoken words, but he was sure Fallon and Ever hadn't heard them.

"Who are you?" he asked. His voice came from a speaker on Lucas's head, and Fallon looked around sharply.

The faceless man studied him, although Reign wasn't sure how exactly. His head was completely smooth, with no eyes, ears, or mouth. He wore the same clothing. A long-sleeved shirt and tightly woven pants with a crisp edge. A short coat in a western style and black shoes. The clothing reminded him of school, and he realized the look might have come from old pictures of a time before the Peace. Abruptly, he felt a jolt travel into his senses.

"I can see the promise, but you lack training," he said. "That won't do. We don't coddle our children." The faceless man waved his hand into the air, and Reign felt himself follow the motion. He tried to return his eimai to Lucas, but he kept floating. Panicking, he tried to pull back into his own body when he realized he'd lost control, and all sensation of the net was gone.

He spun in circles, traveling into the sky faster and faster. Despite the speed and rotation, he felt nothing. No nausea, no sense of gravity or wind, or even smell or sound.

In seconds, he was twenty miles above the ground. Lucas, Fallon, and Ever were distant points on a geography that lost all detail. Then they were gone. After a hundred miles, he flew by the warring Union and Federation vessels. He accelerated faster, going deeper into space.

He passed the thermosphere, then the ionosphere, until in the blackness, all he could see was the sun reflecting off a small sliver that grew into a mountain of metal shaped like a helix in space surrounded by *esclaves*. There was one lead *esclave*, many times bigger than all the others behind that load, pushing it forward.

Out of the back of that *esclave*, a firestorm of ignited gases propelled the helix forward, leaving a trail of ions. His body, still spinning chaotically, fell into that inferno. The fires seared his skin, and the light blinded his vision. He stopped with a sudden implosion of emptiness, cold and dark, combined with a massive weight that left him struggling to breathe.

Reign realized he was the *esclave*. The cold and dark was the emptiness of space, and the mountain in front of him weighed on his chest. His first thought was to escape. When he cast his eimai, a part of him remained. By focusing on that part, he could tip the balance and move his eimai back into his body.

The act was as easy as breathing, but something was wrong. This *esclave* engulfed his eimai, swallowing will and consciousness under a rain of sensors that felt like electrical jabs across his body. He attempted to push past the pain and focus on his sense of self, but each attempt and failure left him shamed and afraid.

Reflexively, he snapped at each jolt and struggled to breathe under the pressure. His only sense of time was counting each breath until the weight lifted, until the cold turned numb, and the inputs faded. That was when he realized he was not alone.

"What are you doing here?" the voice asked. It was a deep voice that resonated, forming a boundary in the darkness.

*I don't know*, they thought. *I'm lost.*

"How did you get here?"

*I'm not sure*, they said. For some reason, they couldn't remember where they came from.

"Who are you?"

*I don't know.* The question seemed important.

"If you are lost, then you are going somewhere," the voice said, encouraging.

That was definitely a quandary. They struggled to remember where they wanted to go.

*Home. I want to go home.*

"What does home look like?"

*There's a bubble. And trees. But there's also the smell of rain after a thunderstorm. There are forest roads and cultivers working in fields. There is warmth and walls under the ground.*

"That sounds like a lot of places," a new voice said. This one was distinctly higher pitched.

"Maybe not," the resonate voice said. There was no sense of direction until the two spoke. One voice seemed to come from in front and the other behind.

"Are you one of the Free People?" the deep voice asked.

Free People. The words recalled many images.

"Do you have any family?" the higher-pitched voice asked.

They remembered their sister. Her name was Riley, and they had a father named Richard. Did they have another brother or sister? Reign wasn't sure, but with sudden recall, he remembered themself and pulled his eimai from dissolution.

"He's here now," the masculine voice said. He wasn't talking to the other voice. His message seemed to shout over a long distance. As Reign understood the voice, the eimai beside him solidified. His name was Tarrell, and he was commander of the Blue Dragon—a ship for retrieving processed ores from the asteroid belt.

"How far have we drifted?" the feminine voice asked. Reign resolved the voice into Suhyun—the primary thruster engineer of the Blue Dragon.

"Not far," Tarrell said. "But we've lost the load."

"Is it still on the right trajectory?" Suhyun asked Tarrell.

"No, the escort *esclaves* are changing its course."

"What did mission control say?" Suhyun asked.

"Nothing. They are looking for a way to regain control to the crew."

"We won't have a crew if we don't get life support back on."

"Duly noted," Tarrell said dryly. Reign felt an icy shiver and feedback from Terrell's scrutiny. "The inputs are completely jumbled. Let me see if I can straighten out life support."

"What's happening to me?" Reign asked.

"When you cast into the ship, the sensors mapped to all different parts of your nervous system," Suhyun said. "You were dying until we shut down the Blue Dragon. Tarrell is remapping life support so that you can activate it."

"Can you release me from the ship?" Reign asked.

"I tried several times," Tarrell said to Reign. "Completely disconnecting you from the cast might kill you. Somehow, you've become intertangled in all the ship's systems."

"It felt like I was being attacked."

"It might feel that way," Suhyun said. "The ship has a crew of twenty, but we had to disconnect all of them except Tarrell and me. The command channel and thruster control require manual input, but somehow you were cross-cast into all the other systems."

"I've never seen anything like it," Tarrell said. "I'm enabling life support. Let us know what you feel."

He concentrated on the Blue Dragon, still icy cold, but he felt information flowing into him instead of a shock of pain. He activated life support with a thought. Visual and auditory readings spilled out of the darkness. With more confidence, he reached out, sensing the accessibility net built into walls and panels.

Cameras added to his perceptions, and he found the crew in acceleration couches. Tarrell was fore and Suhyun aft, both isolated from the rest of the crew. He could feel the soft blowing air from the vents and smell chlorine and unfamiliar disinfectants. He couldn't see outside the ship, and there were no windows on the Blue Dragon.

"Good job," Suhyun said to Reign. "When you are wired in right, you're a natural."

"No offense," Tarrell said, "but I want you off my ship as soon as we figure out how."

"I didn't mean to come here. I was sent."

"How do you get sent into an *esclave*?" Tarrell asked.

Reign considered telling them the entire story. That he was on the run, eavesdropping from a farm *esclave*, when he saw a faceless man who tossed him into the sky. He didn't see how that would help much, so he simplified.

"I'm not sure," he said. "I cast into a *maitre de terrain*, then I ended up here."

"Is that possible?" Suhyun asked Tarrell.

"I don't see how," his replied, voice tinged with frustration. "The identifiers are hard encoded into the hardware. He was mapped into multiple systems, not just one."

Reign spoke, but Tarrell interrupted him.

"I believe you. It's obvious you aren't lying, and what you are saying is too preposterous to be a lie. We still need to get you off this ship. We've already missed our insertion target. The Union will complete the inquiry."

"I've tried to leave multiple times."

"That was before we turned off the Blue Dragon," Suhyun said gently. "Can you feel your body?"

Reign focused inwardly on his eimai searching for a part that remained with his body. He felt amorphous, hazy, and spread too thin. Each thought compounded the problem as the system expanded to accommodate what-if scenarios with endless feedback.

"This isn't a farm *esclave*," Tarrell said to Reign. "In one of these, you feel limitless, and there's nothing like the power of two hundred and fifty million kilonewtons of force. What you need to do is take a single sense. Try to imagine what your eyes are seeing now."

"Or what my ears are hearing." *What are my ears hearing?* The last thing he heard was Fallon and Ever. He listened for them. He listened for Riley and Ailbe.

# 53. THE STARFALL

The sound was a distant thrum of many padded feet, and the more Reign concentrated, the louder it became. *Cultivers walking.* He felt hands holding onto him. A slight feeling of nausea in the pit of his stomach made him want to return to the Blue Dragon, but he held on to the feeling, embracing the sickness until the ship faded and left his awareness.

"His eyes are open," Riley said.

His eyes were open, but he saw nothing. The hard platform gouged into his back, little relieved from the thick exosuit. His head rested on foam, but his arms draped on solid metal and fiberglass exteriors of cultivers folded into shape. He realized his chair had flattened itself. Riley was on his left, and Ailbe to his right. Reign constructed a visual and realized that Fallon knelt by his head.

"You went on quite a ride."

"If you are here," Reign said to Fallon. "Who's directing the *cultivers*?"

"I am," Ever said. Her voice came out of the speaker grill beside his head.

"Are you sure that's safe?" he asked Fallon.

"Lucas knows where he's going. Ever's more than capable of providing oversight."

Fallon trusted them more and more with the daily tasks of setting up camp, but this was the first time he had seen her turn over the *esclaves* to Ever unguided.

"Just keep your eyes on the road," he said weakly and sent the message to Ever.

"I haven't run into anything in a long time," she responded, and he could tell she was joking and focused by the clipped tone of her message.

"This is the second time tonight I nearly lost you," Fallon said. "When we rescue your father, I'm going to have some explaining to do."

"Are you sure we will get him back?" he asked Fallon.

"I am. But what I want to know is what happened. I followed you in the net. You bounced around *sentinelles* and went to a ship."

"The Blue Dragon. They had to turn off the ship because I was tangled in the system."

Fallon nodded. "You can blame that on me. It seemed like you were stuck. However you cast into the ship, both your senses and the ship's controls were routed into a feedback loop. The only thing I could do was tie you into the ship's systems, and I couldn't even add you to all of those. You probably saved them as much as they saved you."

"I thought you knew a trick for everything on the net," Ailbe said. "You knew how to get into the Guardian's FangVolken."

"The Guardians source most of their equipment from Western territories," Fallon said, "but the Union sources equipment from both the East and West. The Union AI platform is built on top, controlling both through intermediary certification."

"The faceless man? Is that the Union AI?" Reign said. "I saw him again. He sent me to the ship."

"No." Fallon shook her head. "The Union's AI doesn't appear

as a person. There are no other intelligences on the net other than the Union AI. There are programs on the net, some of them fairly complex, that think they are human. They appear faceless because they lost their eimai. They are powerless in the system and spend most of their time hiding from the Union."

"How did they get there?"

"Wealth and a desire for immortality," Fallon said. "Historically, the wealth disparity between the rich and poor was high enough for a select few to copy their minds into data centers capable of computation similar to the human mind. They mapped physical neurons in their brain to synthetic coded neurons. After the transfer, they would tweak the maps and add programming designed to mimic life. The results were always disastrous, and while we don't understand exactly what emergent activity creates an eimai, those programs did not have it. The hardware wasn't capable. The programs have memories and a directive to act alive. Was there anything else that happened to the ship? Someone is obscuring their eimai, but maybe if I can understand their motivations, I can figure out who they are."

"I think the ship was okay. We restored life support, and Tarrell, that was the name of their commander, said that after I left, they could restore the other systems. They did mention missing an insertion point," he added as an afterthought to Fallon.

"Did they say what cargo they had?"

"I think the cargo was the ore they were pushing," he said.

"A StarFall," Fallon said bleakly.

"I think they mentioned the *esclaves* were moving it away."

"I wanted to see one of those," Ever said. "We missed that in Dill."

"They aren't that exciting," Ailbe said. "We were too far away to see anything."

"It will be much more exciting and much more lethal if it hits land," Fallon said.

"You think they are using it as a weapon?" Reign asked Fallon. "Why would they do that? They could kill people."

"They will kill people. The StarFall is shaped for reentry and designed to go into the channel, but if it were to strike land, it could destroy an entire city. The rising debris cloud would set back environmental cleanup efforts by hundreds of years."

"Where would they use it?" Riley asked.

"I can think of at least a dozen targets. The closest Union target to us would be the Font, the military-industrial complex of the West. Bragg is not far away. It depends on their motives. It wouldn't be a victory, though. If anything, whoever unleashed a weapon of mass destruction would be vilified by humanity. They would need to pick a target worth the backlash."

"There must be someone we can tell," Ailbe said, but Fallon shook her head.

"They already know. I want to get to Union City as fast as possible, but with the Guardians behind us, we will head east and travel up the coast. The country is mountainous, and we should be able to find a pass that we can travel and leave them behind."

"Can't they just go around and meet us on the other side? There are plenty of old highways."

"They won't go into the mountains, but if they can catch us on this side, they won't need to," Fallon said.

"What if we dig underground and wait them out?" Riley said.

Fallon considered. "If we hide underground, we might come out surrounded. Right now, Captain Matteo's FangVolken is closest to us. He's fallen further behind. He overtook our decoy sooner than I expected and missed several opportunities to turn in our direction."

"Is he going to let us go?" Ailbe asked.

"Captains have more leeway in the field. I don't think he will break orders, but he might be falling behind to create a line we can't get past."

# 54. TACTICAL RETREAT

They rode all night into the next day. Fallon and Ever stayed mounted on Lucas. Reign, Ailbe, and Riley either sat or lay on the *cultiver* platform. On open ground, the *Facere* could travel much faster than the *cultivers*. Paul scouted ahead at first but then fell behind to look for signs of the FangVolken.

Fallon rested while Ever monitored Lucas. She took the job seriously even though she suspected that her mother gave her the task to keep her busy. The *cultivers* had to be rotated in range to Lucas for recharging. Each *cultiver* took only a few minutes to charge, but they had a few hundred *cultivers*. Most of the immersed *cultivers* started working in the early daylight hours, and the rest Fallon simply left behind on the side of the road.

To the east, the sky lightened. The *sentinelles* disappeared in the morning sun, and the mountains became visible as more than dark outlines. She could see the peaks, but there were no direct roads to whichever pass her mother wanted to take, or she was trying to confuse the Guardians. Whatever the case,

Fallon told Lucas the way, and he picked roads north and east at seeming random.

The roads Lucas picked were too small for the FangVolken and almost too rutted for the *cultivers* holding their cargo. The pits and sinkholes in the broken road shook him back and forth, and she looked at the twenty-foot embankment on either side of the road uneasily.

They left the grasslands in the early morning, making Ever feel exposed as they crested every hill. The only thing she could see was red dirt, gravel, and rocks, with the occasional pool of transparent water reflecting the overcast sky, and the ever-present dust that infected her nose. She refused the mask. A wind at her back carried them forward, and it also bore the faint scent of life.

She had a tough time judging distance. A silent query to the net told her they were over twenty miles from the nearest peak. A meaningless number as Lucas turned again, heading down the slope briefly to an open trail heading north. His body tilted precariously as his front legs leapt out to stabilize himself, the blades sinking like a knife in the dirt. Rocks and sand rolled down the embankment while his tracks shot dust and dirt into the sky. Riders in the back had long since sealed their masks, breathing through filters, but not her.

Ever coughed and spat dirt and sand but didn't let the cloud interrupt her concentration. In her mind, she held on to the Axis, and in that Axis, Lucas and all *cultivers* swarmed over the landscape. She even added Ailbe, Riley, and Reign, but every time she tried to add in her mother, the Axis wavered and blurred with double vision.

She added the Witness, the mountain peaks, and the river. The net provided a sense of scale when she added the landscape elements. No matter how hard she looked, she couldn't find the Guardians. She surmised they stayed off the net as much as possible and wondered if the Guardians were tracking them right now.

Paul approached quickly from the rear. The *Facere* made a

cloud of dust, but it was minuscule compared to Lucas and the rest of the *cultivers.* Behind the *cultivers* was a veritable arrow of dust clouds rising slowly in the sky, pointing out every turn.

Fallon woke at his arrival. His *Facere* caught up with Lucas at speed and matched his pace. Using six of its eight legs, the machine flexed and leapt to land on Lucas's back. The *Facere* neatly caught a mount point on the bigger *maitre de terrain* and contorted. Paul stepped off his ride as if they were not moving at all.

Whatever bumps or rocks they hit, he walked to Fallon and Ever with unnerving balance. She watched him do this several times, but she still wasn't sure how he did it. His legs in the exosuit didn't seem to flex, and his knees, like his elbows, were armored in dull black, a color that extended to the fabric of his suit. The armor absorbed the light, leaving the Witness in shadow. As they hit a large rock and Lucas skew-jawed, she wondered if Paul was shifting his weight before she felt the impact.

"How close are they?" Fallon asked him.

"Not far. They have three FangVolken. They have aerial *esclaves* to the south, west, and north of us."

"Do they have any other *esclaves*?"

"No, but they are deploying Bremstur, a small, tracked vehicle, from the FangVolken," Paul said. "Narrower and probably faster than the *maitre de terrain* on these roads."

"Yes, Bremstur are designed for narrow trails or unpaved roads. We won't be able to outrun them. We need to make it to the foothills in front of the mountains."

Paul nodded. "There is no reason for violence. I claim you all Comitium. We can travel directly to Union City."

After Paul's pronouncement, Fallon snorted derisively.

"I don't think they're going to stop for you, but if you want to negotiate, feel free. They won't let us go."

"Why can't we hold them back with the *cultivers*?" Ever asked. "There were twenty Guardians on the FangVolken. That's sixty people. We have three *cultivers* per person. We could hold them down."

"They have stunners," Fallon said. "The *cultivers* aren't insulated against shock. We could hold them back for a while, but the Guardians would easily defeat them. The *cultivers* can't hurt anyone. If the Guardians struggle hard enough, they will release them. Without the *cultivers*, we couldn't carry the food and water we need, although we could pile on top of Lucas as a last resort."

Fallon looked at the mountain. She stared for a long time and seemed to select a foothill at random. She pointed to a ridge on a steep cliff. "That's where we meet them." She turned to the Witness. "Are you going back?" she asked Paul.

"I must try. I may convince them to turn back."

"The Guardians and the Malum have never had a good relationship."

"We deny them access to our city, yes," Paul said, "but there is mutual respect between Witnesses and the Guardians."

Fallon shrugged, and Paul returned to his *Facere*. With a leap, the *Facere* launched itself and the Witness from Lucas. Landing on the rocks in a cloud of dust, the *Facere* adroitly twisted and turned, galloping to the Guardians.

"What if the Guardians try to stun Paul?" she asked, and Fallon just stared at her.

"Well, what if they do?" she asked again, and her mother shook her head.

"I doubt they will even try, but it won't be effective if they do. The Western Federation heavily altered the Malum for their own purposes. All their senses are acute. Their bodies are modular. They have strength and speed, but they have to live apart because they are born with little or no immune system. Many of the Malum refuse transition and die young."

"Paul dove into the river, and you did nothing for him."

"The Malum die unless they choose to become Witnesses," Fallon amended. "Paul is as much a machine as a man. His immune system has been replaced with nanomachines. The *Facere* manufactures the machines and filters his blood along with all kinds of cellular repairs and operations. He has proven to be particularly useful, however. I hope he gets back in time."

"How are we going to stop the Guardians?"

"I hope we don't have to. Release control of the *cultivers*. Until this is over, I want you to avoid directing the *cultivers*. Conflicting commands can slow them."

Ever felt uneasy about turning control of the *esclaves* over to her mother, but she did as instructed. Under Fallon's direction, they increased speed until the *cultivers* bounced off boulders. Lucas led the way, using his front legs like long blades. The rest of the *cultivers* were attached to him, and the force of their combined weight was transmitted through their steel frames like a battering ram.

She looked back to see Ailbe, Reign, and Riley clutching their seats, holding on to the padded bar as their platform twisted. She dropped the Axis she created for directing the *cultivers* and she could no longer feel how far away the Witness was. After about half an hour, they were halfway to the ridge, and she wondered if Paul would make it back in time.

Loose boulders at the top of the ridge sat poised over the edge of the cliff. With sickening certainty, she thought her mother would send those boulders down the cliffside against the Guardians. The cliff was easily fifty feet tall. Taller than Lucas could climb unaided.

When they reached the obstacle, the *cultivers* broke apart from their containers and made a ladder for Lucas, driving their hands and feet into the cliff face like pitons for purchase.

As Lucas mounted the *esclave* ladder, she tilted precariously in her seat and clutched at the restraint to avoid falling out. With every step, he drove his front legs into the sedimentary rock. Layers of stone crumbled as his middle and rear legs found purchase on the *cultivers*. Fiberglass shattered, and steel bent.

Fallon seemed unconcerned about damaging the *cultivers*. When they reached the top of the cliff, at least ten *esclaves* lay broken, either embedded into the wall or lying at the bottom.

Some mangled pieces still twitched and crawled on the jagged rocks and lifeless dirt.

They dismounted from Lucas, and Fallon positioned their stores hidden in the rocks behind them. The ridge swept back a hundred yards before dropping into a narrow valley before another slope.

Like most peaks, craters pockmarked this mountain. On the western face, the entire top was sheared away and collapsed into rubble. Boulders littered the incline up the sides. The rocks were much larger than Lucas. It would take hours to navigate, but she saw jagged caves between the boulders that would make good hiding places.

From this vantage, looking at the desolate plain, she saw a trail of dust heading their way. She recognized the Witness. Behind him, a larger cloud of dust crept through the canyons.

To the north, she saw a FangVolken, a distant gleam maybe ten miles away. No dust trails were coming from that rocky expanse. The FangVolken didn't appear to be moving and she expected the Guardians were either walking or riding Bremsturs. Her eyes sought motion, but in the shadow of the foothills, the Guardians blended into the background.

From this vantage, she scouted the horizon for other familiar features. She thought she could see a distant blue of the Swansong. It sparkled in the late afternoon light. *How far are we away from Union City?* The silent query pinpointed the city center a few hundred miles away. Fallon turned to Riley.

"If I may borrow Varmint for a moment?" Fallon asked Riley.

"Of course," Riley said. She had Varmint holstered to her back. She removed the long gun and, with two hands, handed it to Fallon, who took the weapon.

"Familiar hands," Varmint said.

"Be quiet and find me a target," Fallon said. Scanning the terrain with the weapon, she searched the dust cloud behind the Witness.

"High-value target acquired."

"Hello Captain Mateo," Fallon whispered, and to Ever's horror, her mother's fingers slid over to the trigger, but she stopped. "Do you think they would run if Mateo fell? An interesting proposition."

Her fingers hesitated a moment over the trigger as if she was trying to decide before she pulled back Varmint and handed the gun to Riley. "Paul will make it, but he will need help to get up this cliff." The *cultivers* standing behind Fallon sprang into action again. They dropped off the edge and clamped hands to feet to create a narrow ladder anchored by Lucas.

A dark speck shot into the air from the south, emerging from the rocks. A shrill mechanical shriek reverberated from a flying propeller *esclave* as it circled low, raising dust clouds of its own.

"We've been spotted," Reign said. "Should we launch our hummers?"

"No," Fallon said. "We have better options. We couldn't disable them all with our *esclaves*, and they aren't armed. They use the noise to identify, distract, and sometimes herd."

"It's effective," Ailbe said, covering his ears. More *esclaves* launched into the surrounding sky. Ever realized that each *esclave* launch marked the place of a FangVolken. The three closest to them released several *esclaves*, but some of the aerial alarms flew in from further away until the sky was full of spinning blades. They darted in from different sides. Ailbe tried to run and hide under the boulders, but Fallon grabbed his arm.

Paul arrived, dashing on his *Facere* around the rocks, and with a leap, the *Facere* caught the makeshift ladder, running up the vertical cliff face as easily as flat land and climbing to the top as a flying *esclave* darted in. The *Facere* sprung and grabbed the *esclave* from the air and spun around to land on top of the machine, breaking off the blades and tossing the remains down the mountain. The other flying *esclaves* backed off their aerial assault, immediately climbing to a safer distance.

Paul dismounted to join them, and Fallon looked at him speculatively.

Paul shrugged. "The sound was annoying."

# 55. THE CONFRONTATION

"It's something we are prepared to deal with," Fallon said. She signaled Riley, who raised Varmint. One by one, the propeller *esclaves* rained from the sky as streaks of energy shot from the weapon. The more intelligent ones tried to get to safety behind the mountain. "I take it from their advance, the Guardians didn't listen."

"They say you are wanted for inquiry by the Union."

"And they're here to collect me? How novel."

The *cultiver* ladder climbed the cliff face as the Guardians arrived. They rode short, tracked overland vehicles with a collapsible cage. Smaller than Lucas, but equipped with winches, each transport carried ten Guardians, and behind those three came three others.

Some of the Guardians shouldered short guns with hooks. They took aim at the cliff and fired. Explosive decompression launched the hooks up to the cliff, where they caught on boulders. Riley took aim and severed each of the fibrous lines. Ever recognized Captain Mateo. He wasn't wearing the hood on his suit, and judging by the insignia on the exosuits, he was meeting with the other captains to discuss options.

"Hello down there," Fallon called amicably. "You seem to be on the wrong side of the continent. Ornia is to the west. Keep following the sun, and eventually, you will get there."

Captain Mateo cupped his hands.

"Thanks for the directions. Maybe if you come down, we can go there together."

"No. I don't think I want to go to Ornia right now. I've heard there was a shakeup of the local politics. I try to avoid getting involved in politics. It's bad for business."

"I think you'll find treatment in Ornia much better than in Union City. They seem to think you are responsible for the destruction of *streiters* and sabotage of the Blue Dragon."

"All speculation. I have been testing *cultivers* in the badlands for weeks."

"You're welcome in Ornia may be strained since you have in your custody a known danger to the Peace. If you turn over Ailbe willingly, that would be a mark in your favor."

"That's not going to happen. I have the high ground."

"Eventually, we will get up there. I already have Guardians searching this side, for the best ascent. You can't cover the whole ridge."

"I think you misjudged your position, Captain. You should pull all the Guardian's back."

Fallon walked away from the edge of the cliff. All the *cultivers* came with her, Lucas's tracks spitting rocks as he reversed. Ever and the group followed until Fallon caught Ever by the shoulder and pressed her down into a squat, doing the same with Ailbe and Reign. As they huddled, she whispered to them.

"He's not trained in modern tactics," she said to them. "They've forgotten the consequences of the old stories." Fallon closed her eyes, and Ever searched her face expectantly but found nothing. Her mother was looking to the net.

"Ever," Fallon sent. The invitation was in her thoughts,

but unlike communion, this one couldn't be denied, and when it came into her focus, her perspective wavered with double vision until the solid rock of the cliff edge was gone, and she stood in a room with her mother.

Once again, Fallon wore the olive double-breasted suit tailored neatly to her waist. The straight-legged cut of her pants was unlike any smart fabric Ever had seen, and the medallions on her shoulder had strange symbols of a bird clutching lightning bolts. Fallon held out her hand, and Ever took it.

"I would have preferred an alternative, but they've backed us up against the mountain. There are *esclaves* on the net that you can't query unless you know their eimai. That's where we need to go."

Ever felt information pass to her, and she cast. The distance was greater than she had cast her eimai before. Each thought traveled back to her body slowly.

She couldn't see, hear, or feel, but the net carried a sense of depth as relays spawned a message feeding her a location. They arrived at an *esclave* like no other, holding a massive weight.

Instead of inhabiting the machine, she was at the surface, standing on the edge of a pool but denied entry. There was simply no space. She felt Fallon's eimai close.

"How do we get in?" she said to her mother. Experimentally, she pushed into the pool. The *esclave* was not intelligent and could not see but had an extraordinary sense of touch and feeling. She felt heat below and the vast weight pressing into the mantle.

"The Union has this *esclave*, but a cup can only hold so much water."

Fallon pushed into the pool, carrying Ever along with her. As her eimai filled the pool, the Union withdrew. She couldn't see into the program as it receded, but she felt the complexity of inputs and responses, a wellspring of governance that covered all possible interactions.

"The Union AI?" she asked.

"Even an intelligence as vast as the Union AI can't be everywhere at once. Once we consume the resources in this node, nothing will be left to resist my commands. Think of it as a locked room. The Union has a key, but the Federation built the lock. If we move everything out of the room, only what we bring will be left. This is as far as you go today."

Unexpectedly, her cast collapsed, severed from the source. A wave of nausea and dizziness spasmed through her body. Thoughts fled and she could only feel as she dry heaved onto the ground. The time it took to return to a squatting position felt interminable but could only have been a few seconds as Ailbe pulled her upright.

"Stay down and put on your mask," Fallon said. Following her own advice, Fallon sealed her suit and mask. Ever could tell that Fallon's eimai was mostly absent, but Fallon still managed control as if her body was no more than an appendage.

She tried to connect with her mother but caught only one word—Atlas. Then the ground started shaking. She couldn't stay squatted and fell to her hands and knees on the sharp rocks. They didn't puncture the exosuit but dug into her kneecaps as the ground rose and fell rhythmically.

She stared at the ground vibrating, but a sudden sense of motion threw her to the side. Reign landed on her, and they both scrambled back to their knees before the ground gave way, sucking her stomach into her chest. Just as suddenly, the ground shot back up, striking her. Her arm collapsed, and her head hit her elbow with enough force to stun her and send a tingle down her forearm, numbing her hand.

As quickly as it started, the vibration stopped. She looked around at their group. There was a cloud of dust in the air, and it settled slowly. Blood smeared the inside of Ailbe's mask, running freely from his nose, but he already unsealing the mask to staunch the flow. That was the worst of it, although she knew they were all thoroughly bruised. Only the Witness appeared unshaken. Even her mother had a long red welt across her forehead.

Fallon went to their stores, tucked away in a cargo box that wasn't much worse for wear. She brought back the first aid kit for Ailbe's nose. Reign and Riley helped him sit. The *cultivers* milled around aimlessly, but Ever realized they were undergoing a diagnostic process.

Fallon walked back to the cliff, careful to stay away from the edge, when Ever realized there was no longer a cliff but a ravine that cut straight into the earth, heading north and south as far as she could see. She was on a level with Captain Mateo, but hundreds of feet away. She crept closer to the edge to look down into the darkness.

"Stay away from the edge," Fallon said to Ever as she studied the Guardians across the ravine. The dust was settling, and they were in worse shape. Their transports overturned, and Guardians on all sides were trying to right a vehicle. Paul walked up beside Fallon.

"What do you see?" Fallon asked Paul.

"They are trying to lift the vehicle off a Guardian. They are too late."

Fallon grimaced. "Can you make out anything else?"

"They are investigating who fell in. They still aren't sure how many."

"Do you see Captain Mateo?"

"I do," Paul said, pointing. "He's kneeling in the center of the group."

"Captain Mateo!" Fallon called across the ravine.

Mateo looked and turned from his position beside the overturned Bremstur. He stood shakily and walked near the edge of the ravine. His exosuit was splattered with blood. Ever realized the blood was on the outside of his suit and not his own.

"Fallon," Mateo called. "Peace Breaker. I heard you escaped the Peace, a hard-used animal that bites the hand of the unwary. I didn't believe it. I would have let the child go, but now I will hunt both of you until you stand trial in Ornia."

Fallon nodded. Ever wasn't sure if Mateo could see the

expression in the fading light, but she projected her voice to the captain.

"This is a line you will not cross, Captain," she said, but she stopped mid-dialog. Fallon's face was shadowed behind the mountain, but in Ever's vision, her mother's face reflected incandescent light from the northwest.

Fallon squinted her eyes and put her hand to her forehead to block the unexpected light. Her mouth was a sad line.

Ever peered north into the luminescence. She couldn't look directly at the light and was forced to raise a hand. A dark burning trail followed the light from the atmosphere.

In just those few seconds, the light sent out a shock wave, scattering the clouds. The shockwave swept the Guardians off their feet before the wave crashed into Ever and tossed her onto the sharp rocks.

She sat up and struggled to rise. She realized the entire group lay flattened against the ground. The light was in pieces and wider, many times larger than the sun, and still in the sky. It was so far away it appeared to creep to the earth.

"Where is it landing?" she asked.

"Union City," Ailbe said, shocked.

All at once, the *cultivers* grabbed her and tossed her like a rag doll underneath Lucas who had positioned himself in a narrow gorge before the mountain. He struck four legs into the ground, burying them as far as he could. The others were tossed similarly, even Fallon and Paul.

"Seal your masks," Fallon said. "Put your hands over your heads."

The *cultivers* clamped onto Lucas, making a crude spherical dome over the *maitre de terrain*. There were many holes for the light to shine through until the sky went completely black. Then there was nothing. Silence.

"Are we going to survive this?" Ailbe asked.

"I don't know," Fallon said.

"Why don't we hear anything?" Reign asked Fallon.

"The explosion is too far away. It's traveling faster than the speed of sound."

A sudden high-pressure wave collapsed Ever's cowl to her face. She cried out as both her ears popped, and her lungs contracted painfully. She choked and gasped, rolling on the ground. The wave stripped off the *cultivers* on top of Lucas, then picked up the rest of the hemisphere of linked *esclaves* and tossed it. Lucas hunched down almost directly on top of them. Ever's limbs flailed, hitting Lucas as she struggled to draw in a breath.

Rocks careened through the gorge, and fragments of boulders fell all around her as they impacted Lucas' body with shattering force. Her ears ached, and every sound was muted and hollow.

After harrowing seconds, the force of the pressure wave dissipated, and her hearing returned. She squatted and looked at her friends. Ailbe, Reign, and Riley seemed to be severely affected. Their hands were still over their ears, and blood droplets gathered inside their masks.

"I think we made it through the worst part," Fallon said.

Lucas stood up further and moved aside. He was covered with dirt and scraped in places, and the paint was abraded from his carapace. His steel frame carried large indentations, and Fallon studied him. *Cultivers* appeared, some completely unscathed, but most were missing their arms or legs.

In the distance, she could see a red glow where Union City used to be. A dark cloud filled the sky, blocking the light. Even the *sentinelles* were invisible, and for once, she missed the watchful eyes. There was enough light to see that all the Guardians, along with their Bremsturs, were gone, swept into the trench without a trace.

"It's so dark," Ever said.

"The ash will settle in a day or two," Fallon said

"I'm alive," Ailbe said loudly and then sent. "I can't hear anything."

"Give yourself time to recover. Your hearing will be back to normal in a few hours."

"What's going to happen to the Union?" Reign asked.

"The Union is more than one city," Riley said. "It's part of the Peace."

"It's not the target I would have chosen," Fallon said. "It has almost no military value."

"What about the Union's AI?" Ever asked Fallon.

"That's a distributed system across all territories."

"We need to get in there and help," Ailbe said, and Reign nodded in agreement. "There might be survivors."

"Not in the city itself," Fallon said. "But the blast wave would have spread out in all directions. Most of the Free People shelter underground. That's a minor consolation. The plains to the west are flat but lightly populated. Fewer deaths."

"How can you talk about people's lives that way?" Ailbe asked.

"Prioritization. Right now, our lives are the highest priority. We need to see what we can salvage from our cargo. There's now a trench between us and civilization."

"Can't you close the ravine?" Reign asked, and Fallon shook her head.

"Breaking something is a lot easier than putting it back together again. Even if I could restore these pylons to the correct position, the StarFall damaged the mantle. I can't risk making another change. We are stuck on this side. We need to find drinkable water and food. Everyone should keep their suits sealed."

Fallon gathered the remaining *cultivers* with a thought and sent Ever, Riley, and Paul with an escort in all directions, looking for parts and supplies. The *cultivers* had limited intelligence. They recognized shapes, but they couldn't tell what was salvageable when an arm or a leg was broken into pieces. Fallon stayed at their new makeshift camp to organize and repair the *cultivers*. Ailbe and Reign stayed with her. They were beaten up badly.

Ever's escort led her to a container embedded into a cliff face several hundred feet up the mountain, away from their makeshift camp. Her exosuit light reflected on the layered stone wall. The deep red of the sedimentary rock looked like blood, and when she touched her glove to the stone, it came back wet.

She shivered but realized the moisture was water from the hermetically sealed pouches. None of the *cultivers* from the cargo box worked.

The second cargo box she found was in much better shape. One side of the box was wedged into the mountain, completely crushed, but the *cultivers* on the other side were still functional.

"You need to take apart the cargo box carefully," Fallon said from one of Ever's escorts. "We can't risk losing the water."

"I can do it," she said, creating an Axis. She didn't activate and move the *cultivers* that made up the box. Rather, she used her escort *cultivers* to clamp on to each disabled *esclave* that was part of the cargo box and carefully release a corner and then a side.

"Very good," Fallon said. "Have the *cultivers* bring everything you can get before you try to free the *esclaves* from the rock."

It was a tedious effort. Ever hadn't eaten in a while. She was hungry and dehydrated, but most of the bruising from earlier had faded into only moderate discomfort. She moved the sealed boxes and two tents from the damaged storage container before freeing more *cultivers* and slogging back to camp.

# 56. THE PEACE

Fallon raised two shelters and used the canvas from the remains of the third tent to make a bridge between the two. That gave them enough room to remove and clean the exosuits with some privacy. Ever gingerly took off her exosuit. Her hair caught between the suit and cowl. She was startled at how much it had grown since she left Dill not long ago.

She looked at her arms and legs. Faint yellow bruises covered her entire body. The clothing she wore under the suit smelled of cold sweat in the temperature-controlled tent. She recovered clothes and cleaning supplies but lost their camp stove and bedding. All the perishable food was destroyed from heat exposure.

While she changed, she gnawed on a plant brick. A fate she once considered worse than death seemed like a cruel irony to the smoldering ruin of Union City. She didn't know anyone in Union City other than her grandfather, but his loss was coupled with a look on her mother's face that said so much more.

Ever cried silently, but her mother's face tightened backward at the edges of her lips in an expression she had never seen before. Fallon's unshed tears had gathered in the back of her throat, making her mother's voice sound harsh and even more dangerous.

Ever saw and heard failure, but behind a veneer of failure, she felt her mother's rage, and that frightened her enough to dry her eyes.

When Ever finished cleaning her suit. She hung it in the corner and used the corridor between tents to cross over to the other tent where they were all sleeping. Following her departure, Reign started for their makeshift changing room and stumbled. Catching himself, he pushed on determinately with outstretched hands until Riley jumped up to help him. Without *cultivers*, he was effectively blind, and judging from his listless expression, he was too tired to navigate carefully.

Ailbe passed out completely on the floor, and Fallon used a rolled-up shirt as a pillow to prop his head up. An ugly red bruise ran across his cheek to the base of his nose. Both of his eyes were swollen.

"Paul?" Ever asked Fallon.

"He's communicating with his General. Don't worry, he'll be fine outside, but by morning, we'll be covered in ash."

Ever lay on the tent's floor. Fallon carefully swept away the sharp rocks before unfolding the tent. That left uneven, bare stone, but after spending a day and a night resting on a platform of *cultivers*, stretching out felt wonderful but also wrong.

She felt guilty, but she wasn't sure where the emotion was coming from. The last two days, she'd worried about being caught by the Guardians, and now they were all dead, which made it worse. Since her encounter with the Guardians, she wondered what she was becoming. She lost her grandfather, one-half of the people who knew what that was and she always thought his opinion was more optimistic than her mother's.

When Reign and Riley returned, Fallon dimmed the light.

"Is it wrong I feel better the Guardians are dead?" she asked in the dark.

"No," Fallon said. "What you feel can never be wrong. How

you act on those feelings, what you do with those feelings, that could be wrong."

"The killing has to stop," Reign said tiredly. "We have to stop it. What is the peace if we fight for it?"

Fallon responded to Reign from across the tent.

"The Peace is idealized by the Union, but no one knows exactly when the Peace started. Everyone was fighting either through conscription or fighting to stay alive. It didn't happen all at once, but people threw down their weapons and stopped."

"Did that stop the war?" Ever asked.

"No, those people were killed or lost everything. Sometimes, they gave all their food to others who needed it and then died."

"Then what stopped the war?" Reign asked.

"More people threw down their weapons and refused to fight. Eventually, entire armies defected. At first, we thought it was biological warfare. We identified genetic changes, but they originated decades earlier. Whatever caused it was indiscriminate and infected most mammals and even a few birds. The changes aren't hereditary, but the Peace is pervasive. Shortly after the fighting ended, the Union was formed, and everyone agreed the Peace must be protected. Some people feel the Peace more strongly than others, but sometime after their second decade, the Peace will not be denied."

"If peace is so pervasive, what happened?"

Ever lay quietly, waiting for a response, but Fallon was slow to answer.

"Peace has been tried many times, and it falters and dies when the spirit of the people fails. Peace through strength. Strength is not eternal, and even great empires hemorrhage. Without a shared vision, they feed on the people. The end is dissolution from the contradiction. The founding of the Union was something different. Not a philosophical, but a physiological change. It's peace we can share in, but it's incapable of protecting itself."

Ever woke in the cold, damp air of the tent shivering. The thermostat must have failed and the air conditioning ran all night. The ground was cool, and the tent was dark. Someone was approaching at a run. Many legs pounded the stones, sending rocks flying. She tried to query the net and received a strange response, indiscernible.

"Fallon," Paul said from outside the tent. Ever almost didn't recognize his voice.

Her mother woke instantly, sat straight, and noticed she was awake. Fallon called the others, but they didn't move quickly enough for her.

"Wake them, Ever," Fallon said as she crossed the narrow corridor, grabbing her exosuit. "Suit up."

Fallon unsealed the opening, spilling light out onto the floor. Ailbe and Reign were both moving slowly, but Riley followed Fallon's example before Ever could even get up and get to her exosuit.

She suited while Ailbe wiped the drool off his beaten-up face. Last night's red and purple bruising looked black and yellow this morning. Reign looked slightly better, and he moved confidently in the tent. There were additional lines on his face that didn't seem to go away. She thought they first appeared when she brought back Ailbe from the Guardian's FangVolken.

"Hurry," she urged Ailbe as she unsealed the door to the tent. She wasn't far behind Riley, but Paul and Fallon were already talking in inaudible whispers. Ash sifted down from the sky. The dark powder coated the ground, the tents, and the *cultivers* in filth. Paul and his Facere both seemed unaffected. The black armor hid the streaks that already lined Fallon's exosuit.

"Maybe an hour away," Paul said to Fallon, pointing to a pass between peaks on the north side. "Most of them are coming through that pass, but they are dividing into smaller patrols. The descent is narrow, blocked by the blast."

"If we avoid the pass and go over the top?"

"Then we will be surrounded," the Witness judged. "If it's possible to get Lucas up that cliff, it will take more than an hour."

"Then we go through."

"Where are we going?" Ailbe asked, joining Paul and Fallon as Reign zipped the tent flap behind them.

"Free People are coming down the mountain," Paul said. "Several hundred. They are well equipped."

"That's great," Ailbe said. "Maybe they can help us cross the ravine."

Fallon shook her head. "I'm afraid not. They were camped out on the other side."

"The Free People don't usually cross the mountains," Reign said.

"I don't think these Free People are free," Fallon said. "Paul saw collars over their exosuits."

"It would be quite a coincidence for them to be on the other side of our mountain," Riley said.

"And they are heading right for us," Fallon said. "That's not coincidence. That's a plan. Murdoch's plan. He wouldn't attack unless he had all the pieces put together."

"Should we launch the hummers?" Reign asked Fallon, and she shook her head.

"They were both damaged. We have almost fifty working *cultivers* and about the same number damaged, but mobile. I'll send the damaged ones to the southern pass around the peak. They will only slow us down, and it might encourage them to divide their forces further."

"I can't reach the net," Ailbe said, and Reign nodded.

"I couldn't send you a message," Paul said. "I came to your tent as soon as I could."

Fallon paused for a moment. Her eyes took on the glassy-eyed stare of someone making a query. She frowned slightly.

"He's deployed a signal blocker. It's consuming the band with garbage data."

"Can you control the *cultivers*?" Reign asked, and Fallon shrugged.

"I'm not so easily blocked, and as long as we stay near Lucas, he can retransmit any commands I send to them."

Fallon abandoned the tents in favor of speed. They stuffed their backpacks with rations and water. *Cultivers* mounted Lucas, creating a single platform with as much food and water as they could carry. Everything they couldn't carry was piled under canvas and held with rocks.

Fallon sat at the front. Ever went to sit beside her, but Fallon motioned her to the back.

"I want you and Varmint with me in the front," Fallon told Riley.

"I'm not going to shoot anyone."

"I don't expect you to. There might be other targets."

Ever and Ailbe took the center chairs while Reign took the back seat, with Paul standing beside his chair. The *Facere* disappeared up the mountain as soon as Paul mounted the *maitre de terrain*. Ever watched it go and turned in her chair to Paul with a question on her lips, but he spoke before she could verbalize the thought.

"The *Facere* cannot be disconnected from its master."

"What if they try to shoot it down?" Ailbe asked.

"I don't think we can count on being that lucky," Fallon said. "The *Facere* is more maneuverable and faster than the *cultivers*, but it won't respond with force unless it's attacked."

# 57. MURDOCH

Lucas raised his carapace, and Ever looked back at the tents. The *cultivers* had made hasty work tearing through their provisions under Fallon's direction. With the exception of food and water, their belongings were scattered across the camp, most of them lying broken in thickening ash. Even with the filter, she tasted ash in her mouth, and each breath she drew through her noise was an acrid tingle.

Lucas placed his legs carefully, keeping the platform as flat as possible over the uneven terrain while the *cultivers* followed behind. The ascent was circuitous. If there was a road, boulders and ash covered any sign of it. She knew they were heading for a narrow pass to the north, between the peaks, but Fallon directed them into canyons and over switchbacks.

Over one particular switchback, Lucas came up against a boulder. His carapace was too wide to fit between the boulder and the mountainside. Fallon edged him closer and closer to the rock until he made an impact, jarring the riders.

He forced the boulder over, leaving a long blemish across his already battered body. *He could have just pushed it away.* She sent a message to her mother.

Fallon turned and whispered to the entire group.

"There's a slight chance that most, maybe all, of Murdoch's people will go right by us," Fallon said, "but we need to stay quiet. The ash is muting the sound and making it hard to see. They've cut off the net, but that also hides where we are."

"I feel like we are being followed," Ailbe said.

"How?" Fallon asked, surprised.

"I feel something feral, feline."

"On this side of the ravine?"

"Somewhere in front of us. But a long ways away."

"That could be useful. Try to bring them here."

"I'm not sure if I can do that. I'm not even sure if I should do that."

"Do it," Fallon said with finality, then spoke to Paul. "Does the *Facere* see any movement?"

"They are still deployed along the pass." He hesitated, glancing briefly at Reign.

"Let's have it," Fallon said.

"The *Facere* sees a person who matches Richard's description. He's much larger than the others, and he's also armed."

"With a gun?"

"Many of the Free People carry guns," Riley said.

"Of those that are approaching, only he carries a plasma rifle," Paul said. "It's much like your own. The rest have stunners mounted on catchpoles and long-handled hooks."

"Is there anyone close to Richard who looks unusual?" Fallon asked, and Paul took on the glassy-eyed look that was so familiar.

"Yes, a person in a red exosuit is not far from him. The exosuit is marked with the sigil of the Third Eye."

"That's sure to be Murdoch. He hasn't armed all his people. That could be a limitation. Maybe he hasn't found a way to break the Peace entirely. I expected him to keep Richard close. I would."

"What if we turn back south?" Ailbe asked Fallon. "Find a new road."

"Likely, we will end up surrounded in the mountains. No, I think I like it better this way. He won't be expecting us to confront him. The best plans can be taken apart by moving a single piece. I know."

"All we are doing is meeting violence with violence," Reign said.

"This is our chance to get your father back," Fallon said but turned to Paul. "If he's armed Richard, I assume they have taken the high ground. But not too high, I would expect."

"Yes. How did you know?"

"He will want to talk. He always wants to talk. That will let us get in close."

Fallon cast to Lucas and set him on a path forward. For the next half hour, Lucas continued to a higher elevation, with their small group of *cultiver esclaves* following behind. There were no more switchbacks, just loose rocks, sand, and more ash until they entered a crevice that might have been part of a collapsed tunnel system.

They followed the crevasse north until they reached a wide road cut out of the mountainside but strewn with rubble. Ever caught glimpses of Free People running on the ridges above them. They wore the same color-shifting camo exosuits that Free People wore, and they were almost invisible in the background except for the long, hooked poles they carried.

Lucas made careful steps inside the pass, going much slower than normal. She wasn't sure if Fallon was trying to get Murdoch to underestimate their speed or if she was gauging the reaction of the Free People.

A laser target finder showed up, and a bright red dot traveled from person to person on Lucas.

"We're being targeted," Ever choked as the point of light settled on her exosuit over her heart.

"We have been for a while," Riley said. "My father is accurate from much farther away."

"Please," Varmint said. "That was all me."

"Hush," Riley said, gripping the gun.

As they slowly marched forward, more of the Free People congregated around them. They kept their distance and didn't talk, but they didn't stand still, either running ahead or shambling around aimlessly. They didn't approach Lucas or the *cultivers*.

The Free People wore their masks, but Riley recognized a few and called out to them as they passed. There was no response. The road was full of debris. Lucas lifted his carapace to the max height, putting them safely above observers on the ground, but not the ones that watched them from ridges beside the road.

"We are giving them time to gather their forces," Paul warned Fallon.

"He's up ahead," Fallon said. Ever looked and saw that the road turned south into the mountain, dropping to a tight descent, presumably to the old world beyond. Fallon was certain they would be safe in the remains of the old world.

Before the road turned, two figures stood at the top of the embankment, at least forty feet above the road and well above their platform on Lucas. Neither wore masks, although their cowls were pulled forward, blocking the soft fall of ash.

Ever recognized Richard immediately. His enormous form was easily three times the size of most people. The rifle looked tiny in his hands, and he held it unwaveringly at her chest. The bright red dot hadn't moved a fraction.

The person beside Richard wore a deep crimson exosuit. He wore a gold chain around his neck with a large medallion sporting the Third Eye embedded above a sword and sickle. The skin around his face was loose and mottled, a faint green and purple.

"You can stop," Murdoch said amiably, and Fallon stopped Lucas with a thought. "I've got a lock on her heart."

"Whose heart?" Fallon said. She seemed disinterested.

"You know who," Murdoch said. "It seems like I should have been consulted. There were only two of us."

"I don't think you were available at the time."

"That was not my fault."

"And here we are, anyway. Are you going to let us pass? You could do me a solid for old times' sake."

"After you threw me away?" Murdoch asked, laughing. "My Servants aren't completely obedient, but they are more than a match for your *esclaves*. You seem to have collected quite an odd assortment. I'm looking forward to discovering what's special about each one of them."

"I see you have a nice weapon there. Did you pay a lot for it?"

"I had to go through hundreds of rifles before I got past the moderator on the trigger mechanism. When I walk into a room, their circuits melt in shock."

"That's a pity."

"No worries. I have a huge inventory of spares to work with. Who would have thought it easier to crack the human mind than a dumb machine? All I needed was a little money for collars to transmit commands and a large group of people without implants to experiment on."

"Your Servants don't seem particularly well coordinated. Maybe you scrambled their brains just a little too much."

"Scrambled? You underestimate me. You are confusing patience with ability, Fallon. They wait on my every thought."

"I give you credit where it's due. We both know the Peace is not easily thwarted. That's what makes us who we are or what you used to be."

"A lie perpetrated by an old man."

"A promise of service."

"Promises discarded when they become inconvenient. Do you think I did this to myself? The King under the Mountain thought I had the key, and he went searching for it. I was his plaything for almost fifty years before the Ajat Maata rescued me. Now I have a new accord, power for power."

"Where are your Ajat Maata? They are missing out on our reunion."

"Mine? They serve when necessary for their own rewards,

but they are a little squeamish about killing."

"Your Servants appear equally squeamish. Do you really think you can win with that plasma rifle?"

"My creations may be imperfect, but what I lack in control, I make up for in numbers. This doesn't have to be painful. It's painless to lose the power. I know. When I needed it most, it was missing. All my experimentation on the Free People led to this moment. You can accept freedom from worthless causes and submit. When I negotiate with the King, there will be more than enough power for both of us."

"I think you are confusing power with service to a new master, and I don't think he will negotiate. Do you think the people of this time understand the nuances of power? They understand the Peace and the freedom it affords."

"Freedom is a reward for the brutality of war. Look at these people. They call themselves Free People. They refuse implants and live and die with a dream they don't even understand."

"At least one of them has an implant."

"What do you mean by that?" As Murdoch said the words, a giant fist closed around his neck. He gurgled pitifully and grabbed Richard's arm, but he was already swinging in full motion. Richard launched him down the embankment. Murdoch fell and smashed into the rocks, flailing to slow his fall but plunging from boulder to boulder with the sickening snap of broken bones until he landed in an unmoving heap.

The Free People stopped milling around. With savage snarls, they leapt at Lucas. Some dropped their catchpoles to pick up rocks while others beat at his sides. The *cultivers* pushed them back, and Lucas started forward. There were more Free People than *cultivers*, but most of them were fighting each other, snarling with wild expressions and howling voices.

The crimson exosuit disappeared in the morass of bodies. Murdoch gone. They moved maybe a hundred feet down the slope before Ever saw the Free People reorganize. In groups of eight, they ran up the side of the mountain until they reached a ledge above Lucas. They jumped off, most missing the platform and falling to the ground with broken limbs, but a few landed successfully.

Rough hands grabbed Ever, but startling them all, her chair fought back, pushing the Servant away from the platform to slide off Lucas. More Free People piled onto Lucas's legs, and his head swung around to look at them. He tried to shake them off gingerly but was thwarted by mindless tenacity and overwhelming numbers.

Catchpoles and hooks darted. Reign cried out as one foot was caught in a hook. Before he could be pulled out of his chair, Paul caught the hook in his hands and broke it off at the pole. He moved with frightening speed across the platform, breaking off the long poles, but he couldn't be everywhere.

A stunner looped around Fallon's wrist. The electricity arced from her hand across the platform, and the stunner exploded, burning away her glove. The blast stunned the Free People in front of Lucas, but momentarily, all the *cultivers* stopped and collapsed, releasing a fresh wave of Free People to batter at the *maitre de terrain* as he tried to reorganize the *cultivers.*

In the distraction, Ever forgot Ailbe until she found him desperately clinging to the bottom of the platform. His leg was hooked. She freed herself from the chair and grabbed his arm, attempting to pull him to safety, but he slid inexorably off the edge.

In desperation, she cast into Lucas. The big *esclave* was stuck under the weight of Free People. Every movement he made was met with resistance, as people without fear for their own safety clung to his body and legs.

Ever felt Fallon rejoining Lucas.

"Wait," Fallon sent. "Don't do it."

As Ailbe's hands lost their grip, she didn't have time to wait for her mother.

"I have to." She batted away her mother's mounting control and pushed hard on the *maitre*, overwriting resistance with command and crushing the smaller eimai to take control of his body. Picking up his massive stabilizing leg, she swung it out, sending people flying, and struck down on the hook bearer, flattening the Servant into the ash and smashing her chest into the road.

Lucas's eimai collapsed, ejecting Ever into her own body. A cloud of smoke poured out of his head as the *maitre de terrain* froze into position and slowly settled to the ground.

Ever pulled Ailbe onto the platform, but with him came new Free People diving in from above. Before she could say anything to Ailbe, arms wrapped around her tightly, picking her up off the ground. She panicked, struggling until she realized it was her chair. The *cultiver* was back to life and hoisted her into the air like an empty sack. Her mother's hand whipped out, touching the *esclave*, and smoke rose from the machine near the top of its body.

"You didn't listen," Fallon said in between gritted teeth. Her voice carried more than disappointment. It burned with anger. "This is for your own good." The *esclave* leapt off Lucas, clearing the mass of Free People. Ever struggled to look back or get free, but the *cultiver* continued to run down the slope and then turned east.

She attempted to send messages to her mother, attempted to stop the *cultiver*, and take control, but there was no response. The *cultiver* ran as fast as a bipedal *esclave* could, tearing through the mountain pass and jumping over boulders. She was afraid if she stopped the machine, she might hit a rock or fall off a ledge.

The *cultiver* ran into a lifeless wasteland while she struggled and failed to attune to the *esclave*. Something was missing, and the hot tears on her face didn't give her any answers. She hit the *esclave* futilely, but the mechanical body did not feel pain or fatigue. It ran past midday into the evening when it collapsed into a rock pile, releasing her in its final act.

# THE END OF BOOK 1

In the depths, you'll find the past.
A remnant of the very last.
who keep the truth that they believe.
Truth or lies, there's no reprieve.


The bitter taste of what is left,
reminds us all of life bereft,
of sunshine, rain, and clear blue skies,
of those that couldn't compromise.


Beware the heart confused by love,
of wanting more than those above,
and tangle hope with tragedy
Beware the depths! Heed my plea!


"Laments of the Catastrophe" by Unknown
Recovered from digital archives of the Federation
circa 2149, Western Common Metric

# CRITOS

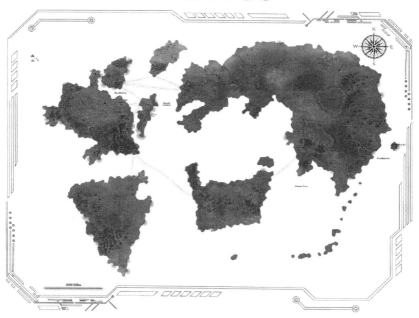

# EPILOGUE

A crack opened in the window, and a light flashed before disappearing into the darkness. Light was always present in the Heliosphere, but this light was unaccounted for, and the photons left an acrid taste in his mouth after millennia of dozing.

He flexed awake, turning his eyes toward the disturbance. As was his habit when something jostled him, Logos cursed Svarog. The light had nothing to do with Svarog. He knew that immediately. The light came from the Gift turned to retribution. No sooner had the humans colonized their world, Credos, than they turned to machinations to destroy him and the Others.

In the warp of space and time, they harvested the material of the Gods. A material so destructive as to threaten the Heliosphere. Not without destroying themselves, but that was a minor concession to the Others, and he'd lost much standing for his support of humankind.

Some of the weak Others attempted to flee, and in the emptiness of interstellar space, their bodies floated as a warning.

Svarog had deceived him, but he expected that. The old man, too, had fooled him. That was something of a shock, and he'd spent many decades considering his error before the old man compelled the Others to look away.

As the Others agreed, it was better for them to turn their eyes elsewhere than risk oblivion. In time, the humans would misplace the burning sphere or use it on themselves.

Patiently Logos waited. The light appeared where it should not, and he listened. The destruction on the surface of the Gift was nothing compared to the power he could bring. The sphere still existed, of that he was certain, but where was the old man?

Made in United States
Orlando, FL
31 March 2025